Ashes and Echoes

Book IX of The Quietus of Fate

By Brian C. Kershner

Acknowledgements

Each and every book in the Quietus of Fate series, while connected, have a character and a life of their own. *Ashes and Echoes* is no different, and in a lot of ways may be one of the more emotional books in the whole series. There are many passages within this novel that have caused me to hold back tears, and no matter how many times I read them, I still am impacted by them.

A lot of time in this series is spent on presenting philosophical and moral questions. Moreover, the characters in these novels act as connection points not only to more fully explore these questions, but also as mirrors into the human condition that is complex and oftentimes beyond simple explanation. Being human is difficult. Living through every day with the pressures, emotions, and aspirations of life is at times the most difficult thing that can be accomplished. We are each different in our humanity, and despite our connections to the same emotions, drives, successes and failings, it is the ability to recognize the humanity in one another that can be lost.

But the one thing that unites us all, and the one thing that will always unite us is that at our very cores, we are human. We love, we strive, we fall, and we find ways to struggle forward no matter what. And just because love may lead to loss, we still love. Just because exertion may lead to failure, we still try. And the greatest hope is the fact that there is a tomorrow.

We draw our greatest strength from one another, and that strength is what unites us as human beings.

B.K.

Table of Contents

Chapter 68

Epilogue

Appendicies

Prosperity reigned in the divine empire of man,
After the bloodshed from the war of Foundation,
Following the mandate of the Creator's flawless plan,
Cadaria was the jewel in the crown of Creation.

However, sin cannot be washed away like blood,
In lands built with the bodies of innocents,
Reinforced with lies and pain like brick and mud,
The unrepentant demanded swift recompense.

And so from the heights of the Divine Heavens,
The Creator delivered upon His beloved servants below,
A test that would cure them of their transgressions,
And let the true light of their dedication show.

They came in the form of a shooting star,
That crashed down upon the land with furious thunder,
The reverberations were felt near and far,
Dark Gods had come to rip Cadaria asunder.

- *The Verses of The Word*
From the High Priestess of the
Church of the Creator

Prologue

Falling from Grace

Time Immemorial, the Heavens

Gwydeon and Midarin stood back to back, Gwydeon was using his wings to shield Midarin from the onslaught of the other angels, while he turned back spear after spear with bursts of his own powers. They were surrounded now, and as Gwydeon looked at the ranks of enemies arrayed before him, he reconsidered the wisdom of wading so deeply into the enemy ranks. But the opportunity had been there. The Wrath had been taken completely by surprise with their tactics, and he fell before the forces of the Creator were able to mobilize. Over the cries of rage and battle, Gwydeon could hear Midarin's bowstring draw and release over and over again, faster than he had ever heard it before. She had questioned the logic of this battle, questioned the need for it, but now that the battle was joined, no more protests would come from her. She was a valiant warrior, a raging soul, and a terrible presence on the field of battle. More and more of the spears of light came flooding toward them, and Gwydeon continued to turn them away the best he could. The angels may have been his betters in the amount of power they could bring to bear, but none of them had fought a pitched battle. And none of them had ever fought against those so well versed in fighting superior opponents.

Another cry of battle came from behind Gwydeon, and he could practically feel Midarin's mood lighten. Impossibly, her rate of fire increased, and she started clearing a path for the onrushing reinforcements. Gwydeon chanced a look over his shoulder and saw another pair of white wings splayed out like mighty shields. Camille held her sword high and cut down any of the opposition that her mother missed. There were plenty of the forces of the Creator whose helms were pierced by gleaming arrows, and Camille spent as many of her strides dodging fallen bodies as she did engaging enemy soldiers. Behind her, Gwydeon saw Pike, Aryx, and Diana clearing out any of those that happened to escape the mother and daughter's fury. It took a scant few moments before the old friends were together again at the heart of the cresting wave of the Creator's army. While they had been slow to mobilize, there were certainly more than enough of them to make up for the lack of speedy organization.

"We have to push forward," Pike yelled above the growing din of death and battle, "those who are following us are lagging behind but will be able to take some pressure off."

A spear of pure energy whizzed by Gwydeon's ear, barely missing his head.

"I don't know how long we can hold out," Gwydeon said, exhaustion starting to fill his voice. "I never thought they could mobilize this fast. If we don't make a push to the throne soon, it will only be a matter of time before the Will and the Voice will be here."

"I'll take care of Evan," Pike growled as he cut down two more of the young angels, "just give me a clear shot and I'll bury the traitor."

Gwydeon grimaced as another three soldiers fell.

"I'm hoping it won't come to that."

Gwydeon surveyed the landscape for a moment and saw a break in the lines. The angels were moving in disorganized patterns to deal with the rebels, but without the Wrath or one of the other Heralds to lead them, their tactics were not sound. It was then that the idea struck him.

"Diana, Camille, I need a hand. Pike, Aryx, Midarin, try to keep them off of us as much as you can. Hopefully we'll be able to take most of their attention and you can make a run for the temple. No matter what happens, as soon as I give the word, start running. Don't let anything stop you until you get there."

There were no arguments, but Gwydeon felt Midarin tense. She never liked when he talked like that, but he was a hero, and true heroes didn't know how to play it safe. Midarin watched as Diana closed her eyes and summoned the power that was hidden inside of her. Though she was now an ascended being, her soul had never been separated from the creature known as Nightwing, and so a part of that energy remained inside of her to be called upon when necessary. The gleaming silver skin encased her body after a moment, and the razor-sharp wings sprouted from between her shoulder blades quickly. With a quick push off the ground and a hard beat with the wings, Nightwing was aloft, hovering above the battle. Gwydeon and Camille lifted off the ground a few moments later, their natural and beautiful angelic wings propelling them. The angels were confused by the tactic for a moment, allowing Pike, Aryx, and Midarin to reform with Pike taking the front and Aryx protecting the flank. Even with one arm, Aryx was more than a match for anything the angels could bring to bear, and Pike with axe in hand was just angry enough to take on the whole army himself. Midarin on the other hand turned her attention to the sky and started picking off those enemies who tried to intercept Gwydeon and the others before they could set their plan in to motion.

In mid-air, Gwydeon pointed to the defect he had seen in the enemy lines. Without any signal of understanding or confirmation, Nightwing opened her jaws and let a bright white beam of energy stream forth. Any angel caught in the blast was destroyed instantly, ripped out of existence before they knew they were even dead. Gwydeon nodded to Camille, and she quickly nodded back. Hovering there in the air they both brought their wings down in front of them, wrapping them around their chests. It took only a second before the two began to glow brilliantly. The glow intensified, heat beginning to radiate from the father and daughter. There was a blinding flash, and then Gwydeon and Camille extended their wings forward. To the opposing forces, it looked as though the sky was burning. Great roiling clouds of pure heat and light energy cascaded across the firmament, quiet for a moment and then bursting forth with a rain of light, heat, and death. Hundreds fell to the assault, pierced in hundreds of places simultaneously by divine energy that defied description. It was as though the air itself had been turned to fire, and the angels immolated in the white-hot heat of it. Between Gwydeon, Camille, and Nightwing, they had burned a huge path through the enemy ranks to the glistening gold and while spires that stretched high in the distance.

"Go!" Gwydeon shouted from above, diving down low to give the three allies cover, "Now!"

Pike, Aryx, and Midarin ran. They were too shocked by the sight of what had unfolded to process what they had seen. There were no words for the death and destruction. No words for the display of power. There was only what would happen next. Behind Midarin, she could hear the charging cries from the angels who had tossed their lot in with Gwydeon. They were outnumbered several hundred to one, but they were loyal to a man who had showed nothing but compassion and heroism his entire life. The Throne of the Creator was just ahead, and the uncertainty of what would happen when they stood before Him with weapons in their hand had not yet cracked the serenity and fear of the moment. Soon enough the fate of not only the heavens, but the very future of all the worlds under the control of the Creator would be decided. All of their fights could not be in vain. All of the losses, all of the misery. There had to be a purpose to it. Midarin swallowed hard as the thoughts began to finally surface in her mind. It all had to mean something. It had to.

* * * * * * * * * * * *

Year Three of the Just Emperor Kaitain "Dragonsbane" Lorien, Creator's Calendar Year 1870

In the darkness of the Vault of Terrors, Dorovar sat cross-legged on the floor, a book in his lap. He had read this book thousands of times during his imprisonment, but he kept coming back to it. The black leather cover defied age and wear, and the crisp white pages were themselves a mystery. They had golden flaking on their edges, and sparkled in even the dim light of the Vault. It was as though the book was proud of its appearance and showed off whenever it had the opportunity. The contents of the book were written in flowing script, the ink also a bright golden color that seemed to glow and lift from the page as it was being read. It was a truly miraculous book, even without blasphemes that it contained. The book was written by an acolyte of Talisia Masile from one of her many failed worlds. It seemed that Talisia herself liked to set her worlds ablaze nearly as much as the Creator did. The story penned by this fallen acolyte read like a laundry list of atrocities. The priests murdered, raped, stole, abused, tortured, and sacrificed the blood of the innocent in Talisia's name just to earn as much favor as they could from the goddess. They were hoping to earn ascendency to her right hand. They hoped to be touched by her divine essence. The particular acolyte woke in the middle of the night, feeling as though he had been guided by the commandment of the Dark Goddess. He took a ceremonial dagger and slit the throat of all of the other members of the church, and then coated himself in the blood of his victims under the light of the full moon. He knelt in the middle of a small village, naked and covered with the blood of his victims, waiting for a sign from the Dark Goddess. He saw a small cloud pass quickly over the face of the moon and he took it for a sign of her pleasure. He described it in the book as the moon winking its approval. He then moved from house to house, killing the men and children, slitting the throats of the women and savaging them as they died. He detailed in the journal how he felt the divine love of his goddess filling him as he committed each of the atrocities. How he felt as though he had lost all control of his body and that she was guiding his actions.

Dorovar closed the book and tossed it across the room. He smiled and shook his head. That was always the passage he read from the book because it comforted him. The poor deluded fool felt guilt deep in his core. That was the only explanation for his words. The guilt in his soul that was born from his doubt in his faith made him believe that Talisia was guiding his actions. If he were to admit to himself that he was the cause of all of that suffering and death for something he did not truly and fully believe it, the knowledge would destroy him. The guilt shattered his faith. Made him weak. Made him mortal and vulnerable. Dorovar had transcended guilt. Dorovar had transcended shame and doubt. He had served a goddess before. He had been a devoted follower of the divine goddess Raenera. That was long ago, on another world, a world that fate and the perverse will of the Creator had deemed was not fit to survive. Like the man in the book, Dorovar too had been an acolyte. He too longed to touch the face of his spiritual guide. Longed to show her the depth and breadth of his devotion to her teachings. That was when the dreams began. Every night, he would hear a woman's voice in his mind, guiding him to a greater understanding of his goddess's will, to his goddess's love. His standing in the church accelerated, and he became the greatest of those in his faith. The voice in his mind soon became a picture, and every night in his dreams he looked on the beautiful and placid face of his goddess, Raenera. In his sleep she would give him new commandments, and new directives to carry out in the name of the church and in the name of his faith. He never once doubted, never once let any bit of disbelief shame him.

It was then that the Demon Dragon Shadowweaver came to Dorovar's world. In his dreams, Raenera directed Dorovar to a deep cave under his church, and there on the shores of a lake of fire, Dorovar negotiated the deal that would sentence his world to death. Dorovar would gain unimaginable power in the name of his goddess, and the dragons would find a new home. But everything would begin to spin out of control. Raenera bred her world to be rigidly ruled by laws and rules and she had achieved through her church and her acolytes an ordered society. Dorovar soon learned that the dragons did not respect order. They did not respect the craft of the goddess or her followers. They each had their own vices, their own way of looking at the universe, and they were greedy. It was only a matter of time before the war began. The followers of Raenera against the dragons. But by this time, many had begun to abandon the teachings of the church. They called out for power, they called out for the goddess to help them, but their crimes against her teaching and her laws made them unworthy to receive her blessings. Dorovar had kept the faith, and he too asked for Raenera's blessings to be showered upon him so that he could defend his word and Her people. But Dorovar had been tainted by the doubt and guilt that had filled the other fallen acolytes. He had lost his way, and he would never feel the touch of his beloved goddess ever again. The dark man arrived soon after. He promised that he could save the people from the dragons' evil. He promised that he could give the fallen acolytes of Raenera's church the power they needed to defend their world. He called himself Emries.

Dorovar remember the day that he met the man called Emries. But he was not a man at all. He was a god, like Raenera; a child of the Creator with powers that defied imagination. Near the Church of Order was a small outcropping of stone and soil that looked over the huge valley and villages below. Dorovar had taken to sitting on that outcropping under the sparse limbs of the tree that clung to the little bit of soil, refusing to die. Dorovar heard the people approach, and when he turned he looked on two people that terrified him down to his core. The man wore simple clothes as though he was a simple human. But his eyes were brilliant blue, bluer than any Dorovar had ever seen, and they practically glowed with power. His long brown hair hung about his face, completely unmoved by the breeze that whipped around them. His skin was perfect, and the look on his face was one of infinite patience and compassion. The woman who stood beside him and held his hand as though they had been long-time companions had skin like porcelain, delicate and perfect. Her bright green eyes were haunting, and to look into them caused all manner of terror to rise up from the depths of Dorovar's soul. Her hair too was long and black, cascading from a part down the very center of her scalp. Her face was also flawless, dark colored lips and deep set eyes creating stark contrast to the white of her skin. The white gown that she wore one had to look several times to realize was not her skin.

Fighting through the fear, Dorovar listened to their offers of power, the man called Emries did all of the talking, but Dorovar could not take his eyes from the woman who called herself Talisia. She was familiar to him. It was then that Dorovar saw the truth. He had been betrayed. He had believed the visions in his mind, he had believed the words of the woman he thought to be his beloved goddess. But the words came from this Talisia. Though her, Dorovar had been responsible for the destruction of his world, for the destruction of everything that he had ever believed in. He turned away from the children of the Creator, decrying their treachery, spitting his hatred upon the wind. His faith shattered, his heart burned, and there was nothing in his soul but a black pit that would never be filled by warmth again. He dove from the rock outcropping, falling through the harsh cold wind into the valley below. With his eyes closing he prayed. He prayed to the very core of his soul for forgiveness. He did not want to be saved. He did not want to be spared his punishment. When his frail body struck the ground, Dorovar knew only blackness.

There in the darkness, there at the very edge of death, Dorovar found something that he never expected. He stood at the edge of a swirling pit, lost from the touch of time, and forever in the shadow of the light cast by the Creator. The pit was filled with the souls of the lost, those who had turned their lives away from the Creator. Those who cursed the Creator for their suffering and their pain. Those who cursed the Creator for the destruction of their worlds and the loss of their loved ones. The number was staggering, and Dorovar could feel their pain. He wanted so to help them find retribution for their suffering. He wanted nothing more than to help them find solace in their eternity, for he knew that hundreds of thousands of his own brethren from his world would soon find their way to this pit of the forgotten and forsaken. Standing there on the edge of the pit, Dorovar could feel them singing to him. Could feel their power inside of him, and their love. They needed someone to redeem them. Needed someone to help them find peace. Dorovar could do that. Dorovar could bring an end to their suffering. The song from the depths of the pit filled him, propelled him back to the land of the living, and when Dorovar opened his eyes again, he was looking up at the burning sky.

The new followers of Emries were clashing with the dragons, and the only suffering was being caused on the world below. Fire rained from the sky, forests burned, seas boiled, and the ground quaked. Dorovar tried to stand, but his body was broken. Over the next few days, Dorovar used all of the strength in him to claw his way back to the top of the cliff where he had escaped the torment in the eyes of Emries and Talisia. At the top of the cliff, he found his home, his church, burned to the ground, its ashes still smoldering in the failing light. With a great effort, Dorovar had pulled himself up to his feet using the old stubborn tree as support. The destruction and desolation before him could not be imagined, and could barely be understood. The land was littered with broken bodies, both human and dragon, and the death toll had to near the millions. It was then that the dragons approached Dorovar with the deal that would make him immortal. He would stand there, clutching that old tree as his world pulled itself apart.

The explosion threw Dorovar into the formless void of space, where he floated on the currents of creation. But Dorovar was not alone. When he closed his eyes, he could hear the chorus of souls singing to him, begging him for their revenge. Before long Dorovar began to hear the cries of souls coming from other worlds in the Creator's universe. They too cried out for retribution for their station. For the suffering they endured under the yoke of the relentless Creator. Dorovar vowed that he would free these suffering souls from the misery of their lives. That he would add them to the growing chorus, and fueled by their love and their devotion Dorovar would ascended upon the wings of their love and topple the Creator. He would then remake the universe as he saw fit. There would be no more suffering, no more injustice, and no more perversion caused by the lust for power. He would remake the universe the way Raenera had once intended, her societal order recreated and perfected. But there would be no place for gods and goddesses in Dorovar's new Order. Their voices would have to join the chorus as well.

Dorovar no longer needed faith. He no longer needed belief. He had transcended guilt, fear, and loss. There was no torment. There was no pain. There was no suffering. There would only be Dorovar. Forever and ever, there would only be Dorovar.

* * * * * * * * * * *

Time Immemorial, the Heavens

Midarin stood just feet away from the Throne of the Creator, her bow at her feet and her hands behind her back. This was the closest she had ever been to the Throne, and she felt its power radiating through her. The scene before her was surreal and impossible. Gwydeon, her husband, the only man that she had ever truly loved stood with his sword drawn, pointed at the nearly insubstantial form of the Creator. Midarin had set her eyes on the Creator many times. While it was a nearly formless power, at times it would assume the shape of creatures or even take the form of a towering giant of a human. Now though while there was definition to the being, there was no clear shape. The Voice, Evan Sinn stood several feet away from Gwydeon, his sword drawn and a look of shock and betrayal on his face. The impassive gleaming helm of the Will was over Evan's shoulder, and Midarin could only imagine the rage that filled its heart. Between Gwydeon and the Creator stood the Spirit. In her life, Midarin had known the Spirit as Sabrina Binosear, the daughter of Anabel Binosear and the niece of the great Cedric Binosear, the Lord Lion of the prophecies. She had been the child of a dark reality where she had been stalked and savaged by a member of the phasia that called itself Draven, a true nightmare born from the mind of Shau-ling. But she had survived. In her frail form had blossomed the mantle of Aerith Seth, the *Chosen One*, and like him she fought, scraped, and clawed her way through hell to reach her ascension. Her trials had impressed the Creator, and Sabrina had ascended to the position of the Spirit.

"You cannot use the human race this way," Gwydeon continued. "We are not puppets for your experiments. We are not toys. Humans worship you, revere you, and you care nothing for them. You tell them how to behave, how to live, even how to die, and then you betray everything that they have faith in just to indulge your twisted whims and the whims of your children. We've seen first-hand what Emries and Halicon can do when left to their own devices. I will not stand by and let you defile everything I stood for in life. I will not stand by and let another world burn."

A wave of power oozed from the form of the Creator and passed over everyone like a calming wind. Sabrina nodded absently and spoke in a calm voice.

"The Creator understands your concerns, and gives you the choice. You may leave this plane, return to the world of the living and you may prove the depth of your beliefs, or you may continue this charade of a rebellion and find destruction. You were once heroes, and you have been given a great gift in this immortality. However, the Creator recognizes the free will that you have, and recognizes the fact that you were once human and as such have sympathy for their plight. Cast yourself down from the heavens if you wish. Cast yourself back to the mercy of those you feel are suffering. But the Creator is sure that you will not find the reception you are wanting. They will curse you. They will seek to destroy you, for you are greater than they believe they can be."

Gwydeon lowered his sword and nodded. Without a word, he walked to the edge of the great temple and looked down on the swirling worlds below. Midarin stepped beside him, and the two embraced briefly, before Gwydeon's lips found his wife's and they held a long kiss. Camille was by their side when the embrace ended, and together the family stepped from the heavens and plummeted to the world of Espre that lay unsuspecting and sheltered in its youth and ignorance. As more of the rebelling heroes who would become the Fallen took the plunge back to the world of the mortals, Pike lingered for a moment. He looked up at the form of the Creator and sneered.

"This isn't over."

Pike then dove into the void, hate leaving a nearly palpable trail behind him. Sabrina watched them all go, and then turned back to the Creator. She drew the sword from the scabbard at her side and laid it at the foot of the throne.

"My part of the bargain is fulfilled," she said with sorrow thick in her voice. "And now I expect that you will fulfill your obligation."

Evan Sinn stepped forward. The Voice did not look pleased at the message he would deliver.

"The Creator recognizes your service, and agrees to the terms of your wager."

Sabrina nodded and turned toward the edge of the Great Temple of the Creator. As she cast herself into the void, she could not help but feel the smile creep onto her lips.

Chapter LXI

Signs and Portents

Year Three of the Just Emperor Kaitain "Dragonsbane" Lorien, Creator's Calendar Year 1870

Fear has many effects on the body and the mind. Some flee when faced with fear, letting it touch their hearts and causing them to fly in the face of that which overpowers them. Others cannot bring themselves to move. They are frozen to the spot as whatever they fear looms over them. Some cower and hold themselves; somehow hoping that a diminished presence will allow them to escape notice, or that hugging their knees tightly to their chest will somehow lend them protection from any threat. Fear can make people so uncomfortable that they become physically ill, unable to sleep, or if the fear is strong enough, can even drive them to madness. Fear can kill too. Fear can cause the heart to give out, either directly or create such a despair and paranoia that the only true escape is that of the dark embrace of death. Fear can hang palpable in air like a fog, making all who pass through it feel cold and desolate. Men can be turned into sheep or monsters by ever-present fear; the cruelty that can be caused by a person whose life has been lost to fear has no limit. No place was ever more fully crushed by the iron grip of fear than the small country inn of Coventry, that now, mere hours after the fall of the Imperial Palace of Aldere, served as the seat of power for the whole of the Cadarian Empire.

The Imperial Guard had shattered the nearly sleepwalking morning routine, bursting through the door as though they were invading enemy territory and then placing armed guards at every access point, grinding all services as well as the comings and goings of the inn's guest to a stand-still. The keeper of the inn and his wife were as jovial and obedient as possible until the Captain of the Imperial Guard, Korin Melcab appeared. The large and belligerent man barked orders in every direction, not waiting until his subordinates responded before moving to the next of his seemingly endless concerns. When he approached the bar, his dark eyes were filled with nothing but hate and his hand rested firmly on the hilt of his sword. Every bit of his posture bespoke a threat of barely restrained violence.

"In the name of the Just Emperor Kaitain Lorien, this inn is now under the direct control of the Imperial Guard, and has been annexed for use by the Emperor as his seat of power after the loss of the Imperial Palace. All guests of this inn shall vacate the building within one hour, and any who refuse or delay will be treated as traitors to the Throne and summarily executed. Those who work in this inn have, as of now, been conscripted into service of the Imperial Family. They will be paid standard conscript wages and will report to a superior officer that will be assigned. Any who refuse to accept conscription will be summarily executed."

Korin turned away from the bar, but the innkeeper reached across and seized the Captain of the Guard's arm in one strong hand. The innkeeper himself was a large man, his shoulders wide and his arms roped with heavy muscle. Scars on his arms and his face told of a violent life before becoming the keeper of a simple inn, and the grey starting at his temples and the cold fire in his eyes were marks that he had lived every minute of his life at the edge. Melcab did not instantly react to the assault, he stood still for a long moment.

"You can't barge in here and talk to me like that. I served the Emperor for thirty long years, and I have more than paid my pound of flesh to the Cadarian Empire."

Melcab whirled on the large man, bringing his free hand down on the innkeepers elbow, the heavy steel gauntlet dislocating the elbow and causing the joint to bend at an unnatural angle. The innkeeper howled in pain, and his wife's face went white as she shrank away from the scene of the assault.

Korin held the man like that for another long moment, his expression not filled with fury, but devoid of emotion; the stone-cold face of a killer staring down at his next prey. The moment passed, Korin reached across the bar and seized the barkeeper by the back of his head and tossed him like a sack of flour over the bar and onto the common room floor. When the Captain of the Imperial Guard spoke again, the walls of the inn reverberated with the unbridled violence in his tone.

"There is no cost that the Imperial Guard will not pay in the protection of the Emperor. There is no threat that will go unanswered. Let this be an example to all of the traitors that nip at the heels of the great and powerful."

His sword was free of his scabbard the next moment, and the quick downward thrust pierced the man between his shoulder blades, driving through his spine and through the wooden floor that lay beneath. A plume of blood flashed into the air for a moment, but gave way to the growing pool of viscous liquid that began to spread from the body. There were some in the Imperial Guard who paled at the display of violence, but none made a sound in protest. Melcab exalted in the fear and shock for several moments before withdrawing his blade, bringing another small plume of blood spurting from the man's back. A barmaid was standing nearby, her knees shaking and the entirety of her exposed flesh had gone white. Melcab reached toward her, and lifted the small white towel that hung at her waist. Looking her square in the eyes, he slowly wiped the blood and gore from the tip of his blade on the towel and then slowly sheathed his sword. He held the woman's gaze for another long moment, before turning his attention back to the innkeeper's wife. After taking a step toward the bar, the barmaid collapsed to the ground, her sobs silent, totally consumed by the fear of what bringing attention to herself might result in. Tears rolled down the cheeks of the innkeeper's wife, but there was still defiance in her eyes.

"I trust there will be no more issues with the orders that I have given."

The woman did not respond, which Korin took as an agreement to his statement. It wouldn't have mattered what she said, the implication of his actions were clear enough. There was no life and no will that would dissuade Korin Melcab from his appointed task, and no amount of blood would sate the demon's violence. As he turned back to the door of the inn, he looked at the two guards holding post there.

"Bring the Emperor's litter in through the kitchen and then leave. The Emperor does not want anyone disturbing him until he has had time to properly attire himself for the tasks of the day. I go back to Aldere now to find Sir Jaccob Aldora. Send a unit to collect the Empress and Lady Chelsea Zarova. They are to be held on charges of sedition and treason until the Emperor has had an opportunity to convene a tribunal. All members of the Imperial Guard have orders to detain those professing themselves as servants of the Church of the Creator on suspicion of inciting rebellion on the order of the Emperor himself. Those who will not be taken into custody are ordered to be executed on the spot and displayed as traitors."

He made for the door and then paused.

"Take the innkeepers body and lash it to a tree outside with a sign hung from his neck marking him a traitor to the Throne."

The two guards saluted crisply.

Korin let his gaze float to the barmaid who was still frozen in a crouch on the floor. She trembled slightly, the tears already making a dark spot on the floor. Her legs also glistened where her fear has caused her bladder to betray her.

"Clean her up and have her brought to me when I return from Aldere. I like her spirit."

* * * * * * * * * * *

Jaccob knelt at the side of his young companion and winced as he saw the blood continue to fight against the bandage and the little bit of healing skill that Jaccob was able to employ. Jaccob knew that he was no healer, and the rudimentary bit of skill that he did have would not have been able to mend a moderate wound, let alone the kind of trauma that Ayden had suffered at the hands of the man Ayden had called Emries. The name had been familiar to Jaccob's ears, but he couldn't place it. It was something old, something from legends, or maybe it had been from his own tortured dreams, but the familiarity tugged at the edges of his mind. Sweat rolled from Ayden's brow, the fever spiking again. Whatever had made the wound in the young man was no natural weapon; it had been of magic plain and simple. It was as if the wound was attempting to eat the young man from the inside out. The morning was advancing on noon, and Jaccob knew that he would not be able to hide in the ruins of the Imperial Palace for much longer. He was after all a member of the Knights of the Flashing Blade, and he would have to answer for his actions during the fall of the palace, and those questions could very well become accusations. If the Emperor had been harmed or even killed during the destruction, Jaccob's life could be forfeit. But after what he had seen, that mattered little now. There was more going on than Jaccob had even realized was possible. The skills that the man Emries and Ayden had displayed were far beyond that of a normal person, even more than the stories said that the Dark Gods were capable of.

A moan came from Ayden's lips, and Jaccob was pulled from his thoughts. The boy's head slowly turned toward Jaccob and his eyes opened slightly. His look was glazed, almost looking past Jaccob to something in the ethereal beyond Jaccob's perception.

"Ash always said I was too stubborn for my own good."

Jaccob knew the words weren't intended for him. Absently he dabbed at the beads of sweat on the young man's head. That act seemed to break whatever fragmented conversation Ayden was having and the glassy look ebbed away. Several blinks later, Ayden was able to focus his eyes on the face of his friend.

"Guess we're even now…"

Ayden's voice was weak and raspy, the strain from talking was evident on his face. The first few minutes after Jaccob had moved Ayden's limp form to safety, he wasn't sure that the boy would last more than a few minutes. Sealing the wounds had been simple enough, but Jaccob could not guess at the extent of his internal injuries.

"You're not out of the woods yet, my impetuous young friend. If I don't get you to a proper healer soon, I don't think you'll make it through the night. But Aldere has fallen, and there isn't a healer within a day's ride, and I dare not take you anywhere near the Emperor's people. They're not totally trust-worthy at the best of times, and these certainly do not qualify as the best of times."

Ayden's hand pawed at his pants pocket, as though he was trying to recover something. Jaccob reached down and moved Ayden's hand away before reaching into the pocket himself. The only thing in the young man's pocket was a small grey stone. Perhaps it was a keepsake, something that was either intended to bring luck, or perhaps just to bring comfort in what were possibly the boy's last few minutes. Jaccob pressed the stone into Ayden's hand and dabbed more of the sweat from his brow.

"Who was he? And why did he want you dead?"

Ayden shut his eyes again.

"Emries," Ayden said with a rasp that could have been from his condition of from hatred, Jaccob couldn't really tell which. "Enemy of everything that humanity could ever be. He who brings destruction. The Coromor."

The word left Jaccob cold. He had never heard it before, but something about it shook him. Suddenly his mind flashed, his vision blurred and all around him was blackness. A red haze crept into the edges of his vision, and when his sight returned, everything was bathed in a harsh red glow. He no longer knelt at the side of the wounded boy, but instead stood in a field, what could only have been the ruins of the Imperial Palace of Aldere far off in the distance. Bodies were strewn everywhere around him, broken from obvious combat. Armor broken, shield ripped in half, bodies twisted into horrifying monuments of cruelty and devastation. Jaccob wandered through the carnage, pools of blood and gore everywhere, soldiers from the same kingdoms with hands still wrapped around each other's throats sent chills through the heart of the Topaz Knight. Then he saw something standing in the center of the carnage. There were several forms, their weapons drawn and pointed at two other forms. Jaccob quickly picked his way through the horrific mass, until he reached the edge of the climactic conflict. There in the center of the tumult stood Emperor Kaitain Lorien, at least Jaccob thought it was the Emperor. His face was covered by a terrifying mask, it features twisted into a cruel scowl. But the eyes that shown through the sockets of the mask were clearly that of the Emperor, but they were wild and mad, filled with rage and rapture. Clutched in the right arm of the Emperor was the limp body of a girl who could have been no more than fourteen. Her eyes were open, but the stare was vacant, her gold eyes flashing dead in the advancing moonlight. Behind the Emperor, his face painted with cruelty and delight was the man Ayden had fought, the man he had called Emries. His crystal sword was covered in blood and at his feet laid a man robed in white with long straight black hair. He was face down on the ground, but Jaccob had the feeling that the man was a stranger, but important. Standing against Kaitain was a small contingent of people, most of which were unfamiliar to Jaccob, but two stood out. The first was Hannah Ironheart, but she looked much different than the last time Jaccob had set eyes on his ally. Her hair was shorter, but there was a power that radiated from her that was beyond anything Jaccob had ever felt before. She no longer wielded her mace Spirit, but instead held a pure black blade that seemed alive in her hands. Its form changed and undulated like a living thing, but at the same time appeared solid and deadly. Standing opposite Hannah was a man that Jaccob had never laid eyes upon, but he felt as though the man was familiar. There was something about the man's eyes. Fire cascaded down from the sky in sheets harder than the hardest rain, and the sky was ablaze with exploding stars. A form was hanging there in the firmament above, a form without definition, but a presence that could not be ignored. Screams resounded, from the girl, the Emperor, Emries, and the form in the sky and then a flash of brilliant crimson light, and Jaccob's vision went dark again.

"You saw it didn't you?"

Ayden's croaking voice brought Jaccob back to the here and now, shaken to his core, and his head throbbing from the experience.

"That was the dream…" Jaccob's voice trailed off. His mind had been plagued with that dream for so long now, but he had never experienced it with that level of detail, or with that immersive feel. It was as though this time he was really standing there, really seeing what could only be described as the end of everything.

"Prophecy," Ayden rasped. "What will come if things continue."

The suggestion sent a shiver through Jaccob, as though an army had just walked over his grave.

"I've been seeing the future?"

Ayden shook his head slightly.

"Possible futures. Paths, contingencies. Not true vision. Not like the seers."

The assertion did not fill Jaccob with any sense of peace. Whether it was a true vision or not, if there was any possibility that it could come true, he would have to make sure that it never did, no matter what it cost him.

"I'm sorry Jaccob," Ayden said finally. "I'm sorry that you have to set this in motion. I'm sorry you are the key. But your death will not be in vain."

Jaccob's stare was blank. Had he heard the boy right? Was it just the fever talking?

"Quickly," Ayden said after a moment, holding the grey stone up. "They're coming."

Jaccob took the stone in his hands. For a long moment, there was nothing, until suddenly warmth began to flow through the piece of rock. It was as if the stone had grown slightly in his palm. It had, and then again, nearly double the size it had once been.

"Pull it open," Ayden forced through clenched teeth.

Feeling equal parts silly and curious, Jaccob took a different grip on the stone and lightly pulled. To his astonishment, the stone actually got bigger. He continued to pull, until the stone had elongated and grown to reveal a swirling portal in its center. It hovered there in the air of its own volition. Without being bidden, Jaccob helped Ayden to his feet and held the boy at the edge of the portal.

"Wish I could take you with me," Ayden said slowly. "I'm sorry my friend. I will miss you."

With that, Ayden pushed himself forward and fell through the portal. Once his feet had gone through, the portal closed in on itself and winked out of existence. Jaccob stood there, his hands and shirt covered with the blood of his young friend, his mind still reeling from what he had seen and what Ayden had said about his death. He was only alone for a few moments before hearing the clanking of armor approaching. He could have run of course, he could have even put up a fight had he thought it would do any good. But Jaccob Aldora knew that his fate could not be fought any longer. Ever since the Sacred Weapon Temperance had been placed in his hands, he had been on a collision course with this moment. No matter what would happen, he would meet it walking forward, not running away.

* * * * * * * * * * * *

Kaitain Lorien sat upright in a high-backed chair in the largest bedroom available at the inn. It was a quarter of the size he was used to, and the thought vexed him. Nearly a year had passed since his wedding, and in that time the empire had crumbled around him. All morning he had been reading reports about the states of the various engagements with the dragons, the Dark Gods, the newly minted rebel forces, and a host of other small annoyances. Everything he read made his blood burn. Geoffry Aramour's report had been the most vexing. His best assassins had failed and Kaitain's brother and niece were still alive somewhere, and no doubt they knew that Kaitain had been behind the plot on their lives. Moreover, it seemed that Seraph Kore and other members of the Knights of the Flashing Blade had been behind the attempt on his life on his wedding day, and now those that had not disappeared into hiding like the cowards they were, were leading the rebellion backing his own daughter. Kaitain threw a stack of reports into the fire and stood quickly, kicking the chair backwards. The action threw Kaitain's balance off, and he tumbled forward, barely catching himself on the fireplace's mantle.

More than just twisting and contorting his features, it seemed that the poison had weakened Kaitain's equilibrium, as well as some of his senses. His vision felt blurry, his hearing sometimes was as though he had cotton stuffed in his ears, and his tongue felt swollen and he could taste nothing but ash in his mouth. He pounded his fist against the mantel and felt a bone crack in his hand. Yes, his body had been weakened, but he no longer felt pain the way other men did. Pain no longer had a hold on him, it was no longer a weakness that could be exploited.

The door to the room opened slowly, but Kaitain kept his back turned. While some of his senses had been diminished, others had been heightened. It was as though he could feel the presences around him by the emotions and energy they exuded. He could practically smell them coming. The person entering the room had been expected, and though Kaitain was not pleased with Geoffry Aramour's performances of late, he was still a devoted servant, and as loyal as any Kaitain had seen.

"My Emperor, I have returned as you have asked."

Kaitain kept his back turned.

"Do you have it?"

"Yes, my Emperor."

Kaitain turned finally, and caught the slightest wince in Geoffry's eyes. The assassin was adept at keeping his emotions in check, but the little slip was magnified because of it. Kaitain had looked in a mirror for a long time once he had gotten into the room, and he burned the sight into his mind. The skin on the right side of his face had shriveled and twisted, drawing down the corner of his right eye, and exposing some of the musculature and bone that lay beneath. His right cheek was sunken in like that of a corpse, and the tendons and muscles could clearly be seen in his neck on that side, as the skin had faded to near translucence. The hair on the right side of his head had also changed, fading from his normal lustrous and shining black to a stark white. The hair also appeared now to be brittle and thin, but was in fact stronger than it had ever been.

In Geoffry's hands he held a mask. It was made of the strongest steel and had been etched with dark filaments of obsidian. Kaitain had ordered its construction when the war with the dragons broke out, as he knew he would inevitably be driven into battle with the beasts, and he wanted to meet them as a foreboding and intimidating figure. The face on the mask itself had been molded from a cast made of his own face, the lips turned into a snarling frown, and the shape of the eyes holding nothing but disdain and contempt. It would be perfect for the days and the challenges ahead, and it would also allow Kaitain to continue to project himself into the minds of his subjects. They would not see the infirmity that had been inflicted upon him by those cowards on the day of his wedding. They would only see the strength of the Lorien family, and the true righteousness of his task.

Taking the mask from his servant, Kaitain quickly turned and moved to the large mirror in the corner of the room near the wardrobe. Without having to be told how, Kaitain pulled the mask onto his face and tightened the tri-point strap system that would hold it in place. The metal felt cool against his skin and after a moment, the alien sensation felt almost natural. Hanging on one of the corners of the mirror was a dark robe with cowl that had been used for Kaitain's secret arcane academy. He pulled it over his head and secured the cowl tightly in place. His hair would now be hidden, and the bright steel would be all that his subjects and opponents would see. The display of strength was important now more than ever.

When Kaitain turned again to face Geoffry, he felt his lips curl into a smile when a small shudder escaped the man. To cover the reaction, Geoffry bowed slightly.

"Is there anything else, Geoffry?"

Kaitain heard his voice as he spoke through the mask, and he was pleased with the effect. There was a harder edge to his tone as it reverberated through the metal. He sounded crueler and colder.

"As you requested, the Knights Jaccob Aldora and Chelsea Zarova have been brought here, as well as the Empress Dominique. Irene Drage is still counted among the missing, but searching through the remains of the palace may take several more days to complete. We've prioritized recovering the Imperial Sword from the remains of the throne room, but digging though that deep into the ruins has proved challenging."

"Conscript as many workers as it takes, and work them as long as necessary."

"As you command, my Emperor."

24 – ASHES AND ECHOES

Kaitain hesitated for a moment before speaking.

"I will come down in a moment to deal with Aldora and Zarova, but in the meantime I want Dominique confined to the smallest room you can find. Her discomfort should not be a concern. Do you understand?"

Geoffry bowed again.

"Of course, my Emperor."

Geoffry turned to leave, and as he opened the door, Kaitain spoke again.

"And send for Alise. I have a job for her."

Geoffry stopped, but did not turn around.

"She is currently tracking the blood scent of the man who prevented the deaths of your brother and niece. She will not be pleased if she has to abandon that hunt."

Kaitain let a low growl escape from his throat.

"She is my daughter and the only member of my family that has proven loyal and trustworthy. She will come if I tell her to. And if she has any issue with having to change assignments, I will make sure she visits that aggression on the one who ensured that her involvement in the botched job was necessary in the first place."

Geoffry could not suppress the shudder.

"As you command, my Emperor."

Geoffry closed the door behind him, leaving Kaitain alone in his room. Soon the declaration about the future of the Empire would spread like wildfire on every set of lips from the farthest eastern climbs to the western reaches. No sedition would be tolerated, and the whole of the Empire if not the whole of the world would be brought back under the control of the Lorien family. Then Kaitain could set his sights on those that were the true threats. The Dark Gods, the one calling herself Talisia, and the creature whose name was most feared these days in the countryside. Kaitain would soon deal with Dorovar, and he would show the creature what true fear was.

Embers of the Dying

Year Three of the Just Emperor Kaitain "Dragonsbane" Lorien, Creator's Calendar Year 1870

"Fire!"

The sounds of cannon fire filled the silence that followed the command, and the thunderous blast echoed across a considerable distance. The first volley of cannon fire was followed by three more volleys from the other ships in the small fleet. The lead ship, the *SeaFox*, quickly let loose with another salvo of cannon fire, the experienced gunners earning every bit of their share of the spoils. The four pirate vessels had pounced on a merchant fleet being guarded and escorted through pirate waters by ships of the Imperial Navy. Luckily for the pirates, these vessels were simple patrol craft, not the larger galleons made in the Kingdom of Iron, Pellatori. Patrol craft were not designed to stand up to the kind of firepower that the pirates could bring to bear, and obviously the merchants either could not afford larger escorts, or they simply did not believe that massive firepower was needed this close to the shores of the continent of Cadaria. The powder magazines of two of the patrol ships exploded after well-placed shots coming from the gunners of the *SeaFox*, and another of the craft had its main mast split in half by a volley from one of the other pirate vessels. The last of the patrol craft was turning to put distance between itself and the pirate fleet, using the merchant vessels as a shield.

"Cowards," the first mate of the *SeaFox* cursed in the direction of the fleeing ship. "Orders, captain?"

The blond woman in command of the vessel looked out at the array of vessels for a moment and then back at her first mate. They had been together for nearly five years now, since her last first mate was killed in a skirmish in the Pritan Islands. She reached up and pulled on one long braid that had escaped from under her hat. Something about this felt wrong. That was why she had made such a good and successful pirate all this time. She had a way of knowing that things were going to happen before they did.

"He's not running; he's trying to lead us back to the rest of the fleet. They've got big guns on the other side of that point, and he's using the merchant vessels as a screen to force us to pursue."

Coli looked at his captain for a moment and then back at the array of ships. He knew after all this time not to doubt the word or the hunches of his captain.

"Shall I call up the rest of the flotilla to secure the merchant vessels?"

Taya Viruci looked out at the ships for a long moment before finally nodding.

"Secure the vessels, but only use our recovery ships. I have a feeling we may find a few surprises waiting for us below decks. Have our gunships make speed for the point with the *SeaFox* and the *Old Fool* as the spearhead. If we're lucky, they'll be dumb enough to fire when they catch the first sight of us."

She pondered for a moment and then smiled.

"Strike the colors, and pull the *Thief's Blood* up from the flotilla to support us."

An evil smile crossed Coli's lips, and he quickly began barking orders to the crewmen. A large cheer went up from the crews of the vessels when the red flag with two crossed daggers was hoisted to the top of the mast. Pride swelled through the ranks, and Taya turned aft and watched as the massive war galleon *Thief's Blood* emerged from the cove where it had awaited orders.

The *Thief's Blood* had been an incredible victory for the pirates under Taya's command. The original plan had been to raid a small supply depot at the southern edge of Celidar in an attempt to procure enough supplies and materials to make repairs and upgrades to some of their smaller aging vessels. What none of the pirates on the raiding mission had expected was a massive war galleon using the port on its shakedown voyage. But because it was on a shakedown voyage, it was only sailing with a skeleton crew, and it was rigged for a smaller crew to operate efficiently. The Cadarians had practically gift-wrapped one of their most advanced warships for the pirates. The plan had evolved on the spot. Best case scenario, the pirates would capture the ship and have a new centerpiece for their armada, but if they were unable to take the vessel, they could at least deprive the Cadarian Empire of their prize. Not only did Taya and her crew make it out of the port with the *Thief's Blood* intact, but they were also able to secure a hull full of supplies. The raid was daring and made Taya even more infamous than she already was. It was after that raid that Taya was officially branded an enemy of the Cadarian Empire, to be killed on sight. A death mark turned out to be the best thing for her ability to recruit for her armada.

As the spearhead formed up, Taya felt a familiar twitch in the back of her mind. There was a primal surge of power around her, and she cursed loud enough for her first mate to hear her.

"What's wrong, Captain?"

Taya shook her head.

"That damned fool never did have any sense of timing," Taya muttered to herself.

She sighed to herself after a moment and barked a new set of orders.

"Come about! Signal the *Old Fool* that she'll be taking over the mop up work, but not to overextend. Xehm knows what he's doing and he'll use the superior firepower of the *Thief's Blood* to make those Cadaria bastards pay. Clear the deck!"

Her sailors moved quickly to follow orders, and the signalman was the last to leave the deck after the execution of his duty. Coli stayed well back from his captain, but Taya knew that he would not leave the deck unless she specifically ordered him to. They had been through much together, and Taya couldn't ask for a better sword at her side. But given the circumstances, if Aerith was coming through the portal that was about to form of the deck of her ship, then hell would likely be two steps behind him, and Coli would be severely overmatched.

Taya stepped to within five feet of where she knew the portal would form and waited; her hand on the sword at her hip. Unlike other members of the Fallen, Taya had been trained to feel the flows of power that came from the stones that Aerith often used to travel from one location to another. Granted, there were few others who were still alive that had enough opportunities to study the stones and learn how and why they worked. The stones themselves, at their cores, were little more than focal points with connections to two specific points. One of the points was always where the user of the stone was. That was the origin point. The second point could be coded by the user to any destination that they had been to. Of course, the person had to be in that location to code the stone. What was brilliant about the stones was that the destination didn't have to be a place. It could be a person. To that end, Aerith always had a stone coded to Taya, and one to Bryn. That way, no matter where he was he could always get to them. It could be annoying, and it certainly had led to some uncomfortable entrances. More than once, Aerith had come into her bedroom when Taya was entertaining. That more than anything had prompted Taya to want to know how the stones worked so that she could feel them coming.

The swirling blue portal opened a moment later, and Taya steeled herself. She and Aerith had never gotten along, would never get along, and if it weren't for her relationship with her grandmother, she probably would have nothing to do with the old man. But for better or worse, he was family, and that fact grated on her every time she had to set eyes upon him. As soon as the portal had opened, a large black ball of fur bounded through. It opened the second it hit the deck, its bright eyes, huge sharp teeth and swaying tail enough to strike fear into the heart of even the bravest man. When it locked its eyes on Taya, its purr lowered, and Taya could immediately feel anger and fear coming from the Snag. Taya was not as adept at reading emotions from the Snag as Aerith was, but she had enough of a connection with the creatures over time to be able to pick up the basics. But the last time Taya had seen the Snag, it was with Sabrina, not Aerith. Her stomach began churning as thoughts raced through her mind. Something bad had happened, or worse, was about to happen.

As if on cue, two more figures tumbled through the portal. Their exit made it clear that they had never navigated through that mode of transportation before. As soon as they were on the deck, Taya drew her sword and dagger from her belt. Coli followed suit the next moment, and Taya was about to call for her sailors to return, but hesitated when she saw the Snag take a protective stance in front of the two men. It too knew what she was thinking, and it was ready to defend the two men no matter the cost. Taya knew her sailors well, and knew that they were all valiant and skilled men. But mortals could not match the savagery or power that Snag could bring to a conflict, especially in close quarters. Perhaps a mob of her men could kill the Snag, but the cost of life would be great, and even in its dying, the Snag would probably take the whole *SeaFox* down with it.

Both men were bruised and bloody, the winged Onyx Knight of the Flashing Blade, Devlin Rannoch being the worse for wear. Both men were unarmed, which was a small relief, but the fact that they were both well-known Cadarian loyalists made Taya's blood burn. Devlin was a half-breed, and the other man, Gabriel Shadowfall had been the personal protector of the Celestial Princess Marlae Lorien for many years. Perhaps she wouldn't have to kill them. Maybe Snag would allow them to be her prisoners.

"Call for the medic," Taya said over her shoulder to Coli. "And bring some irons."

A moment later, two more forms emerged from the portal, and it quickly closed. As soon as Taya saw Sabrina clutched in Rhain's arms, a burned patch covering her chest, Taya feared the worst. Without a word Rhain set Sabrina on the deck and then moved to check on Gabriel and Devlin. The medic was there a moment later, and Rhain directed him to Sabrina. It took only a few seconds for the medic to pale, and he looked over his shoulder at Taya and slowly shook his head. The meaning was clear. There was nothing that he could do for the young woman. Taya nodded and the medic moved away to deal with the wounds on the two members of the Knights of the Flashing Blade.

Taya returned her sword and dagger to their sheaths, and knelt by Sabrina's head. The young woman was still alive, but she was barely holding on. Her hair was matted with sweat, and Taya gently smoothed it away from her face. Sabrina's eyes fluttered open, and she forced a smile when she saw Taya.

"Sorry to drop in on you," she rasped, blood trickling from the corner of her mouth. "It was Aerith's idea."

Rhain had returned to Sabrina's side, and took the older woman's hand in hers.

"What happened?" Taya asked looking up at Rhain.

Rhain kept her eyes trained on Sabrina, trying to keep a warm smile on her face.

"The rebellion was going to execute Aerith on the command of the Will. Camille, Devlin, Gabriel, and I were trying our best to get him out of the Heart of Stone. Then the Voice showed up and the Will and they blew us apart like we were nothing. We had to leave Camille behind, but I think she's already dead. We were just able to escape thanks to Sabrina. Unfortunately she took a direct blast in the chest from the Will. Healing was never my talent, mother didn't approve of such reckless use of power."

Taya nodded. Bryn's stand on healing was well known. She was bred to be a killer, a destroyer, why should she waste her time on healing people. Because of that she would not allow her children or her grandchildren to bother trying to learn the skills. Aerith did have a minor amount of talent, but he respected the wishes of his wife and never attempted to teach his family what he knew.

"Bryn was always stubborn," Sabrina coughed out, "but that was just part of her charm."

Rhain finally looked up and met Taya's eyes. The unspoken conversation was brief and painful. There was nothing either of them could do to save Sabrina, and in a matter of agony filled minutes, she would be gone. Taya looked up to see Devlin Rannoch approaching. His wounds were serious, but the medic had done a good job getting the bleeding under control. He knelt on the other side of Sabrina and took her hand into his. When he spoke, his voice was distant, almost as if it were coming from somewhere else.

"She can't die here. She is too important, and there is still too much work to be done."

Taya looked at Devlin, and watched in fascination as the air around him began to shimmer and change. Suddenly, there was another form there, sharing the same space as Devlin, but with its own shape and definition. The second form stood and moved away from where Devlin knelt, and as it moved into its own space on the deck, the form began to solidify more and more with each second that passed. Finally, the form had completely solidified into that of a man. He stood looking at the scene for a moment, and then knelt beside Devlin.

Taya had never seen the man before, but for some reason he seemed very familiar. He wore light gray robes, that when the light hit them a certain way, they looked white, but in the shadows they looked black. There was some kind of pattern stitched into the robe, like peaks of flame or something similar. His face was common, nothing about his feature stood out, except his bright golden eyes that at the same time were filled with such caring and also a tinge of malevolence. When the bright eyes locked on Taya's, she could not help but shiver, no matter how hard she tried to suppress it. His gaze made her feel as though she could never be warm again. Sabrina looked up when he touched her forehead. There was the barest trace of a smile that came to her lips, all that her strength would allow her to manage.

"Should have known you couldn't stay away."

Her words were broken, strained, and forced. It wouldn't be much longer, Taya knew.

"Quiet child," the form said, in a voice that was more reminiscent of a hiss than of a human voice, "your connection with Aerith has made you unable to keep your mouth shut when you should."

With one hand on her forehead, the form put his other hand on her stomach and closed his eyes. Taya, Rhain, and Devlin all pulled their hands away as Sabrina was suddenly wreathed in green flames. The fires danced across her skin, not burning her, but rather forming almost a protective shell around her. When the new form's eyes opened again, a small smiled showed across his lips.

"For a long time I have been looking for the opportunity to repay the debt that I have owed to Aerith Seth. Once, a very long time ago, he came to my defense when he had no reason to. He was my mortal enemy, the enemy of everything that my children and I stood for, and yet, his stand was closer to the truth than any of us could have seen. He was the one who showed me that I had lost my way. He was the one who helped me to see that it was my own failings and my own hatreds that were the source of suffering, not my brother Emries and his reckless need for power."

Taya's eyes widened.

"Halicon…"

Rhain took several steps back from Sabrina's body and quickly found the hilt of her sword. Taya was too shocked to make any moves, and Devlin did nothing but sit still, watching in wonder. Halicon held up a hand in Rhain's direction.

"There is no need for that, my granddaughter. You are as much my family as any that walk this world. And I am glad to see that you are so much your mother's daughter. Perhaps some of my legacy has meant something after all."

The words did nothing to ease Rhain's hand away from the hilt of her sword, but she did not draw the steel from its sheath. Halicon regarded her for another moment, and then sighed.

"Perhaps she is more like her mother than even I expected. Her hatred and distrust is plain, but I think that the love in her heart is more than even she knows. That was what always impressed me so much about Bryn. Despite all her cruelty, despite all of the destruction created in her name, her thoughts always turned to the man that she loved, the one that her heart would always belong to, no matter how much time and distance separated them. Her redemption is one of my proudest moments as a father."

Taya worked her jaw, but no sound would come out. She knew who the being was that sat before her, knew his power, and knew his history. Halicon was a child of the Creator, one of those chosen to help make reality and the Cosmos into what it was. For a time he had been the dark being known as Shau-ling, the creature born out of the nightmares of men to take retribution against his rogue brother Emries. But that had all ended with the death of the world called Onea. Emries had been defeated, Halicon had been redeemed. And yet, after Onea's death, Halicon had simply disappeared. And now, here he was, on her ship.

"But this is not about Bryn," Halicon continued, looking back down at Sabrina. "This is about Aerith, and the injustice that he has been shown by me and those whom I created. Aerith is my child no different than you are, Taya. Aerith is the blood of my blood, and I willingly sacrificed him to get my revenge upon my brother. That is how far down the road of revenge that my madness had taken me. I cared not for the people that I hurt, whether they were my own blood or innocents. My phasia killed indiscriminately, and the cruelty and wickedness that they showed in the execution of their duties has never been matched on this or any world. My atonement has brought me to this point."

Sabrina's eyes fluttered open again.

"And you tell me I talk too much."

Her voice was stronger this time, as though whatever Halicon was doing to her was fighting back the damage that the Creator's servants had done. Taya finally was able to find her voice.

"Are you able to heal her?"

Halicon shook his head.

"I only wish it were that simple, child. These wounds were inflicted by the Heralds of the Creator. They do not damage the flesh as your simple weapons do. The Creator influences spirits and souls. The wounds you see here are just physical manifestations of the true damage that has been done. Her soul has been wounded to a degree that her body can no longer be supported by its strength. It is only the mantle of power that she inherited from Aerith that has allowed her to survive this long. Were she only possessed of the powers of a Dark God, she would not have made it through the portal to your vessel. Without repairing the damage to her soul, she will die. But the immortal soul is neither the province of the Creator, nor the Heralds, nor the Dark Gods, nor any other creature that calls this reality home. The soul is a piece of the living Cosmos, sent here to learn all that can be learned before its time is at an end, and it rejoins the whole."

Taya's heart sank. While she and Sabrina had never been close, and truly she had never cared for the girl because of her connection to Aerith, she couldn't completely begrudge Sabrina for her lot in life. She didn't ask to be the chosen vessel of Aerith's power. She didn't ask to inherit his abilities and share his bad habits and terrible jokes. She was as much a victim as anyone. But there was something in Halicon's eyes that said she should not lose heart.

"Once, very long ago, Aerith Seth was there for me when my own children had turned against me. He saved my life then, and was the salvation of millions who were relocated to Espre following Onea's demise. At that point in time, Aerith had given his powers to his successor, Evan Sinn, and wanted nothing more than to know the truth about his purpose. He wanted to know if all the suffering he had gone through, and all the suffering he had caused, actually meant something. At that moment, at what he perceived as his end, he sacrificed as much of his power as he could to save one of his mortal enemies. At that moment I envied Aerith, and I envied the fact that he could give away all of the powers that he had gained, and still have the courage of his convictions to carry him. His bravery was unmatched, and it served as an example for what I knew I must do. I told him then that I envied his ability to give away his powers and I wished that I could do the same. Perhaps now I have the opportunity to do just that."

The smile was gone from Halicon's face a moment later, and a look of concentration replaced it. The green flames around Sabrina's body intensified and started to pulsate rhythmically. After several moments there was a nearly blinding flash of light, and the green flames around Sabrina disappeared. However, they didn't just evaporate into the ether; they were instead absorbed into Sabrina's skin. Her eyes opened wide the next moment and a spasm rocketed down the entire length of her body. Her muscles tightened and relaxed in random patterns and it looked like she would shake herself apart if the violent spasms didn't stop soon. Then, just as suddenly as the reaction began, it abated. Slowly, as if coming out of a long and restful sleep, Sabrina forced herself to a sitting position, and locked her eyes on Halicon. Though Taya could not see directly into the woman's eyes, there was no doubting that her eyes were glowing that same golden glow as Halicon's had.

"What did you do to me, old man?"

There were so many different emotions rolled into Sabrina's question. There was anger, frustration, and amusement mixed in with the confusion and a little bit of fear. Halicon took a long breath, and then let his shoulders slump. There was something different about his appearance. As though he was somewhat diminished and somewhat ghostly. As though any moment he could fade from their view completely.

"You are far too important to what is to come to lose your life here, for nothing, Sabrina. You must carry the mantle that Aerith has given you, and you must make the most of the path that has laid itself before you. Aerith is right when he says that the Creator has lost his way, and we his children are as much to blame for it as He is. The Creator depended on us to make this universe a thriving place, but all it has become is a warzone for us to fight our ideological battles in. That is why the Creator has become so fascinated in finding out which forces are stronger. That is why so many worlds have fallen to destruction in the name of his experiments. His thirst for knowledge was created in part because we, His children could not let go of our own petty bickering to see what we were creating. If Aerith is ever going to succeed in his plan, he must ensure that all of us are destroyed. And so, I sacrifice myself to save that which he needs to make this universe what it always should have been."

Halicon took a long deep breath, and Taya could tell that he was struggling to maintain his focus and his control.

"As I was once the master of the Blaze, you Sabrina now wield all of its power. Just as it was once the force that acted as my life essence, so now is it as much your life as your beating heart. But I give you this word of caution. Despite what you may have once been, you are not divine. The part of you that belonged with the Dark Gods died when the Will struck you down. You are as mortal as Devlin or Gregor. But you do have power at your disposal thanks to Aerith, and also to the Blaze. You may extend its power to others as I have, but be careful in how you use it and how far its boundaries are pushed. You are now responsible for my children that walk this world, as well as those who have been given the ability to embrace the Blaze. You may breathe new life into the phasia if you so choose, but do not make the same mistakes that I have, my child."

The form was fading more and more from view, and only the barest trace of Halicon's outline could still be seen in the bright midday sun.

"I join my brother Pyrrus in eternal rest," Halicon said, his voice barely a whisper. "Seek out the rest of my siblings, and give them the peaceful rest that they deserve. Then, shake the heavens and topple the Creator from his perch."

With those last words, Halicon faded. Sabrina sat staring at where the form had been only a heartbeat earlier and then forced herself to her feet. She could feel the power of the Blaze pulsing through her, and she felt more powerful than she had ever felt at any moment in her life. And for the first time in her entire life she felt as though she were a whole person. She had stepped fully out of the shadow of the greatness that had always been around her, her mother, her uncle, her allies, and of course Aerith. Now she could stand on her own.

"Was he serious?" Coli was saying in a fear and disbelief drenched voice. "Was he really talking about killing the Creator?"

Sabrina turned and smiled.

"Yes, he was."

There was no comedy in her voice, and a new deadly light glowed in her golden eyes.

"Captain Viruci," Sabrina said turning to the still kneeling blond woman, "I have need of your assistance, if you are willing to extend it."

Taya stood up and extended her hand to Sabrina.

"I suppose I can take some time out of my busy schedule of raiding Kaitain's supply lines to help family."

Sabrina took Taya's hand and held it firmly.

"Don't worry, Taya," Sabrina said after a moment, "I hold no love for Cadaria, and I would like nothing more than to help you make them pay."

What Monsters Fear

Year Three of the Just Emperor Kaitain "Dragonsbane" Lorien, Creator's Calendar Year 1870

Deep in one of the most ancient forests on the face of Espre, a huge tree grew. This tree was the center of power for the oldest mortal creatures in the universe, the race known as dragons. The tree was actually not a single tree, but a grove of nine separate trees that wound together. Their roots had become so entangled that it was impossible to distinguish where one tree ended and another began. For this reason, the Great Tree was revered by the dragons, as they held it as a symbol of their own existence. They were many breeds and many races, but they were entwined together the same as the Great Tree. They could no longer function in any meaningful way apart. Though more often than not, some tried to forget that fact. The older the dragons found themselves growing, the more fragmented their breeds became. Factionalism was nothing new to the dragons, but it had gone so far since their coming to Espre. Perhaps something on this world had poisoned them, had set them apart from one another and no longer enabled them to see the truth of their purpose. Dragons were the most noble of the Creator's children, and they had been ordained with incredible power and responsibility. They were the stewards of the universe, even more so than the gods themselves. There had been some talk that the Creator itself was a dragon, at least in some ways, and that the entire dragon race had been crafted in His image. And therein lay perhaps the root of every conflict between the humans and the dragons. Humans held themselves as the paragons of the Creator's blessings. They erected churches and statues in His honor, and yet they were not truly graced by His light. They were pretenders to the throne where Dragons were the most-blessed. But the decree that had set the race of dragons at the mercy of the fragile and short-lived humans was hard for most breeds to take. They had tasted human blood, and though it had cost the dragons dearly, many hungered for more than a taste. Some, like the Demon Dragon Shadowweaver wanted nothing more than to wipe the whole species off the face of every world in the Creator's domain. The grudge was there, and it ran deep, and could very well last as long as any dragon drew breath on any world.

Lord Tarot sat in the depths of the Great Tree, deep under the ground, looking at the marvel of the strong roots and the way they chewed through the ground to find the nourishment they required. For many centuries now, Tarot had pondered the war that had been ignited by the arrogance of some of the younger dragons. Shadowweaver had been at the heart of it all, though he too had been deceived. Perhaps that was why his tactics had changed and he now favored eradication. Tarot stroked his long white beard and felt the bones in his spine and in his wings ache. It had been too long since his wings had felt the strong breezes, and he wondered now if he even had the ability to lift himself off the ground. Tarot was old now, older than he had any right to be, and he had fought alongside gods and against gods in his time. He once faced off against the chosen of the Creator and fought the one called Emries to a standstill. But that had been early in Tarot's life, when he was idyllic and stupid. The dragons had felt slighted because of the worlds that Emries had created, the humans that he had sprung into existence like ants on the plain. That debate raged until finally it had come to blows. But the Will and the Voice put an end to it quickly before any serious blood could be shed. But that was before. Before the rebellions, before the Fall, and before the war that brought the death of one of the Creator's Chosen. Once the sacred trust had been broken, once divine blood had been spilled it seemed that everything changed.

Tarot exhaled deeply. The spilling of divine blood had changed a great many things, but the dragons' crime had long since been committed then. Dorovar was the dragons' greatest sin. Not the worlds that had been destroyed or the millions of lives that had been lost. No, it had been the abomination of Dorovar. Perhaps now it was fitting that the dragons found themselves trapped on the same rock that served as Dorovar's prison. There was strange and miraculous symmetry there. It had the feeling of the Hand of the Creator, like so many other things that had come to pass on this world. The death of a herald, the Fall, the creation of the Tear. In his ancient heart, Tarot began to fear that the time of the dragons was about to end.

Down the corridor that lead to Tarot's personal study, the ancient dragon heard the slow movement of heavy talon-laden feet. Tarot knew immediately who it was before she was half-way to him. Her scent was unmistakable, and though Tarot knew that many of his senses had begun to fail, he would know the scent of his betrothed anywhere. Mariti Brightblade was fully half of Tarot's age, but she was still ancient by any standard. She would be a fitting successor to Tarot, if there was anything left to leave her. Dragons mated for life, but dragons only ever chose one mate. Once that mate was dead, a dragon would never find another. Tarot's mate died early in the rebellion that brought death to the Creator's chosen, struck down by the vengeful god Talisia Masile, and it pained Tarot to go the rest of his existence without companionship. Mariti too had lost her mate, and so the two found each other in the only way left open to them. They were betrothed in loss, and betrothed in sorrow. Forever bound together by the forces that kept them apart.

"My Lord Tarot," she said her voice full of trepidation and reverence, "there is an outsider who has been brought to the Council by Khalas Skydancer. He has requested, perhaps one would say demanded, an audience with those members of the Council who are still present."

Tarot hung his head. He had expected this weeks ago, and in fact, he felt the man's presence the moment he set foot in the protected forest. He had the mark of power, but it was a power that was unfamiliar to Tarot. One thing was clear however, this man was old, and the power that inhabited him was even older.

"Very well," Tarot said after a moment of hesitation, "convene the Council, such as it is. We will give this human a hearing."

Mariti stayed in the doorway, and did not move.

"A problem, Mariti?"

Tarot could hear her grind her ample teeth together.

"Why are you doing this? It's another action that Shadowweaver will use against you. Letting a stranger address the Council, and a human no less? If you take this path, Shadowweaver may challenge you to the Trial of Combat. Are you willing to risk your life and the leadership of this Council to hear the words of a pathetic water sack?"

Tarot turned, and locked eyes with his betrothed. There was so much that she should have known, so much that he should have told her over these centuries. But it was not his place to tell those secrets that he had been entrusted with. He could not betray those who had placed their faith in him. Could not betray those who still needed his protection.

"Shadowweaver is many things, but most of all he is a coward. Even at the height of his power, he would not risk openly challenging me. More likely he would send Charnada or Stormbane to make the challenge. If one of them were to defeat me, Shadowweaver could either manipulate their decisions or challenge them, knowing full well that he could defeat either one of them easily. I am not yet weak enough to be unseated by either of those pretenders, so Shadowweaver will bide his time. In his way of thinking, he would expect me to allow you to challenge me, and mercifully take my position from me. But I am not the coward he takes me for. No, if Shadowweaver wants my throne, he will have to take it from me by force before time is done with me. Otherwise he will lose whatever chance he might have had. He is strong my dear, but you are much stronger than he gives you credit for. All he sees is a female. Not a warrior who ripped angels to pieces."

Mariti sneered. She did not like to be reminded of how she earned her name. She was barely an adult when the war broke out. Barely old enough to know the result of her actions. And yet she fought, she fought with all the vigor that was within her, and it was true, she did taste the blood of angels, did smite them with their own glowing weapons. She had been awash in divine blood, so much that her talons glowed with their power.

Tarot saw her discomfort and waved away his comments with a wag of a single golden talon.

"We shouldn't keep our guest waiting."

Mariti bowed slowly, and Tarot could feel the irritation rolling off of her. But there was another feeling that was pulling his attention away. It was older, more primal, and much more dangerous. Fear had gripped the hearts of some of his brethren. Fear unlike he had ever felt before. Something was happening, something that fate and destiny had conspired to bring about. Tarot left his chamber and made his way to the Council chamber, the weight of providence growing with every step.

* * * * * * * * * * * *

The chamber at the heart of the Great Tree was the meeting place where the Council of the Winds gathered to discuss all matters relevant to the various breeds of dragon that called Espre home. There were places for a representative of each of the ninety-nine breeds that inhabited the world, and a central platform that a speaker held. In the whole existence of the Great Tree, no human had ever stood in the center of the Council chamber and looked up at the sky through the bowl shaped opening at the top of the chamber. Sunlight always shown through the top of the tree, and at night, the moonlight gave the center of the chamber the same amount of light. But the cloaked man who held the center of the chamber now did not take in the breathtaking sights. He did not lift his eyes to look at the wonders of the representatives of the dragon breeds taking their places, and did not even seem to realize that all eyes were upon him. He stood, his hands nonthreateningly at his sides, and his eyes cast down to the floor. Only when Lord Tarot entered the chamber did the cloaked man change his stance. But it was not to address the leader of the Council, nor was it even to show a level of deference with a bow or some other recognition of his station. It was merely to step aside, and let the much larger creature take his place on the platform. Tarot seemed to ignore the human at first, his eyes scanning the chamber to mentally take stock of the few representatives that were still within the bounds of the Dragon's Forest. Perhaps a third would hear the important words that were to be spoken. Perhaps half of those would truly understand what this moment meant. In his heart, Tarot felt that such a failing of understand was his burden to bear, his failure as leader.

"We have a guest, one that many of you would not have expected to be given leave to speak before us. But these are not normal times, and we must be willing to listen to even those whose voices we may not have respected centuries ago."

There was some grumbling from the assembled representatives, but no one gave clear voice to their protestations. Tarot turned to the human and wordlessly gave the floor to their mysterious visitor.

"Dragons of Espre, beloved children of the Creator, I come to you as a man outside of the Creator's love, outside of the love of the one who gave humans life, and outside of the love of even his own people. Once, I was a man, a man like any other, but fate and destiny, and the touch of the Creator made me more than I ever could have dreamed. But in my arrogance, I sacrificed everything I held dear. I put the will of a tyrant ahead of the duty he willed me to perform. And now I stand before you, less than I have ever been, but at the same time greater."

The man reached up and pulled back the hood of his cloak to reveal an old man's face. His gray hair was a mottled mixture of both gray and silver, but the silver did not glisten, as the dull gray dominated. His face was a weathered mass of wrinkles, scars, and imperfections. His grizzled beard clung to his chin and cheeks like moss to an ancient tree. But as Tarot looked into the man's eyes, he could see nothing but power, a power he knew well and had grown to fear. This man was known to Tarot, known far and wide once as the Voice of the Creator. As if sensing the ancient dragon's thoughts, the old man nodded and sighed.

"Yes, Tarot, I was once the man known as Evan Sinn. I was once a chosen of the Creator, and I was once the Voice. But before then I was simply a man. A man with a destiny that I could not even begin to understand. I bathed in the glow of those with more power than I could even imagine, and for a short time, I drank from a river of that power. But I was not worthy of that gift. Was not worthy to be a successor of a man who was truly touched. I think deep down I knew that I was not worthy of the power that the Creator gave me. And perhaps that is why the Voice chose to be done with me. Or maybe it was because I had that other power within me that the Voice was never fully attached to me. Whatever the truth may be, the simple fact is that I am no longer any of those things. I am not the Voice, I am not touched, and I don't even believe that I am human any longer."

There was a growl from collected representatives, and a dragon named Brux let his voice rise above the din.

"This creature wastes our time. It does not matter what he was or what he is. Be gone creature and do not stain our chambers with your presence ever again, or we shall have to make an example of you."

Tarot was about to chide Brux for speaking out of turn, but a great roar of laughter came from Evan that caught everyone by surprise and ended all of the arguing and raised voices in an instant. Evan turned slowly so that he was looking directly at Brux.

"Should I fear you, dragon? Should I fear what you can do to me? What can you take from me that hasn't already been taken? But please, strike me down, seal your fate by crushing me before I can give you the means to save yourself from the destruction that Dorovar is bringing to your doorstep. Rip the beating heart from my chest and mark the final hours that you will draw breath. It would almost be poetic justice that you should be the ones to destroy me, as it was my orders to help you free yourselves from your bargain that led to my own downfall. So strike! Strike if you have the courage of your convictions! Strike me down and we can all burn together!"

Tarot began to raise his hands to lend calm to the situation, but another voice rose. This was from the dragon known as Serentis, perhaps one of the wisest of them all.

"Let visitor speak...words are not only words....wisdom comes in forms unexpected..."

The low hissing voice of Serentis was like a wave of calm descending on this tense situation. Emotions and perceptions were still heightened, but at least the opportunity to listen was still there. Evan took the opportunity to reposition himself in the center of the platform, and when his voice rose again, it was filled with a richness that should have been coming from a man in his twenties.

"This world stands at a crossroads, but both paths lead through unimaginable darkness and pain. The Emperor of Cadaria, the beast wearing the name Kaitain Lorien will bring unparalleled suffering to those who once defended his name, and those that curse him will suffer even more. The demon you call Dorovar will soon find a way to escape his prison, and you dragons are as much responsible for his escape as you are for his creation. It is through your recklessness and your arrogance that you will suffer, and nothing that you do now will prevent that. It is even possible that through your haughty dismissal of the danger that you have sealed your eternal fate. But as always, that choice will rest with you. You have one chance left to see the error of your arrogant and short-sighted ways, and one chance to embrace a future that still has your kind living within it."

Charnada Ivorytooth was the first to scoff at the man's words.

"What can you know about the fate of the dragons? No matter what you may have been, you are now just a pathetic human. Lower even than those creatures we choose to grace with the privilege of being our food. Dragons are beloved by the Creator. No matter what darkness befalls the humans, it is the problem of the humans. You can all burn and we will prosper, as we always have."

Evan shook his head.

"You see? This is why you will fall. You are all so confident in your position within the Cosmos. You are all so haughty in the love that you feel the Creator has for you. But where is the Creator when your kind is being slaughtered by the Cadarians? Where is the Creator when you have had record low numbers of new hatchlings to bolster your ranks? Are you so confident in the love that the Creator has for you that you will allow yourselves to be as blinded by that faith? How very human of you."

Roars of displeasure and insult came from all directions. Threats of violence were shouted in a myriad of tongues, but the old human weathered them all.

"The Creator has lost His way!"

Evan's voice only carried so far before it was lost in the din. Tarot's eyes found Evan's after his words first hit the air, and the words pierced Tarot's heart as surely as any spear ever could. Again Evan repeated the words, this time their permeated the chamber like smoke. Silence reigned again.

"The Creator is blind to the role that He Himself has created in this darkness. Blinded by his ambitions and his desire to know what should not be known by any being. He has forgotten that there is more to the Cosmos than His will. Forgotten that he too is a child of something greater. And so, you, just as the humans, just as his Chosen, just as the gods who once flocked to his banner, you have all been forsaken. You are all just part of his grand game. Do not be blind as He is. Do not fall into the trap that has made so many worlds burn for his pleasure. You must choose now. Will you stand against the Creator, will you make the choice that could very well damn you all to fire, or will you do nothing and find your way to the fires through your own arrogance and inaction? Fight on the side of those who can see what is coming. Stand against the one who is truly bringing the suffering to your kind."

Silence filled the chamber. There were no words for the shock that the human's words had caused, and there was no easy answer to his challenge. Evan looked around at the great creatures, and he could feel their fear rolling off of them like tidal waves. It was the kind of fear that kept people stuck in place in the path of a great storm. But unlike a creation of wind and water, this storm could not be weathered by any creature. Those in its path would be destroyed; ripped from existence as though they had never drawn breath at all. Finally Evan's shoulders slumped. He pulled the hood of his cloak back over his head and turned toward the exit of the chamber. He had taken two slow steps when he felt a claw touch his shoulder.

"We shall have to consider your words, Evan," Tarot said slowly, "we have known for some time that there was a change coming, and now perhaps we will have to take steps we never thought we would ever have to take."

Evan breathed hard.

"Do not take too long to consider your actions, Tarot. When the stars fall again, you must have a decision, or it will be made for you."

* * * * * * * * * * * *

Evan Sinn walked, the hood of his cloak drawn up around his head. His mind was filled with so much, all of the things he had seen over his centuries of service to the Creator. All the death, all the life, all the wonders that the universe held, and still he felt as though he had missed so much. He had allowed himself to become so blinded by his duty and his pain that he became that which he had struggled so hard against. He had become the arm of a tyrant. He had hidden behind the orders and responsibilities that he had been given and had taken comfort that he had no choice in the atrocities that he had committed in the Creator's name. Whole worlds had burned because of his actions, and no longer could he say that he had no responsibility. Gwydeon and Pike had stood up to the Creator, and though their motives may have been misguided, their cause was just. And instead of fighting with them, instead of helping them to throw down the Creator and stop the suffering and pain, he followed orders. He led the armies of the Heavens against the Dark Gods, and he was the one who held Gwydeon's unconscious body above his head and threw him down to Espre. Evan had stood watching as the greatest hero he had ever known tumbled like a broken doll, disgraced and destined to be forgotten in the greater scheme of the Creator's grand game. But heroes could not be defeated by cowards who followed orders.

Evan's chest heaved, and he fell to his knees. His heart ached with the exertion that he had just put himself through, but that was not what caused most of his pain. Memories wounded him more fully than any weapon that had been taken to his flesh. He tried to force his way back to his feet, but his body would not respond to his urging. The ache moved through his chest down to his hips and knees. With some effort, he was able to fall back into a seated position, his back finding a large stump to lean against. It was a labor to take any breath at all, and time it seemed had caught up with the man who once held the power to move mountains with his bare hands. There was a soft light that glowed briefly to his left but winked out of existence as quickly as it had appeared. He felt the woman beside him before she ever entered his peripheral vision. Evan lolled his head to the left and smiled when his eyes found his visitor.

"So, he sent you?"

Diana Terian looked down at Evan and gently smoothed his hair back. She smiled lovingly down at his and nodded softly.

"We knew it would come to this when we saved you," Diana said softly. "Without the powers of the Creator or Aerith's abilities, you would just be a very old man whom time would eventually catch up with. I'm sorry that there wasn't more than we could do for you. If you want, I can take your pain away."

Evan shook his head, and then coughed hard. The pain radiated through his body, and the cough brought the taste of blood to his mouth.

"I'm sorry Diana," Evan said, his voice rough, "I never should have sided against you. I never should have forgotten who I was. I betrayed Aerith, I betrayed everything he trusted me to be."

Diana stroked his hair and smiled her best smile. She knew the pain inside of him, and tried her best to comfort him.

"Aerith trusted you," Diana cooed, "and because of that, you became a member of our family. Aryx looked at you almost like a son, and he was so proud of everything you accomplished. And believe me when I tell you that Aryx made some of the same choices that you had to make, and so did Aerith. They both understood the burden that duty and responsibility can place on a man of conscience. And you have more than proven yourself to be a worthy member of our family. You have shown incredible bravery. Even when you knew that your time was at an end, you used the last of your strength to come here to try and make a difference. That is what makes you a hero, Evan. That is what defines you as the good man that you have always been."

Evan tried to force a smile, but his strength was beginning to fail. Already the corners of his vision were beginning to fill with darkness.

"My only regret is that I won't get a chance to say goodbye to Aerith and tell him I'm sorry."

Evan's eyes fluttered and started to close. Diana reached down and took Evan's hand into hers and held it tightly. His breathing was slowing, and the beat of his heart was the faintest sound. Before his eyes finally closed, his strained voice, barely above a whisper floated to Diana's ears.

"Will I see Meredith on the Other Side?"

She wasn't sure he heard her say yes. And she tried to hold off her tears until she was sure that he was gone. She sat on the ground for a long time, Evan's head in her lap, stroking his hair, finding what solace she could for her broken heart.

The Limits of Faith

Year Three of the Just Emperor Kaitain "Dragonsbane" Lorien,
Creator's Calendar Year 1870

Aerith Seth stood looking first at the Voice who stood before him, and then back to the Will that had taken up position behind him. The Will stood in front of the still kneeling form of Hannah Ironheart, and Aerith stood over the fallen form of Camille Sandar. It felt wrong to think of her with any other name, and Aerith was not one to follow the rules when it didn't suit him. Besides, he was about to kill two of the Heralds of the Creator, he doubted that the Creator would begrudge him using a forbidden name after that. Aerith steeled himself and then set both of his feet for the assault he knew was coming. Fighting the Heralds would be different than any foe he had ever fought, so his standard tactics would not avail him this time. The Will launched another salvo of brilliant white streaks of energy, and Aerith brought the Sacred Weapon that Devlin had relinquished, the sword called Discipline, up to defect the blow and was shocked when the metal of the sword not only blocked the blows but seemed to absorb the energy. If Aerith had any doubt that there was a consciousness within the blade, something that willed the Sacred Weapons into his hand, it had now been erased. But Aerith did not have time to spend pondering what had just happened. The Voice was speeding forward, making the most of its newly reconstituted form. The gleaming crystalline blade came crashing down, and Aerith had to use nearly all of the strength and speed at his disposal to block the blow. As it was, the force of the blow pushed Aerith down to one knee, and he was so close now that he could feel Camille's chest rising and falling with each labored breath. If he allowed himself to remain in this defensive posture for too long, it would be the death of him. The Will could be on him any second, and Aerith may have been good, but even he wondered if he was that good.

Aerith braced himself for a moment and then pushed a great deal of his energy into his legs and sprang away from the fallen form of Camille and backwards toward the Will. He twisted in mid-air, and lashed out with the long curved blade of Valor, forcing the Will to bring up his massive crystalline sword to block the blow. Instead of continuing his strike, Aerith tucked his legs up under his body into a flip and after he had passed over the head of the Will, he twisted again in mid-air, kicking with both feet. He wasn't able to land a square blow, but at least one of his feet contacted the armored back of the Herald with enough force that it was sent stumbling forward. Aerith landed flat on his back, and he quickly hopped back to a kneeling position. He stole a glance over in the direction of Hannah, prepared for her to lash out at him. However, he was surprised to find her still kneeling, her head bowed and her eyes closed, silent prayers being mumbled from her quickly moving lips. On second thought, Aerith realized he shouldn't be surprised. Hannah was a devout woman, a believer. And here she was faced with two of the most divine beings that she could ever be in the same room with. Well, Aerith felt he should have included himself in that, but thought better of it. Such things were not for battlefields. He would have time to gloat later.

The Will recovered from the blow a little too quickly for Aerith's liking, and spun around, swinging that massive sword in a long downward slash. Aerith wasn't there when the blade connected with the ground, but was not prepared for the shockwave that erupted from the strike. Pebbles, stones, and massive slabs of rock from the walkway were thrown in every direction, and a wave of pure white energy radiated in every direction from where the blade struck the ground. Aerith, instead of throwing himself away from the blast launched himself toward Hannah, where he tackled her and managed to get her just out of the blast radius of the Will's strike. Before Hannah had recovered her senses, Aerith was back up on his feet, swords held high and waiting for the next clash.

"Get out of here!" Aerith called back at the Knight of the Flashing Blade. "You'll just be in my way, and I don't want to be held responsible for your death."

Aerith didn't wait for the next assault from the Heralds; he instead turned his designs to attacking. He knew that the Will was slower but much stronger than the Voice, and he hoped to use that to his advantage. He also hoped that the process of merging with a new host had weakened the Voice somewhat, or at least didn't allow him full access to all of his abilities. With a quick crouch and push off from the ruined floor, Aerith launched himself at the chest of the Will, darting in and dodging the hard swat from the creature's free hand. Aerith feinted to the left, and then darted back right, using his superior speed, the blade of Discipline flashing in. However, Aerith knew he made a mistake the moment before he felt the Will's other hand grasp him by the shoulder. He was not fighting mortals, nor was he fighting creatures that had to abide by any natural laws. The Will had left his massive blade hanging in mid-air and then simply reached down and struck Aerith on his left shoulder. The once-mortal simply closed his eyes as the armored hand grabbed hold of his shoulder and then flung him down the hallway as though he was a doll. A dozen feet down the corridor, Aerith's back and left side struck the hard stone wall, and he heard several of his ribs break. His left knee too struck the wall, and the ache in that joint would be a problem in the remainder of the battle.

Finding his feet again, Aerith called the two Sacred Weapons back to his hands from where they had clattered to the ground after his impact. Ever since Aerith first began to learn what he could do with his abilities under the not-so-gentle tutelage of Saurn and then the more encompassing training by Bryn, he had found ways to compartmentalize the use of his powers. It had come in handy to be able to set his powers on some task while performing another. The unconscious parts of his mind became very adept at processing those tasks. In a battle like this, such a talent could mean the difference between a victory and defeat. Reaching into his mind he felt for the roaring green flame that was the Blaze. He knew well from both Saurn and Bryn of its ability to not only be directed in a true offense manner, but also in a more defensive, physically augmenting way. Not only that, while augmenting his physical prowess, the powers of the Blaze could also act in a healing capacity. He reached down into the depths of the Blaze and pushed every ounce of the power that he could draw upon into his muscles and bones. The simple application made his heart race, and he could practically feel the blood pumping through his veins. Aerith drew on the Blaze as deeply as he dared, just to the point where he could feel the burning begin itching under his skin. Any more, and the life giving energy would start to eat him from the inside out, and he would be doing the Heralds' work for them.

Aerith stole a glance in the direction of Hannah, and she was still trying to pick herself up off the floor. The impact with the ground from Aerith's attempt to save her had obviously not saved her entirely from the barrage of stone. Pieces of her armor were heavily dented, and he could see a wide gash on the side of her head, blood cascading down the left side of her face. It was a serious wound, and if she didn't get some kind of treatment soon, she could very well bleed to death. Her left arm too seemed to be damaged, as it hung limp at her side. Two of the fingers on that hand were distended and pointed in nearly unnatural directions. The brave knight was leaning heavily on the Sacred Weapon known as Spirit, and Aerith was sure that without it, she would still be lying on the cold stone floor. Camille was still lying motionless, but at least she was out of the path of battle now. The Voice and the Will were advancing on his position, and only Hannah was still at risk.

His ribs on the mend thanks to the power of the Blaze, Aerith decided to try a new approach. It was a risky gambit, but perhaps it was off the wall enough that the Heralds would not expect it. Aerith launched himself toward the Will again, this time though, instead of feinting one way or another, Aerith released his grasp on the hilts of the Sacred Weapons and dove toward the feet of the larger creature. The Sacred Weapons, bidden by not only Aerith's will, but also their own intentions, sped forward, one aimed at the head of the Will, while the other arced in toward his heart. A new blade appeared in Aerith's hand, one made purely of Blaze energy, a tactic that while he knew was not wise, was necessary in this case. He felt the blood in his mouth from the exertion of drawing too deeply on the Blaze, but quickly turned his focus. These next moments could be pivotal in the battle and he could not afford the distraction.

The Will reached out with one hand and attempted to catch Valor before it struck his heart, while at the same time brought the flat of his crystalline blade up to block the on-rushing point of Discipline. For the moment the creature ignored Aerith, and focused instead on stopping the Sacred Weapons. Discipline was harmlessly turned away by a well-placed block, but Valor would not be dissuaded so easily. The Will's armored hand found the blade of the sword in mid-air, but instead of arresting its advance, Valor ripped through the armor, bringing an unearthly roar from the Will. But the act of cutting through the heavy armor changed the trajectory of Valor's strike, and the tip of the blade struck true in the Will's left shoulder. Bright white light poured from not only the wound in the Will's shoulder, but also from the large jagged cut that spanned the palm of the Will's left hand. However, the Will was not going to let a third blow pierce his defenses. In a deft move, the Will allowed Valor's impact with his shoulder to propel him to the right, away from Aerith's intended strike. With his full weight shifted to his right leg, the Will brought up his left knee, and smashed it hard into the left side of Aerith's face. Aerith was caught completely by surprise by the blow and rocketed into the wall leaving an impact crater that nearly took him through the wall into the adjoining chamber. The blade of pure Blaze energy disappeared from Aerith's hand that next moment, and a hard cough brought forth more blood from the obvious internal injuries.

The Voice darted in, ready to end the battle once and for all. The gleaming crystalline blade crashed down on the nearly helpless form of Aerith Seth, but instead of contacting with flesh and bone, was instead intercepted by the cold steel mace known as Spirit. Both the Will and the Voice seemed shocked by the impertinent act of the High Priestess Hannah Ironheart, her broken form protecting the fallen Dark God, but they would not let shock rule their actions. The Will pressed in, his much heavier and broader blade sweeping toward both Aerith and Hannah. The priestess would have been no match for the strike even if she were in a position to block it, but Aerith was a different matter. He had recovered much quicker than the two Heralds had anticipated, and not only blocked the blow from the Will using a newly reconstituted Blaze weapon, but also reached out with his off-hand and sent a plume of the roiling fire into the face of the Voice. As both Heralds fell back, Aerith turned his attention to the Sacred Weapon Discipline which lay motionless on the other side of the corridor.

A single exertion of thought vaulted the weapon from where it lay to a hard strike at the left shoulder of the Will. The blades of Valor and Discipline met somewhere in the sinew and bone of the divine creature and severed its left arm at the shoulder. The massive creature roared in something that must have been pain and surprise, as a fountain of light energy erupted from the exposed joint. Once the limb hit the floor, it dissipated with a flash, and the two Sacred Weapons clattered to the ground again. The Will was not out of the fight though, and the next slash of its sword was possibly the strongest it had ever managed. Aerith wasn't foolish enough to try to block the blow; instead he turned into Hannah and flattened them both into the floor. The crystalline blade passed just a hair's breadth over the both of them. The tip of the sword ripped through the wall behind them, sending more rock and dust cascading into the room. However, the blow must also have struck a support beam. Aerith heard the cracking of wood and the rumbling of stone from above, and knew they didn't have much time before the ceiling would collapse upon them. There wasn't time to jump, nothing to kick off of, and standing up would make him a target for the Voice. Aerith reached into the back of his mind and took hold of the Blaze once again. This time, the swirling blue portal appeared beneath them, and without warning they fell through.

Using portals was never something that Aerith had been comfortable with, which is why he created the stones to begin with. The difficulty for Aerith had nothing to do with finding the power or creating the portals, it was more with aiming the destination. The farther the destination, the harder it was for Aerith to keep track of it in his mind while he was doing anything else. The stones allowed Aerith to move from place to place without ever having to worry about the destination. But this was an emergency situation, so Aerith risked a short jaunt to further down the corridor where Camille lay. Just as Hannah and Aerith tumbled from the other end of the portal, the ceiling collapsed on the two Heralds.

"They'll be free from that in a moment," Aerith said picking himself up off the floor, without looking in Hannah's direction. "Get Camille out of here and get out of Albitonin if you can. There may not be much of this place left the way this battle's going."

As if on cue, the wreckage from the walls and ceiling that had covered the Herald's exploded in all directions. Aerith crafted a quick shield out of Blaze energy that melted and burned any of the debris that came in their direction, but he could not completely blunt the force of the shockwave that accompanied the debris. Both Aerith and Hannah were tossed off of their feet, and sent flying back a good ten feet where they landed heavily on the floor. When Aerith got back to his feet again, he was surprised to see Hannah out of the corner of his eye, dusting herself off and bringing the Sacred Weapon Spirit to bear. Aerith tried to will Valor and Discipline back to his hands, but they lay motionless behind the Will and the Voice. As Aerith let twin swords of Blaze energy form in his hands, he looked down the corridor to where Camille lay. She was now back in the center of the conflict, and he was sure that if the Voice or the Will wanted to, they would finish her off before Aerith could make a move to save her. It was too risky to try to create a portal under her, especially in her condition. He had no idea where he could safely put her, or even if she would survive the transition. Portal travel was never advisable for those who could not control how they exited the portal. Portals had to take some queues from the traveler, and if the traveler was not conscious, an uncontrolled portal could have disastrous consequences.

"HANNAH IRONHEART," the Voice spoke in its hard metallic tones, "YOU STAND AGAINST THE HERALDS OF THE CREATOR. REPENT NOW, OR BE DESTROYED ALONGSIDE THESE BLASPHEMERS."

Hannah held her ground.

"You cannot be emissaries of the Creator. The Creator preaches love, forgiveness, and devotion to peace. How many innocents have you robbed of their lives through your actions? The men you have killed here were devout followers of the Church of the Creator. They were pious men and women. Yet to you they were collateral damage in your quest to exterminate this man. And you call that woman there blasphemer even though she nearly sacrificed her life to save all of the lives of the devout men and women of Albitonin."

"IRRELEVANT," the Will growled. "AERITH SETH WILL BE DESTROYED."

"Then I shall strike you down in the name of the Creator as the pretenders and lies that you are," Hannah called back bringing her Sacred Weapon to bear.

The two sides began to advance on one another when the wall of the corridor near Camille exploded in a fountain of flame and light. The light was nearly blinding, and Aerith had to shield his eyes. Even when he knew that the light had faded, he had to blink several times to force the tears from his eyes, and his vision to clear. The blurry vision finally cleared, and Aerith was beyond shocked at what he saw. Standing in the newly created hole in the corridor wall was a young girl, perhaps fourteen or fifteen in appearance. She wore only a tattered white nightshirt that was matted to her body by rain and stained with soot. The rips in the fabric allowed nearly all of her body beneath the shirt to be clearly seen, but the girl seemed to care nothing for modesty. Her eyes were locked on the crumpled form of Camille that still lay motionless where she had finally fallen.

"Camille!"

The girl's voice was one of shock, pain, and sorrow. She rushed to the fallen woman's side, and scooped Camille's head into her lap and stroked her hair softly. The girl rocked back and forth slowly as though her mind had been shattered by what she had seen, and she sang softly to the unconscious woman, stroking her hair.

"Tess," Hannah called, "get out of here, it's too dangerous!"

Aerith made mental note of the name. He had never seen Pike's youngest, But the entrance was certainly one befitting her father. As though locked in a dream, Tess turned her head toward Hannah and Aerith, and Aerith could feel the brave knight shiver. Tess's eyes were wide and the iris was bright yellow, a color that Hannah's reaction told Aerith was not normal. Aerith could also see that at the edges of the iris was a dark red glow, one that had unmistakable power. Tess smiled briefly and then turned her attention back to Camille's fallen form. The Voice hesitated for only a moment, and then darted forward, his blade intended to take the head of the new arrival as well as finish off the fallen Dark God. Aerith moved as well, his intention to block the blow and give Tess and Camille time to escape, with Hannah's help if the girl was not in possession of enough of her faculties to get out of the Heart of Stone herself. A foot from their intended targets, both the Voice and Aerith were seized by some invisible force. They both hung, suspended in the air, all of the powers and abilities rendered moot. Hannah and the Will too seemed to be seized by the same force, as they were unable to make any motion to assist or take advantage of the situation. The threats removed, Tess gently lifted Camille from where she lay on the floor and held her closely as Tess made her way back to her feet. The young girl seemed totally oblivious to anything that was going on around her, and her attention was solely focused on Camille. In a matter of moments, the two were gone, and as soon as Tess had left the corridor, the invisible force that was holding all of them simply vanished. It took both the Voice and Aerith a moment to recover their footing. Aerith looked over his shoulder at Hannah for a quick moment.

"When we get out of here," Aerith said turning his eyes back to the two Heralds, "you're going to have to explain to me just what the hell just happened."

Hannah grimaced.

"I was hoping you would be able to tell me."

Aerith frowned. What the little girl had done was beyond the abilities of any of the Dark Gods, let alone their children. Aerith doubted that even the children of the Creator could have managed such a thing. Craning his neck from one side to the other, Aerith prepared himself for the next part of the battle to begin, and inwardly wondered if he had enough left to be much of a challenge to the two Heralds that were set on his destruction. Hannah would be a nice distraction for a few seconds, but once one of the Heralds got a clean blow in on her, it would be over. If anything, Hannah's participation in the battle hurt Aerith's chances of walking away from it alive. Despite his inclinations otherwise, Aerith knew that he would kill himself trying to defend Hannah so long as she was part of the battle, and with the stakes this high, that is probably exactly what would happen. Well, he always had been told that he would lose his head over a woman one day, and he had always hoped that it would never be literally. Then something truly unexpected happened.

Aerith first felt it as a twitch in the pit of his stomach, something akin to hunger, but deeper, and much more violent. It radiated outward, like a wave of nausea and revulsion, but soon changed from unpleasant to warm and soothing, like being wrapped in a blanket. All of the pain and discomfort in his body was suddenly washed away. He felt stronger, faster, and as though he had just woken from the best sleep he had ever had. The exhaustion was wiped away from his muscles, and his breathing was calm and even. The broken and cracked bones had all been healed, and the wounds that littered his body just simply pulled themselves back together as though they had never been there at all. Even the scars on his arms from previous battles simply disappeared. The Blaze that he felt at the back of his mind suddenly flared to five times its previous brilliance, and the power at his disposal increased to a factor he couldn't even begin to fathom. Information flooded into his mind, too much to process, but at the same time almost instinctive.

"Sabrina, you brilliant girl," Aerith said to the emptiness around him, "I could just kiss you."

The sword of Blaze blinked out from Aerith's hands, and he stood straight, looking at the two Heralds. Hannah could tell a change in the man instantly, not just his posture, but his entire being. He may have been looking up at the faces of the Heralds, but he was most certainly looking down on them now.

"Well," Aerith said finally, "this is a much more even fight now. Tell you what. Give me a second to confer with my ally here, and we'll get back to fighting."

The Will roared and rushed forward. Aerith seemed ready for the tactic and reached out with his left hand, sending a sheet of green flame coursing down the whole of the corridor. The crest of the wave struck with such force that the Will was knocked off his feet and sent flailing backwards. The Voice too was swept in by the wave and sent careening out of control for several feet before the wave subsided enough for him to bat his wings and regain balance. The Will simply dug the tip of his sword into the floor and opened a huge furrow down the center of the corridor until he was able to arrest his backward momentum.

"That wasn't a request," Aerith yelled down the corridor at the Heralds before turning to face Hannah.

Hannah saw a new light in Aerith's eyes. It was frightening while at the same time comforting. His eyes were a brilliant blue, almost glowing with power. At the very edge of his iris, she could see a pulsing rim of green which blended into the blue to form an almost ghostly haze at the edge of the iris. He put a hand on each of her shoulders, and immediately Hannah felt all of the pain and exhaustion flee from her body.

"Hannah, I'm going to give you a choice," Aerith said firmly. "All your life you have followed the teachings of the Creator and tried your best to follow His tenants. Now you see what the Creator truly is. You see the pain that those working in His name can cause. The Will and the Voice are just the most direct extensions of that perverse view. You and yours have been lied to all this time, and now you have a chance to make it right. You've already split from the Cadarian Emperor, your rebellion will crumble around your ears now that Gregor, Devlin, and Gabriel are gone, and it's only a matter of time before Marlae shows her true colors and shows you just how much she is her father's daughter. Principle is not going to get you where you want to go in this Hannah."

Hannah felt the sting of his words, but could not put voice to any objections.

"You've got a bright mind, Hannah, and you've seen what faith can truly do. I can give you the opportunity to see that balance returns to this world. I can give you what you need to stand up to the false gods and the perversions that call themselves the Heralds of the Creator. The game is changed now. Sabrina has opened a door for me that I don't think anyone realized was possible. She was mortal when she received the touch of Halicon's might, and while it may have made her the equal of a Dark God again, she could no longer wear my mantle. So, Hannah, I'm offering it to you. Become the first *Chosen One* of this world. Help me put these things right."

Hannah didn't realize that she was nodding until she saw the wide smile on Aerith's face.

Chapter LXII

The Shadow and the Fox

Year Three of the Just Emperor Kaitain "Dragonsbane" Lorien,
Creator's Calendar Year 1870

The Keep of the Serpentine Knight of the Flashing Blade had returned to its more common silence and emptiness after the departure of the fugitives from Kaitain's justice. Servants had been dismissed early, and Isa, the long-time companion of the Serpentine Knight, Vallic Ultiv had retired early. Vallic as he did many nights sat in his private study, a book open in his hand. However, as was usually the case, his attention was only half-focused on the book. There were so many things going on in the Empire now for him to focus his attention on anything fully. Between the continued troublesome followers of Dorovar, the Dark Gods, and now the rebellion in Albitonin, there was certainly enough for a Knight of the Flashing Blade to do. But the Knights of the Flashing Blade were not what they once were. The once proud organization had been splintered by one man, Kaitain Lorien. Vallic had known the boy since he was an infant, and watched with revulsion at what the boy would become. Kaitain was a spoiled child, not in a material sense, but in the sense that he felt as though he were entitled to everything he wanted simply because he drew breath. He was the heir to the throne of the Cadarian Empire, but before Kaitain even knew what that meant, he acted with power and a feeling of impunity. Many parallels could be drawn between Kaitain's early life and that of his daughter Marlae. They both felt as though the world was theirs, and they only needed to show the rest of the world that it was so. Vallic had collided with spoiled men like that all of his life. Men who felt they were above their station. Men who did not know the meaning of honor, duty, or respect. They only wanted what they could not take into their own hands. The more they had, the more they wanted. And the simple truth was, that men like that only brought one thing to the world; suffering. So many friends had been lost in the wars caused by such men. So many loved ones. Many philosophers said that for a hero to rise, there must be a villain to struggle against. While Vallic knew this to be true, he often mused that the line between hero and villain was much thinner than most ever thought about. It was all a matter of perception. To Kaitain's supporters, he was a hero rescuing the great and noble Cadarian Empire from the evils of the dragons and the Dark Gods and the rebels. To the rebels, Kaitain was a vicious young man whose desires would lead the Cadarian Empire to ruin. Who was the villain? Who was the hero? Were the rebels in the right? Were those loyal to Kaitain? Were those men doing their duty in Kaitain's name villains as well? Vallic himself had done many unsavory things in the name of his Emperor over the years, and in the name of his superiors in his time before becoming a member of the Knights of the Flashing Blade. He was revered as a hero, but how many saw him as a villain? Plenty of good men had been the perpetrators of incredibly evil deeds, just as many evil men had hidden behind their own good deeds.

As Vallic continued to muse about the fine line between light and darkness, there came a sound from the dining room. It wasn't a random creaking of the wood, or something that could have been caused by the wind. There was a definite sound of moving liquid and something heavy being placed onto metal. Vallic looked over to the large scythe standing in the corner, and inwardly sighed. The Sacred Weapon had been in his possession since his ascension to the rank of Knight of the Flashing Blade, but he had never felt comfortable wielding it. Like all of the Sacred Weapons, Harmony granted abilities to its wielder. Vallic could feel all of the flows of power coming from all over the world and feel where imbalances were. He could feel pockets of evil, good, hope, despair, and all other types of imbalance. It was overwhelming the first time that Vallic felt the power course through him, and it forever changed his perceptions of the world around him. But as the Empire of Cadaria and by extension the rest of the world descended into the chaos of Kaitain Lorien's rule, Vallic could stand to hold Harmony in his hands less and less. He felt a malignancy in his heart every time the haft of the weapon was in his hands, and he could no longer see past the evil of his own actions. One could not be an extension of Harmony when one did not have harmony within themselves. But Vallic's worried mind would not give him peace. Even in Isa's loving arms, Vallic's mind could find no rest and his soul no peace.

When Vallic rose from his chair to investigate the sound, he wanted to reach for Harmony, but he did not. There was a sickening twist in the pit of his stomach at the thought of holding the weapon in his hands, and he could not stand the thought. Instead, Vallic drew a longsword from a scabbard that hung on the back of a chair near the door. He emerged from the library and stood in the hallway looking into the dining room. Most of the room itself was cast in darkness, except for a handful of streams of moonlight that flooded in from the large windows high in the east and west walls. One of the beams of moonlight illuminated the center of the large dining table, and Vallic tensed when he saw a pair of boots propped up on the table. The stream of light revealed the form of a person up to the top of the thighs, and while Vallic could make out parts of the rest of the shadow-covered form, he could not make out enough to attach an identity to the person. The sound Vallic had heard was a person pouring a drink from the large cistern that sat in the center off the table.

"Intruding into the home of a member of the Knights of the Flashing Blade is not wise," Vallic said standing straight, leaving his sword at his side. "And it is rude to help yourself to food and drink without first being invited."

The form sitting on the other side of the table made no move, but a distinctive woman's voice rang out from the empty hall. Vallic thought the voice sounded familiar as soon as he heard it, and the possibility made his blood run cold.

"Consorting with Kaitain Lorien and doing his bidding is also not wise," the woman's cold hard voice intoned, "and because of it, you won't see another sunrise, Vallic Ultiv, Serpentine Knight of the Flashing Blade."

The woman's feet dropped from the table the next moment, and with a single hard kick to the table's edge, she sent it flying across the chamber toward where Vallic stood. When the table hit the walls of the chamber, it splintered, but the center of the table continued into the hallway with such speed that Vallic was unable to react in time to dodge the blow. He was struck in the chest, and landed flat on his back, the sword clattering from his hand and spinning across the floor away from him. The woman was also on top of him the next moment, a gleaming blade of steel speeding toward his heart. Vallic's eyes flashed to the tip of the blade, and the woman was forgotten for a moment. He reacted fast enough to get his hand up to catch the blade before it pierced his heart. Unconsciously, he channeled some of the power within him to harden the flesh of the palm of his hand, but it was not enough to keep the feel of steel ripping skin from rocketing through him. However, the damage was not what it could have been. Vallic wrenched the blade out of the woman's hands and let a bubble of force form around him. With a single exhale, the bubble popped, sending a shockwave of force billowing out in all directions, shattering the fragments of the table, and sending the woman flying backwards through the air. To her credit, the woman landed on her feet in a crouch, near the center of the dining hall. She stayed in the feral crouch as Vallic made his way back to his feet. He didn't bother to look at his hand, he knew blood was flowing freely from the wound. He clenched his hand tightly and let a small trickle of power flow to his hand to help knit the wound. It would still be tender, but at least it would not hamper him for the rest of the fight.

"Your actions are crimes of the highest order against the Throne of Cadaria. To take arms against a member of the Knights of the Flashing Blade carries the same penalty as if you had raised arms against the Emperor."

Vallic could almost feel the woman smile.

"Well, as I intend to kill your Emperor as well, it is a fitting piece of trivia. Not that anyone will ever have the opportunity to charge me with these crimes. I consider what I do a service for everyone that draws breath in this pathetic Empire."

Vallic's blood boiled. Such blatant disrespect was an affront to everything he had sworn to defend, and yet the woman's voice brought shivers through his body. It was so familiar, but impossible.

"Well, if you are going to kill me, at least give me the honor of your name."

The woman rose the next moment, and Vallic felt his heart almost stop in his chest. While she was not wearing one of her token red dresses, Lady Bryn Seth was still strikingly beautiful and fearsome in the same breath. Her smile was wide and wicked, and the red shirt that she wore seemed at least two sizes too small for her frame. As it was, she had slit the collar as to create a plunging neckline that was just on the other side of decent. She wore a simple black pair of pants that could have been painted on her as tight as they were, and a simple pair of soft leather boots. Her hair was pulled back, held by a red ribbon, but the streaks of red in her brunette hair were still quite apparent. Bryn's eyes flashed in the moonlight, and there was no doubt in that moment why the woman was called the Lady Fox.

"I am Lady Bryn Seth," the woman said, a slight hesitation in the pronouncement of her last name, "and I have been sent by the leader of the Dark Gods to take retribution on the Knights of the Flashing Blade for their attempts on the lives of the Dark Gods in blatant violation of the decree of Emperor Lorien the First. And on a personal note, one of you was stupid enough to actually draw a weapon against me. For that, all of you will burn."

Vallic wanted to open his mouth and respond to the woman's charge, but there was no time. She darted forward the next moment, a blast of fire erupting from Bryn's outstretched hand. There was no way for Vallic to respond to the strike or even attempt to dodge. The stream of white-hot flames sped toward him and connected with the very center of his chest. A cry of pain tore from Vallic the next moment as he was propelled down the hallway where he crashed into two suits of armor that stood as ornaments at the end of the hall. By all rights, that strike would have killed an ordinary man, and most extraordinary ones. But Vallic was able to draw one tortured breath, followed by another, and he instinctively brought his hand to the still smoking patch on his chest. The simple black shirt had been burned away, and his skin was bright red and hot to the touch. Blisters would begin forming in a matter of seconds, but he had no time to worry about the pain. Vallic barely got to his feet and then dove to the floor as a ball of fire streaked through the space where his head had been only a heartbeat before. The ball of flame exploded against the wall, sending a shower of flame and sparks, as well as melting stone into the air. Some of the debris caught Vallic on the back and shoulders, and he could smell the smoldering of what remained of his shirt. Scrambling back to his feet, Vallic ripped the remains of his shirt from his body and tossed it to the ground. His eyes scanned for his opponent, and he found her a moment before her next strike.

Bryn rose high into the air and thrust both hands forward, a massive sheet of roiling flames crashing toward their target. Vallic reached into himself again, pulling forth the power hidden there. Just in time, he was able to form another bubble of force around himself, enough he hoped to protect himself from the assault. The wave of fire collided with the bubble, and while some was diverted toward the walls and floor, still more poured over the entire surface of the bubble, enveloping him in scorching heat. The force of the crashing wave was almost too much for Vallic to keep the bubble intact, and he sank to his knees to minimize the size of the bubble he needed to maintain. Blood began to stream from Vallic's nose and he kept the bubble up against the assault. Drawing this much power was taking its toll on him, and he wondered how long his body would hold out. If he allowed Bryn to just keep assaulting him, there would be nothing left of him. He had to take the fight to her. He took some of his concentration off of maintaining the shield and poured what energy he could manage into his left hand. The energy began to coalesce as a ball of water that floated above his palm. Vallic could hear Bryn's laughter over the roaring flames. He sneered and committed himself to ending her enjoyment of the battle. Vallic released part of the shield and then thrust his left hand forward, sending a stream of water back through the wave of fire toward Bryn. The fire and water collided, canceling each other out into super-heated steam, and the force of the collision of fire and water created a shockwave of heat blasting in all directions. Both Vallic and Bryn were caught in the blast, and Vallic was thrown backwards into the now melting suits of armor, while Bryn crashed to the ground on the far end of the dining hall. Vallic's gambit had worked, but it had been a costly one. As he got back to his feet, he knew that several of his ribs were broken, and the skin on his back and chest must have looked more like melted candle wax than skin. There was little strength left in his left arm, and while it hung limp at his side, he knew it could still be used if necessary. His right hand had been broken by his collision with the wall, but he was channeling a little of his remaining power into it to make it useable in the remainder of the fight. There was little energy left now, and he had drawn on more than he had in dozens of years.

Bryn brushed herself off and frowned. A Knight of the Flashing Blade shouldn't have been this much trouble. They were pests to be sure, but they were not nearly on the level of competition that this Vallic was turning out to be. He fought more like Logan and Pike had in their day. Too stupid to realize they were hopelessly overmatched. But no matter, she was after all the Lady Fox, at the height of her abilities. Brute force had never been her strong suit, but she felt that such direct assaults would have easily reduced this would-be hero to ash. But, no matter, she would simply employ different tactics, but the outcome would be the same. Vallic Ultiv would not see the next sunrise, and the Cadarian Empire would be put on notice that the Dark Gods would not stop until all of the Knights of the Flashing Blade were exterminated. And the name of the Lady Fox would be feared once again.

Vallic knew the next assault was coming, but was unable to defend against it. Instead of a wave or burst of fire, small needles of flame erupted from the darkness, looking like shooting stars. They cut through Vallic all over his body, passing straight through as though he were so much paper. Hundreds struck true before he was able to form a bubble around himself again, and blood trickled from all of the wounds. He could not rise back to his feet again, even if he wanted to. The damage done to his legs was too great. The hail of needles of fire intensified, and the bubble around Vallic burst. Vallic fell under the intensified assault. His fallen body convulsed in pain and he writhed on the ground. Bryn approached slowly, ready to strike again if the fallen knight managed to mount some kind of surprise assault. Vallic's body smoked and his breathing was ragged and labored. Bryn was impressed that the man was still alive and that he was breathing at all. It was a testament to how stupid the man truly was. If he was as wise as the stories wanted people to believe he would have realized that he was dead and stop hanging on to pointless hope. Smiling to herself at the thought of his absurd stubbornness, Bryn walked slowly over to Vallic's fallen form, a blade of pure fire forming in her hand. Perched over the fallen Knight of the Flashing Blade, Bryn held the point of the blade at Vallic's throat, and then lifted the sword high, ready to strike the final blow. The blade came streaking down, but suddenly a roaring noise filled the chamber and something struck Bryn from behind. The cold raced through her body, and she instinctively released the blade of fire from her hand and it winked out of existence. Bryn was thrown clear of Vallic's fallen form, and she landed hard on her stomach on the far end of the hallway near a pool of melted metal that had once been the ornamental suits of armor. She managed to get to her feet quickly, the pain in her back nothing more than an annoyance. However, when she realized that she could not see, she realized she had been hit harder than she imagined possible. It took only a moment for the darkness to clear from her vision, and when she turned, she was surprised by what she saw before her.

A woman in a stark white nightdress stood in at the end of the hallway, her hands extended in front of her, panting hard. Whatever she had done had been a massive exertion, and probably was the one trick that the older woman had up her sleeve. Vallic had done well in choosing his mate, even if it meant that she would know death before he did. Bryn wasted no time in extending her power once again, thinking that a simple direct assault would be enough to overwhelm the exhausted woman and bring an end to her interloping. Bryn channeled fire into the ground at the older woman's feet, and a column of fire engulfed Isa. For the next few moments, all Bryn could see was churning flames, then suddenly the fire became a wall of steam, and from it emerged a ball of ice that moved so quickly that Bryn was unable to dodge it. The blast took her full in the chest, and she was slammed to the ground by the force of the impact. Isa stepped from the wall of steam, her nightshirt nearly disintegrated, but the skin on her face and body showed no signs of blistering. In fact, if anything the woman looked younger. Bryn fought hard to breathe, the impact having broken several bones. She could have taken a few moments to channel healing flows into her body, but this woman was full of surprises and there was not time. Any hesitation could be costly.

Bryn felt the air around her cool, and could almost taste ice on her tongue. Her eyes widened with realization, and hurriedly brought a shield of fire up around herself a split second before the assault began. Shards of ice shot from the coalescing vapor in the air, sharp as daggers. They battered the shield, hissing angrily as they turned to steam. Once the assault had ended, Bryn released the shield of fire, but did not counterattack.

There was something far too familiar about this battle, something far too familiar about the suddenly youthful woman that stood across the hallway from her. The way she held herself, the way those defiant cold eyes stared back at her. Sudden realization hit, and the shock melted into a smile.

"At least you didn't try to bore me to death with some over-analyzed scheme."

The woman calling herself Isa smiled and nodded.

"And at least your combat tactics have improved since last we met. I was hoping that all these years with Aerith that something would have rubbed off."

Happiness would not allow Bryn to scowl at the remark. She started slowly, making her way across the chamber to the slowly approaching older woman. Finally the two women stood eye to eye, and finally, they embraced. When Bryn pulled back, she could not erase the smile from her lips.

"You certainly still hit hard, Ellis."

Isa smiled.

"I haven't been called that in a very long time, Bryn. Its Isa now and it has been for a good long time. Ellis died the day that Onea burned."

Bryn nodded.

"But you're here? How can you be here? And why are you with one of the Knights of the Flashing Blade? Why aren't you with the Dark Gods, or in hiding like Aerith and I were?"

Isa smiled and shook her head.

"So many questions," Isa said moving past Bryn and kneeling at Vallic's side. "You always had so many questions. That is what got us in trouble all those millennia ago. Questions. Can you help me get Vallic into the library?"

Bryn stood firm.

"Ellis, Isa, whatever name you want to go by now," Bryn said coldly, "he is a member of the Knights of the Flashing Blade, and so he is my enemy. I've come here to kill him and all of his confederates. Don't stand between me and my goal, sister, or I'm afraid I would have to kill you as well."

Isa looked up at Bryn and sighed.

"But still not grasping things as quickly as you should. Some things never change Bryn. Look closely at Vallic. Look him in the eye. Isn't there something familiar about him? Something familiar about the way he fights? We were together for all those generations, fighting side by side, trying as hard to kill each other as we were the enemy."

Bryn looked at Isa quizzically and then approached Vallic's fallen form. He was still alive, if barely, and his dark eyes stared up at the ceiling. If he was conscious, it was just barely, and Bryn doubted if he would recall any of what happened after his defeat. But then Bryn looked into his eyes, deep into his eyes almost into his soul, and her blood froze. She took two steps back, shaking her head. It couldn't be, it was impossible. And yet Ellis was sitting there, still alive.

"That's right, Bryn," Isa said looking back down at Vallic, "Vallic is Jeroch."

To Set the Soul Ablaze

Year Three of the Just Emperor Kaitain "Dragonsbane" Lorien, Creator's Calendar Year 1870

Leonora Wastri looked on in horror as her boots sank into the bloody ground. Paces from her Bernhardt Yeoman still lay on the ground, his face ruined, and blood flowing freely from his wounds. The Moonstone Knight had certainly seen difficult times since his ascension to the rank of Knight of the Flashing Blade, and now with the loss of the sight in his left eye, and perhaps even loss of his ability to speak clearly, along with his already missing leg, his time of retirement may have been upon him. It would not be the shortest tenure in the history of the Knights of the Flashing Blade, but his mercurial fall would be remembered for the rest of the history of Cadaria if he lived to see another sunrise. However, such an eventuality was not assured. The naked force arrayed against the two armies of Cadaria was awe-inspiring at the least, terrifying at the worst. Never in all of Leonora's time in Galateria did she ever see a force of Jeresei and Shadowwalkers this large amassed. In a single charge, they would overwhelm what remained of the Jade Army and the Iron Legion. The Jade Knight had fought against the beasts many times over, and had spent a great deal of time learning their tactics. It was the others that concerned Leonora. The names Rael and Trece Starlin were well known to her. They were Dark Gods, members of the Fallen. This was the second time that the

Dark Gods had made their presence known at the Academy of Arcane Arts in Jelan, and both times Leonora had been present. The last time had meant her defeat and near execution at the hands of Emperor Kaitain Lorien. This time however, she would not retreat so easily. She took two long strides forward, and as she did, she reached into the deepest reserves of her strength and power granted to her by Wisdom, and tried her best to knit her injuries. It would take some time, and that small trickle of power would be useless to her in the fight against the Fallen, but there were other tools at her disposal. She was easily within striking range of the two Dark Gods when she stopped her advance and planted the butt of Wisdom's haft into the ground at her side. She must have looked like a mess to the two Dark Gods; her armor shattered at the shoulder and her breastplate cracked, her clothes tattered and her hair a tangled mess. No matter her appearance, she was still the Lady Leonora Wastri, the Jade Knight of the Flashing Blade, and Protector of the Kingdom of the Soul.

"Lord and Lady Starlin," Leonora began in the best voice she could manage, "you hold no claim over this kingdom or over the people who dwell within its borders. The Academy of Arcane Arts is not open for claim, and whether it chooses to recognize rule by the Emperor Kaitain Lorien or the Empress Marlae Lorien is a matter of internal Cadarian politics."

"I beg to differ," Rael said quickly. "The Iron Legion came here to invade."

"Where is the choice in that?" Trece continued, flawlessly picking up the continuity of the sentence. "And what would the Jade Army have done if the Academy chose not to accept the rule of the spoiled princess?"

"What then, indeed." Rael finished.

Leonora tried hard to keep her tone even.

"Regardless of their status, the students and administrators of the Academy of Arcane Arts are citizens of the Empire of Cadaria, and so are subject to the laws of the Empire. Failure to cede to those laws has led us here."

"Failure to cow-tow to a tyrant is what has led us here," Trece began.

"And so we have come to give another option," Rael continued.

"A better option," Trece concluded.

Leonora could not keep the look of incredulity from creeping onto her face. Her distrust of the Dark Gods was plain, but this was bordering on lunacy.

"And what makes you think that the members of the Academy would even welcome your intervention? The Masters have been the staunch allies of the Emperor of Cadaria for generations."

Rael and Trece looked to each other for a moment, and then back to Leonora. Rael's smile was wider now, and the one from Trece had disappeared completely.

"Things change," Trece said coldly.

"We were invited by the Academy to ensure their protection," Rael said in a tone that could only be interpreted as mocking.

It felt like something exploded inside of Leonora's mind. Her thoughts raced, and the betrayal soared through her heart like poison. She squeezed the haft of Wisdom so hard she could hear her knuckles crack. The rage that was normally so well controlled was building to a breaking point, and she didn't know how much longer she could let this insult go unchallenged.

"Withdraw from this field," Rael said after a moment.

"Once both armies stand down, the Masters will be willing to hear petitions from the two sides to determine whether or not they want to align with either side or be an independent entity that governs itself."

That was it. That was all Leonora could take. Long ago she made a promise to herself that she would follow the course of action that her mind and heart were screaming for her to follow. She had learned to touch the heart of evil, the soul of the wicked, and channel that for her own purpose. If she had known the true nature of that power when her teacher offered her the secrets, she never would have let the foul power sully her. Even now she felt the taint, like a greasy stain upon her soul, one she could never remove. But here, faced with this untenable position; faced with letting the fate of the Academy of Arcane Arts slip into the hands of the Dark Gods… It could not come to pass.

Reaching down into the depths of the core of her being, Leonora found what she was looking for. There locked away was a small, nearly insubstantial emerald green flame that had been reduced by neglect to barely embers. However, as though it knew it was being observed, it flared into life, bright and seductive and hungry. The moments she considered reaching for the power that lay dormant within her would only take heartbeats to the outside world, but felt like an eternity to her soul. The siren song of the crackling flame was hypnotic and powerful, like the voice of a long lost lover. Finally she reached for the power of the Blaze. Almost instantly, Leonora felt the sensation of power flood through her. In a matter of heartbeats the feelings changed to that of pure joy and contentment. The feeling mounted until she felt as though she was swimming, immersed in pure sensation. Her chest heaved and her heart beat so fast she thought that it was going to burst forth from her already damaged ribs. She could feel the power of the Blaze surge through her. But the cautions from her mind were screaming louder now. The recriminations and rebukes from years of discipline and purity demanded that she stop what she was doing. They begged her to fight back against the invading and tainted sensations. This was the moment she knew was coming. She could feel the doubts wane for a moment, and the power of the Blaze hovered there at the edges of her perception, waiting to be let it. Waiting to be given control. She could still turn back now. She could shut the power away, never to let it feed upon her doubt and her fear again. She still had time to decide, but the time was growing short. Suddenly the Blaze was there, bright and powerful, threatening to make her choice for her. Leonora felt part of her mind lash out, trying to fight against the flows of power. The inner conflict began to boil as she felt her control begin to slip. But then the Blaze flared once more inside of her, and all doubt, all fear, and all chances to put the monster back into its cage were gone.

The whole scene took the length of a blink, but Leonora knew the Dark Gods felt the change within her. Leonora drank deeply of the unbridled power and let it fill every part of her to the fullest. Her sweat burned as it rolled down her skin, and her aura radiated with the brilliant green energy.

The looks on the faces of the Dark Gods had changed. The haughty confidence was gone, and a new uncertainly replaced it. It was then that Trece pulled on the sleeve of her companion.

"Rael, look at her eyes."

Rael nodded absently. The woman's eyes had lost all of their natural color and were now a brilliant jade green. They shone brightly like tiny stars, flaring with power that raged against its containment.

* * * * * * * * * * * *

Year One of the Just Emperor Ender Lorien, Creator's Calendar Year 1782

The year of mourning for the Tenth Lorien Emperor, Kaldawyn "Peacebringer" Lorien had come to a close with the coronation of his oldest son, Ender. For the first time in nearly a hundred years, a new voice would be leading the Cadarian Empire, and all indications from the year without an emperor were that Ender would be a fitting successor for his father. However, Ender's first days at the helm of the Cadarian Empire had been rocky ones. Rumors travelled throughout the Empire that Kaldawyn had been murdered by agents of the Dark Gods, and the cries went up in the countryside for vengeance. It had sparked off the Third Shadow War, and the whole of Galateria was alight with the fires of battle. Men and beasts fell in equal measure, but there was no direct sign of any involvement by the Dark Gods. Innocent blood was being spilled everywhere. The Jade Army had been dispatched to deal with the mounting armies of beasts in the fields of Oradrim and Menoris, and the teenaged Leonora Wastri watched her father and older brothers be called off to war. She may have only been thirteen years old, but she understood war, and she understood the needlessness of fighting in one. That belief struck firmly home when none of her family came home from the war. Her father had fallen to the claws of a beast known as a Shadowwalker, and no one could know for certain how her two brothers had died. Their bodies were too broken to even be returned for burial. All that returned from the battle were her father's armor and his helm. The helm itself was a ruined mess, the claws from the beast had cut massive long gashes into the polished metal, and the stains of blood would never come clean from the sharp edges. Her father had died in violence, leaving Leonora and her mother alone.

A letter came from the Just Emperor himself weeks later extending his condolences, and the letter assured that no taxes would ever be demanded from the Wastri family so long as he sat on the throne. In the Emperor's words, the family's debt to the empire had already been paid in blood. Leonora's mother made some money as an instructor in the Imperial Academy in Menoris, and was gone for several months out of the year. While Leonora was too young to attend the Academy, her mother decided that she did not want the girl to be alone in their house with only the ghosts and memories to keep her company. And so Leonora was fostered to a tutor for the months that her mother was away. But young girls are not ones to take the decree of their mothers without argument. And so the first two tutors were met with equal parts disdain and disinterest by the rebellious nature of the young Leonora. In fact, the parting with the second tutor was so explosive that Leonora's mother had to take a leave of absence from her post at the Imperial Academy to deal with the issue.

One evening, Leonora had left the house to go walking after another fight with her mother over her future. The village where Leonora grew up was small, and everyone knew everyone. But just outside the village, Leonora saw a small camp fire and a simple tent set up. Visitors to this area of Oradrim were rare to say the least, and for the most part strangers were not a welcome sight. These days however, strangers had as much chance of being run out of town at sword point as they did finding hospitality. Though Emperor Ender Lorien was doing his best to put the pieces back together after the death of his beloved father, no one could deny that the soul of Cadaria had changed. The peace that Kaldawyn Lorien worked so hard to create and maintain had been shattered, and with it had been a measure of the trust and security that so many had taken for granted.

Leonora had never been a shy child, and with two older brothers had learned quickly to take care of herself. Though her brothers would have been there for her in an instant if she had been in any real trouble, they had a propensity for causing her enough trouble without having to go look for it. But since the loss of her brothers, Leonora had been more adventurous and much more curious. She had gotten into several scuffles with other children, and had been regarded as a bit of a bully by other parents. Other girls, while they looked up to Leonora, felt she was too much like a boy, and boys wanted nothing to do with her because they were scared of her.

The path she was on was going to make her very lonely, or very dead. She had thought many times of enlisting in the Jade Army when she was old enough, to follow in the footsteps of her father and brothers, but her mother would not hear any of that talk. Leonora's mother was going to make her daughter into a proper lady, even if it killed her.

As Leonora approached the campfire, she couldn't see anyone sitting around it, and there were belongings on the ground, but no one was in sight. The opening of the tent was facing her, and from her viewpoint, there was no one at the camp at all. An empty camp held no interest for her, and she was not a thief, so she turned to head back to her house and ran headlong into a man. The collision startled her, but she was able to stifle the scream before it escaped her lips. She did however take two steps back and look up at the man, wishing she had remembered to bring her dagger that her oldest brother had given her for protection.

"So, just passing through, or did I catch a thief before she had a chance to go through my things?"

Leonora frowned and gritted her teeth in anger. To be accused of being a thief was insulting at the least. She put her hands on her hips and looked up at the man's cold gray eyes. He had a full beard and long dark hair that looked as though it had not seen any soap in a good long time. His clothes were not fine by any means and were covered in soot and dust from long travels. What was strange though was that he didn't smell. Someone who had been on the road as long as this man obviously had should have smelled of sweat and dirt and the ugliness of the road, but this man didn't smell at all, and neither did his clothes for that matter. He was a full head and shoulders taller than Leonora, and she was tall for her age.

"I'm not a thief," Leonora said firmly. "We're just not used to seeing strangers here, so I wanted to see who you were, and warn you off coming into town. People are not very kind to strangers these days."

The man regarded the girl for a moment and then nodded.

"War makes everyone a little paranoid. I should know, I've been in enough of them. This one won't last too much longer. But it does seem that everyone is drinking a little deeper from the cup of vengeance than they normally do. I suppose its natural when someone like Kaldawyn is cut down."

As if suddenly remembering that she was standing there, the man looked down at Leonora and patted her lightly on the shoulder.

"Thank you for your warning. I'll be passing through in the morning and I'll make sure to keep my distance from the village proper. Your people will have nothing to fear from me."

With that the man walked past her toward his camp. There was something about the man that sparked Leonora's interest, something about the way that he talked and held himself. He was more than just a traveler, no matter what image he was trying hard to present. After a moment he had settled back in front of the fire and was about to start roasting a lizard he must have caught before Leonora disturbed him. Despite herself, she found herself walking toward his camp. When she was standing just an arms-reach from him he looked back over his shoulder.

"I think maybe I can find you a better meal," Leonora said suddenly shy, "and maybe a bath, if you want."

* * * * * * * * * * *

Year Five of the Just Emperor Ender Lorien, Creator's Calendar Year 1787

It had been five years since Leonora had found her tutor. She had no way of knowing the night she literally collided with the stranger that he would be an integral part of her life over her teenage years. The strange travelling man, as Leonora expected turned out to be far more than he appeared. After that first dinner, Leonora's mother had been so impressed with him that she offered to let him stay on to do some work around the house if he wanted to stay in one place for a while. Over the next week more about the man became apparent, and Leonora was soon learning all manner of lessons from the man she came to know as Cedric. He seemed to be a fountain of knowledge on so many subjects. Diplomacy, courtly matters, philosophy, law, religion, combat, battle tactics, and also seemed to be familiar with a variety of weapons and fighting styles. And Leonora, to her credit, was a sponge. She constantly was in Cedric's company, soaking up all of the information that she could manage. For a time, Leonora's mother thought that the connection between the man and his daughter was harmless, but as Leonora grew, she began to see a different look in her daughter's eyes. One that did not speak of the admiration a pupil had for her teacher.

Cedric was asked to leave, and not wanting the conflict, he agreed. But Leonora would not be denied her tutor. Nor would she allow the love that was blossoming between them to be cut down in its infancy. She told her mother in no uncertain terms that she would follow Cedric wherever he went, if he would have her, and packed her things and left the village after him. It took her two days to catch up to him. Cedric was adept at not being followed when he did not want to be, and even all of the tricks that he had showed Leonora were barely enough to help her find him. Just as she found him five years earlier, there he sat by a simple fire, roasting a lizard.

"You should go home to your mother, Leah. It's not safe for you to be out here, even with all that I've taught you. And out in the world it's not safe for you to be with me, either."

"You aren't finished teaching me yet."

Cedric looked back over his shoulder, and saw the look in the young woman's eyes. She had changed so much in just five years. As she approached, her determination was clear. All of the anger that had been with her as a child was gone. She was controlled, elegant, and beautiful on both the inside and outside. He could not help but laugh.

"I'm old enough to be your great-grandfather."

Leonora shook her head.

"Your lies never make sense."

She leaned in and kissed him hard on the lips.

* * * * * * * * * * * *

Year Thirteen of the Just Emperor Ender "Just Hand" Lorien, Creator's Calendar Year 1795

Leonora and Cedric sat around the fire laughing. Cedric had caught another lizard and was about to stick it on the end of a spit to roast over the fire. Leonora took an apple out of her bag and threw it at him.

"You never liked my cooking, Leah," Cedric said as he let the lizard go.

"You've never cooked anything for me to like," Leonora responded.

They had been together for almost thirteen years now, the last seven as lovers. Cedric had shown Leonora more of the world than she ever dreamed possible. He saw the bonds of reality not as walls, but as windows, and he had taught her to see things the same way, but it had taken her learning to touch the Blaze. The way Cedric taught her, the Blaze was the life force of nature, and learning to tap into it made it possible to experience reality the way it was intended to be experienced. It had taken her a long time to learn to touch the flickering green energy, but once she had, her learning accelerated in a way she never thought possible. Touching the Blaze made her faster, stronger, and more capable in all tasks. It also seemed to make her mind work faster. She grasped information quicker. The biggest shock was the first time she looked in a mirror after touching the Blaze. She had had many years to get used to her appearance. The small imperfections that all women have that they obsess over for the rest of their lives were burned into her consciousness. However, when she looked at herself in the mirror, all of those imperfections had been washed away. Her skin was flawless, her features perfect, and her body toned and timeless. The Blaze had made her beautiful. Men looked at her differently; women looked at her either with jealousy or hunger. Cedric had explained that the Blaze helped a person become who they truly saw themselves in their mind, and a conscious application of that power could accentuate that.

"Cedric never could cook."

Cedric was on his feet and facing the voice before Leonora even saw him. When she got to her feet, recognition had seeped into her mind. The man was Vallic Ultiv, the Serpentine Knight of the Flashing Blade. Cedric had his hand on the hilt of his sword, but had not drawn the weapon yet. With his off hand, he signaled for Leonora to take a step back.

"And Vallic here always had questionable timing."

The two men sized each other up for a long second.

"You look pretty good for a dead man," Vallic said quietly.

"I could say the same for you," Cedric returned, a low growl entering his voice.

"It took me a long time to track you down. I nearly caught up with you in Oradrim, but when I heard you took a student, I feared the worst. It seems that my suspicions were correct. What you did was unwise, old friend."

Cedric drew his sword.

"We're not friends, Vallic, or whatever name you're wearing now. We've never been friends, and we'll never be friends. So, if you're here to kill me, just make your move and spare me your patronizing."

Vallic brought the Sacred Weapon to bear, the huge vicious scythe that could sever a man's head with a single stroke.

"I don't have a choice, Cedric. You shouldn't be here. This world isn't for you."

Cedric fell back to a defensive stance.

"Neither should you, Shadow. Let's end this once and for all."

A blinding flash came from the corner of Leonora's eye, and she was struck by something unseen. Her vision went black and she lost consciousness.

* * * * * * * * * * * *

Leonora awoke in a temple, a cold compress on her forehead. She turned her head to the left, and there sat the Serpentine Knight, Vallic Ultiv. She felt the anger rise in her, and she reached for the Blaze, but it wasn't there. It had fled her control.

"I've suppressed your ability to touch the Blaze," Vallic said after a moment. "It's an ability you never should have been able to learn, and Cedric is someone you never should have been able to meet."

She wanted to scream. She wanted to strike out at him, but her body would not respond. He stood after a moment and approached her, and he put a hand on each side of her face and looked deeply into her eyes. For a moment the defiance in her kept her gaze away from his, but soon her resistance melted. His gaze was not angry, but sorrowful and understanding, and it filled Leonora with a sense of peace.

"What you touched," he began, "what you allowed into yourself is evil. You were tempted and lied to. The Blaze is the life of an evil god, and if you touch it, it will consume you to the core and kill you. Do you believe me?"

She didn't want to. She had been communing with the Blaze for so long, and it never hurt her. But she listened to his voice, and she knew he was telling the truth.

"I believe you."

She felt dirty. She felt betrayed. She had loved Cedric, and he tricked her and betrayed her.

"You will spend the rest of your very long life trying to distance yourself from this power. Meditate, teach, learn. Become a paragon of virtue. Become everything the Blaze does not want you to be. Do not give in to power. Power is an illusion. Power is evil."

"Power is evil," her voice intoned.

"When you have attained your new status, I will find you again. You will be needed. You will be a Knight of the Flashing Blade, and you will help to defend this Empire from the likes of Cedric and the Dark Gods."

He was gone when she awoke again, and the next morning, she was taking her vows at the monastery.

* * * * * * * * * * *

Year Three of the Just Emperor Kaitain "Dragonsbane" Lorien, Creator's Calendar Year 1870

Leonora felt the power flow through her, and all of the rage and the hate surfaced again. She felt once more how she had all those years ago when she was a girl. She felt whole again.

"I was trained by a Lion," Leonora said bringing Wisdom to bear, "now prepare to feel my roar."

Mending Broken Hearts

Year Three of the Just Emperor Kaitain "Dragonsbane" Lorien,
Creator's Calendar Year 1870

In her room deep in the heart of the Palace of Celidar, Felicia Lorien removed her armor and tried hard not to think of the events of the past days. It seemed like a lifetime had passed since she and her father had left their keep on the edge of the Imperial Province of Lordhill. Contrary to his position as the brother of the Emperor, Felicia's father had foregone any improvements to the keep, and had simply wanted to maintain some level of humility and normalcy despite his elevated status. Felicia had always respected her father for that. She knew that at his core, he had it within him to be as spoiled and ruthless as his older brother, but it was the qualities of nobility and strength that won out more often than not. Make no mistake, her father was not a diplomat, and would never be courtly or well-spoken. She often thought that deep in his heart he was a simple farmer who had somehow been born into the body of a noble. The thought had been a joke between the two for many years. She was a warrior in the body of a princess, and he was the farmer in the body of a lord. They made for an interesting pair, and by all estimations were the more tolerable members of the Lorien family. Time had tricked the world by making Kaitain the older brother and his daughter the next in line to the throne. The poetic injustice always brought a wry smile to Felicia's face, but this night, it was not enough to break her sour mood. The audience with Lord and Lady Mistic had left an incredibly sour taste in her mouth, and even through the meal where the moods were superficially light, her palate would not sweeten. Food and drink tasted like ash on her tongue, and every stolen glance in the direction of the man named Wynne made bile rise in the back of her throat.

How strange it was that a simple word could change the perception of a man, and how it can change the way one person reacts to another. From the moment Felicia heard the word wife, everything about Wynne changed. She could no longer see how handsome he was. She could no longer revel in his strength or his compassion, or his bravery. She no longer saw the way that his eyes sparkled, or longed to run her hands over the scruff on his chin. His smile lost some of the sparkle, and his skin no longer begged to be touched. She no longer longed to feel the softness of his lips. All because of one simple word; and the thought sickened her.

Her armor clattered to the ground, and the sound was like the one her heart seemed to make now. Beats ached where once they soared. How could she be impacted so much by that man? She had not known him that long, and though he was approachable, he certainly never showed any inappropriate attention to her. He was kind, devoted, focused, and utterly, disarmingly charming. Felicia growled at the thoughts and twined her hands in her long curly red hair. She wanted to scream. She wanted to pull her hair out. But who was she mad at? Was she mad at the woman she had never met? Was she mad at Wynne for not saying sooner that he was married? But what cause would he have had to even bring up his family? It wasn't as though there were many opportunities for a good long chat. They were running for their lives, and Wynne was doing everything in his power to keep both Feyd and Felicia alive. Honestly, Felicia hadn't given a single thought to the possibility that Wynne had a family, or a life outside of his heroism.

Felicia unbuckled her sword belt and let it fall to the floor. She should have felt bad about the dishonor and disrespect she was showing to the weapon. But now her mind was on a great deal less responsible things. Her mind was on her heart, and the sick feeling in the pit of her stomach, and how stupid and irresponsible all of those things were. She dropped down onto the edge of the bed and sighed hard. It was then that the first real wave of sorrow hit. It was totally unexpected and though she had tried hard to keep it at bay, she couldn't any longer. The first tear streaked down her cheek, feeling scalding hot. When it hit her lips, all she tasted was the salt, but only for a moment. The wave of emotion crested again and more of the hot tears began to stream down her face. She could feel the blood and heat rush to her cheeks, and unconsciously her hands went to her face, and the uncontrollable sobs increased in tempo and strength. Every breath was ragged, and every crash of emotion sapped more of her energy. She felt her shoulders and back slumping, and was about to collapse onto the bed, when suddenly she felt that she wasn't alone. The warrior in her screamed in the back of her mind, and she sat up as straight as she could manage, and rubbed her eyes trying to clear her vision. Blinking her puffy and swollen eyes, her vision finally cleared enough to see a blond woman sitting in a chair across the room from her. Her eyes were filled with such an immense sorrow that Felicia could feel it crushing her own soul. But that wasn't the only look in her eyes. There was also pity there. As much as Felicia's pride bristled at the thought of being pitied, she could not pull herself away from the soul-shaking sorrow that radiated from the woman, nor the way that it echoed and bolstered her own pain.

"It hurts, doesn't it?" the blond woman said finally, her voice small and sorrowful. "And the tears can do nothing to quench the fires rolling in the pit of your stomach or fill the void that opened in your heart. You feel like your whole world is ending and that your soul is just one big gaping wound. A wound that could never possibly be healed."

Felicia opened her mouth to speak, but her mouth was dry and she wouldn't know what to say even if she could speak. Her shoulders slumped again, and she surrendered to another wave of sorrow and pain. She felt as though she closed her eyes for only a second, but when she opened them again, the blond woman was sitting beside her on the bed, holding her hand with both of hers. Felicia should have been shocked. She should have pulled away. But there was comfort in the woman's touch. There was understanding on a deep unspoken level that can only be shared by those who have gone through similar sorrow.

Felicia had never let her defenses down before with a man. There was always her duty, there was always the protection of her family, her status, and her position. She was a warrior, and could not show the weakness that the doe-eyed girls did when they flushed and flustered around some boy that captured their affections. She would never be the one to stare longingly at some man; bat her eyelashes and become a slave to the beat of her heart. But somehow, without even wanting to or knowing it was happening, Wynne had broken through her armor and her practiced detachment. Like the heroic and unstoppable force he was in the physical world, he was twice as potent against her unwilling soul and heart. Without even knowing it, she was his if he wanted her. She shouldn't have felt betrayed. She shouldn't have felt anger or rage at a woman she probably would never set eyes upon.

The woman sitting beside her rubbed Felicia's hand gently between her own, and a feeling of peace swept through her. The sobs were coming less frequently now, and some of the conscious control was returning to her emotions, but the raw and ragged quality remained just at the edge of her control, as if another wave of the uncontrollable emotion could be set off at any moment.

"I felt you," the woman said after a moment. "I felt you and your sorrow from so far away, I could not resist coming to you. Sitting there in the dark watching you, I began to realize how much you were just like me. How much you and I could be mirror images of one another. And it was then that I knew, that you had to be the one that I passed my gifts to. You had to be the one to take the path that I cannot walk any longer."

"Who are you?" Felicia managed to croak out, feeling a little strength returning not only to her body but to her mind.

The blond woman patted Felicia's hand reassuringly before standing and taking three long steps to the center of the room where she turned to face the princess. It was the first time that Felicia took a good long look at the woman. Her blond hair was cut short and was so light that it was nearly white in the soft candlelight of the room. She wore a blue tunic with long sleeves that had a white collar and an almost snowy pattern woven throughout it. Looking at the tunic more closely, Felicia realized with astonishment that the tunic was not made out of fabric at all, but was made out of what could only be something akin to chainmail, and the snowy pattern was actually the glistening of the edges of the tiny rings in the light. She wore a wide studded leather belt around her waist, and twin sword belts hung low on her hips, but there were no scabbards attached to the belts. Her grey pants were nondescript, and were mostly covered by the flowing bottom of the tunic and her thigh high light grey boots. Her skin was flawless, her neck long and her stance spoke of a long tradition of pride and courage in battle. The woman's lips were slightly pale, and her clear blue eyes were like miniature storms. They smoldered with such fire of emotion that it could be felt between every long slow blink. She pulled herself up to her full height before she spoke, her shoulders pulled back hard, and Felicia could only see the warrior now, all hint of emotion and sorrow eradicated.

"My name is Lady Diana Terian, formerly Diana Geoffry. I am the wife of Lord Aryx Terian, the sister of the great Lord Arathorn Geoffry, and the Wind *Erieal* of the first generation of the prophecies of the *Coromor*. I am the mother of Lissa Terian and Lord Alderin Terian. But those names mean nothing to you. A name you will know however is this one. I am a Dark God."

Shock pulsed through Felicia and her mind raced. So many thoughts collided within her the next moment, and she was frozen by them. The warrior part of her wanted to dive for her sword and mount some kind of defense. The rational part of her warned against such a stupid action. She was mortal, and no matter her skill with a sword, she knew she was no match for the power of one of the Dark Gods. This woman had sought her out for a reason, and if she had wanted Felicia dead, the woman calling herself Diana could have struck Felicia down before she even knew the Dark Goddess was in the room. Terror competed with the sorrow for control of her mind, and it took every ounce of her control just to sit still on the edge of the bed. As if sensing the younger woman's confusion and trepidation, Diana raised her hands and let a small smile come to her lips.

"My visitation here is not to threaten you, Princess Felicia Lorien, nor is it on some errand for the Dark Gods. As I said, I felt your sorrow, I felt the pain in your heart, and it was those feelings that drew me to you. You see, I too know the feeling of a broken heart, and the feeling that wound makes on your soul. I recently lost my husband, a man that I have loved and been devoted to for longer than you could imagine. Together, he and I fought against the forces of heaven and hell. We would have given our lives if it would have meant saving one innocent. And somehow, in the face of all that destruction, in the face of all of that turmoil and torment, we found one another."

Felicia watched as the woman's warrior exterior melted away. The woman shown through again, the same woman that had sat beside Felicia and comforted her as she wept. The weight of her sorrow and loss was almost visible on her shoulders.

"Aryx and I loved more deeply than two people should, and our love allowed us to blur the lines of our lives into one another. At some point we ceased being two distinct people. At some point our hearts and our souls melded together in a way that could never be undone, no matter the distance, and no matter the trial. But now he is gone. I will never gaze into those beautiful eyes again, and never hear his soft words in the twilight hours as we lay together. And I will never hear him sing me to sleep again."

Felicia felt a kind of helplessness and panic fill her. She wanted to shake her head, to protest and fight against the resignation in the woman's voice.

"Surely you'll see him again on the other side," Felicia finally found the strength to say. "Love like that can never be severed, not even in death."

Diana smiled at the younger woman, and Felicia felt it as though it was a look of pity for someone who could never understand just how wrong they were.

"I wish I could believe that, Felicia," Diana said the smile on her lips starting to crack slightly, the left corner of her mouth quivering. "But I know the truth. Aryx and I were both ascended beings. We were gods serving the will of the Creator. But now we are Fallen. We are outside of the Creator's love. I don't know what happens when we pass beyond the veil, and I don't know what is waiting for me in the embrace of death. I hope that I will feel my husband's arms once again, but the conviction in my heart is not as strong as it once was."

There was a slight shake of the woman's head, and Felicia felt as though Diana was trying to get herself back to the purpose of her visit. As if a simple shake of the head could push the unpleasant thoughts back into the seclusion of her mind.

"But I will not sleep alone again, and my time in this world is at an end. But before I fade into memory, I must complete one task, a task that has been planned for quite some time, but I hoped would never need to be done. I have a gift for you, Princess Felicia Lorien, if you will accept it."

Felicia steeled herself.

"Before I was ever a Dark God, and before I felt the touch of the Creator upon me, I was a warrior, just as you are. But from my birth, I was blessed with a power that I didn't know I had until I met a man who was locked into a fate that would cost him not only his life, but his soul. Eventually I learned more about the powers locked inside of me, and I honed them into a weapon. But even that was not enough to fight against the forces of a god. Nor was it enough to save the man that I loved from the dangers he could not see massing around him. For that, I made a deal with someone whom I thought was my enemy, but turned out to be the true hero of my world. I became the host of a being known as Nightwing, a creature of great destructive power, and a great weapon against the forces of tyranny and destruction. Your world is on a collision course with the same destruction and devastation that befell my home, Felicia, and it will take more than a sword and your wits to save the innocent from the fire that is coming. I wish to give you the powers that are mine to give. The powers I had as a mortal, and the powers that helped to make me the hero that the world needed me to be."

Felicia didn't know what to say; didn't know if there was anything for her to say. How did one respond to such things? After a long deep breath, Felicia stood, pulled her shoulders back and tried to stand as straight as possible even though it felt as though her knees would give out at any moment.

"I am honored that you would choose me for this responsibility, Lady Terian," Felicia said in her best courtly voice, though she could not banish the waver fully from her tone, "and I humbly accept this gift, and vow to use it to protect all that I can."

Diana smiled.

"Well said," a hint of comedy in her voice, "but this gift is not for a diplomat, or a chaste virtuous princess. This gift is for the warrior whose heart raged with such fire and such ferocity that it called to me from across the face of Cadaria. That fire and that passion alone will help you wield the weapons that I am giving you. That love and devotion turned toward the innocents of this world is all that you will have in the face of what is to come. Protect those who cannot protect themselves. Defend the weak and those mired in fear. Fight back against the real enemies of this world, and do so with your eyes open. Don't accept what you think you know. And most of all honor your heart, for without that, nothing you do will have any meaning."

Felicia let the sage words penetrate her and cast her eyes down to the floor. Diana was right, the practiced veneer of the princess had no place here.

"I understand," Felicia said finally. "I accept."

Diana nodded wordlessly and put her hands on Felicia's shoulders. For a long moment, there was nothing, just the feeling of the woman's warm hands on her shoulders. But as the seconds passed, Diana's hands began to get warmer and warmer; until they were so hot it felt as though her touch could sear Felicia's skin. A heartbeat later a flood of heat blasted through Felicia and enveloped her. It felt like she was being immersed in pure joy and rapture. It was as if all of the worldly pleasures had been concentrated into the woman's touch. Felicia saw the blue sparkling tunic that Diana begin to melt off of her body, leaving only the simple white shirt below it. The metal began to solidify into a single large thin sheet, it glided slowly across the floor, until it was close enough that Felicia could reach out and touch it. But it would be the metal that would reach out and touch her. The metal started to mold to her legs first, and she could feel her skin searing and burning beneath her clothing as the metal seemed to pass through the pores of the fabric to get to her tender flesh. Any pain that she might have felt during the process was immediately doused by the overwhelming feeling of joy. The metal bonded slowly, and as it passed her waist, she felt a tail begin to grow slowly out from behind her, and she could feel her balance shift as her body adjusted to the new appendage.

Her mind whirled at the changes, but somehow was acclimating to them nearly instantly. Her arms were soon coated, and then she saw the black metal talons extending from the tips of her fingers. They were not thick and clumsy as though they were mounted to some gauntlet designed for a man's thick hand. They were almost delicate, and feminine. They were extensions of her own form. The metal continued upward, crawling up her neck and a small sheet broke away from the whole and approached her face. This burning sensation was the worst of all that Felicia felt, but unlike the others, this burning was not immediately extinguished. She could feel the metal bend and pull at her skin, but the searing heat never lessened. There was more to the change than physical transformation. The tendrils of metal seemed to reach inside her, burrow into her mind. She could feel all the memories from the older woman creeping into her consciousness. Unspoken instructions on how to use her abilities, fighting tactics, uses of the primal powers now at her disposal. A hundred lifetimes of experience exploded into her brain at the bat of an eye. It was then that the pain suddenly and inexplicably disappeared. The red film that covered her eyes was no longer strange or alien. It was simply part of who and what she was now. The being that was Nightwing was every bit a part of her as her right arm was. And for the first time, she felt the haunting and melodious call of the Blaze from the back of her mind. She could feel the bright green flames at the edge of her vision, feel its touch caressing her skin, and knew the depth of its power. The revelry in her ended the moment she realized that Diana had collapsed. Without a thought, the metal skin retracted beneath her human form and Felicia dropped to the floor, taking Diana's head into her lap, and smoothing the sweat-soaked and matted hair away from her suddenly much older face. Felicia didn't have to be told to know that the woman was dying, and only had a few breaths left. Diana looked up, first at Felicia, and then past her. The soft and sweet smile returned to the woman's face that next moment, and when she opened her mouth to speak, the voice was weak but still beautiful and melodic.

"I see him, Felicia," Diana said the love filling her voice, "and he is as beautiful as he ever was. I can hear him singing."

At her last words, her eyes closed for the last time, and her body slowly went limp in Felicia's arms. As the moments passed, Diana's body became lighter and lighter, growing insubstantial and passing beyond the veil into whatever world where her love waited for her. Though the tears rolled down Felicia's face, she could not help but smile. Finally, the body of Lady Diana Terian was gone, and in her heart she knew that wherever she was, she was with the man that she loved, and they would be together until the sands no longer ran, and time stopped moving. The mixture of emotions held Felicia to the spot where she sat on the floor for quite some time, until she felt a twinge in the back of her mind. While it may have been unfamiliar to Felicia's conscious mind, it certainly was not unfamiliar to the memories of the Blaze. Someone had opened a portal into the throne room of the palace. Felicia didn't bother recovering her sword or armor from where they lay on the floor, instead rushing out the door and down the hall. This late in the evening, the halls were practically empty, and she emerged from one of the back entrances to the throne room, typically reserved for use by the Lord and Lady of the kingdom. The throne room stood empty except for one woman who stood near the dais, the person who must have been responsible for the power she felt.

The woman's clothes were tattered, covered in soot, ash, and what could only have been marble dust. Large rips and tears were apparent in both her shirt and pants, and there were stains around most of the tears that could only have come from dried blood. Her hair was mussed, barely being held together by a strip of green cloth, and the look on her face could only be described as annoyance. There was a sword hanging in its scabbard on her belt, and in one hand she grasped a bow that looked as though it had seen better days. The woman's eyes found Felicia almost instantly.

"I'm looking for Lord Jerrard and Lady Erika. I need to see them now."

Felicia took the demand in stride. Obviously the woman didn't know who she was addressing.

"I'm not sure how people do things where you come from, but there is something known as courtly protocol here, and I suggest that in my presence you follow it. Lord and Lady Mistic have retired for the evening, and if you want an audience, you'll have to wait your turn like everyone else."

The woman clenched her teeth.

"And I would suggest that you exercise more decorum when you meet the Lord and Lady, and that you apologize for your rudeness to me."

The woman stared daggers into Felicia's chest.

"And why should I do that?"

Felicia frowned.

"Because you are addressing a Princess of the Lorien family."

"And you are addressing a Dark God," the woman said sharply, "and if you don't get out of my way, I'll make sure you understand your place in the greater scheme of things. The future has no place for spoiled and entitled little girls who play at being important."

Felicia took a step forward and then set herself.

"Before a few minutes ago, I might have been afraid of you, Dark Goddess, but now, I think I'll make you pay for your impudence."

The woman dropped her bow to the ground and slowly drew her sword.

"Any other day, I might have let you live," she said coldly, "but today, I'm going to make you regret the day you crossed blades with Midarin Sandar."

Pulse of the Heart

Year Three of the Just Emperor Kaitain "Dragonsbane" Lorien, Creator's Calendar Year 1870

"Even prisons can have lovely walls."

Quyhn's voice echoed slightly off the walls of her spacious room in the small keep that served as the nerve center for the Imperial operations in the mining community of Lordhill. For nearly two weeks, Quyhn had been in residence in Lordhill, and everyone had been extremely nice and pleasant to her, but it was just on the edge of condescension. Connor and Gabrielle Peregrim had been all smiles and had given her guided tours of all of the mining operations, but Quyhn could not help but feel that something was being hidden from her. There was nothing overt, that much was certain, but there was an underlying feeling that something was just, wrong. Now, two weeks into her posting, Quyhn felt more and more like the outsider that she was. As per Dominique's request, tutors were made available so that Quyhn could continue her studies, and even Rhionna had been convinced to give her lessons with the bow. But that agreement was grudging to say the least.

The woman assigned to be Quyhn's protector both maddened and inflamed Quyhn at the same time. On the outside, which is all Rhionna ever allowed anyone to see, she was a professional soldier, utterly and completely devoted to her duty. She served to the letter of her orders, and very little more. But despite her military background and her sparkling service record, Rhionna stood out like a polished coin in a bag full of tarnished ones here in Lordhill. The post was dominated by men, and most of those men were rejects, failures, trouble-makers, and those who were on their third or fourth last chance. They were loyal to the Empire, but more importantly and perhaps subversively, they were loyal to Connor Peregrim. And so, Rhionna and Quyhn, two outcasts from the situation around them should have been able to find some common ground to become more than just a ward and her protector. But that had not happened. To Quyhn's surprise, Rhionna spoke little, and was obviously not interested in sharing her thoughts with her charge, even though Quyhn had tried to engage the woman in conversation on several occasions. Rhionna was respectful in those moments, but only just. She deflected any personal questions about herself, and only engaged on the most superficial level on other matters. She seemed to know much about Quyhn and her situation, but again would not elaborate on what she knew, or how she came to know it. The one strong link between the two women was their connection to Chelsea Zarova, but that too seemed an avenue of conversation that Rhionna was unwilling to go down. The blond woman was a stone wall, and it infuriated Quyhn to no end.

And then there was the other side, the frustrating and inflaming spark between the two women. At least, it was a powerful spark that Quyhn felt. Early in her life, Quyhn knew she was different than most girls her age. She was not chasing the boys trying to steal a kiss, nor was she staring when she thought they weren't looking. Boys were disgusting. They rolled around in dirt, used foul language, and generally tried to disgust one another for fun. They were preening, posturing, and petulant. Nothing about them was attractive, and nothing about them filled Quyhn with anything but the most stomach-churning disgust. She didn't hate boys, but the thought of one of them touching her in any meaningful way made her skin crawl. Girls on the other hand were something entirely different. All her time in the Academy of Arcane Arts, most of her time was spent with other girls her age, and some slightly older. Aris Ebonsight had been a very close friend and confidant, and Quyhn could remember how good she always smelled. She wore the finest clothes and always had a smile on her face. Quyhn wasn't sure when she began noticing the smell was intoxicating. She wasn't sure when she started noticing the smooth skin or the way her clothes hugged her form. She wasn't sure when she started to feel the heat rushing through her when Aris was near to her. But it was clear from that moment that no boy could ever bring her those feelings.

Quyhn was trapped by her situation when it came to the new and blossoming feelings that she had. Her closest friend, the one who she felt she could confide in, was the one person that she couldn't talk to about what she was feeling, and without her mother to lean on, there was only her father. And how would her father ever understand something like that? So she stayed silent. She stayed silent for a very long time; suffering in a way that she didn't know was even possible. Until the day she caught Aris and the insufferable Ayden Seth kissing in a dark corridor just before lights out. When she saw Aris shove Ayden into her room, Quyhn felt as though her heart was being ripped from her chest. The hurt inside her was more than she could bear, and she contained the tears only as far as the kitchen. That was where Fiona Ebonsight found her. Her head on the table, sobbing uncontrollably. It took almost an hour in Fiona's room for Quyhn to finally open up and start talking, but when she did everything came out at once. Her pain over her mother's death, her hatred of Irene, her feelings for Aris, and lastly, the scene between Fiona's daughter and Ayden. That last came out in a much harsher and unvarnished way than Quyhn would have wanted, but she was in no emotional state to control her words. Fiona was obviously shocked about both Quyhn's revelations about her preferences as well as her daughter's dalliances, but whatever personal feelings she had about the situation with her daughter, she never gave it voice. Instead she smoothed Quyhn's hair and dried her tears and spent most of the night trying to make her feel better. All this time later, Quyhn had nothing but the utmost respect for what Fiona tried to do that night. She fumbled through the talk the best she could, but at the end of the day, the message was what ended up being important, not the method in which it was delivered. We can't control what we feel or whom we feel it for. The important thing is that we feel and we hold on to those feelings.

This brought Quyhn's thoughts back to Rhionna. Quyhn had had feelings for women in her life before, including the brief shadow of attraction that she had for Dominique. But Quyhn was more mature in her designations of feelings now, and what she had felt for Dominique in those brief moments before she banished the thoughts were nothing but lust. But then, there weren't many that didn't lust after Dominique Lorien once they set eyes on her. She was a striking woman in every way that the word could be applied, but she was more enthralling when you got down to her heart. Aside from her mother, Dominique was the most caring and devoted woman that Quyhn had ever met, and those comparisons to her own mother made Quyhn able to dismiss whatever tension could have been between the two women. Besides, Dominique had another admirer that was much closer to her than Quyhn could ever be. Rhionna was another woman whose physical beauty had inflamed Quyhn. It was different than the impact Dominique had, to be sure, but Rhionna's sculpted features, long curly blond hair, and dark eyes would have made most men melt were it not for her intimidating strength. Most men possessed of the military mind were intimidated by women who could keep up with them, or even surpass them physically. What bothered Quyhn about Rhionna's obvious physicality was not the advantage the woman could have over her, but the way that her features made Quyhn feel about herself.

When Quyhn was around Dominique and Chelsea, and even earlier in her life with Aris, Quyhn's image of herself from a physical standpoint was not in doubt. Dominique was so beautiful that she made every woman fall into her shadow. Chelsea was attractive, but her ruggedness and military manner made her more approachable. Rhionna was a completely different story. She had a statuesque beauty, but her unapproachability made Quyhn feel as though she were being rejected on two levels. Not only that, because the woman was her personal protector, Quyhn felt weaker and smaller in the woman's presence. She felt like a little girl, under-developed and sexually unattractive. Not ugly, but she didn't feel that she had anything to offer someone like Rhionna, even if the woman did give her a second glance. Quyhn found herself laughing at the thoughts, and didn't realize that she was laughing out loud until there was a sharp knock at the door, followed by Rhionna letting herself in.

"Is everything alright?" came Rhionna's clipped words. There was a hint of an accent there that was certainly not Saldarian, but Quyhn couldn't place it. She was normally very good with those things.

Quyhn smiled and nodded.

"Everything is fine, Rhionna. Just reveling in the absurdity."

There was a puzzled look on the woman's face for a long moment, and then she finally gave a curt nod.

"Lady Peregrim has requested time with you today between your studies. She felt as though the two of you have not had much time to talk in the past few days, and she wanted to remedy that."

Rhionna started to close the door, but Quyhn motioned her into the room. The blond woman hesitated for a moment, looked back over her shoulder into the hallway, and then came into the room slowly, shutting the door as she did. Quyhn noticed she was not wearing her armor that day, and instead had opted for a loose-fitting white shirt that laced up the front, the top laces of which were left open showing a considerable amount of cleavage. Her bow was slung over her back, and the bowstring caused the shirt to bunch in such a way that the sheer material hugged the woman in noticeable ways. Quyhn felt heat rush through her, and she had to stand to keep from squirming on the chair.

"You seem to have some level of relationship with Lady Peregrim," Quyhn said after clearing her throat. "You've had more than one private meeting with her since we've been here, and up until now you haven't been very forthcoming with the contents of those meetings."

There was a spark of annoyance that flashed across Rhionna's features, and her dark eyes narrowed.

"Are you ordering me to tell you what we talked about?"

The defiance in her tone was unmistakable, and though Quyhn wanted to shrink back, she didn't. She stood her ground and put her hands on her hips.

"I have no intention of ordering you to do anything but your duty, Rhionna," Quyhn said finally, "but how am I supposed to trust you as my protector if you keep secrets from me during my imprisonment here."

Rhionna's eyes widened, and she looked over her shoulder at the door before taking two steps closer to Quyhn. Immediately, Quyhn could feel the heat radiating off the woman's skin, and the strong smell of the wind and the outdoors. She had been out in the training grounds that morning keeping her skills sharp, and her skin still smelled of sweat and exertion. Quyhn's head swam with the smell, but she kept herself strong and tried hard to project the defiant and confident exterior, despite how weak her knees were getting.

"You shouldn't speak like that, Quyhn," Rhionna said, her tone becoming more conspiratorial. "Remember that you are here as a Ward of the Empire, and that you are on a personal mission for the Empress of Cadaria. That tends to make people nervous. So you should expect that they will keep you at arm's length until they get to know you. I think that is perhaps what the meeting with Lady Peregrim will be about."

Quyhn forced a frown.

"If they have nothing to hide, then they have no reason to keep me at arm's length."

Rhionna glared at her for a moment.

"That is a very naïve way to look at things."

Quyhn pulled her shoulders back and stood as tall as she could manage. The blond woman was still considerably taller than Quyhn was, but the younger woman tried her best to call on all of the regal manner that she had learned from watching Dominique in court.

"I was sent her by the Empress as a measure of good faith, but also to discover whether or not there was something to be worried about here in Lordhill. In the short span of time, if I were to go back now, I would have to tell Empress Lorien that I have no uncertainty at all that there is something more than the unwavering support that is portrayed by the Peregrim family at work, and if I had to take a guess, there is theft at the least, and outright rebellion at the worst at work here. With the Emperor in a weakened position, and the hand-picked military assets at the disposal of a military veteran like Connor Peregrim, I would have a hard time not characterizing this as a threat to the stability of the Empire. Not only that, with the way you've been acting, I would have to consider very highly reporting your behavior to Lady Zarova."

Rhionna didn't flinch, but Quyhn could tell in the woman's eyes that something she had said had touched a nerve.

"So I suggest that you start sharing information with me," Quyhn said finally, "or I shall be returning to Aldere before the week is out."

The two women held each other's gaze for a long moment before Rhionna let a small smile break her lips, and she nodded slightly.

"Chelsea told me that you had a lot of your father in you, and she told me that you could be formidable when you wanted to be. I guess taking all those classes with the Empress had to make an impression."

Quyhn was taken aback by the woman's words, and tried her best to keep her proud posture, but the softness and familiarity of the woman's tone was disarming. Quyhn felt her irritation lessen slightly, but she tried in vain to keep hold on it.

"I think that's the most you've said to me at one time since we've been here."

The woman reached back and pulled her bow up over her head, and freed herself from it. Quyhn's eyes were immediately drawn to where the bowstring caught the woman as she moved, but tried her best not to let it show. Gracefully, Rhionna stood the bow in the corner closest to the two women. When she turned back to Quyhn, it seemed that her features had softened somewhat, and that Quyhn was finally getting to see glimpses of the woman underneath the warrior.

"I'm sorry for that, Quyhn," Rhionna said in a voice that ensured her words were genuine, "but you have to understand, that in my position, I had to be sure about you. Chelsea vouched for you, and while ordinarily that would be enough for me, you are a friend of the Empress, and you are a ward of the Empire, and that makes you a very different kind of charge. The Ward of the Empire part of it, I can get through rather easily. I've guarded high-level members of both the Saldarine royalty as well as been part of the Imperial Guard detachment for Princess Felicia Lorien on her visit to Saldarine."

Quyhn nodded, understanding what the woman hadn't said.

"So it's because of Dominique."

A small frown came to Rhionna's face.

"You have to understand something, Quyhn," the blond woman said, her left hand balling into a fist. "That woman's name is a curse among the military in Saldarine, at least those of us who were recruited by Chelsea and know her at all. Chelsea is a proud woman who has sacrificed everything for our Kingdom. She is our Knight of the Flashing Blade, and she gave up her life and her freedom not only to serve the best interests of the Kingdom and the Empire, but also because she was forced to marry that lecherous bastard, Seraph Kore. Most of us wanted the man dead before we found out that he was having an affair with some common woman, but once that became common knowledge, there were more than a few members of the army that wanted to desert just to go after him. Chelsea would have none of it though. Her orders were clear. Anyone who tried to execute some vendetta on her behalf would answer to her, and to her blades."

Quyhn nodded.

"She is a good woman who understands her duty, even if she doesn't always agree with it."

Rhionna's fist tightened even more.

"Chelsea is not just a good woman, she sacrificed everything that she could to be where she is today. She was in love before she became a Knight of the Flashing Blade. She was ready to retire and have a family before she got the call. Her duty to the Empire was more important than her happiness, or the new life that she had started to build."

There was a slight hesitation in her voice. Like something caught in her throat that she desperately wanted to say, but couldn't bring herself to. A practiced lie by omission.

"The daughter that she never allowed herself to know."

Quyhn never felt the shock. She never felt the surprise. All she felt was the sorrow that rolled off of Rhionna like waves. Looking at the woman,

Quyhn would have never guessed her relationship to Chelsea, but then again, Quyhn had never seen the two women standing side by side. Quyhn had also never thought Chelsea old enough to have a daughter in her middle twenties. As if understanding where Quyhn's thoughts had gone, Rhionna nodded.

"Chelsea was very young, and my father was her superior officer. They kept their relationship secret for quite some time. My father had been married before, and his wife had been killed in a raid by Thorigald soldiers on a small staging area that was used for gathering information on troop movements. Chelsea and my father began their relationship not long after. But she was on the fast track to glory, while my father was a shadow of the man he had been. He quickly faded from contention for the position of Knight of the Flashing Blade, where for a time it seemed that that was his destiny. Then there was the Plains of Steam incident, and the Wolf of Saldarine was born. No one knew that as she plunged again and again deeper into the enemy ranks that she was carrying a child. Me."

Quyhn was awed by the story, and thoughts sprang into her head of a pregnant Chelsea throwing herself with reckless abandon into enemy lines. It was Rhionna's sorrowful voice that broke her from her thoughts.

"So when the time came, and Chelsea was to take her place among the Knights of the Flashing Blade, she requested a short leave of absence to settle some family matters before accepting her post. It was granted without question. Chelsea's sister was also a member of the Saldarine military, but she had been married to a lord of Saldarine in a match to improve the station of both families. Rupert Winter, the lord of Saldarine who has been my father since shortly after my birth, and his wife Jacinda, are both good people. They've never known who my father is, as Chelsea kept the identity to herself until just after his death. I know very little about him, and Chelsea has never been very forthcoming with information about that time in her life. What I know I have only barely been able to piece together after all these years. My foster parents confided in me my true parentage just before my thirteenth birthday. I sought Chelsea out then, trying to understand more than anything why I was cast aside. It was then that I got my first lesson in duty, and though I tried to hate Chelsea for a very long time, I never could."

Despite herself, Quyhn found herself reaching out to take Rhionna's balled-up fist in her own hands. The woman wanted to pull her hand away, but Quyhn gently massaged the fist until it relented. Quyhn held and patted Rhionna's hand as she continued her tale.

"When it was time for Chelsea to give birth, she went to the one place that she knew she could be alone, and be safe. She went to Rashaleb to the home of a family friend."

"Gabrielle Peregrim," Quyhn filled in.

Rhionna nodded.

"Rupert's half-sister. They have the same mother, but different fathers. Veronica Maupin, the mother of Victor Maupin was originally Veronica Lorien, aunt to Kaitain Lorien. Veronica's youngest daughter was Gabrielle Maupin, who is now Gabrielle Peregrim. Rupert was fostered to his father's family when Rupert's father died not long after his birth. So, when Chelsea needed to hide, Gabrielle opened her home, and even helped to deliver me. Once Chelsea had recovered, she returned to active duty. Gabrielle raised me for a few months until a woman in her household died during childbirth. It was common enough in the cold reaches of Rashaleb. I was given that woman's last name for the purpose of shrouding my true identity, and then sent to Rupert and Jacinda. They had the story they needed that would save everyone from shame and questions. Of course Rupert and Jacinda never treated me as anything other than their own daughter even though I was really Jacinda's bastard niece."

Quyhn nodded and smiled up comfortingly at the taller woman. Suddenly she didn't seem so fierce and so distant. The wall between them had come tumbling down in those moments, and Quyhn saw her protector in a much different light. There was a softness and a vulnerability in her eyes that had been hidden behind the warrior's façade, and now that Quyhn could see it, she felt her heart beat even faster.

"So that is why you and Gabrielle have been meeting in private. She's trying to find out why I'm really here and if I can be trusted."

Rhionna's lips curled into a half-frown, and then she nodded.

"So there is something more going on here."

It was a statement, not a question, and Rhionna could not help but nod her ascent. She had to admit that she had slightly underestimated the girl. There was no doubting that she was astute.

"I'll leave that for Gabrielle and Connor to tell you, but just go in with an open mind, and I'm sure you'll make the right decision. Chelsea and Dominique trust you, and I can see now why they do. After all, you're a Ravenheart, you have a reputation to uphold."

A sly smile came to Quyhn's face.

"I'm a Lorien now too, what does that do to my reputation?"

The frown disappeared from Rhionna's face, and a hint of a smile glistened in her eyes.

"I'm not sure you really want to know."

There was a sudden wave of discomfort that passed between the two of them, something between apprehension and uncertainty. Rhionna looked down at Quyhn's hands holding hers, and Quyhn kept her eyes on the taller woman's face. Rhionna made no effort to pull away, and Quyhn moved her left hand and let her fingertips touch Rhionna's face. Slowly, Rhionna raised her eyes again, and she was looking down into Quyhn's eyes. The smaller woman couldn't resist looking at the glistening of the blond woman's lips, and the feeling of butterflies in her stomach rose as she stroked Rhionna's cheek. She bit her bottom lip slightly, and moved in gently, starting to feel Rhionna's hot breath. She closed her eyes as she felt the taller woman's lips gently brush against hers.

A sharp knock at the door broke the stillness and silence, and when Quyhn's eyes shot open, Rhionna had already moved several steps away, her hand taking hold of her bow and her other hand on the hilt of the sword she wore on her hip. There was another sharp knock, and the door opened to reveal Gabrielle Peregrim. There was no smile on the woman's face, in fact it looked as though she was none-too-pleased. Behind her, already with his sword drawn, was the advisor to the Peregrim family, Arent Fox. He stayed outside the door as Gabrielle entered, and Rhionna positioned herself between Quyhn and the door, her eyes floating back and forth between Arent and Gabrielle.

"I was really hoping we would have more time," Gabrielle said curtly, "but it seems that whatever questions we had about your loyalties are now moot. We've just received word from Aldere. The Imperial Palace has fallen, and the Emperor is awake. The man seems bound and determined to destroy everything that his predecessors worked for, and I'm afraid you're now more of a bargaining chip than we ever thought we would need."

Panic and confusion filled Quyhn's face.

"We're now the hosts to the Imperial heir," Gabrielle said some coldness edging into her voice, "at least until Kaitain decides that you're expendable like Marlae was."

Chapter LXIII

Awakening the Dragon

Year Three of the Just Emperor Kaitain "Dragonsbane" Lorien, Creator's Calendar Year 1870

Darrien Annis knelt at Alderin's side, his head in her lap, his eyes closed but fluttering. He was still breathing, but the breathing was labored. Several minutes before, Darrien had extracted the hard and cruel black metal blade from Alderin's back, and she had expected the regenerative abilities granted to all of the Dark Gods and their children to take over and quickly heal his wound. But Darrien had sensed something was wrong almost immediately. The gaping wound in the center of Alderin's back had begun to spider-vein with a black pulsing puss. It was starting to heal, but so slowly that it defied Darrien's understanding. The wound smelled rotten, like meat that had been left out in the hot sun for a week, but there was a strange sweetness to it. Additionally, as the black blade lay on the ground it had begun to secrete a viscous black fluid that smoked when it collided with any living matter, like grass. Whatever the demonic woman calling herself Seraphina Masile and her followers had imbued into this weapon may not have been enough to kill a Dark God or one of their children, but the wound inflicted was certainly more than could be shrugged off. Darrien and Alderin unlike their parents, had only known life as immortals. They had never been wounded seriously, and had never known the fear of death. Darrien had sat up many nights with her father listening to his war stories from both their former world of Onea and also of the rebellions in the heavens. Darrien had never known her mother, and so all she ever had in her life was Pike. He had been a good father, even though he was equal parts cold and domineering. He demanded the best of her, in everything that she did. She spent much time when she was a young girl with Lissa and with Sabrina, but most of her time was with Pike, trying her best to learn everything she could. She had an insatiable thirst for knowledge. And then there had been Alderin. Alderin was already much older than Darrien when she was born into the world of Espre, and he took up the task of ensuring that the daughter of the leader of the Dark Gods was always protected. As Darrien grew, the relationship became less about a protector and his charge, and more about a budding need for affection. Since that point Darrien stopped trying to escape Alderin's watchful eyes so that she could get into the very trouble that he was trying to keep her from, and became about trying to steal as much time with him as possible. They all had responsibilities in the Citadel of the Dark Gods, but both Darrien and Alderin had become quite adept at ensuring that the work schedules coincided and they could create private time for themselves. Of course once their relationship was discovered, there was a small outbreak of tension between Pike and Aryx, but Diana and Midarin were able to put an end to it quickly.

Darrien smoothed Alderin's long blond hair away from his face. The cold sweat was beginning to break, and his skin no longer felt clammy. His natural regenerative abilities were beginning to take over, and before long he would be back in fighting shape. Out of the corner of her eye, Darrien could see a bright flash of light. She placed Alderin's head back on the ground and got to her feet as quickly as she could. It took only a moment to form the axe of ice in her hands. If Seraphina or any of her followers were coming back to finish the job they had started, she would be sure to be ready. The flash came again, and Darrien set her feet in the soft soil. Finally there was a larger flash, one so bright that Darrien had to shut her eyes and turn her head to keep from being blinded by it. When the light had ceased, Darrien turned her eyes back toward the opening in the wall that Lucian had emerged from during the fight with Seraphina. Her eyes widened with shock, and her grip on the haft of the ice axe weakened enough that the weapon slipped from her hands. Her jaw went slack and there were no words to be found.

Emerging from the opening in the wall was Darrien's younger sister Tess. While they did not share the same mother, they had become so close that it didn't matter. Through her formative years, Tess could best be described as sweet, naïve, and hopelessly inquisitive. She thirsted to know anything and everything possible, and she did so with a wide-eyed eagerness that belied her age and her status as a daughter of the leader of the Dark Gods. Her eyes were always warm and kind and engaging. But even now as Darrien looked into the young woman's eyes, that softness was nowhere to be found. Where her eyes had once been bright blue, presumably like her mother's, her eyes were now golden, flashing and glowing brighter than should have been possible. She stood with her back straight, her thinly muscled arms holding the limp form of Camille Renar. It was obvious that Camille had been seriously injured, and her angelic white wings hung limply from her back, shedding feathers against the light breeze. There was little of Tess's white night shirt remaining, and what did still cling to her rain-soaked form was stained with both grime and blood. Tess's long dark hair was matted against her face but she seemed to pay it little mind. Darrien covered the distance to her little sister and her wounded protector quickly, and reached out to help Tess carry her burden. Tess's eyes went wide, and she extended one hand toward her sister. A burst of invisible force erupted from Tess's outstretched hand and claimed Darrien firmly in the chest. Darrien was hurled backward several feet, landing on her back just a few feet from where Alderin lay. She recovered quickly from the blow, and Darrien sat up quickly in time to see Tess gently lay Camille on the ground and stroke her hair once before standing straight again.

"I will not let anyone hurt my Camille. Never again!"

* * * * * * * * * * * *

Xaran Firesoul sat cross-legged on the floor of his small room in the Heart of Stone and felt the world around him go mad. All around him he could feel power bursting like exploding stars. Some of the powers he could pick out, but others made no sense. Hannah Ironheart and Gregor Quicksilver were powerful, and the little he had been exposed to Devlin Rannoch and Gabriel Shadowfall, he was able to feel their powers as well. However, those stars were pale compared to the brightness of Aerith Seth's power. When Xaran came in the proximity of the man, Xaran could practically smell his power. It crackled off of him like lightning. It was like standing next to the sun. Surprisingly, when Xaran was near the woman who was the protector of the Empress Marlae Lorien he had a similar feeling. Granted it was not as powerful or as developed as Aerith's power, but the woman who called herself Rhain was also very powerful. But then Xaran felt a huge power blossom into existence. It had always been there, that much was for certain, but something had forced the power to bloom. In the back of Xaran's mind, he could feel the voice of Faith call to him. The Sacred Weapon could feel all of the things that Xaran was feeling, and whether those feelings were independent or simply joined through their shared connection, both were aware of this new power. Faith thirsted to be closer to this new power, wanted to know what it was, and it was clear that this power was important. But there was another voice in Xaran's mind as well. The gift that had been given to Xaran by his dragon ally Khalas, the belt known as Kadon, also had a strong voice and strong consciousness. Despite his attempts to ignore it, Kadon's voice was strong and powerful. Where Faith was curious, Kadon was cautious. There was something about this new and blossoming power that worried the dragon's artifact. Xaran found his way to his feet, and collected Faith from where it stood in the corner near the mattress that lay on the floor. At the door, Xaran paused. He intended to leave Kadon behind, but there was a concern that burned somewhere deep in the back of his mind. This power was unlike anything that Xaran had ever encountered, not necessarily greater in magnitude than Aerith's power, but it seemed to have more far-reaching possibilities. At the last moment, Xaran returned to the bag where Kadon rested and recovered the belt. He strapped it on slowly and then made for the door again.

The power flooding in from all directions made it difficult to keep focused on the direction that Xaran wanted to go, but eventually he locked in on the source of power, and slowly made his way towards it.

* * * * * * * * * * * *

Darrien scrambled back to her feet with one hand extended, both shocked and dismayed at her little sister's display of power. In her off hand, Darrien let small flows of power begin to coalesce. They took no form yet, but Darrien had learned long ago that the more prepared she was for a situation without committing to a singular course of action, the more she would be able to adapt when things inevitably went horribly wrong. It was one of the first lessons she learned when she began to duel her father to learn better control of her abilities. Pike in battle was brash and always moved forward. But that did not mean that he wasn't able to think laterally or adapt to situations. What it did mean however was that more often than not, Darrien was on the defensive. And that was the very position she found herself in now. Tess took one step forward onto the soaked ground, her foot sinking into the mud. Darrien let her weight fall to her back foot and prepared herself for the inevitable attack. Tess did not disappoint, another burst of force lancing out from Tess's hand in the direction of Darrien's chest. Pushing off her back foot, Darrien spun away from the assault, and returned the attack in kind, sending a bolt of pure energy aimed at the smaller girl's side. Unprepared for the attack, Tess took the blow fully to her side, and was thrown like a rag doll against the stone wall of the Heart of Stone. Darrien held her ground, not willing to give up the little bit of advantage that she had won for herself.

"What are you doing, Tess? I'm not going to hurt Camille! I don't want to hurt you!"

The young girl forced her way back to her feet, using the wall of the keep as leverage. Darrien knew that she hadn't hit her sister with enough force to do any real damage, but Tess's abilities had never lent themselves to combat. Her knees shook, and even as she pushed herself away from the wall, Darrien could tell that she was barely keeping herself upright. But it was not the attack that had caused her instability. It was as if there was a war going on inside of Tess, something was pushing to come out, whatever it was that was making her irrational seemed to be winning. A matter of moments later, Tess was back on her feet fully and standing on her own. She closed her eyes for the briefest of moments, and suddenly a golden haze descended around her like a fog. When it dissipated, the tattered white nightshirt had been miraculously repaired.

"You are not my sister."

Tess's voice was suddenly eerily calm. The bright glow in her eyes changed, and instead of the brilliant golden color it had been moments before, her eyes had gone completely white. Around her hands and arms a golden glow appeared, and Darrien could feel energy radiating from her sister unlike any that she had ever felt before. The drizzling rain that was falling began to create a nimbus of steam around the smaller girl, and as the seconds passed, small rocks began to levitate around her.

"What did you do with my sister? Why are you doing this to us? Why can't you just leave Camille and I alone?"

The young girl thrust her right hand forward the next moment, and a stream of golden fire burst in Darrien's direction. No matter her divine birth, there was nothing that Darrien could have done to prevent the attack from landing. From the minute the flames hit Darrien's skin it felt like she was being roasted from the inside out. Every part of her burned and froze at the same time. Her joints ached, her muscles flexed and contracted in a schizophrenic rhythm. Her heart began to beat wildly, tortured, frantic. She felt as though she were dying. Darrien's vision began to cloud over, but just before it went completely black, Darrien saw movement out of the corner of her eye. Alderin was making his way back to his feet.

* * * * * * * * * * * *

By the time Alderin was back to his feet, Darrien had been forced to her knees by the continued assault of her deranged younger sister. He was still feeling weak, the assault of the creature calling itself Lucian had taken its toll on his strength. But if he could manage to break Tess's concentration on Darrien, if he could somehow focus her attention on him, if only for a moment, it might give Darrien the opportunity to break free and either get out of the line of fire, or mount some kind of counterattack. He dared not attack with pure force, because in her current state, he was unclear if such an attack would even be felt by the young girl. There out of the corner of his eye, he found it. The jet black dagger that seemed to ooze hatred. As if sensing the threat, Tess turned her eyes in Alderin's direction and reached out her other hand in his direction. The gout of fire moved impossibly fast, so fast that Alderin had to flatten himself to the ground to prevent being struck by it. As it was, the heat of the flame burned the exposed portion of his back. From his prone position however, Alderin was able to reach the dagger. There was no time to get back to his feet, and if he tried, Tess would have been able to quickly counter the threat that his diminished power would present. In one smooth and deft motion, Alderin seized the dagger with his right hand and immediately felt a wave of revulsion pass through him. It was as though total and complete evil had been consolidated into the blade itself. There was no malice, no intelligence, but simply evil. Alderin did his best to suppress the need to vomit, and pulled himself up to his knees before reaching back and then slinging his arm forward in one smooth motion. The hilt of the blade slipped free from his grasp and sped fast and true toward its target, the stomach of the young girl. What happened next, Alderin could never have dreamed possible.

The black blade gleamed as it traveled the distance between Alderin and Tess, and though Alderin had hoped to catch Tess completely by surprise, part of him knew that would never be the case. Though what Alderin had hoped would happen, did. Tess's eyes widened when she saw the dagger approaching. She ended her twin assaults against Darrien and Alderin and extended both her hands in the direction of the rapidly approaching dagger. She extended both of her hands, palms out, toward the weapon that hurtled toward her. Inches before the black blade tore into the young girl's flesh, it simply began to unravel. It was like the weapon itself was knitted from metal yarn, and somewhere in the midst of flight between Alderin's hand and Tess's form, it had struck something that snagged its construction. The unraveling began at the tip, and continued down the length of the blade and the hilt until all that was left was a pile of metal shavings at the feet of the young woman. Tess looked down at the pile of refuse that was once the threatening dagger, and then looked back up at Alderin's kneeling form.

"Not you too! You're trying to take Camille away from me! Why are you trying to hurt her? Why are trying to kill us?"

Tess took a step toward Alderin, her hands still extended and Alderin felt a tingling begin in his right hand. Alderin could not help but to look down at his right hand. At the very tip of his middle finger, a small trickle of blood emerged, and as the heartbeats ticked past, Alderin watched in horror as the edge of the nail on his middle finger peeled off like a thread being pulled from the edge of a tapestry. Pain shot through Alderin's arm and yet he could not withdraw his hand. Tess took another step forward and the unraveling continued in Alderin's hand. Now four separate strings were being pulled from Alderin's hand, one from each of his outstretched fingers. Blood flowing freely from the stumps that remained behind.

When the unraveling reached the level of Alderin's thumb, a fifth strand joined the others. The pain flooding through Alderin was beyond comprehension, and as the unraveling reached his palm, he was barely able to keep conscious. By the time his entire hand had been rendered to a pile of shredded flesh, Alderin's eyes began to flutter closed, and what was left of his vision was filled with darkness and bright flares of white hot searing pain. Just as Tess began to take another step forward, the thick haft of a staff interjected itself, striking Tess in the chest and forcing her backwards.

Alderin felt the pain ebb, and the unraveling ceased just above his wrist, half-way to his elbow. The stub had healed over as though Alderin had never had a right hand at all. A man stood between Alderin and Tess now, a thin man who held a thick wooden staff in his hands. Tess kept her back against the wall, but Alderin could see the frown painting her face. The white hot glow still encased her eyes, and the golden fire wrapped itself around her hands once again. Alderin could not keep himself within the moment any longer, and he collapsed to the ground.

* * * * * * * * * * * *

"I am Xaran Firesoul," the man said proudly, holding his staff in a fighting position, "Tiger's Eye Knight of the Kingdom of Knowledge, Menoris, sworn protector of the rightful Empress of Cadaria, Marlae Lorien. I do not know how you have gained this level of power that you now wield, nor do I know what you intend to do with that power, but I cannot allow you to exist as a threat to the Cadarian Empire, or to the Empress. Yield now, or I shall have to take you by force."

Tess stood straight again, one finger extended toward Xaran's heart.

"I am Pirotessa Rhuiden, daughter of the leader of the Dark Gods, Pike Rhuiden, and of the goddess Raenera, first born daughter of the Creator. The laws and nature of the universe are at my command, and I could erase you from existence as though you were never born. You know me as a Dark Goddess, but I have another name. A name from prophecy. A name from legend. I am the Dragon's Tear."

Xaran felt a shudder go through him, the kind that made him feel that he would never be warm again. The two additional voices screamed in his mind. Faith wanted him to run, to retreat, to get as far away from the demonic presence as possible. Kadon on the other hand roared with pure hatred. The very existence of the girl was an affront to everything that Kadon was created to protect. Xaran had to make a choice, and unfortunately there was no good choice left open to him. He could not see the girl with his dead eyes, but the outline of her power was clearly visible to him. The power was unbelievable, and it defied even the most rudimentary description. Xaran's choice was made. Without warning he struck out with the staff, intending to impact hard against the girl's outstretched wrist, crippling it. Perhaps that would slow the girl down enough that Xaran would be able to press an advantage and bring an end to this fight before someone got killed. However, either the girl was prepared for such a tactic, or her reflexes were much greater than Xaran had anticipated. With her free hand, Tess caught the strike inches before it connected with the target. She pulled the staff back toward herself, drawing Xaran in. The strike that connected with Xaran's sternum easily shattered not only his breastbone, but several of the ribs that were attached. For several long moments, Xaran could not catch his breath. When he was able to drag several tortured breaths through his lungs, he knew that he was no longer in any kind of fighting shape. The girl had debilitated him quite effectively, and now she held the Sacred Weapon Faith in her hands. She regarded it for only a moment, and while Xaran could not see the scowl that turned her lips, he could certainly feel it.

"You dare imprison a servant of a goddess in this manner? Who do you Cadarians think you are? The arrogance to stand against the will of the Creator. The arrogance to stand against those that were once the Creator's chosen champions. You will all suffer for the indignities you have inflicted upon us. I will make this whole world burn if need be. And there is nothing that you or your puppet Emperor can do to stop me."

The voice was ghoulish, cruel, and filled with such benevolence that Xaran felt as though he had been struck again. With one smooth deft motion, the girl brought Faith up, and then crashing down upon her knee. The Sacred Weapon, the symbol of the Kingdom of Menoris, and the charge of the Knights of the Flashing Blade for nearly two thousand years snapped with the sound of tides crashing against unfeeling rocks, and a million trees crashing to the ground in unison. Tess tossed the pieces of

Faith to the ground and then wiped her hands on her nightshirt as if they were stained with something foul. Whatever restraint was within Xaran snapped that next moment. He called deep within himself and reached for the power that the ancient artifact Kadon had offered to him.

* * * * * * * * * * * *

The strands of consciousness began to return to Darrien, and from where she lay slumped on the ground she could see a sight that in her wildest dreams she could never imagine. Alderin laid several feet away, one half of his right arm missing, and his face buried in the mud, unconscious. Tess was wreathed in golden fire, her eyes bright white, and her hair beginning to float upwards as if it was carried on some breeze. At her feet lay a tangled mass of metal and the broken halves of a staff of some sort. A man lay on his back several feet in front of her, and he was just beginning to make his way back to his feet, but as Darrien watched, a change began to take over the man.

His body was suddenly drenched in an aura of red energy that seemed to manifest out of nowhere. The man's eyes were open wide, and his face had begun to take on more reptilian features. Skin was becoming black scales, and the eyes were beginning to go into a deep red. His arms began to thicken, and the scales began to turn black. The middle two fingers on each hand grew together, and then became one as the hand flexed back and looked more like a great paw than a hand. At one point, the elbows straightened and then bent the opposite way. Each arm now looked like a leg with the giant paw on the end. The new paws grew gleaming golden talons. The man's pants ripped and then were shredded as the breadth of the limbs increased. The black scales seemed to cascade down each leg, and the talons grew out of each toe. Again, the middle two toes merged, and soon, his legs were almost identical to his arms. His torso expanded and the black scales seemed to grow from the human-like pours, his neck started to lengthen. When the neck was finished growing, the still very human head began to grow. His jaw jutted forward and lengthened as his nose sank back into nonexistence and his head flattened. The top part of the man's mouth then began to lengthen and stopped when its length matched that of the jaw. Where a human's head seems to sit atop the neck at a square angle, this new creature's neck and head seemed to sit in a straight line. When the head and neck moved to their new locations, there was a sound like snapping bones and ripping flesh. The unnatural angle the face formed made Darrien's stomach turn. The tail of the dragon was the next piece to be formed. That same sound of skin breaking accompanied the formation, and as she watched, a small snake-like projection came into view. It twisted and moved as if it were fighting to pull itself from the rest of the body. More and more pulled itself out as the seconds passed until it had grown to at least sixty yards in length. But the transformation's most spectacular part had yet to be seen. The dragon now rolled onto its side, and two large slits appeared in the dragon's back. The scaly liquid substance that had formed on the legs and chest of the creature now dripped from the open wounds, and then started to solidify the further they dripped away from the rest of the body. It was like the wings formed from the tips inward. Most of the wing was a lighter color, almost a gray. Black veins arched across the seemingly thin skin and attached to the black tendon-like framework of the wing. The wings themselves looked like those of a bat. When the transformation was complete, the haze of energy dissipated, and the newly formed dragon glared down at Tess with its brilliant red eyes.

"You will pay for what you have done."

The dragon's jaws opened and a massive gout of fire exploded from its maw. The white flames licked in all directions from where they struck, melting the stone wall of the keep creating a bubbling crater where Darrien's sister had stood only moments before. But within the white flames, Darrien could see something glimmering. As the seconds passed during the dragon's assault, the golden glow within the roiling white flames began to strengthen. Darrien could barely believe her eyes, when the golden glow began to extend, pressing back against the unrelenting assault of the dragon's flame. Somewhere deep in the conflagration, a chain reaction was ignited which set forth a massive explosion that engulfed both the combatants. The flash was so bright that Darrien lost her vision for several long moments, and when her vision was finally restored, the wreckage before her could barely be believed. A large portion of the keep's wall had been totally melted away, and a massive crater had been dug in the ground in front of the ruined wall. Miraculously, Camille's broken body lay completely undisturbed outside the remains of the fray. A man's broken naked body lay in pieces at the edge of the crater, the only clothing was a shredded belt which lay in pieces around what was once his waist. Darrien scrambled on her hands and knees to the edge of the crater, and her breath caught in her throat as she saw the body of her sister laying in a small pool of blood at the very bottom.

Darrien scrambled down the steep face of the fifteen foot deep crater and made it as quickly to her sister's side as possible. She was comforted to find the girl still breathing. Ignoring the blood, Darrien pulled the girl's head into her lap and smoothed her hair away from her face. Tess's eyes fluttered open, and relief swept through Darrien when she saw they were back to their normal color.

"Five more minutes, Darrien," Tess's distant voice said as her eyes began to flutter closed again. "Just let me sleep a little longer."

Wind of a Thousand Chills

Year Three of the Just Emperor Kaitain "Dragonsbane" Lorien, Creator's Calendar Year 1870

Standing atop a low hill at the edge of the Plains of Steam, Jerah stood looking down on the small procession of people below. All had been set into motion perfectly, and yet Jerah took no joy in what was to come. However, that was nothing new. Jerah took no joy in anything done in service of her master, they were simply necessary steps taken toward a greater resolution. Thousands of years ago Jerah had entered the service of Dorovar, long before he had been imprisoned on this world, and long before he would truly understand the plan that drove him since he was cursed by the dragons with immortality and was made to watch as his world died around him. Thousands of years later, after her own world had died, Jerah, though she wore a different name in those days, first collided with Dorovar. Like many before her, she had been tasked as an emissary of the Creator, attempting to pull Dorovar away from his destructive path. But even with all of the additional powers granted to her by the Creator, Jerah had been no match for Dorovar, and he defeated her quickly, but painfully. Jerah lay there on the ground, broken, dying, and Dorovar stood over her, looking deep into her eyes, through them into her very soul. He saw something there, in those dying moments, something that intrigued him that he could not simply let be extinguished. Perhaps that was when he finally understood the true nature of his plan, or perhaps that was simply when he decided that killing the servants of the Creator was no longer gaining him anything. Whatever the case, Jerah was reborn that moment. The life that had been hers before that moment ceased to exist, and she was dedicated to the building the Chorus of Souls and helping her master rise up to his rightful position in the heavens.

But something had begun to change in Jerah, she could feel it stirring in what passed for her heart and in the back of her mind; something ancient beyond words. Ever since she saw him, something had changed, and she could not reconcile it. He should not have even existed let alone been there defending the so-called Lady of Cadaria. What was she to him? What was he to her? It wasn't until she felt the ground tremble beneath her feet that she realized that she was angry. The emotion was almost alien to her. She could not remember the last time, since Dorovar's touch had remade her, that she had felt anger. She could not remember the last time she felt any strong emotion. There was no love, no pity, no rage, nothing, only the duties that she was assigned to perform. Nothing held passion, not even the ultimate goal. But when she stared down at him, at his face, her bright green eyes locked upon his, she felt something stir within her. Something powerful, something primal, and something that defied all description. Memory rose in her; the touch of his hand, the feel of his breath against her neck as he walked close behind her. She had longed after his passing that she could have truly felt the tenderness of his lips against hers.

But then she felt a presence approaching, one nearly as powerful as she. Breaking her solid stare down at the doomed band below, Jerah turned to see the approaching Gray Man Pestilence and the newest member of the followers of Dorovar, the hulking beast known as War. The former Knight of the Flashing Blade Seraph Kore had embraced the teachings of Dorovar, but not in the ways that the other Heralds had. Pestilence had come to the services of Dorovar through greed and a need to have more than he could possibly do with. He was a thief, a braggart, and his arrogance laid him low at the feet of a god. Famine had been hurt and angry. And her hate of the people who stole her life from her made her an easy target for the will of Dorovar. She came willingly and visited her hatred gleefully upon the world. Death was dutiful and committed, but to a fault. He was a true believer, a zealot, and devoid of any existence beyond his adherence to his righteous calling. Seraph, now War, was afraid. Fear motivated him, fear made him stronger, and Jerah could smell it rolling from him like a fog. That which weakened him now became his greatest weapon, and the very tools that he would use to bring conflict to every corner of the world. There were none that could feel his presence that would not become paranoid with fear, and they would lash out. They would lash out against their neighbors, they would lash out against their loved ones, and they would lash out at anyone and everyone that could be targeted. Fear would drive them into a frenzy, and the world would burn and feed millions of souls to the chorus. Dorovar would delight in the tumult of voices that would sing to him in his prison.

Jerah watched as War approached and marveled in the way that the touch of Dorovar had changed the once proud and powerful Seraph Kore. Where Seraph had been barely six feet in height, War stood nearly twice that, the sweeping crests of his massive helm brushing well over ten feet. From his feet to his shoulders, every inch of his body was covered with armor, the plates thick and forbidding, their texture pocked and wrinkled, as though they had seen many lifetimes of constant warfare. Where once the color may have been the brightest bronze, now the plates were tarnished, the color uneven and a mixture of oxidized greens, stained browns, and faded bronze. The great helm too continued these colors, wide crests like the wings of some great bird sweeping back from the temples. Two demonic horns protruded from the front of the helm which covered the creature's forehead, and wide plates swept down over the ears, to under the chin. There was no faceplate on the helm, and the creature's face was fully exposed. No one gazing on the beast would have seen a resemblance to the once renowned Emerald Knight, as its face was now the color of slate; cheeks, lips, and nose pocked and deformed like the armor. But below craggy brows, bright red eyes glared out. The fires of war manifested in the creature's eyes. Long white hair emerged from under the helm and was dirty with ash, soot, and dried blood, a halo of regret circling the creature's head. Clutched in one mighty hand was a sword nearly as long as the beast was tall, jet black, with a cruel saw-like blade on one edge that swept into a vicious hook at the end. It was a weapon of death to be sure. Despite herself, Jerah found herself proud of the creature.

"Master has plans for our newest addition," Pestilence said in his haunted voice, "already the forces of Saldarine and Thorigald march upon the Plains of Steam, and War will ensure that none leave this valley alive. He will incite them to a new level of violence."

Jerah extended her hand and then pointed into the valley. Pestilence moved to the lookout where Jerah had stood only moments before and looked down upon the small procession of travelers. A low laugh escaped the creature's lips.

"Perhaps War shall make his appearance earlier than expected and rid us of the troublesome Lady of Cadaria and her protector."

Jerah instead of turning her attention to Pestilence looked up into the face of War. If the larger beast felt Jerah's eyes, he ignored her. He instead looked out past Pestilence. That instant Jerah knew where War's eyes had gone. His attention was drawn to the largest threat on the field, and that undoubtedly was the man who wore the name Dane Rhuiden. But that name was a shroud, a disguise to protect him from those who would know the danger of his true name. Finally, War looked down and met Jerah's eyes. Something passed between the two of them that instant, something that Pestilence could not have understood. Something that required a person to have loved something other than themselves so completely that it changed them forever.

"Dorovar wants the woman," War said finally. "The monk will not be killed, it is not his time."

Pestilence turned to protest, but it was too late. War had already taken two long steps toward the edge of the cliff and leapt high into the air. His massive body plummeted toward the ground below, and hit with enough force to create a crater a hundred feet wide, and shake the ground for a mile in all directions. The travelers were taken off of their feet, and recovered as quickly as they could to meet the aggressor. Pestilence turned away from the scene below and moved toward Jerah.

"Flaunting the will of Dorovar is not wise, dear Jerah, no matter how you feel you are entitled. Despite your power and your station, none are above Dorovar's will."

Jerah clenched her fist and Pestilence felt its throat begin to tighten. But it was more than its throat that was being constricted. Every joint felt as though it was being compressed, every inch of its body. Its lungs and heart were being squeezed as though they were in a vice, and though his knees wanted to collapse, they would not move, the joints themselves were locked in place. The pressure continued, tightening more and more as the seconds passed. Bones began creaking under the assault, threatening to snap. From somewhere deep inside her, Jerah felt a pain. It was not unpleasant, but it was jarring enough for her hold on Pestilence to slip. Her master was in pain, but not enough to put him in danger. Dorovar was testing the strength of his bonds, and it was sending intense pain rocketing through him. None of the other heralds would be attuned enough to their master to feel it, but Jerah was different. She was a child of the universe as Dorovar was, intrinsically linked to the power that flowed through all of the chosen. The pain was gone the next moment, and Jerah turned her attention back to Pestilence. The servant of Dorovar had managed to regain a measure of his composure, but the assault had drained him of a great deal of his vitality. A whisper thin rapier appeared in Jerah's hand the next moment, and she slid forward across the ground like fog rolling in. Pestilence had no defense as the needle tip of the rapier pierced it through the shoulder. Pain unlike anything the beast had ever felt or ever inflicted swept through its body like a fire. Every portion of its being was on fire and freezing at the same time. The torture and torment robbed its lungs of the ability to scream, and paralyzed every muscle. When Jerah removed the point of the blade, the torture continued, and Pestilence was locked there, the echo of pain mounting on itself, doubling and tripling with every stolen moment. Jerah watched impassively as Pestilence suffered the true Touch of Dorovar. Every soul that had been taken by one of the heralds had added its pain to the Touch, and Pestilence lived through their suffering over and over again, all at once and then mounting in waves, the torment and torture of a million dedicated souls visiting their pain upon him. It was then that Jerah felt something new. Dorovar was again testing the bonds of his prison. This time however, the pain had not answered his actions. Instead the prison had ceded to his desires and had shattered under the pressure of his will. Dorovar was free. With a thought Jerah released Pestilence from his suffering and walked away, fading into the air like retreating mist. Pestilence stood several minutes later. He could hear the conflict below, but it held no interest. Hatred burned within him, white hot and threatening to consume his weakened form. Hatred for Jerah, and hatred for her position of influence over him. Jerah would pay for her treachery, and soon Pestilence alone would stand at the right hand of Dorovar.

* * * * * * * * * * * *

Jillian looked around the desolate land called the Plains of Steam and couldn't help but shiver a little. This land had been the site of more than one battle in the constantly escalating conflict between the Kingdom of Fire Saldarine and the Kingdom of Water Thorigald. But the land was the home to more than the ghosts of dead soldiers and unrequited hatred. It was also the home of one of the most feral of the dragons of Cadaria. As one of the foremost experts on the dragons of Cadaria, Jillian had many opportunities to study the beast that called itself Nessus the Hovering Rain. It made itself quite well known to all of the villages in the area, and had also on many occasions taken it upon herself to swoop in during conflicts between the warring armies and bring peace back to the land that she considered her own. What most people did not know was that Nessus had a mate that shared the lands with her, a mate that was perhaps more fearsome than she was. Thalasia Steelbiter was twice Nessus' size and could breathe a cloud of noxious vapor that would instantly cause any metal that it touched to rust and become useless in a fight. His very touch could also instantly rust armor and any other metal object. He was the bane of armies and anyone foolish enough to attempt to slay him. Many dragon hunters had tried over the years, and none stupid enough to venture into his haven returned to tell what they had seen there. Jillian could feel Scaleripper vibrating in its scabbard, and knew that at least one of the beasts was close. Dragons didn't like anyone intruding on their lands, especially not armed groups the size of the one Jillian traveled in.

Dane looked back over his shoulder and his gaze met Jillian's. While at first she smiled in response to his gaze, the smile quickly faded and her stomach fluttered. The man who consorted with Dark Gods and used a false name was more than a worry to her, and yet she could not help but trust him. Nothing he had done had been overtly threatening, and he did seem to honestly have her best interests at heart, even if he kept his motives very tightly guarded. But even as he turned back to watch the road ahead,

Jillian did not let her gaze fall back to the landscape. She continued to watch him for a long moment, lost in thoughts of his words in the clearing with the Dark God. She was important somehow, to something larger than even she could understand. Suddenly Dane stopped in his tracks and looked up toward the high peaked cliffs that flanked the Plains of Steam on the southern side. He stood for several long moments looking at seemingly nothing. He turned back looking not at Jillian but at Blade. The unspoken exchange lasted only a moment, but the diminutive man drew his large axe and scanned the horizon for the threat that Dane had detected. Dane's walking staff was quickly discarded, and he set his feet into a ready stance. Jillian needed no further prompting to take action of her own. Scaleripper was freed from its scabbard a moment later, and quick hand signals to her fellow dragon hunters sent them into practiced motion. Angelina immediately took to guarding the flank, while Kiara slid to the center of the formation, ready to bring her healing abilities to bear if needed. She also drew a long thin rapier from a sheath that hung from her back, a weapon that suited her smaller and more lithe frame. Jacqueline brought a large studded club to bear, one that she had fashioned herself out of the hide of one of the larger dragons they had disposed of.

"Dane, to the north!"

Jillian whirled in the direction that Blade had indicated, and her breath caught in her throat. Emerging from the mist were the bright red banners of the Army of Fire, the feared fighting force of the Kingdom of Fire Saldarine. Their numbers were easily in the tens of thousands, armor gleaming in the advancing morning light.

"And the south!"

Jacqueline's voice was full of irritation and edge, no different than any other day, but there was also a twinge of fear there. Jillian turned her head and saw brilliant blue banners, the mark of the Army of Water, from the Kingdom of Thorigald. They were trapped in the middle of bitter enemies, and the term non-combatant would not avail them once the charge was sounded. The Plains of Steam were vast, as were the front ranks of the armies that flanked them on each side. Once the battle was joined, the small band would have to fight their way through enemies on all sides to make for the borders of Albitonin, a line that neither army would cross without cause. Word must have already reached the Heart of Stone, and the forces of the Stone Legion would already be on the move. If the rumors were true, and Gregor Quicksilver had taken control of the rebel army as their military commander in the name of the so-called Empress Marlae Lorien, then both the armies of Fire and Water would think twice about encroaching on their borders. Jillian turned back to Dane to give a suggestion that they move quickly, but she found him not looking at the forces arrayed against them, but rather still up at the cliffs above. Something leapt from the cliff that next moment, something huge. The sunlight gleamed off every inch of it, nearly blinding anyone foolish enough to look directly at it. When it finally crashed to the ground below, the whole of the valley shook, and despite their best efforts, every member of the small band, save Dane, were taken off their feet. When everyone had scrambled back to their feet, they watched in horror as the massive beast trudged its way out of the crater its fall had created. The creature's armor seemed to glow in the mist, a hateful stare set upon its ashen face, bright red eyes burning through.

"There is no surrender," a deep booming voice echoed from somewhere inside the beast, though its lips did not move in the utterance. "There is no escape. There is only defeat."

Dane took a step forward, but the larger beast raised its cruel sword from its side and pointed it at the chest of the much smaller man. The huge creature was still a great many paces away, but with the length of its arm and the length of its blade, it could cover huge distances. Dane stopped in his tracks at the unspoken threat, but balled his fists.

"You're the last of Dorovar's heralds," Dane said confidently.

The creature didn't respond.

"Big isn't everything," Blade said after a moment, stroking his beard with his free hand. "I've killed bigger."

A look between the two men was the only signal that was given. Dane rushed quickly forward, Blade a pace behind, but losing ground to the other man's longer legs. Dane leapt high in the air, ready to deliver a strong palm strike to the side of the creature's face, but moving with a speed that belied its great size and bulk, the creature swatted Dane out of the air and sent him sprawling through the air like a broken doll. Blade didn't fare much better, as his long swing with his great axe was intercepted by the saw-like blade of the creature's sword. Blade may have been strong, but he was no match for the larger creature. A moment later Blade too was sailing through the air, his axe coming to rest a few feet from where he hit. The massive beast drew itself up and raised its cruel weapon high into the air.

"Tremble before me mortals. I am the last of the Heralds of Dorovar, the greatest of his generals, and the immortal bringer of destruction. I devour worlds, shatter families and kingdoms. I am eternal, fed by hatred, nourished by fear, and succored on blood. The broken bodies of the fallen are the proof of my passing, and my footprints can be seen in the ashes of the worlds I have burned. You cannot escape. You cannot retreat. There is nowhere that you can hide from my touch or my influence. Blood will spill at the sound of my call. For I am War!"

A deep bellowing laugh filled the whole of the valley. The laugh was answered by the signal horns first from the Army of Fire and then from the Army of Water. War's call had started the inevitable conflict, and a moment later tens of thousands of throats let loose a war cry. The sound of clattering metal was like thunder rolling across the Plains of Steam. Dane and Blade had recovered their feet, but made no attempt to rejoin the group. The two shared another quick conspiratorial glance, and Blade charged in again, his axe left where it had embedded itself in the ground. Dane too advanced, moving as though to flank the beast, but darting back at the last moment when War attempted to swat him with its huge free hand. The saw-like blade flashed forward, its intent to take Blade's head off, but the smaller man had other plans. He skidded to a stop, his hands out in front of him as if he intended to catch the blade. Jillian started to call out, to call him a madman, but the cry caught in her throat. A sheet of green fire erupted from Blade's hands, forming a shield before him. War's blade collided with the shield, and gouts of fire erupted in all directions. The sparse grasses of the plains caught fire, and burned quickly, but Blade and the beast War paid the burning no mind. Dane darted in, a blade of pure pulsing green energy appearing in his hands a moment before he leapt into the air and struck at the creature's sword wrist. The pulsing green blade struck the armor, and a flash of blinding light flared at the contact. It was as though an explosion had gone off at the point of impact, and a wave of force burst out in all directions. Dane was again tossed into the air, but there was no control to his fall. He was unconscious and broken. When he collided with the ground, Jillian could not tell if he was breathing. Blade too seemed to be worse for wear after the impact. He lay face down in the ground, one shoulder visibly dislocated. War took a step forward and raised its huge sword above its head.

"I cannot know defeat! War cannot be stopped!"

From somewhere above the massive creature, a form emerged, streaking down from the skies like a falling meteor. It struck down on War with such force that the ground shook again. Wings buffeted for several moments, the sound of claws and teeth scraping against armor filling all ears with shrill sounds that chilled the blood. The gnashing and grinding continued for several long heartbeats, until War found strength to dislodge the massive winged beast and send it hurtling into the air. It took only three beats of its huge leathery wings to bring itself back under control. Huge clawed feet touched down, and the dragon held itself upright, long neck and massive head looking down at Dorovar's herald.

"You are not welcome in my lands, puppet," the dragon's harsh voice boomed from its massive jaws. "But as you say, there is no retreat, and no surrender. So prepare to meet your end as I rip you to shreds. You have earned the ire of Thalasia Steelbiter."

* * * * * * * * * * *

Tolon Moor stood on a high cliff looking down at the Plains of Steam that stretched below him and unconsciously held his breath. Jerrica had been right, there was something terrible that was going to happen in Saldarine, something that defied even the most basic of descriptions. He felt the weight of Strength in his hand and knew that the massive axe wanted to be down in the valley adding its own part to the battle. For himself, Tolon thirsted for battle as well, but there was something more going on than just the clashing of two great armies. There was a massive beast below, clad in stained and well-worn armor, its cruel sword matching blows with a dragon whose size defied description. And there, in the middle of it all was a smaller group of travelers. Two had already been rendered either unconscious or dead by the creature that had bellowed its name, War, to all who had ears to hear. Unbelievably, Tolon recognized one of those who remained standing. It was the woman he had collided with before his audience with the Emperor, the woman who called herself the Lady of Cadaria. What was she doing here, and more importantly, what was he going to do to get her out of the middle of a war zone? After taking in the scene below, Tolon turned away from the cliff and quickly moved back to where Jerrica sat. The closer they had gotten to the Plains of Steam, the weaker it seemed that she became. It was as though her strength was being leeched from her by something nearby. She looked up at him, and more bloody tears were streaking down her cheeks.

"I have to go," he said after a brief moment. "I'm needed down there."

He turned, and she held his arm.

"We're needed," her meek voice came softly. "You cannot face what is down there alone."

He wanted to argue, he truly did, but he knew better. Whatever she had seen that had driven them to this moment would not occur without her at his side. Taking hold of her gently at the waist, Tolon lifted Jerrica and made his way to the winding path that would lead them into the heart of the battle. In his heart, Tolon worried if he would be able to protect both himself and Jerrica from what was to come, but no matter what doubts he had, Strength quickly erased them. He was where he was needed, that much was assured, what happened after was of no consequence. The future would see to itself, no matter what happened next.

A Cold and Broken Hallelujah

Year Three of the Just Emperor Kaitain "Dragonsbane" Lorien,
Creator's Calendar Year 1870

The Vault of Terrors, the greatest collection of power in the entirety of the Creator's universe was also its most effective prison. For thousands of years, Dorovar had called this place home, the first home he had known since the loss of his world. The devices and records in the Hall would have taken a thousand thousand lifetimes to fully understand, but Dorovar had patience, and more than that, he had time. The power that he had accumulated in just the first two hundred years would have been enough to shatter any world, or lay waste to any civilization. But Dorovar had no interest in killing. Yes, killing was a necessary task in the new world that would be forged by his hand, but there was no joy in the task. The enemies of the will of Dorovar did not deserve the honor of bringing joy to the one who would deliver them unto death, and those who were being freed from their bonds of servitude to the Creator were to be pitied. There was no joy. There was no fear. There was no hate. There was only the work. The task at hand was one that could only be done by Dorovar himself, and the Creator would pay for the hellish dominion that he visited upon those who could do nothing but endure. But Dorovar felt something new in the air. The stale and stagnant coldness in the Vault of Terrors seemed to have lessened, and the heaviness of foreboding had begun to lift.

The door to the Vault of Terrors was easy enough to find, but it was a door that could never be opened, for it had no hinges, no locks, and no mechanisms. It simply was. Much like the Creator's laws, they served a purpose without explanation. Before the actual threshold of the door was a barrier of force that hung invisible to the eye but apparent to the perception of any marginally intelligent being. Dorovar was considerably more than intelligent enough to perceive the barrier, and he could also feel its strength hanging heavy in the air. Today was different though. The barrier had been weakened somehow; not slightly, not in minute degree, but as though it's very foundation had been breached. Wordlessly, Dorovar extended his hand and pressed against the invisible wall, feeling it give slightly at the application of pressure. The pain radiating through his hand would have killed a mortal, but Dorovar pushed away the pain and concentrated. All of his heralds were loose now in the world, bringing his love to those who were ground into the dust by the boot of the Creator and his minions. But there was something else...something new. It was as if the universe was holding its breath, waiting for something to happen. Dorovar could wait too, and whatever it was that was about to happen, it would bring Dorovar one step closer to making everyone pay for what happened to the innocents and to his world.

* * * * * * * * * * * *

The common room of the Inn at Coventry had been converted to a type of throne room. There was no finery and the throne was nothing more than the largest dining chair that could be found in the inn's meager storeroom. When Emperor Kaitain Lorien emerged from the top of the stairs, the members of the Imperial Guard around the room snapped to a quick attention. The only man who did not move was the Captain of the Imperial Guard, Korin Melcab, who continued to stand in his rigid and unapproachable guard. The bar had been removed from the edge of the common room, ripped free and tossed out like so much garbage. What stood now in the void were a set of six Imperial Guards, two holding the entrance to the kitchen and four to hold the manacles of the two prisoners who waited judgment.

Jaccob Aldora stood as casually as he could manage, but the whole of his capture and imprisonment by the Captain of the Imperial Guard had solidified his worst fears about the fate that was waiting for him at the hands of the Emperor. The manacles did not weigh on him as much as he thought they would, but the cold iron around his ankles had started to itch in a most unexpected way. There was an absurdity to the situation that seemed to set in as soon as he came to peace with the fact that he would never see another sunrise. Temperance lay just feet away, on a low table that sat ten feet from the pseudo throne. The guards in the room probably would not have been much competition were Jaccob to wish escape, especially if his fellow prisoner chose to assist him. He looked to his left and found the statuesque beauty of the Wolf of Saldarine, the Garnet Knight Chelsea Zarova staring out; trying to be the single stone standing after the torrent of the hurricane had passed. It looked as though she was simply trying to will herself through this latest incongruent cruelty. Jaccob knew as everyone seemingly did about the affair between the now Empress Dominique Lorien and Chelsea's husband Seraph Kore. There was no one that did not inwardly wince when Chelsea became the adulteress' protector, nor did anyone not feel pity for the great and powerful knight when her husband was labeled a traitor to the throne and was on the rapidly shortening path to execution. But through it all, the woman stood tall, vigilant, and strong. She was the best example of what a knight should be, and now she was standing beside the worst example of what a knight should be, ready to meet her judgment. Jaccob knew he was a drunk, a carouser, and a disgrace to his station. But perhaps he would be able to summon enough dignity to meet his end, and redeem himself in the eyes of one that truly deserved adoration.

The Emperor took a long time to descend the staircase, carefully measuring each and every step. Uncharacteristically, he was clad in black from head to toe, with a heavy gray and black fur wrapped around him that dragged the ground, leaving a sheen of dust and debris on the very bottom edge of the garment. When his face finally came into view of the common room, there were barely stifled gasps from some of the soldiers and nearly all of the inn workers who had been conscripted into imperial service. Where once Kaitain's bearded face was an imposing and fearsome visage, the new steel mask that adorned the Emperor's face was ominous in the best light. Veins of black covered the steel in a strange pattern, like a demon from stories designed to frighten even the bravest soldier. Kaitain's bright eyes shown from deep behind the mask, furious stars in a midnight black sky. He stood in front of the throne for a long moment, letting his presence fill the room and deepen the foreboding fog of confusion and fear. When finally he sat, there was no lightening of the room's mood, if anything it solidified that the Emperor was once again in control of his lands, and he would not brook defiance from anyone under any circumstances. Silence held the room until a voice boomed from behind the Emperor's mask. It was hard; hard as the steel that covered the man's face, and was filled with the most pitiless and cold tone that any in the room had ever heard.

"Once a man walked upon the face of this countryside who believed that all manner of men could live together in peace. He fought under the banner of that peace, and gathered men to his cause that believed as he did. Together they forged the greatest land this world had ever seen, and through blood, sweat, and dedication they forged the first Empire of Cadaria. The man's vision had nearly become a reality, and he sat upon the first throne, not much different than the one I sit upon now, as the first Emperor of Cadaria. But Terrik Lorien had one challenge left to him, and it was the evil that rained down from the Heavens. The Creator had cast out the Dark Gods and let them wreak havoc upon the face of this world. But my forbearer still believed in his heart that peace was possible. So while standing in a pool of blood spilled from the headless body of the leader of the Dark Gods, he forged a pact with the Dark Continent of Mythryn to create the thirteenth kingdom of Cadaria and create a peace that would last until the suns burned no more."

Kaitain reached into the pocket of his cloak and pulled out a small wooden sphere that was painted with green and blue.

"This was to be Terrik Lorien's legacy. A united Espre. An Espre blessed by the Creator with eternal peace and safety."

The Emperor regarded the sphere for a moment and then in one quick deft motion crushed the sphere. The cracking sound resounded through the room, much louder than it should have been. When Kaitain opened his hand, all that was left was dust.

"My ancestor's dream turned out to be fragile and ill-conceived. Cadaria cannot be ruled through peace. And it certainly cannot be ruled so long as the Dark Gods, the dragons, or any other disciples of the so-called Creator roam this land. The clergy would say that the challenges facing this Empire are tests from the Creator to prove our worthiness. Other more militant members of their order would say that our hardships are visited upon us because we are not pure in the eyes of the Creator, or perhaps we are being punished for some misdeed from another life. Or even that we have become so morally corrupt that the Creator no longer holds us in His heart. Those are words of treason!"

The voice boomed from his chest and radiated through the room as though a burst of thunder had struck the very center of the room. Before anyone had time to recover, Kaitain pressed on.

"You need look no further than the actions of the High Priestess and the most devout of their order Hannah Ironheart or her husband the pious and above-reproach Gregor Quicksilver. Was it not they who freed the traitor Leonora Wastri from the dungeons and spared her the execution that was sentenced upon her? Was it not they who broke away from this Empire when it was in turmoil? If they were the bringers of peace and mercy that they have always purported to be, then why were they not attempting to heal the wounds of the countryside while their Emperor lay on the edge of death from an assassin's arrow? Why are they now conspiring with that very assassin, Seraph Kore, who has seized power in Thorigald through murder and propaganda? Have they renounced him for his deeds? No. They are sanctioning the attempted murder of the rightful ruler of this land!"

The doors to the common room were open, and Kaitain's voice billowed from it like smoke from a fire on a cold night. It drew in the waiting ears of the commoners, and before long a crowd had gathered. They had heard the rumors of the awakening of the Emperor and the fall of Aldere. From the crowd there were murmurs of acceptance, mumbles of outrage. A fire had been started by the Emperor's fury-filled words, and though it burned slowly, if he continued to stoke it, it would explode.

"I challenge all of those who follow the path of the Creator to look at those who are preaching to you. Do they truly practice what they preach? Are they as firm in their convictions as they are in their words? Or are they simply buying your obedience with the promise of something better on the

Other Side? How much suffering in this world is worth an empty promise of contentment at the feet of the Creator?"

With this Kaitain stood, spreading his hands wide.

"We have all suffered in these past few years. Is it the vice of our own making that has caused this suffering? No! We did not bring the Crawling Plague to this world, but we all have watched as those we loved have suffered and died on their knees. And yet we are supposed to bring ourselves to our own knees, begging and praying for some Creator to visit his love upon us and ease the suffering of those we care most for. Did the Creator send his angels down and lift my father up off his knees and restore him to health, or did the Creator simply watch as the beloved Just Hand Ender Lorien withered away like burning paper. Did the Creator show mercy on my family and spare my own wife and unborn child from such a horrible end? And did that healing come to any of your loved ones?"

Someone yelled from the gathering.

"No!"

More yelled in support of the first man's voice.

"No!" Kaitain continued. "What came next was the Wasting Disease that made us all watch as loved ones gorged themselves to death, or died slowly, starving. How many of you had to hold a blade to the throat of a loved one to spare them from that pain?"

The murmurs increased in volume, individual words and sentiments lost to the greater tide of unrest.

"And then the tragedy in Rashaleb. The whole of the capital city wiped out. Nothing left living there. A wasteland that may never recover." Kaitain's voice added a touch of manufactured sorrow, his tone deep and sonorous.

"But Albitonin was spared!" a woman's voice cried out. She was almost instantly shouted down, but some bolstered her words with cries of their own.

"The Creator spared them!"

"They followed the teachings and were spared!"

"Open your eyes!" Kaitain bellowed, silencing the throng. "Were those men and women, the so-called most devout among us truly saved by the love of the Creator? No! The Creator did not even deem those sheep worthy of his shepherding. It was a Dark God! A Dark God who came to the rescue of the people of Albitonin. She spread her wings and pushed back the hands of the Death itself. Where was the Creator? Why was one of the evil creatures that He cast down more concerned about the so-called faithful than the true angels of the Creator? Perhaps it was not the Creator that the so-called devout amongst us have been praying too. Perhaps the true power that they worship resides on the Dark Continent of Mythryn!"

There were disbelieving stares for a long moment, the whole of the group holding its breath, teetering on the brink of the madness Kaitain was stoking within them. His next words would shatter that resolve.

"Is not the very sister of the High Priestess the wife of the leader of the Dark Gods?"

Insanity erupted from the crowd. It was a frenzy expertly stoked. The guards did their best to keep the mob under control. Kaitain allowed the surge to continue for several long moments, ready to drive the dagger deeper into the heart of those that wounded him so deeply. He would tear down everything that they valued, crush their hopes and their dreams, and wear their broken faith as a badge of honor.

"From this moment on, the Church of the Creator is to be considered a treasonous and seditious organization whose only goal is the subjugation of the wills of the people of Cadaria and the undermining of its rightful government. It has if not directly, indirectly participated in the most heinous crime possible, the attempted murder of the Emperor of Cadaria, as well as two other members of the royal family. They have consorted with enemies of the Throne, and have raised arms in rebellion. Those who are members of that organization are traitors to the Throne. Their possessions and lands are to be seized. All direct members of the organization are to be put to death."

The momentary shock was followed by a cheer that turned Jaccob's stomach.

"The family members of those within the organization will also be examined for their loyalty. If they are found above reproach, they will be offered conscription into the service of the Empire to cleanse them of the stain upon their honor. Those who are deemed questionable will be stripped of their lands, rights, and belongings and will be forced into servitude to repay the debt they have to our wounded Empire."

There was some trepidation at the decree, but Kaitain knew it was coming and had prepared his master stroke.

"My own daughter is not above this decree. She has been hopelessly corrupted by the teachings of this cult. She has rebelled against not only the empire, but against her own blood. She is hereby stripped of all title, rights, and inheritance, and henceforth is no longer recognized as a member of the Imperial Family. She is a non-entity. My daughter died, and the demon wearing her face should be made to suffer for the indignities she has perpetrated."

To Jaccob's surprise, there was almost a wave of sympathy that held the crowd. It was equal parts sickening and aweing. The Emperor now turned his attention to the prisoners.

"But there are more pressing indignities that have to be dealt with."

Kaitain pointed in Chelsea's direction, and the two guards stepped forward, pulling at the lead of her manacles. Chelsea stood firm, her eyes sparking with defiance. She would not be dragged before the masked man like this, not so long as she could still stand and fight. The guards pulled again, and Chelsea would not budge. One of the guards reached for his sword, but the Emperor waved his hand.

"Lady Chelsea Zarova, Garnet Knight of the Flashing Blade, Commander of the Army of Fire, and the dreaded Wolf of Saldarine, the Just Emperor requests that you present yourself before him."

The Emperor's tone was even and Jaccob was surprised at the concession that was made for the prideful woman. And while Chelsea may have been a woman of principle, she was also not a fool. She did not hesitate once the invitation was made to move from her place to where the Emperor indicated for her to stand. She would see this to the end, but she would do it with the dignity that she had earned through blood and sacrifice. Chelsea and the Emperor stood looking at one another for a long moment before the Emperor motioned to one of the guards.

"Remove her bonds."

The guard seemed taken by surprise by the order, but snapped to it quickly, releasing first the manacles at the woman's wrists and then at her ankles. Chelsea made no move to rub her irritated wrists, and stood stark and straight in the face of the Emperor, her face impassive, showing no contempt.

"Lady Chelsea Zarova," the Emperor began, his tone just bordering on sympathetic even through the coldness of the mask, "you have also had many indignities heaped upon you since I have been upon the throne, and through all of them you have displayed nothing but the utmost devotion to not only your position but to the Empire that you have sworn to protect with your own life if need be. Your husband, the traitor Seraph Kore has been a source of humiliation for you for many years, flaunting his many affairs while still calling himself your husband. He made war upon you, both physically on the battlefield as the general of your sworn enemy the Kingdom of Thorigald, and emotionally on the battlefield of your marriage. And yet you stood tall, sacrificing of yourself to try to hold the peace between Thorigald and Saldarine together from the marriage bed."

Jaccob could feel the venom in the words. The compliments were hollow, spiteful, and meant to strip away Chelsea's pride and humiliate her. It was a carefully and cleverly constructed ruse that would fool the masses, but would not be lost on those who truly heard.

"And again, when your husband's mistress became your better, when she became the Empress of Cadaria, you showed your dedication to this Imperial Family by becoming her protector. Willing to give your life to save someone whose betrayals to you would have ripped a normal woman's heart to shreds."

Chelsea's posture never shifted, her eyes blinking impassively and naturally, but Jaccob knew that inside she was dying. He could almost feel her blood boiling.

"For this service to your Emperor and to your Empire, and your initiative in protecting the life of the Empress of Cadaria during the fall of Aldere, I am hereby absolving you of any responsibility in the fall of Aldere, or in any of the questionable acts taken while I was not able to sit upon the Throne. I find that you have acted in the furtherance of the best intentions of the Throne, and you are to be rewarded for that service. From this moment forward, Lady Chelsea Zarova of Saldarine is now the master of Saldarine. All of the nobles that currently rule there owe allegiance to the Lady Zarova, and will follow her commands as she will follow mine. But as the leader of one of the Kingdoms of Cadaria, you cannot be seen to have any attachment to the improprieties that are swirling around your husband. Therefore, I dissolve your union with Seraph Kore. You are hereby free of him, but the terms of the treaty between Saldarine and Thorigald cemented by your marriage will still be in effect. I shall not allow his dishonor to tarnish your sacrifice."

There was a cheer that came from the mob that had grown ten-fold since the Emperor began speaking. Chelsea bowed a proper amount, but when she straightened Kaitain began to speak again.

"Unfortunately, Lady Zarova, your escalation to the ranks of nobility precludes you from fulfilling your oath as a member of the Knights of the Flashing Blade. I hereby relieve you of that position and will take custody of the Sacred Weapon Tenacity until such time that a suitable replacement from Saldarine can be found. Your days as the Garnet Knight are over Lady Zarova. The Throne thanks you for your tireless service."

Chelsea felt as though she had been struck by the open hand of the Emperor. Nonetheless she bowed again and waited to be dismissed. The wave of the Emperor's hand came a moment later, and Chelsea took her place out of the way of what would follow. She felt diminished, in more ways than just the loss of her connection to Tenacity. Emptiness was forming in her heart, and an ache resounded in her the likes of which she had never felt before. The rattling of chains broke Chelsea from her thoughts and she looked up to see Jaccob Aldora being led to the

Emperor's presence. Unlike Chelsea, there was no move to release Jaccob's bonds.

"Jaccob Aldora, Topaz Knight of the Flashing Blade, of the Flying Kingdom of Hedorah," the Emperor began, his voice cold and distant, "you have been charged with grave dereliction of duty in your role as a Knight of the Flashing Blade. Though your direct action may not have prevented the fall of Aldere, you were however in the vicinity of the Imperial bedchambers, and you made no effort to protect the Emperor from harm. You also made no attempt to thwart the activities of either the member of the Dark Gods who was spotted in the Imperial Palace, or the creature Death who was also seen within the palace walls. There is no excuse for these actions, and therefore I have no alternative but to condemn you to death."

Silence filled the common room. There was no expectation that this would be the result of the fall of Aldere, even though everyone knew that someone would pay the price for that very visible failure. Jaccob simply bowed his head, nodded slowly and then raised his head.

"Does the condemned have any final words?"

Jaccob took a long deep breath.

"I have never been the model knight. My failures are many and varied, and perhaps there were paths that I could have taken over the years to be more than what I have become. But here at the end, I realize more than anything that the choices we make have greater ramifications than we can ever dream, and I know now that the moment I became a member of the Knights of the Flashing Blade, all doors that led off of this path were closed to me. My pride and arrogance led me here, and I accept my fate. It has been an honor serving the Empire of Cadaria, and I can only hope that the path I see before it is not one that anyone here ever sees the end of. There is only cold and desolation there. For everyone."

His last words spoken, Jaccob knelt; the proudest act possible for a condemned man, to meet his death on his own terms, not held down like a sacrifice. Korin Melcab stepped forward, taking Temperance from the low table where it lay, pulling the ends apart to reveal the gleaming blades that lay beneath the ornamental housing. Melcab stood before Jaccob and placed one blade on each side of the Topaz Knight's neck. Feeling the cool steel, Jaccob felt the sobering wave wash over him one last time, as if the Sacred Weapon was saying goodbye in its own way. Jaccob looked up; his eyes clear, into the face of the Captain of the Imperial Guard, and saw not the face of a man, but that of a massive beast, its face covered in blackened scales, and burning red eyes glaring hatred. Horns protruded not from a helmet, but from the top of its head; it's snarling mouth full of razor sharp teeth. Their eyes locked and the beast that wore the name Korin Melcab swung both blades in unison, cleanly taking Jaccob Aldora's head from his body.

A sound like the death wail of a thousand men filled the room followed by the sound of glass shattering at different pitches and octaves. In Korin's hands, the twin blades of the Sacred Weapon Temperance shattered, breaking in hundreds of small shards, the ornate hilts fracturing and crumbling in his massive hands.

* * * * * * * * * * * *

Deep in the Vault of Terrors, a shudder passed through the room. The walls, floor, and ceiling rippled with pain and spasmed with power. Dorovar felt the tumult and pressed his hand again to the barrier before him, the one that barred the door and prevented his escape. With a simple push, the barrier shattered. A long moment later, a low creaking sound filled the room. It was the sweetest sound that Dorovar had heard in a dozen lifetimes, and he watched with idle fascination as the huge glowing stone door slowly began to swing open.

Chapter LXIV

Legacy of the Viper

Year Three of the Just Emperor Kaitain "Dragonsbane" Lorien, Creator's Calendar Year 1870

Natalia Pressen watched in horror as the whole of the Imperial Palace of Aldere collapsed in on itself. Only a few minutes before, Natalia had escaped the coming destruction by jumping out of a high window in the personal chambers of the Empress. There had only been a few moments for Natalia to make her decision and for many if they were aware of the decision that she made, she could be regarded as a coward at best, or a traitor at worst. Natalia was a member of the Knights of the Flashing Blade. Her first responsibility was to the protection of the Emperor and to the Imperial family, including the Empress Dominique Lorien. However, part of that responsibility had been mitigated in the Empress's case by the presence of Chelsea Zarova. Not only was Chelsea a member of the Knights of the Flashing Blade, but she was also the personal protector of the Empress. Protection of the Emperor on the other hand was less certain. Natalia should have made her way across the palace to try to rescue the Emperor, but another member of the Knights of the Flashing Blade, Jaccob Aldora was also in the Palace and he was probably in a better position to make a move on the Emperor's chambers. Also, the Imperial Sorceress Irene Drage had made it quite clear that the protection of the Emperor was her primary concern. There would be enough blame to go around if something had happened to the Emperor, and while Natalia would not escape her share of it, she certainly would not bear the brunt of the responsibility. In fact, Natalia's escaping enabled her to fulfill a much greater responsibility.

As a member of the Shadow Guild, Natalia had taken several oaths. The most important of the oaths was that no other duty superseded her duty to the Guild. Even when Natalia accepted the position as the Sunstone Knight of the Flashing Blade, she knew in her heart that her life belonged to the Guild. For that reason, and that reason alone, Natalia needed to take all that she knew back to the Grand Master of the Guild. As things stood, the Shadow Guild had not been tasked to take direct action against the rebels in Albitonin, but that was mostly due to the Empress and her lack of will when it came to doing things that needed to be done. Natalia had been very interested in the way that Dominique had handled the rebellion. While she had declared the rebel members of the Knights of the Flashing Blade traitors to the empire, she had not authorized any direct action, either military or covert against Albitonin or any of the other rebel kingdoms. That had frustrated not only the military commanders, but had also made Dominique very unpopular with the Masters of the Shadow Guild. There had been talk, at least from some of the more militant Masters of the Guild that the Empress needed to be removed from power. If Dominique's more forgiving nature was no longer in power, the more hardline elements of the Imperial Government, namely Irene Drage, would not hesitate to use all of the powers available to them to crush any opposition. However, the Grand Master had unilaterally forbidden any action against the Empress, just as he had forbidden any direct action against any of the members of the Knights of the Flashing Blade long ago.

The Shadow Guild kept a presence close to the Imperial Palace, and the Grand Master liked to be close to the seat of Imperial Power at all times. The fact that one of the Masters of the Shadow Guild had a prominent position within the Imperial Palace had never sat well in Natalia's heart, but the fact that the Grand Master was close made her concerns lighter. Even more than that, her relationship to the Grand Master assuaged her concerns even more. For all members of the Shadow Guild, family was a prime concern. That was the only way one got into the Shadow Guild. Members had to be fostered into the Guild by a member of their family who was already in the Guild. Natalia's mother had been an exceptional member of the Guild, and her specialty had been assassinations. For those who knew her reputation, she was feared and respected. Many of her assassinations were considered perfect, a blend of terror-inducing example and deniable accident. While Natalia was not possessed of those abilities, she had ascended to a much higher rank than her mother had ever attained. A perfect assassin was too valuable to take out of the field, which is why her mother was never considered for Master status. So perhaps it was a bit of an insult that Natalia was granted the rank of Master. But Natalia was a Knight of the Flashing Blade, a well-respected servant of the Empire, the perfect cover for someone of her standing in the Shadow Guild. Natalia's mother had fostered her into the Shadow Guild, just as her grandfather had been responsible for that induction. And now, Natalia's grandfather was the Grand Master of the Shadow Guild.

Tripping the access shaft in the sewers around the Imperial Palace was not easily done, and could never be done by accident. A very specific pass code spoken in a long dead language triggered wards that had been in place for thousands of years. It was said that the first Grand Master of the Guild had been a very gifted wizard, and though he was the Grand Master of the Shadow Guild, he was also one of the first Masters of the Academy of Arcane Arts in Jelan. He had been instrumental in the creation of both entities under the rule of Terrik Lorien, before he became known as the Godslayer. There was still much strife coming out of the Founding Wars, and the Lorien dynasty was still in its infancy. The Shadow Guild was created to protect that which the people of Cadaria had fought so hard to establish. But Shadow Guild fought against enemies that the common people could never know about, and would never be able to stomach. They had to be protected from the truth about how dynasties actually became dynasties.

* * * * * * * * * * * *

Year Five of the Just Emperor Terrik Lorien I, the Creator's Calendar Year 55

Terrik Lorien sat on his throne, the crown feeling heavier on his head than it ever had. Though he had ruled in theory for five years, after the bloody conclusion of the war that was now being called the Founding War, it was only in the past year that he was truly crowned and recognized as the ruler of the twelve kingdoms of Cadaria. He had just been married to the woman who would be called Empress, Liette, but his heart still grieved for his first wife and two sons who had found their deaths during the war. One of his rivals in the Founding War had cut them down ruthlessly, hoping to take the fight out of Terrik. That warlord had been named Grawn, a monster of a man with gray hair and a fearsome gaze that could curdle milk. Grawn was ruthless and cunning and had wanted the throne of Cadaria for his own purposes, but most of those motivations never came to light. One thing that was never in doubt was his viciousness, and the fact that he would do anything to achieve his goals. Such a man could never be allowed to sit on any throne, and it was that more than anything that had compelled Terrik to stand against Grawn. But it had taken many years and too much blood to create the Empire of Cadaria, and it had taken far too many years off of Terrik's life. But a new chapter in the Lorien family's story would be written, as Liette was with child. There would be a dynasty, and Terrik would be able to pass on a better world to his child than he himself had grown up in.

The doors to the throne room were still being hung, and only one of the massive wooden doors was on its hinges. Soldiers from all of the twelve kingdoms were gathered in the throne room, the start of an Imperial Guard. There were so many logistical challenges still to be undertaken, so many threats still to be dealt with, and until the lands were at peace, and protection of the newly crowned Emperor was foremost in everyone's minds. But the old hatreds and mistrusts were still there. Saldarine and Thorigald hated each other, and they constantly accused the other of schemes and plots. The same went for most of the other Kingdoms. They fought hard to retain their sovereignty even in the face of the newly formed Empire, the long-standing royal families were not willing to give up all of their power or become marginalized in the new government. The constant bickering made Terrik's head hurt, and made him wish at some moments that a tyrant like Grawn had actually succeeded. Then once the tyrant was overthrown, the greedy and the entitled would have already been taken from their perches and a true Empire could have been forged without all of the petty squabbles. However, that way would have incurred so much death, and a man like Terrik probably wouldn't have been alive to see the aftermath.

Terrik looked up when he heard the clattering of armor. Ranks of soldiers were moving to clear a path for the man who walked through the entryway to the throne room. For the first time in what seemed like weeks, Terrik could feel a smile creep on to his lips. It had been too long since he set eyes on his friend, and it seemed like it had been forever since the two men had stared down the warlord and ended his life. Terrik rose from the throne and in a very uncharacteristic display from a man in his position, Terrik met the man half-way down the carpeted path and embraced him. When Terrik pulled back his eye found the violet eyes of his friend, teacher, and advisor Saurn Macco and smiled.

"It's been too long my friend," Terrik said warmly, "to what do I owe the pleasure of this visit? I thought you had gone home to Menoris."

Saurn nodded and smiled a faint smile. Terrik had never known Saurn to be an emotional man. He kept his thoughts to himself, but was very powerful. Terrik had no doubt that had Saurn wanted, he could have been Emperor of Cadaria. But he was content to act behind the scenes, to be an advisor to a man of conscious like Terrik.

"It does me well to see you, my Emperor," Saurn's reply was coldly measured as always, but still showed proper deference. "I was home for quite some time before matters compelled me to return to your side. There are many rumors in the countryside my Emperor, and a great many confused and frightened people."

Terrik nodded. He put both hands on his friend's shoulders for a moment and then returned to his throne. As soon as he was seated, he motioned for Saurn to approach.

"Tell me what concerns you, my friend."

Saurn bowed slightly.

"There are many stories in the countryside, my Emperor. While a great deal of them can be passed off as simple superstition and fear, others cannot be ignored. There are stories of men and women who have terrible powers at their disposal. It is said that some can conjure fire from their bare hands, while others can make the ground shake with a thought. As you may remember, the Lord Grawn himself had legions of these fantastic soldiers at his disposal, and a small force of these men were almost able to destroy your entire army."

Terrik barely suppressed a shudder at the thought. The men that Saurn spoke of were fearsome indeed. They shook the battlefield and leveled whole units of his men with just a wave of their hands. It took tactical brilliance on the part of both Terrik and his lead advisor Saurn to win the day, but the death toll was amazing. Even though they had won the day, the losses were such that it looked as though the Founding War would be won by another of the factions. But Grawn was indiscriminant in the use of his special troops, and caused as much damage to the other rivals as he had to Terrik's forces. Grawn was a force of nature, killing any and all who stood in his way, but as Saurn had pointed out in the early days of the conflict, Grawn was not a tactically sound general. He was ruled by his passions, and without something to focus his aggression, he would strike wildly and randomly, dealing with the threat of the moment, rather than the root of the opposition. If Grawn had focused his attention on one of his rivals, wiping them out completely and then moving on to the next rival, there would have been no one powerful enough to defeat him. His recklessness was his downfall.

"And what is to be done with these people?" Terrik asked coldly. "Shall I order that they all be exterminated? How would that look as one of the first actions of my rule? Will the people understand that I am protecting them from a great threat, or will they simply see me as a tyrant bent on eliminating any possible threat to my rule?"

Saurn seemed to ponder for a moment.

"My Emperor, these people are possessed with a great power that can be of benefit to the Empire. Imagine the great wonders these people could achieve if they were taught to control their abilities. They could build houses, prevent disasters, and ensure plentiful crops and good weather. They could be the greatest boon to this Empire."

"And what do you purpose?"

Saurn straightened, his violet eyes flashing.

"I would beseech my Emperor to issue a declaration creating an Imperial Academy for the Instruction in the Arcane Arts. I have a large property in the town of Jelan that would be perfect for housing the Academy. All those able to touch the arcane would be fostered to the Academy and taught to control their abilities and use them for the betterment of the Empire. It would remove the risk and the worry from the simple folk of the countryside."

Terrik pondered for a moment, and a concern blossomed in his mind.

"And who would control this Academy? Surely this is too much for one man to control, and surely it should not be something that the Emperor himself should oversee."

Saurn nodded.

"Quite astute, my Emperor," Saurn said calmly. "To that end, I would propose that the Academy be presided over by a Council of Masters; the most learned and powerful of the group would also act as the advisor to the Emperor. The Emperor should have the wisdom of the Academy at his disposal at all times, and I would also recommend that the Emperor create a position for a Court Sorcerer, to assist the Emperor in dealing with matters of this nature."

Terrik smiled.

"A sound argument. Very well, my old friend. I hereby decree that the Academy of Arcane Arts will be founded in Jelan. In one year's time, I expect to have a charter for the Academy as well as the creation of this Master's Council. One year after that, the Academy will name the first Imperial Court Sorcerer. While the Court Sorcerer will still abide by the rules of the Charter of the Academy, his loyalty will be to the Emperor and the Emperor alone. I will not accept dual allegiance for an advisor of this power and import."

After he had finished speaking, Terrik looked to his left and saw that the Court Scribe had dutifully recorded every word, and he looked up to acknowledge that he had finished the transcription. Terrik nodded, and then turned his attention back to Saurn. While the man seemed pleased with the declaration, it was obvious to Terrik that there was more on the man's mind.

"What more, old friend?"

Saurn took a deep breath before speaking. He seemed to mull his words over carefully in his mind, and his pattern of speech was slower than normal. Each word was measured, careful, and chosen precisely.

"My Emperor, now that the Founding War is over, and all of the factions have united under the Lorien banner, there are bound to be those who are unhappy with the end of the war, and the fact that their faction was not successful in their bid to control the fate of the Empire. While I do not know of any specific threat, my Emperor, it is clear that such threats will always be present where the light of the Cadarian Empire fades to shadow. There will be those that choose to move directly against you, and there will be those cowards that target your family, your generals, and your sworn servants. These threats my liege are more dangerous than that of open rebellion will ever be. As you know, my Emperor, one fanatic is more powerful than a thousand hired mercenaries."

Terrik considered Saurn's words for a moment, and then nodded. Fanatics would always be a problem, and while the walls of the Imperial Palace would be shelter against an army, where in the world was there shelter enough against a motivated fanatic?

"And how, my old friend, do you propose we deal with such threats?"

"My Emperor," Saurn began, "these threats are born in the shadows, they rely on secrecy, and they thrive on the dissatisfaction caused by misinformation. You need a way to combat that. You must control the secrets, control the flow of information, and ensure these threats are neutralized by any means necessary before they become true threats to your rule or to those that follow your rule. To that end, I propose the creation of a guild whose only purpose is to protect the empire from itself. To find out all the secrets and expose the traitors in their hiding places. This Shadow Guild will be your eyes in the dark places that your will does not travel normally. And where necessary, it will be your sword."

"Are you saying that you wish me to authorize the creation of a group of assassins?"

Saurn shook his head quickly and put up a purple-gloved hand.

"My Emperor, you misunderstand. While the elimination of these threats may require the skills that you would find in an assassin, the mandate of this guild would not merely be assassination. They will go where you cannot, where your soldiers cannot. They can find out about and eliminate threats before they happen. They will safeguard the soul of your empire the same way that your Imperial Guard will safeguard the body. I know it is an unpleasant thought, my Emperor, but it is necessary."

Terrik thought for a long moment. It felt wrong in the pit of his stomach. He tried turning over the words Shadow Guild in his mouth, but his throat filled with bile. But Terrik had been forced to consider a great deal of unpleasant and unsavory things on his path to the throne. Was he really convinced that the days of doing terrible things for the greater good were at an end simply because the war was over? Perhaps Saurn was right. The war may have been over, but the grudges and the hatred would never be.

"I will cede to your wisdom in this matter on one condition, my old friend."

Saurn steeled himself and waited for the words of the Emperor.

"This Shadow Guild may be created with my blessing, but under the condition that you take up the position as Master of this Guild. You are the only one I can trust to take this post, and from now until the end of the Lorien line, you and your closest disciples and descendants will be entrusted with a priceless treasure. From this day forth, the Shadow Guild will be the defender of the soul of the Empire."

With that, Terrik turned to face the Imperial Scribe.

"I want no record of this," he said sternly. "There were no mentions of the Shadow Guild here today, and no mentions of the creation of a position manned by the man named Saurn Macco. In fact, eliminate his name from all records today. The land that the Academy of Arcane Arts will be built on was generously donated to the Empire by an unnamed supporter of the Lorien family."

"Yes, Emperor Lorien."

When Terrik turned back to face Saurn, he was gone. The man had slipped out of the throne room without the Emperor noticing, but just before he turned back, Terrik was sure that he had seen a flash of blue.

* * * * * * * * * * * *

Year Three of the Just Emperor Kaitain "Dragonsbane" Lorien, Creator's Calendar Year 1870

Natalia sat in an antechamber waiting to gain an audience with the Grand Master. It had been several years since she had set eyes on her grandfather, not since her ascension ceremony that made her a master in the Shadow Guild. After several minutes, a door opened, and Natalia knew that to mean she was expected. Even in this most secret of Guild fortifications, security was subtle but deadly. At all times Natalia knew there were a dozen eyes of well-trained assassins on her, and there were more false hallways and passages in this honeycombed outpost than she could count. The layout was constantly changed to insure there could be no attempts on the grandmaster, and all of the traps were deadly. The Shadow Guild did not take threats against their leadership lightly, and any such attempt would only happen once. If an attempt was made, not only would the assassin find his end, but the Shadow Guild would not stop until all of his confederates and family had met with fiery retribution.

Natalia passed through the small doorway into a larger chamber. The chamber itself was filled with wispy black curtains hanging at odd angles from the walls and ceiling, as well as dozens of mirrors, that bounced reflections around the darkened room. Somewhere in the chamber sat the Grand Master, but even Natalia's heightened senses could not tell the reflections from the real man. She knelt obediently on a small patch of floor where the symbol of a viper, the ancient symbol of the Grand Master of the Shadow Guild, had been carved. She kept her head bowed and waited to be acknowledged.

CHAPTER 64

"Lady Natalia Pressen, Sunstone Knight of the Flashing Blade, Master of the Shadow Guild," an old voice came from somewhere in the chamber, "welcome home."

Natalia pressed her forehead to the floor for several seconds before sitting back in her kneeling position. She picked one of the reflections and locked her eyes on it. The reflection was nothing more than a shadowy outline of a figure sitting cross-legged on the floor.

"Grand Master," Natalia said in a respectful tone, "I bring news from the Imperial Palace of Aldere. The Palace has been destroyed, but from what I have been able to gather, both the Empress and the Emperor were able to escape."

There was a short burst of laughter.

"Yes, Master Pressen," the Grand Master said coolly, "the Emperor and Empress did escape, as did the Imperial Sorceress and the Captain of the Imperial Guard. Your confederate Lady Chelsea Zarova also escaped, and fulfilled her duty well in protecting the life of the Empress. But that is what everyone seems to know at the moment. What is it that is not known?"

Natalia could not suppress her smile.

"A Dark God was in the chambers of the Empress moments before the destruction of the Palace, and there is no doubt in my mind that she had a hand in the destruction."

The Grand Master seemed to straighten.

"A Dark God you say? Why was a Dark God meeting with the Empress?"

"The Dark God was attempting to broker a deal with the Empress to end the war between the Cadarian Empire and the Dark Continent of Mythryn. However, instead of a truce, the Dark God was demanding that the Kingdoms of Cadaria accept direct rule by the Dark Gods themselves to ensure that no punitive action was taken in violation of the peace."

The Grand Master reached up and scratched his chin.

"And what of the Emperor?"

Natalia frowned.

"Any such deal with the Dark Gods would require the murder of Kaitain Lorien."

The Grand Master nodded.

"And you were present for this conversation?"

Natalia nodded.

"I was in the room for the whole conversation, until black cloaked figures burst into the room and attempted to kill not only the Empress but Chelsea, myself, and the Dark God. The Dark God dealt with the men quickly using a bow whose construction defied my understanding. I knew that the information was too important to be lost, so I made my escape once I was sure the threat to the Empress had been disposed of."

At the mention of the bow, the Grand Master leaned forward. A beam of light caught the shadow-covered face for a moment, and Natalia caught the faintest flash of violet.

"And do you know the identity of this Dark God?"

"Midarin," Natalia and the Grand Master said at nearly the same time.

The Grand Master leaned back.

"You have done well to bring me this information, Master Pressen. Do not stray far; I believe I will have an assignment for you very soon. We have received word that the Emperor is awake and that he has executed Jaccob Aldora for gross dereliction of duty in his failure to defend the Emperor and the Imperial Palace."

Natalia felt her breath catch in her throat. The Emperor had executed a member of the Knights of the Flashing Blade.

"But more interesting is what happened to the Sacred Weapon. Rest now, Natalia," the Grand Master said slowly, "you have a long road ahead of you. There are questions we must now have answered."

The End of Beginnings

Year Thirteen of the Just Emperor Ender "Just Hand" Lorien, Creator's Calendar Year 1795

The Serpentine Knight Vallic Ultiv stood grasping hard the haft of the Sacred Weapon Harmony, confusion filling him. Cedric Binosear, the Lord Lion of the dead world Onea stood before him, his student to his left, ready to fight. But Cedric had gently reached out his hand in the direction of the young woman, and a bright flash of light erupted from his fingers and enveloped the woman. A moment later she was slumping to the dusty ground, unconscious. Cedric moved quickly to catch her falling form and laid her down gently. He carefully brushed the shimmering blond hair away from the girl's face and then leaned in to kiss her lightly on the forehead. When he rose and turned to face Vallic, any tenderness that he had displayed moments earlier had been erased from his features. The look that hung on his features now was one of a trained killer.

"What is between us is not for her to know, or to see," Cedric said after a moment. "She is an innocent, and deserves a chance to have her life mean something in the years to come. You know the fire that is coming for this world, and while it may not begin in her lifetime, I want her to have the tools to fight if it does."

Vallic shook his head.

"She ceased being an innocent the moment you interfered in her development. You taught her how to touch the Blaze. Don't you know what that means?"

Cedric nodded.

"It means she's special. She is destined to do all of the things I was never able to do with my gifts. Emries cursed me all those lifetimes ago and turned me into his unwitting implement of evil. What Shau-ling gave me in those last few years I was too broken to understand. My recklessness caused so much death and suffering, and my own selfishness trapped others in the lies that Emries was selling. But it's different now. I know the truth, and I can help make a difference. Not like the Dark Gods. Not like you who hides behind another man's face. I can teach the truth to those who need to hear it, I can give them the tools they need to fight."

Vallic frowned.

"You're dead, Cedric. Your kingdom is dead, your followers and your loved ones are dead. You should have never been brought back to this world, and I will make sure that I correct that oversight."

* * * * * * * * * * * *

Year Three of the Just Emperor Kaitain "Dragonsbane" Lorien, Creator's Calendar Year 1870

Vallic Ultiv was still in very poor shape from his confrontation with Bryn, but he sat upright in a soft chair in his private study. Isa had helped prop his feet up on a small padded foot stool before excusing herself to an upstairs bedroom where she recovered a new nightshirt and a change of clothes for Vallic. She would have offered to get clothes for their violent guest, but Isa knew her sister too well. None of her clothes would be scandalous enough for the Lady Bryn. Bryn stood near the fire, her eyes flickering with the flames, her gaze never straying far from Vallic's slowly breathing form. She had not uttered a word since the revelation of Vallic's ancient identity. When Isa had finally returned and knelt beside her companion, Bryn broke her silence.

"I think someone owes me an explanation."

Isa looked over to Bryn and then back to Vallic. He sighed and nodded slowly, and at that indication, Isa rose and smoothed her nightshirt before beginning to speak.

"Onea was more than just an experiment for the Creator," Isa said after a long moment, "it was a battleground of ideology fought by the Creator's children. What we stumbled on, you and I, during our time as members of the phasia was just the first piece of a larger puzzle of truth that we were too arrogant and self-centered to realize was not the whole truth. And a lot of it has to do with your husband, and more of it has to do with Emries and Halicon."

Bryn frowned.

"Why does everything always come back to Aerith? We knew he was special, we knew he had power that defied our explanations, but we all thought he was just some bauble that Saurn had picked up and wanted to play with."

"Saurn was far smarter than any of us gave him credit for," Vallic said softly, his breathing labored and his voice raspy.

"Aerith was an unexpected heresy," Isa started.

Bryn smirked at the characterization.

"He's been called many things, a great deal of them by me, and I have never quite heard him described quite that way."

"It's a more appropriate title than you realize," Isa continued trying not to let annoyance at the interruption slip into her voice. "He should never have been born. He was an accident, something that neither Emries or Halicon had expected, and I wonder if even the Creator knew something like Aerith was possible. Aryx was a child of Halicon, one of the first of the phasia, like the three of us, but his power was different. He was supposed to be the anti-Emries. He was supposed to take all of the best attributes of Emries' creations and turn them against Emries. He was noble, vigilant, self-sacrificing. He was equal measures the best of us and the worst of us. And he rebelled because we were killers. He could not stomach what the phasia were at their core, and he could not abide the suffering of the innocents trapped between the warring brothers and their servants. Halicon let him go, his powers still nearly at their full strength. And most importantly, he could still touch the Blaze. That proved to be the most important point of all."

Vallic began speaking now. His voice was still weak, but conviction of his words seemed to bolster the power of his voice.

"We were led to believe by Halicon that the Blaze was his life-force, that it was the life-force of all of nature and that to draw on it was not only to weaken his life, but to weaken the life around us. That is why he put the controls in place so that we could not draw so deeply that we would injure him. But it was all a lie."

"A lie wrapped in truth actually," Isa corrected.

"The Blaze was indeed derived from Halicon's life-force, but it was so much more than that. When Halicon was spawned by the Creator, he was left to gestate and grow in the limitless reaches of the Universe. He learned its lessons and became the being we knew as our father. But there were worlds before Onea that Halicon was the lord of. Those worlds were successful but for the meddling of Halicon's brother Emries, and his sister Talisia."

Bryn frowned.

"What sister?"

Isa too frowned.

"It has taken us many lifetimes, and a very high price to learn these truths, dear sister, and that is one of the reasons that Vallic and I have worked so hard at crafting new identities for ourselves over these millennia. We have both worn many different faces and many different names in an effort to hide from the forces that are working to tear this world and by extension the whole of this universe apart. The Creator knew that this world would be a final battleground. An ideological purging."

Bryn's head ached. There were too many questions, as always, and getting answers out of Ellis and Jeroch had been challenging in the best of times, but now they were being downright cryptic.

"What do you mean he knew? Why this world? Why now?"

Vallic laughed.

"For the worst reasons," he said finally. "He made a wager."

* * * * * * * * * * *

Year Thirteen of the Just Emperor Ender "Just Hand" Lorien, Creator's Calendar Year 1795

Vallic's words burned in Cedric's mind, and he charged, his sword ready. Vallic too was ready for the tactic, and swung the massive blade of Harmony low, at Cedric's knee level. The unorthodox weapon made approaching Vallic difficult, but Cedric leapt high into the air, the soles of his boots barely clearing the rising blade of the scythe, and dove in with hard downward slash that would have parted Vallic's skull. Vallic stepped deftly to the side and brought the haft of the scythe around to catch Cedric in the ribs. Despite his training and skill, Cedric had no counter for the blow, and the hard iron haft slammed fully into his right flank, and the unmistakable cracking of ribs resounded through Cedric's body. The force of the blow sent the powerful warrior sailing through the air, and he crashed into a rock outcropping. Vallic held his ground, but turned to face his fallen opponent, his face blank and emotionless. Cedric coughed a ragged wet cough, blood spurting from his mouth and nose. Still he reached out, recovered his sword, and forced his way back to his feet.

"You still are a talented warrior, Cedric," Vallic said coolly, "but you are out of practice. You've been fighting mortals for too long. I've been hunting down and killing phasia. We were all brought back to this world in one manner or another, and I've gotten to most of them. Before long I'll have removed all of the Creator's pawns from the field, and I can't have you training more innocents to be used in a battle they have no chance of understanding."

Cedric sneered.

"When did you become the moral compass for this world, Vallic? You're evil, just like all the other phasia. You hate humanity, you want us all to burn. Remember?"

Vallic shook his head.

"I saw at the end what you were capable of Cedric, both in victory and defeat. I saw the futility of a dying man that turned into triumph in death when I was cut down by Gwydeon Sandar. I saw the heroes of our world battling against things they could not understand even as the whole of Onea crumbled around us. But it was Aerith, at the end it was that insufferable bastard who changed me. He rescued me from myself, and he put me on this path. I will hate him for the rest of my days for it, but I will walk it nonetheless."

Cedric pulled himself back to his feet, but his legs were buckling. Vallic had been right, Cedric hadn't been in a real fight since he had been brought to this world, and if Vallic had indeed been out killing members of the phasia, that experience would be more than enough to overcome whatever muscle memory still existed within the former hero. But Cedric Binosear would never surrender, and would never admit defeat. He had come too far and had seen too much for that. Cedric raised his sword as high as he could manage and charged.

* * * * * * * * * * * *

Year Three of the Just Emperor Kaitain "Dragonsbane" Lorien, Creator's Calendar Year 1870

"A wager?" Bryn croaked incredulously. "All this for a wager?"

Isa looked down at Vallic, and Bryn read the expression as puzzlement. Vallic too seemed to be confused, but it didn't show on his face as clearly as it had on Isa's. When Isa tilted her head up again, her lips were twisted into a frown.

"You didn't know?"

Bryn put her hands on her hips.

"Know what?"

Isa looked down at Vallic again.

"We just thought that you knew," Vallic said after a moment. "After all, it was Sabrina that made the wager with the Creator while she was serving as the Spirit, and we assumed that it was done at Aerith's behest."

Bryn's fists balled so tightly that both Isa and Vallic could hear her knuckles crack. She spoke after a moment through gritted teeth.

"He swore to me that we were out. He swore to me that we were just going to hide out and live out our lives quietly. Even after Rhain and Ayden were born, we tried to shield them from everything we could. I knew that he would have a connection to Sabrina, but I thought that since most of his powers were with Evan that the connection would just be an echo and nothing more. Are you telling me that he always intended to get his powers back? That he knew we would have to take an active part in the war?"

Isa frowned.

"Would you really have had it any other way Bryn? You were always a fighter, and you knew what Aerith was from the moment you laid eyes on him, despite your constant arguments to the contrary. Do you think it's a coincidence that both Evan and Sabrina found their way into roles as heralds of the Creator? Do you think that it is such a coincidence that you two were allowed so easily to stay out of the line of fire as the Dark Gods and the Cadarians continued to clash? The Creator gave you all a measure of immunity from the conflict until it was Aryx and Aerith that pressed the issue. Of course Aerith knew it was coming. Ayden finds himself in the Academy of Arcane Arts just before it becomes a rogue state? Rhain is joined at the hip with Marlae Lorien right before she becomes part of the rebellion? You go back to being the Lady Fox just when all hell breaks loose and Pike wants to go hunting for the heads of the Knights of the Flashing Blade? You aren't that naïve sister."

The annoyance that filled Bryn a moment before dissipated like the morning fog under the bright sun. Perhaps she had always known that there was more to their seclusion than met the eye, but even her devious mind could not have pierced the depths of Aerith's planning. Perhaps he really had been listening all those years to her and to Saurn. But why had he chosen to leave her out of the plan? Obviously both Ayden and Rhain were in on it to some degree. Then the realization hit her. Bryn would never have allowed for the time it would have taken to set the plan in motion. She was as rash as she was conniving, and the plan could not have played out if she were complicit. Aerith had needed her to be natural and to act as he intended her to, and she never would have done that had she known. Her admiration for her husband as well as her disgust with him grew in equal measure.

"What is the wager?"

Vallic smiled slightly at Bryn's question, knowing the war that must have been raging within Bryn.

"Humans had been tools and pawns in the fight between the Creator and his children for a long time, and on many worlds before this one and before Onea. And many had been touched with power like the phasia and the *Erieal* had. Sabrina argued that on a level playing field that the humans' capacity for adaptation, strength, faith, and will were more powerful than anything the children of the Creator could muster, and was greater even than the dragons that were so beloved by the Creator. It was the creation of this level playing field that proved to be so…complex."

Isa continued.

"The Dragons were brought here and given an ultimatum that they had to make things work here, once Gwydeon's fall and death trapped them."

A light went on in Bryn's mind.

"Gwydeon knew that and staged his own death because he was in on the wager."

Isa smiled and nodded.

"There were a few of us that knew more than others. Gwydeon had to know because he led the rebellion in the heavens. It was Sabrina that finally convinced him to do it. The Creator allowed the person who bargained with the dragons for sanctuary to be targeted by Gwydeon's fall, trapping the dragons here until the battle is over. But there was more. Bringing the Dark Gods here caused both problems and opportunities. While touched by the Creator, Emries, and Halicon, the Dark Gods were truly champions of the human race, but casting them as demons fallen from heaven kept the playing field even."

"And made it so that no mortal would trust them," Bryn added. "It left humanity on their own against not only their own failings, but the imagined horrors of fallen gods. Which is probably why the servants of the Dark Gods ended up being Jeresei, Stone, Shadowwalkers, and Kalbraks, making the Dark Gods even less trustworthy."

"And so the poor mortals," Vallic continued, "flanked on one side by dragons, on the other side by fallen gods, become paranoid. Leaving them open to being seduced by the children of the Creator, the teachings of the Heralds, and even corruption by the other powers that were secretly introduced into their midst."

Bryn looked first at Isa and then at Vallic and then back again.

"Yes," Isa answered the unspoken question. "Because the phasia were children of Halicon, and thus extensions of the Creator's power, they could be brought back from the beyond at the Creator's leisure and repurposed for whatever goals he saw fit. We were all brought back to this world to act as a sort of counterbalance to the Dark Gods. But what the Creator didn't count on was that someone was brought back who was not born a phase. Someone who carried not only the heart of a mortal but the power and devotion to ensure that another world would not fall to indiscriminant application of power."

Bryn's eyes went wide.

"Logan?"

Vallic nodded gently.

"Between the three of us, Gwydeon, Logan, and myself, we devised a plan to ensure that humanity had the best chance to succeed. Logan and I started hunting down the other members of the phasia that were brought to this world. We found most of them quickly, as they didn't make it too difficult."

"We were almost too late with Grawn," Isa added, "he was well on his way to making it the Aplee dynasty instead of the Lorien imperial family. It was Logan and Warron that actually took him down in the last days of the war to unite Cadaria."

"Of the rest," Vallic continued, "only Taron, Saurn, and Draven are unaccounted for. Once they have been removed from the game, Isa and I have made a pact with Logan and Warron to ensure we do not hamper the battle to come."

Some color drained from Bryn's face, but she tried hard to cover her reaction. Isa saw through it. She knew her sister far too well.

"You aren't like us, Bryn. You aren't one of the Creator's pawns, and you shouldn't assume that Aerith or one of the others has you on some hit list. You were purposely kept out of the game because of Aerith."

Bryn shook her head.

"I was never out of the game, Isa. I am being used in this, just as you are."

Vallic sighed.

"That's what Cedric said, too."

* * * * * * * * * * * *

Year Thirteen of the Just Emperor Ender "Just Hand" Lorien, Creator's Calendar Year 1795

Cedric Binosear lay on the dusty ground, bleeding profusely from a long wound across his chest that spanned from his shoulder to his hip. Vallic's scythe had cut him nearly to his breastbone, and Cedric could feel the pounding of his heart slowing in his ears. There was not much time left. For the hero of one age and the villain of another, the last sands of time were running out. Even now, the edges of his vision were beginning to darken, and what he could see was distorted and fading. Vallic was kneeling beside him, and as Cedric looked up, the two men's eyes met. Despite himself Cedric found his lips curling into a smile. A cough ripped from his throat, thick blood causing him to choke.

"You always said you would kill me, Jeroch," Cedric said in the strongest voice he could manage. "It took you long enough."

Jeroch held back a grimace. The two men had been enemies from the day that Cedric was born, and even now at the end, thousands of years later, they had not progressed from where they began. Enemies to the last breath. Perhaps that made it all simpler. No confusion about motives, no confusion about which side of the greater issues that each man stood upon. Between them there was only hate. Only disdain for the other's existence. But now, as he knelt beside his fallen opponent, Vallic felt only emptiness.

"Don't talk," Vallic said softly. "Just close your eyes and let death take you."

The incredulous look that came to Cedric's face quickly faded when the two men's eyes met again. It was not a taunt or a jibe as Cedric had expected, but honest and heartfelt concern. Cedric broke eye contact and let his head fall to the side where his eyes found where Leonora lay. His heart hurt for what she would feel from this moment forward. The hatred and pain that she would have to live with. Just as Cedric suffered at the loss of his first and only true love, Leonora would suffer at his loss. Cedric straightened, tears starting to stream from the corners of his eyes.

"I never saved anyone, Jeroch. Everything I touched crumbled in my hands. No matter how strong everyone thought I was, I was weak and frightened. Anabel was always stronger than I was."

He was rambling, and as hard as Cedric tried to keep his mind on what he wanted to say, it continued to drift on the tide of consciousness that was being drawn to the Other Side. Gritting his teeth, he pulled as much of himself back to reality as he could. His vision sharpened for a moment, and he could see the starts of tears in the corner of Jeroch's eyes.

"Promise me." The words came out garbled at first, but Cedric swallowed and tried again. "Promise me. Leah is important. More than just to me, but to everything. I couldn't save her, just like I couldn't save

Erika, or Logan, or any of the others. Save her from what I have done, and save her from the pain that my loss will bring her."

Vallic nodded silently.

"We never mattered, Jeroch," Cedric said, his eyes closing slightly and his voice beginning to trail off. "Emries used me, Halicon used me. Caught in the middle without ever knowing what it was all for. I never mattered..."

Cedric's eyes fluttered for a moment and then closed, his chest rising and falling one last time, before the one last exhale seemed to stretch on for minutes, the last of the essence of the great Cedric Binosear being extended into the universe. Vallic put his hand on the fallen man's shoulder and closed his eyes for a long moment.

"You mattered, Cedric," he said gravely, "none of us would be here if it wasn't for you."

Tempered by Flame, Tempered in Blood

Year Three of the Just Emperor Kaitain "Dragonsbane" Lorien,
Creator's Calendar Year 1870

Leonora Wastri stood on the battlefield a changed woman. The power of the Blaze flowed through her as it had all those years ago, and now, well into her hundredth year of life she felt as though she was seventeen again. Though no one on that battlefield would immediately notice, all of the subtle lines of age had been smoothed away, and her wounds nearly instantly mended by the white-hot energy flooding through her. The beat of her heart slowed and steadied, and she felt a calm wash through her body like the gentle winds that covered the land after a hurricane had ripped through. There was no breeze, but her hair fluttered around her, staying away from her face. Her skin bristled with power, though her eyes had returned to their natural color, the brilliant green seemed to have a more intense edge to it. Opposite her stood two members of the Dark Gods, and no matter their words about being invited by the Masters of the Academy of Arcane Arts, it was their true intentions that were clear. They were here to corrupt the members of the Academy, no different than Kaitain would have were Bernhardt Yeoman to be allowed to march the Iron Legion into the Academy's central courtyard. It didn't matter if the Emperor was awake or asleep, and it didn't matter if the Empress was giving the orders. The implication was the same. No one could be allowed to dictate a change in policy for the Academy of Arcane Arts. They had to be forced if necessary to maintain their stated adherence to non-violent applications of their abilities. No matter the cost, the Dark Gods and the Iron Legion would need to be driven from the field.

"I give you one last chance," Leonora said, raising her left hand and pointing a finger directly at Rael's chest. "Take your army and leave this field. If you do not take this chance to save yourself and those that serve you, I will have no choice but to destroy you."

Neither Rael nor Trece made a move, and that was implication enough that they had no intention of leaving the field. The next moment a beam of bright green fire flooded from Leonora's extended hand and struck the black-clad man in the center of his chest. Rael was thrown back several feet, and Trece leapt backward of her own volition in an effort to avoid the surely oncoming assault from Leonora. Trece continued into a long slow backflip and landed at Rael's side, where he was already getting back to his feet. A patch of burned and charred skin was visible through the front of his ruined shirt, but he did not appear to take notice of it, and no tell-tale marks of pain or distraction appeared on his face or in his eyes. He simply brushed off his pants and looked once over to Trece before locking his dark eyes back on Leonora.

"I suppose we should have expected nothing less than a sneak attack," Rael said coldly, "but if that is the kind of fight you want, we will gladly oblige you."

Leonora didn't wait for either Rael or Trece to make a move, and she unleashed another stream of Blaze fire, this time it took the form of a broad fan at waist level that would have easily cut the two of them in half. Rael dove for the ground while Trece jumped high into the air and then floated back down once the assault had passed. This time though, Rael was ready and counterattacked, sending dozens of blades of dark energy speeding toward Leonora. She twirled the Sacred Weapon Wisdom in her hands to shield herself from the blow. The daggers of chaos energy struck true on the reinforced haft of the weapon, but instead of dissipating, they stuck where they struck, adding weight to the weapon and making it clumsier to wield. It also caused Leonora to focus more on the blocking attempts than she had initially intended, and she didn't see the beam of white energy streaking down from where Trece floated until it was too late. But instead of striking Leonora, the white beam struck where the dark shards had impacted the Sacred Weapon. There was a bright flash of light, and Leonora found herself encased in a translucent bubble of force that rotated between light and dark aspects. Leonora saw the two Dark Gods advancing, but they were being cautious. She channeled more of the Blaze fire from her fingers, filling the bubble of force with it. She was completely obscured from sight, but then the tip of Wisdom's blade burst through the bubble, sending a torrent of flame in a vertical scythe jetting toward the approaching duo. This time both of the Dark Gods were sent diving for the ground. Trece proved to be slightly slower than her mate and the whole right side of her shirt and pants were smoldering when she made her way back to her feet. When they were both standing again, Leonora had strengthened her grip on the haft of Wisdom, and the blade of the Sacred Weapon glowed with an angry intensity. Green flames danced around the metallic bladed head, and the weapon seemed alive in the woman's hands.

Ready to meet the woman's aggression on her own terms, the Dark Gods allowed weapons to form in their own hands. Rael's sword slid out from his hand like a living thing. It started as several long thick and roiling tendrils of black energy, which moved and congealed together until they formed a sword's shape. The shape was never consistent, and the blade reformed and refocused itself constantly. Trece's sword on the other hand had a more definite shape. It was brilliant and pristine, beautiful and shimmering with a crystalline structure. Rael charged forward first, Trece half a pace behind him at most. They both slashed together, hard, Rael's blow targeting the Jade Knight's left shoulder, while Trece's low blow targeted the woman's knees. Leonora's accelerated reflexes and military training allowed her to spin the Sacred Weapon, to bring its blade down hard on Rael's sword, knocking it away, while at the same time intercepting Trece's blow with Wisdom's haft. Leonora whirled, bringing the haft around and sweeping Rael's legs out from under him, while the blade just barely connected with Trece as she attempted to dodge out of the way. The long slender blade opened up a cut across the red head's left cheek. The Jade Knight continued her spin, bringing the head of the Sacred Weapon to bear again at Rael's fallen form, trusting the head down to where he lay.

Trece recovered quickly enough that she sent another beam of pure Order in Leonora's direction, and it claimed the woman firmly in the back, causing her to stumble and miss her mark. The blade of Wisdom sliced into the ground mere inches from Rael's head.

Rael rolled out of the line of Leonora's assault and found his way to a crouch. Trece too had taken the opportunity to withdraw slightly from the duel, and she too fell into a crouch. As Leonora looked on, the very human blue eyes of the man named Rael started to take on a different appearance. The pupil widened and then elongated vertically. As this was happening, the blue of the eyes became sharper and brighter. Within a few heartbeats, Leonora was staring at a pair of cat's eyes. Rael's short black hair then began to grow longer, and the pores in his face and his arms also began to sprout thick black tufts of hair that almost resembled fur. The undulating sword of black energy was quickly discarded as Rael's hands grew wider and his finger's shortened and got fatter. The hard callused hands quickly formed huge powerful paws that were armed with hard black nails that gleamed with sharpened points. The change took only a matter of seconds, but where Rael had crouched now stood a huge muscular black panther. There were hints of Blaze energy around each of the cat's extended claws, and though it was a beast, the panther had intelligence in its eyes as well as the malice that Leonora most certainly would have expected from a member of the Dark Gods. Once that metamorphosis was complete, Leonora looked quickly over to Trece who also had begun to change. Her piercing green eyes became more beautiful as they morphed into cat's eyes. The color retreated from her bright red hair and was left stark white. The slim frame of the beautiful woman widened and grew muscles atop muscles as the form of the huge white tiger became prevalent. The tiger also had powerful paws whose claws glowed green with the powers of the Blaze. Leonora already had respect for the abilities of the pair, but in their transformed forms, a new dimension of lethality was revealed and needed to be accounted for. She stood steady, waiting for the inevitable assault to come. There was no way that Leonora could create an advantage with an attacking posture against the two oversized cats, so she would have to be more conservative in her tactics. The panther was the first to move, stalking in a large circle around Leonora. It became obvious what the two creatures were trying to do. They wanted to divert Leonora's attention so that the other could strike. Despite the fact that the three faced off in the middle of a larger battlefield occupied not only by the Iron Legion and the forces of the Dark Gods, the Jade Legion was also present. However, it seemed that the change in Leonora and the display of powers from the three combatants had caused all of the mortals on the field to give them a wide birth.

Leonora took several steps backwards, attempting to keep both the tiger and the panther in view. However, the tiger had begun to move and when Leonora looked again over her shoulder, she realized she had lost track of the tiger, then when she looked to where the panther should have been, it was gone also. Several times Leonora spun around looking for the beasts catching glimpses of them from the corner of her eye. They were using the fog that still enshrouded the battlefield, created by the interference of the Masters of the Academy, as well as the natural crest of the hills and the furrows created by the conflict. There were too many shadows and darkness-filled holes to search, and Leonora was left out in the open, practically begging to be attacked. She held the haft of Wisdom close, and tried to calm her senses. She stretched out with her hearing and felt the changes in the wind and fog around her. She could almost feel the movement of the two creatures amid the hundreds of breathing men, women, and creatures arrayed around her. A low deep growl filled Leonora's ears the next second, and it was answered from a growl elsewhere in the fog. The attack would come at any second, and Leonora set her feet and waited. Scanning the desolation around her, she caught a glint of motion out of the corner of her eye. A white form broke from a bank of fog for only a moment, and then only the tail was visible.

Behind Leonora, a pair of sharp blue eyes burned through the fog. It watched as Leonora tried to track Trece's movements. Wordlessly, the two creature's interconnected minds relayed information to each other, and Rael advanced slowly, using the places that Trece found in her feints to get within striking distance. By the time the blow came, it would be too late for the Knight of the Flashing Blade to do anything. She would be caught completely unaware, and hopefully could be subdued before the conflict escalated too much farther. But the Jade Knight was cagy, and her awareness of her surroundings was impressive. Each time the knight would turn and look, the panther would close its eyes and wait, melting in with the shadows and the fog, allowing the constant feed of information from Trece keep him informed as to what Leonora was doing. Rael knew that Trece was keeping Leonora as busy as she could, and he could hear her thoughts echoing in his mind. Trece knew exactly where Rael was, and she was doing her best to keep Leonora jumping at shadows until the panther could get into position. Leonora had turned again, so Rael continued to crawl forward, inching ever closer to his prey. Only a few more steps would be needed and then a powerful leap would take the panther the rest of the way.

Leonora spun again looking for the movement out in the fog and advancing shadows. She had caught mere glimpses of the tiger out of the corner of her eye, and she was sure that the panther was just out of her field of vision playing with her also. Then, just in front of her, the tiger appeared. It stood straight and tall, looking at Leonora with those impossibly bright green eyes. Before the Jade Knight could make any moves or look over her shoulders to try to locate the panther, Rael leapt from behind her and raked his huge set of claws across Leonora's ribcage. The Jade Knight gritted her teeth to keep from howling in pain and tightened her grip on the haft of Wisdom. If she were to let the Sacred Weapon drop from her hand, the battle would be over. The tiger was on her the next moment, clawing at Leonora's face and arms. The Jade Knight had been able to get the haft of Wisdom up in time to defend her throat, but was not able to concentrate enough to draw on her newly rediscovered powers. Had she been in full control of her abilities, she could have burned the tiger where it stood, and the beast's jaws would be able to do no further damage. But as long as Leonora could only act on the instinct of the moment, she would have to depend on her warrior's prowess, not the abilities granted to her by the Blaze. The jaws of the tiger descended and took a powerful hold on Leonora's left arm, ripping and tearing at it, as if trying to rip it off of the woman's body. The panther was just recovering from its distracting leap and was moving in for the kill. If Leonora did not act soon, she would have to fend off both Rael and Trece, and such a situation would likely end with Leonora lying dead on the battlefield. Desperation began to set in, and Leonora had only one option left. With all the power that the Jade Knight could manage to draw upon, she channeled the pure and unadulterated power of the Blaze into all of her limbs and tried to make peaks of bright green flame erupt from her pores. She could tell her success when the tiger released its hold on her mangled arm and yelped in pain. Leonora scrambled to her feet and intensified the defenses that she had erected. In a matter of seconds, a nimbus of green flame surrounded her. Now any direct attack against her would have to pierce the veil of Blaze flame, and anyone foolish enough to try such a maneuver would certainly pay for the attempt. So long as she was able to keep both of the monsters in view, she would make it out of the battle alive. Balance had been restored to the situation, and the two beasts, sensing the shift in the tide of battle backed away from Leonora, sizing her up again.

The pain in Leonora's body was immense, but she tried her best to keep her mind calm and to block it out. If she allowed the pain to distract her for even a moment, her control over the shield of Blaze would falter and she would be at Rael and Trece's mercy again. Blood flowed from a variety of cuts on her face, legs, arms, and side. Her right arm was practically useless as it hung limp at her side, looking more like shredded animal meat than a human limb. She continued to hold tight to the haft of the Sacred Weapon Wisdom with her left hand, and though she was not as adept at wielding the weapon with that hand, she was still more than a match for most warriors. She would have channeled some of the Blaze energy into healing her extensive wounds, but she knew that would require her to drop her defenses. Additionally, it seemed that Wisdom's natural abilities to gently knit her wounds had been suppressed. For the second time, Leonora was faced with a Dark God, and despite the new powers at her disposal, again she was losing badly. Fortunately enough, she had gotten the fight to a stalemate, but that was a tenuous one at best, and that was a great improvement over the thrashing she received at the hands of the woman who called herself Serrina. However, if the beasts regrouped and split up again, the chances were good that she would not survive the next assault. She had to figure out a way to disable one of the attacking beasts and still keep her defenses up. However, time was against Leonora as that she was slowly bleeding to death. The Blaze energy that was coupled with each of the claw strikes from the beasts was eating her from the inside, and until she had an opportunity to negate the necrotic effects, it would continue to eat living tissue and kill her before the loss of blood would. The twins seemed to be plotting their next attack as they stood looking at the Jade Knight. It was then that the tactic came to Leonora's mind.

Keeping her concentration on the shield of Blaze flame that surrounded her, she poured as much of the potent energy into the blade and haft of the

Sacred Weapon, Wisdom as she could. If the tactic she were about to employ failed, she would be defenseless, and Rael and Trece would meet no resistance as they tore her apart. She watched and waited as the panther and tiger began to slowly advance again. In a moment they would split, moving to either side of Leonora and robbing her of the opportunity to strike. Whether she was ready or not, it had to be now or never. She turned the point of Wisdom down to the ground and thrust the point into the soil. A carpet of Blaze energy swept out from the blade of the weapon, covering a width of several yards. At the same time, Leonora pushed the shield of Blaze around her into a single wall, and pushed it forward, sweeping just behind the advancing edge of the carpet. Rael and Trece were fast, but no matter the speed at their disposal, they were not fast enough to dodge out of the way of the assault. Rael tried to leap to the right, but he was slow, and slammed front shoulder first into the burning wall. Trece's tactic was to attempt to vault over the wall, but Leonora extended the wall to try an intercept the tiger's arc. She managed to elevate the top of the wall enough to catch the tiger's trailing paw, leaving her landing at the mercy of gravity, which brought the white tiger crashing down on the carpet of Blaze energy. Both of the beasts cried out in pain and Leonora continued to pour on the assault. When she could maintain the attack no longer, she collapsed to one knee in exhaustion, and looked up to see that both Rael and Trece had reverted to their human forms and were hanging on the edge of consciousness. If she moved quickly enough, she would be able to finish off the two Dark Gods, and then deal with her extensive injuries.

As she forced her way back to both feet, she caught movement out of the corner of her eye. Something large and metallic came crashing in on her, and she barely was able to bring Wisdom up in time to block the blow.

* * * * * * * * * * * *

Bernhardt watched from where he lay on the mud and blood soaked ground horror beginning to fill him. Leonora Wastri was glowing with brilliant green energy, and flames danced across her skin. She set upon battling the two members of the Dark Gods, clashing with both weapons and powers, even when the two Dark Gods transformed themselves in to creatures, the woman who was once counted as an ally of the Throne of

Cadaria, continued to battle as though she too were possessed with the wicked power that emanated from Mythryn. The longer the battle went on, the more Bernhardt became convinced that Leonora was as much a threat to the stability of not only the Academy of Arcane Arts, but also the Empire of Cadaria.

The Moonstone Knight tried to pull his good leg under him so that he could make it to a knee. It took several attempts but finally, the proud warrior was back onto one knee and supporting himself heavily on the haft of Gravity. The massive head of the Sacred Weapon was pushed into the soil, and Bernhardt was still shaking as he added weight to his damaged limbs. Blood was streaming from the open wounds on his face and chin, half of his face nearly hanging off of his skull. It didn't matter how much healing Gravity was trying to pour into his broken body, Bernhardt knew he was dying. But he needed to live long enough to see that this newest threat to the Empire was dealt with.

The two creatures circled and swarmed Leonora, looking for an opening, and then finally the tiger struck and began ripping and tearing at the skin of the Jade Knight. Bernhardt held his breath, hoping that the responsibility to rid the ranks of the Knights of the Flashing Blade of the corrupted being of Leonora would not fall to him. Even in peak fighting shape, he would barely be a match for Leonora, and more often than not, she would be able to defeat him. Now with these frightening new powers at her disposal, Bernhardt would be like a flea trying to fell a bull. She would swat him away easily, and he would only be a champion of futility. A bright green flash drew Bernhardt's attention again, and he watched as the two creatures were thrown clear as a haze of flame enveloped Leonora's form. It was a stalemate, with neither advancing nor retreating. It was then that Leonora struck, sending a wall and sheet of bright flame in advance of her kneeling form. Both the panther and the tiger were swept up in the assault and at least momentarily incapacitated. This would be Bernhardt's only chance. Using the last bit of strength at his disposal, he pulled the head of Gravity from the mud and called upon the innate powers of the Sacred Weapon. With both hands, he swung as hard as he could, sending the massive war hammer spinning through the air toward Leonora. The head of the Sacred Weapon spun around just as Bernhardt had hoped, on a collision course with the Jade Knight's chest. Whatever new power possessed her gave the woman a few seconds warning before the blow struck, and she brought the haft of her own Sacred Weapon up in an attempt to block the strike. When Gravity collided with Wisdom, the massive iron head split the haft of Wisdom in two, and continued through, impacting Leonora hard in the chest and sending her crashing to the ground. Gravity fell to the ground, and Bernhardt could see that the solid head of the Sacred Weapon now had a long fault running down its axis.

The sound that filled the battlefield was like that of a thousand voices screaming in a thousand unrecognizable languages all at once. The voices were tortured, screaming out in pain and horror, and Bernhardt sank back down to the ground, all strength gone from his body, the last sound he ever heard was the cacophony of death filling the air.

* * * * * * * * * * * *

When Leonora Wastri was able to open her eyes again, she hurt in ways she didn't think possible. It was hard to breathe, and she knew that her sternum and most of her ribs had been broken by the blow she had been barely able to block. She tried to sit up, tried to find the haft of Wisdom, but when she was finally able to get back to a sitting position, she saw the broken Sacred Weapon lying on the ground in a pool of her own blood. The blade was tarnished now, lifeless and mocking in its simplicity. Gravity too was lying nearby, the source of the blow that struck her. The head had been cracked nearly in two, and when Leonora looked for Bernhardt, she quickly found him sprawled out not far away. He was not moving, and his chest neither rose nor fell. He had died trying to kill her, and in the back of her mind, Leonora wondered if it was the last desperate act of a dying hero, or the futile tactic of a fool and brigand who wanted to win at any cost. Rael and Trece were getting back to their feet, and they each looked worse for wear after Leonora's assault. There was no way that she could press the advantage now, so she poured all of the power that she could manage into healing her significant wounds. It wasn't until then that the Jade Knight noticed that the sky had darkened.

Above the battlefield, four massive swirling blue portals appeared. From three of the portals, huge dragons emerged, taking hovering positions. From the fourth, a woman emerged, her long dark hair streaked with gray, and her stark white, almost porcelain colored skin clear to the naked eye; impossibly bright green eyes shown against the tapestry of darkness behind her.

"I am Talisia Masile," the woman called in a chilling voice. "None of you will leave this field alive, and by the dawn, the Academy of Arcane Arts will no longer exist."

Check and Mate

Year Three of the Just Emperor Kaitain "Dragonsbane" Lorien,
Creator's Calendar Year 1870

The Universe is a conscious being, one that has broken itself into countless tiny pieces and invested itself into everything within its massive frame. People, animals, plants, flowers, the wind and the streams all carry a piece of the greater entity that is the Universe drinking in all knowledge that it can about the boundless reaches of itself. Is it any wonder that rooms then can take on different temperatures based on the happenings within it, or that people within those rooms change attitudes and tones based on the temperature in the room? Everything feeds off the energy of everything else. So it should be no surprise that the vast receiving hall of the Palace of Celidar was suddenly ice cold, but seemed to be priming itself for an explosion of heat and fury. Midarin stood, her ancient blade in hand, a barely restrained hatred burning in her eyes. While her hatred may not have been for the woman that stood before her, Midarin was happy to make her the target of that rage for the time being. Felicia Lorien to her credit took the palpable wave of hatred in stride. Of all the things that had happened to her in her short life, it seemed that she was prepared for this moment. Her call to become a warrior, sparring in court with her cousin Marlae, the assassin, Wynne, Diana, Nightwing, and now this Dark Goddess. Her life had driven her to this point. She felt for the first time that she was no longer chasing what she was supposed to be, but instead was being everything that she had been destined to be. A new excitement flooded through Felicia. She was going to take the fight to a Dark God, and not only that, all of the tools that Diana had given her sprouted fully into her mind. And what's more, she wanted to try all of them.

Midarin advanced several steps, but was still well outside of striking distance with her blade. She could have simply channeled several flows of power at the girl and ended the battle quickly, but the fight with the woman calling herself Irene Drage and the creature Death had left her more than a little drained. Besides, it would feel good to fight again like a mortal. It had been too long since her last really good fight, as the battle with Natalia Pressen had been over too quickly and had taken too little effort. This would be a chance to actually get some swordplay in. It was then that Midarin noticed that her opponent was unarmed. That would not do at all.

"Where is your sword, little girl?" Midarin growled. There was no mocking in her tone, and the anger oozed with every syllable. "Though it would not hurt my feelings to strike you down unarmed, I am in no mood to waste this blade on your pampered flesh. So either take up a weapon or get out of my way."

Felicia looked down for a moment and then cursed. She had been in such a hurry to track the portal that she had left her sword sitting on the floor of the bedroom. Her armor as well. But then, she had no need of those mundane items any longer. She had Nightwing living beneath her skin and the powers of the Blaze at her disposal. Not only that, there was something more. Something deeper. Diana's essence had given her powers that were beyond that of Nightwing, something that defied description. Calling upon that power, Felicia concentrated harder than she ever had in her life, touching that cord of power deep within herself, a mix of thought, emotion, pain, and love. A bright flare erupted in the back of her mind, and she could feel everything around her as though she was seeing the world for the first time. Not only could she feel her surroundings in a more crisp and clear perspective, there were people and places outside of her conscious perception that were suddenly so clear, it was as though they were in the same room with her. A man standing in the cold, a man and woman on a blood-soaked hill, a husband and wife in a crumbling castle, three ancient and powerful people sitting around a table, a burning bright image of a man laughing, and two women on a ship. It was one of the women on the ship that kept pushing her way to the forefront of this new consciousness. She was important, so important that she could not be ignored. But almost as brilliant was the laughing man. Where the woman was soothing and comforting, the laughing man was both awe-inspiring and terrifying. But as much as his visage scared her, she could not help but feel drawn to him. Felicia suddenly realized that she was being drawn too deep into the powers themselves, and pulled back. She could not surrender to the knowledge that her new abilities brought her, not when she was on the cusp of a battle. The sword formed in her hand with little to no exertion, as solid and substantial as her own weapon, and with a cursory examination she realized that it was in fact her own sword. The smile flashed onto her lips. The Dark Goddess would surely interpret the smile as something else, but Felicia was reveling in her own surprise and satisfaction.

Midarin stopped briefly as the sword simply blinked into existence in the woman's hand. She knew that the Knights of the Flashing Blade had special weapons with powers, and perhaps this one could be summoned back to the hand of its master with a thought. Such things were not out of the realm of possibility, but it would take more than simple parlor tricks to impress Midarin. She continued her advance and a full two strides from Felicia, she lunged forward in the practiced strike that Gwydeon had drilled into her head all those years ago.

* * * * * * * * * * * *

Palace of Dalx, World of Onea, Time Immemorial

Midarin lay with her head on Gwydeon's chest, listening to his heartbeat and his ragged breathing. She wasn't sure what she was expecting when he carried her to the small bed, but whatever it was it was not what had occurred. The unrelenting warrior that Gwydeon had been on the battlefield had faded and his soft kisses and tenderness would stay with her for as long as she lived. Now they lay together, more than new-found lovers, and much more than the relative strangers they had been before that night. Gwydeon had been an oddity to her, a bit backwards, but no doubt loyal to his friends. Logan was the charismatic leader, Pike the carousing thug with his equally insufferable counterpart Talon, Elwyne was the heart and the conscious, Eldar was the lady in farmers clothing, Lane the intellect, and Aryx the grizzled war veteran trying to keep order in the nursery. And what did that make her? Maybe she had just been in the wrong place at the wrong time in that tavern. Maybe she should have just gone her own way when she learned what these farmers were up against. But now, lying in Gwydeon's arms, everything was so clear. She felt Gwydeon move slowly away from her. He leaned down and kissed her on the forehead and slid gingerly off the bed and stood up slowly. She could tell that he was still unsteady, but as much as she wanted to take credit for his lack of energy, she knew that it was from the near death experience during the fight with the phase Zarsi. She could scarcely believe that he was still breathing after seeing that massive shard of ice impale him. He stretched slowly and then crossed the room to recover his sword from where it lay across the arms of the chair. Midarin pulled the covers up over her and propped her head up on one hand as she watched him go through simple movements with his blade. There was no doubt he was a master with the sword, and while Midarin had always favored the bow, she knew that in the days and weeks to come, there would be many more battles where she would need to rely on steel far more than the wooden bow. She lay there for several minutes watching, the awe and respect rising within her. She watched as he moved from a simple en guard position to a quick hard forward thrust that covered a greater distance than Midarin thought a simple lunge possibly could. Gwydeon moved on to another set of practiced moves, and Midarin gracefully pulled herself from the bed and pulled Gwydeon's shirt over her head. She liked the smell of him that still clung to the shirt. It took him a moment to realize that she was standing there, but when he did, he lowered the blade and smiled. She smiled in return, walked to him, and instead of giving him the kiss that he expected, she reached out and took the sword from his hand.

"Show me how to do that lunging strike."

* * * * * * * * * * * *

Year Three of the Just Emperor Kaitain "Dragonsbane" Lorien, Creator's Calendar Year 1870

Felicia was not ready for the speed at which her opponent moved, and had it not been for the new abilities at her disposal, the battle would have been over before it began. Felicia flowed to the side of the surprising strike and parried the woman's blade away from her chest. Midarin was ready for the counter, and let her momentum take her past Felicia and the slashed back hard at the woman's undefended flank. Again Felicia was pushed into a defensive posture, parrying each of Midarin's precise strikes. Felicia was impressed at how light her opponent was on her feet and her ability with the sword. But no matter her prowess, Felicia knew that her training was superior to her opponent's. Midarin had obviously been taught by a master swordsman, but while she may have been an exceptional student, there were flaws in her form. Felicia herself was a sword master and had not only her own techniques at her disposal, but had also inherited the techniques of a master swordsman from Diana Terian. Three thrusts and parries later, Midarin made her first mistake. It was a minor one, an opening in her defense that a more practiced fighter would not have allowed to show. Felicia planted her lead foot and slashed for the opening. However, halfway into her strike she realized that the hole in the defense had not been one left open from lack of practice or deficient skill. She had been baited in, and in her arrogance, Felicia did not think laterally to the possibility that the woman was testing her. The pommel strike that collided with her cheek was enough to send Felicia sailing across the room. When Felicia looked up, she fully expected to see the Dark Goddess advancing on her, but instead Midarin had fallen into a defensive posture, her blade wheeled up over her head, her weight shifted to her back foot.

* * * * * * * * * * * *

Inn of Barer, World of Onea, Time Immemorial

Midarin could tell that Gwydeon was angry, she could always tell. Normally during his instruction sessions, his tone was understanding and soft. He corrected without being demanding. Tonight he was like an instructor who had to deal with the worst student he had ever seen.

"No, no. You can't evenly distribute your weight in that stance. All your weight has to be on your back foot."

Midarin wanted to argue. She could feel the bile rising up in the back of her throat, but she kept her tongue in check. They were all a little ragged. First Leane Torne had suddenly reappeared and then Logan started acting like a rabid dog that was barking at the end of its leash. What was worse was that Logan was purposefully sending them into danger; a meeting with at least two members of the phasia, and only a handful of the group were tasked. It was almost as though Logan wanted them to get killed. Gwydeon hadn't felt very much like training that night, but Midarin insisted, so she knew that she would be the target of some of his wrath.

"The sword has to be straighter; otherwise you won't be able to strike or defend evenly to both sides."

His hands were on her the next moment, correcting her posture. He put one hand on the small of her back, forcing her to pull her shoulders back and let her hips move forward. It was a little uncomfortable, but when she shifted her weight to her back foot, it felt better. With the other hand, he held her wrist, straightening the sword in her grasp. She could feel his breath on her neck, and while it was maddening, it was also comforting. His hands left her body, and he stood in front of her. She watched his eyes, and saw the anger melt and be replaced by a lightness that eventually bloomed to a smile.

"Do I look that ridiculous in that position?"

* * * * * * * * * * * *

Year Three of the Just Emperor Kaitain "Dragonsbane" Lorien, Creator's Calendar Year 1870

Felicia saw the smile of the face of the Dark Goddess, and it unnerved her. This woman was playing with her, and Felicia could feel the annoyance growing. The time for simple swordplay was at an end. From where she sat on the floor, Felicia started to rise, but as she straightened, she thrust out her left hand, and a stream of fire erupted from her outstretched fingers. Midarin was unprepared for the strike and took the full burst of flame to her chest. The Dark Goddess had no time to erect a defense and was sent flying across the room where she slammed hard into the wall, sending stone flying in all directions with the impact. The sword was knocked free from her hand and went skidding across the room. Felicia stood and pulled her shoulders back proudly, but the pride and self-satisfaction faded as soon as she saw Midarin pull herself away from the wall, and pat down the scorched front of her ruined shirt. The look on her face was not one of surprise, but rather irritation.

"So, you want to turn this into a real fight," Midarin said extending her hand and calling her sword back to her clutches, "then we can certainly do it your way."

The Dark Goddess was on Felicia before she knew what was happening. The sword flashed in and disarmed the young princess, and then Midarin's off-hand thrust into the woman's chest and an explosion of force violently erupted into the young woman's midsection. Felicia was tossed backwards, and she collided hard with the stone wall, breaking through it into the chamber that lay beyond. The collision sounded like a bomb exploding, and Midarin smiled at her handiwork. However, she was not expecting what happened next. From the hole in the wall, the familiar shining form of the creature Nightwing emerged. The form was slightly different from the last time that Midarin had set eyes on the creature, but there was no doubting what the beast was. Midarin smiled despite herself and let her body fall back into the practiced defensive posture again. Shock would have to wait until the battle was over. If this princess of the Lorien family had somehow gained access to the powers of Nightwing that could only mean that Diana had given the powers away willingly. Not only was that worrisome, but that made the woman far more dangerous than Midarin had expected.

"NOW YOU'VE MADE ME MAD," Nightwing's scratchy metallic voice intoned. "I'M GOING TO KILL YOU."

The beast whirled in the next moment, bladed wings flashing and metallic skin gleaming in the dim light. Midarin was ready for the strike and had seen Nightwing fight enough to be ready for its tactics. The flash of blades was a feint, and Midarin treated them as such and was ready with the blade of her sword to block the true strike, the thin razor-sharp tail that swept in toward Midarin's heart. Midarin's block was perfectly timed, and the tip of Nightwing's tail collided with Midarin's sword and was driven off its deadly course. Midarin kicked with her left leg, the heel connecting solidly with Nightwing's right thigh. It was enough to drive the beast back a pace, but not enough to do any kind of damage. But Midarin's strike was not intended to hurt, just to create enough space for her next assault. Her sword swept across Nightwing's midsection, but again was not intended to strike a target. Instead, Midarin expended some of her powers and created a spray of ice shards that materialized in the space between the two combatants. Many of the projectiles hit home, perforating the breastplate of the metallic beast. Nightwing howled in a mixture of pain and anger. From its open mouth, a beam of pure white energy emerged. Midarin was able to spin out of the way, but not in time to prevent the beam from connecting with her shoulder. The burning was intense and would have been deadly to any being that was not touched with godly power. It was a weapon of last resort granted to the creatures known as Shadowwalkers, but could be used freely by Nightwing. It was pure unadulterated Blaze energy, and whatever it touched was destroyed by its might. The wound on Midarin's shoulder smoked, and her eyes filled with tears of pain that blurred her vision. She barely saw the flash of steel that sped toward her defenseless neck. It was the strike that would end the battle. But at the last moment, another weapon flashed in, a curved and elegant blade intercepted the cruel blade wielded by the beast Nightwing.

* * * * * * * * * * * *

Wynne heard the explosion and practically felt it rock the palace. He grabbed the curved blade he had taken from the assassin and raced out of the door of the simple yet elegant room that Jerrard had given him and headed toward the direction of the tumult. It took only a few seconds to pick up the sounds of battle and they had been coming from the throne room. He skidded to a stop as soon as he burst through the door and saw the combatants. It was like a bad dream come to life. He knew the metallic form as soon as he lay eyes on it, and the woman Nightwing was pummeling was more than familiar to Wynne. He saw the column of Blaze strike Midarin in the shoulder and knew the finishing strike would be coming in a moment. He drew the assassin's blade and flashed in, catching Nightwing's blade with his own, sparing Midarin's life. Nightwing disengaged, but Wynne pressed the advantage that his shock had given him, lashing out with several strikes. He knew that he was no match for Nightwing, but if he could give Midarin enough time to recover, she would be more than enough of a match for the metallic beast.

CHAPTER 64

Felicia could only react as Wynne intervened and saved the Dark Goddess from the finishing strike. Anger boiled up in her, the anger at Wynne for being married, and the anger at the assassins that had stalked them since leaving the Imperial Palace at Aldere. The anger at her inability to defend her father without Wynne's help. She didn't want to kill Wynne the way the she wanted to kill Midarin, but if he wanted to bring the fight to her, she would prove to him and to herself that she didn't need him. She had everything that she needed now, and she was strong enough to leave Wynne behind. Nightwing parried Wynne's strikes to the left and to the right, occasionally thrusting or slashing back at him, but his form was nearly perfect.

Midarin got herself back to her feet, and found her sword quickly. She had been saved from Nightwing's strike by the form that she could barely make out through her blurred vision and swollen eyes. The pain continued to make her eyes water, and no matter what she did, she could not make her vision clear. At once she realized that it was not just tears that clouded her vision, but also blood. Nightwing's strike had done far more damage than she had originally thought. Staggered a little, Midarin watched as the mystery man poured on the assault, and though he was good, it was only a matter of time before Nightwing unleashed another assault that the man could not handle. Even with her blurred vision, Midarin saw an opening and sped forward. Her blade would penetrate Nightwing in its damaged breastplate and pierce the woman's heart, ending the battle for good. Mere instants from the strike, the man's curved blade arced away from where it had blocked another Nightwing counterattack and intercepted Midarin's own strike. Midarin dropped back, anger filling her. Her savior had become her enemy, and she lashed out equally at the mystery man and the creature Nightwing.

Felicia breathed a quick sigh of relief at Wynne's defense of her life, but the relief was replaced again by anger that he interfered. He was always interfering and proving that she really did need him in her life. Urged on, Felicia continued to strike and thrust not only at Wynne, but at Midarin as well.

Wynne went totally defensive. All he was trying to do was keep Midarin and Nightwing from killing each other. The three blades danced among one another in a deadly blur. One combatant's block flowed into a strike on one of the others, and they continued to circle and strike. Wynne rarely lashed out on his own, unless he was trying to prevent harm to come to one of the others. Finally the dance moved to a speed that Wynne was having difficulty keeping up with. Once he had been powerful enough to end this battle before it began, but now he was struggling to keep up. Another strike flashed out from Midarin, and Wynne was taken completely off his feet. Nightwing howled and lashed out at Midarin, but the Dark Goddess was too quick, and a beam of pure energy struck Nightwing in the face sending the creature toppling backwards uncontrolled. The metallic beast slammed into the wall, and lay limp on the ground, rendered unconscious by the blow. No longer bidden, the metallic armor retracted and Wynne was shocked to see the unconscious form of Felicia Lorien laying on the ground. Wynne turned his attention back to Midarin, who was advancing on him. She pawed quickly at her eyes, trying to clear her vision.

"Now, you'll pay for interfering in this."

Wynne had one chance. He waited until she struck, and darted under the assault and buried his shoulder into her stomach. It was like running full speed into a brick wall, but they both went down, Midarin landing hard on her back, her sword skidding away from her grasp again, and Wynne landing on top of her. When he realized where he was, Wynne pulled himself up, and Midarin's hand was on his throat the next instant. She opened her mouth as if to speak, but closed it again suddenly. Her bottom lip was quivering, and her brilliant eyes locked on his.

* * * * * * * * * * * *

Year Nineteen of the Just Emperor Terrik Lorien I, Creator's Calendar Year 69

Gwydeon lay curled up with Midarin in the depths of the Citadel of the Dark Gods. They both knew what the dawn would bring, and Gwydeon knew more than anyone the cost of the actions he would take over the next few days. But this is what it had come to. The Cadarians were becoming more of a threat to themselves, and as long as they made war with the Dark Gods, the danger was real that the Dark Gods would have no choice but to wipe the face of Cadaria clean of the impetuous mortals. Midarin rolled on top of Gwydeon and looked down into his beautiful eyes and kissed him slowly and passionately. Instinct made Gwydeon wrap his arms around his wife, and he held her a long time before pulling away slightly so that he could speak to her. Her eyes held some disappointment, but there were so many things he still needed to say. So many things he wished he had time to tell her about what was to come.

"As much as I want to leave you in charge, my love, you know I can't."

Midarin sighed and stifled a laugh. Of course she understood. She had understood from the moment that Gwydeon told her, but he just would not accept that she wasn't upset.

"Pike needs to be in command so he won't do anything reckless," Gwydeon continued. "As long as he knows he is responsible for all of you, he'll abide by the bargains that I make with the Cadarian emperor."

Midarin felt her stomach turn.

"And what if this Terrik Lorien doesn't want to make a deal?"

The flaw in Gwydeon's plan had been depending on the mortal emperor to make a rational decision as Gwydeon would. The Cadarians were out-classed in all respects, and had not fully recovered from the Founding Wars that had put Terrik Lorien on the throne. If the Dark Gods truly wished to put an end to the fledgling Empire, they could easily do so, which is what Gwydeon hoped to prove with his all-out assault on the Imperial Palace. From a position of strength, Gwydeon could dictate the terms that he wanted, and the Cadarian Emperor would have no choice but to accept. Either that, or Gwydeon would be forced to do the unthinkable.

"I'm not going to follow Pike's plan and put myself on their throne," Gwydeon countered.

He kissed Midarin again and rolled them both so that he was lying atop her. He shifted his weight so that he wasn't pressing down too hard on her, but then smiled and kissed her again. She looked up into his eyes, and just for a moment, she felt as though things would be alright.

* * * * * * * * * * * *

Year Three of the Just Emperor Kaitain "Dragonsbane" Lorien, Creator's Calendar Year 1870

Midarin blinked hard, her eyes finally clearing and her vision returning. But what she was seeing wasn't possible. The eyes that stared down at her, those lovely, soft, passionate, and understanding eyes. As impossible as it was, they could only belong to one man.

"Gwydeon?"

Iron Crucible

*Year Three of the Just Emperor Kaitain "Dragonsbane" Lorien,
Creator's Calendar Year 1870*

For all of Hannah Ironheart's life, there had been a path and a plan. Her early childhood was a vague and hazy memory filled with laughter, love, and acceptance. Hannah and her sister Sadrina were happy children, loved by their parents and their extended families. Sadrina was older, but not by any measure that strained the relationship between the two young girls, and though there were fights and arguments, the two girls were almost inseparable. But it all changed the day that the Reverend Mother of the Church of the Creator came to the home of the Ironhearts. Hannah was only five years old, barely able to understand what was happening to her. The last memory she had of her parents was looking back through tear-filled eyes over the shoulder of the Reverend Mother. Hannah's father had been a soldier in the service of the Church of the Creator, and her mother had been a promising acolyte before they found one another. A condition of their release from their service to the Church of the Creator was that one of their children would be welcomed into the fold and fostered to the Church. Originally the bargain had called for the first-born, but that all changed the day that Sadrina was born. Their eldest child had been born under ominous portents, and the Church would not accept the girl. The rejection of the Church, and the hatred spurred by losing her sister to the cold and dispassionate clergy turned Sadrina forever against the worship of the Creator. Perhaps that was why she eventually found solace in the arms of a member of the Dark Gods.

While Hannah never forgot her parents or her sister, her mind was quickly filled with the business of life in the Church of the Creator. Even from that tender young age, her mind was constantly being filled with the lessons from the Book of the Creator. Everything had an explanation there, and any questions that her growing mind would bring forward would always be answered by the Creator's will. From the day she stepped into the church, Hannah excelled. She was a perfect student, perfectly devout, free of all temptation and doubt, and most of all, unlike a great many others who called the Church of the Creator their home, Hannah truly believed. The first five years passed in the blink of an eye, with Hannah quickly becoming the prodigy of her order. It was then that the war in Galateria flared again, and her parents were called to duty. The war was bloody, brutal, and completely unnecessary. The only thing that came out of that war was blood and death, and unfortunately that fact was true for most of the wars in the history of Cadaria. No war since the War of Founding where the Loriens took control of the Empire of Cadaria, or the war with the Dark Gods had any true meaning. Hannah cried for two days after the loss of her parents to that unnecessary war. She vowed in her heart that day that she would never allow wars to claim innocents again. She would never allow the needs of petty and selfish men to overrule the rights that the Creator granted to all beings who brought glory to His name.

But to truly understand war, Hannah would have to know war. Against the wishes of the Reverend Mother and most of her order, Hannah began to train with the members of the Sanctified Guard, the protectors of the church. While Hannah was not the prodigy with weapons that she was with scripture, she was still better than most. Within two years Hannah was training and keeping up with the elite, which brought her to the attention of Gregor Quicksilver, who had already made his meteoric rise to the rank of Ruby Knight of the Flashing Blade, and favorite of Emperor Ender Lorien. The two became fast friends, and fierce combatants on the training grounds, and while Hannah would never be his equal with a weapon in hand, she was certainly his equal in force of will and strength of character. In fact in some ways, Hannah had something that Gregor would never have. She believed. She believed with every fiber of her heart and soul that she was doing the will of the Creator with every breath that she took. In every sense of the word, she was a holy warrior, doing the Creator's bidding in the world of the living. Saving souls and saving the innocent from the touch of evil. Not even the defection of her sister to the arms of the Dark Gods could damper her devotion to her Creator. What was more shocking was that no one even batted an eye in Hannah's direction when the news became known through the upper echelon of the Church of the Creator about Sadrina. No one questioned Hannah about her loyalties or her motives. Hannah Ironheart was above reproach. And when she was called to do the bidding of the Emperor, when she was called to become the representative of the Kingdom of Stone at the right hand of the Emperor as one of his champions, there were no expectations. It was merely accepted that she would be everything that everyone knew she could be, and that she would never falter for one moment in her devotion to her duty or to the Creator's will.

Belief and Faith are strange constructs. For so long they can seem as hard as steel and as unwavering as stone, but once a crack has formed, even the smallest crack, it takes only one good hard blow to shatter the veneer and expose the delicate web of doubt and fear beneath. Aerith Seth had been a great many things in his long life, and this latest role was that of the bearer of the hammer of truth that shattered Hannah's resolve. She had seen the naked force that the Will and the Voice had brought to bear. She had seen their single-minded devotion to carrying out the destruction of a man who on the surface seemed more devoted to the principles described in the Book of the Creator than the Heralds themselves did. Hannah knew that Aerith Seth was not a good man, and certainly was not a pious man. But what he was, was a man of principle. And those principles had brought him into direct conflict with not only the Creator, but all of those who served the Creator's will. By all rights, Hannah and Aerith should have been the fiercest of enemies. And until a few moments before she stood face to face with the man, his hands on her shoulders, Hannah looked on him as a heretic who needed to be stopped. However, Hannah had been able to see the truth, the brutality that utter devotion to the Creator brought. Faith and knowledge were incompatible. The Heralds knew the voice of the Creator, they had heard it with their own ears, and knew the Creator to be a real thing that they could touch and could touch them.

Those in the Church of the Creator had faith in the words of the Creator that they read in books and heard spoken by those in the hierarchy. But no one truly knew the face of the Creator, no one felt the power of his voice radiating through their bodies. They believed. Those who believed could be motivated to do anything; their faith could be incited against any threat, loosed against any enemy. The faithful would become zealots that would unfailingly defend their beliefs against those whose only weapons were doubt and fear. Hannah was a faithful and devout servant, until her faith was tested, not by the doubting words of a non-believer, but by the very vision of all that she had held sacred. She saw the naked power that she had once revered, and the fear and revulsion that awoke in her was something she would never have been prepared for. She found herself taking up arms against the vessels of the Creator's power, bringing her weapon to bear to defend the man that was once her enemy.

All of the years of devotion to the teachings of the Creator were washed away. She was now a renegade, an enemy of the Creator, and marked for death by the Heralds of His will, and all because she wanted the needless killing to stop. There were too many dead there in the corridor, struck down in equal measure by the forces of the Creator, and the wrathful Dark God. But the men that Aerith Seth killed, he killed in self-defense. The Heralds killed devout followers of the Creator indiscriminately and for only one purpose, because they stood between the Heralds and their prey. It was an abuse of power that would not be tolerated in the world that Hannah had once been a part of. But that world no longer existed, and as she looked into Aerith's eyes, she knew that there was nothing left of her old life. Perhaps her sister had been right all along in her devotion to anything that fought against the Church of the Creator. Or perhaps the Church of the Creator was an ideal that even those who served the Creator in the Heavens, and perhaps the Creator himself were unable to live up to. The blasphemy would not leave her mind; a flawed Creator whose teachings were mere parables about how He wished He could be, than a description of what He really was. Was the Creator really so much better than those who struggled every day to be better than they were?

Aerith's smile brought Hannah back to the moment. She had accepted his offer, but being lost in thought and weak from exertion in battle had not given her time to process exactly what she had just agreed to. Someone named Sabrina had done something, and now Aerith was stronger. He was different now, she could see it in his eyes, and feel it in his tone. The man who seemed allergic to anything serious was now suddenly so serious that his gaze could turn the blood to ice. There was a power in his gaze that sent shivers through Hannah's body, and only his bright smile kept her from shrinking away from his touch. His presence demanded respect and fear.

"I need to hear you say it, Hannah," Aerith said, stealing another look over his shoulder at the Heralds of the Creator. "I can't take just a nod. Not this time, not with so much at stake. Too many have worn my mantle without a choice. You have to accept it, and you have to do it willingly."

Hannah too took a moment to look past Aerith at the Heralds. The latest display of power from Aerith Seth had sent the two toppling down the corridor, and they were just now beginning to recover. They obviously sensed that something was different in their opponent and were changing their tactics. No longer could they overwhelm Aerith with brute force, and seemed content to judge the situation for a little longer before launching the next crippling offensive. Suddenly a feeling rushed through Hannah. There was warmth and a comfort like being wrapped in a warm blanket, and all of her doubts seemed to melt away. At first she thought that the feeling was radiating from Aerith's touch, but then she realized that the wave of peace and tranquility was coming from Spirit. The Sacred Weapon that had been her ally for so long seemed to be pushing her to make her decision, and it was almost as if Spirit wanted her to accept Aerith's offer. The thought sent a stream of joy from the weapon, right to her heart. She had understood. Spirit wanted her to accept this role as the *Chosen One*, and to wear Aerith Seth's mantle. Her decision was made.

"I accept," Hannah said, though she was unable to keep the doubt or the fear out of her voice, "I will wear your mantle, and become the *Chosen One*."

Aerith nodded.

"Don't worry Hannah," he said, the joviality returning to his tone for a moment, "this is going to be fun."

Aerith removed his hands from Hannah's shoulders and rubbed them together in front of his chest. Hannah at first thought it was an absent gesture, an affectation while he was concentrating on whatever he was about to do to transfer his mantle. But soon Hannah realized that there was purpose in his gesture. After several long seconds, a green glow began to become visible around Aerith's hands. The glow clung to his hands like moss to an old tree. Finally he looked up into Hannah's eyes.

"Ready?"

He didn't wait for her reply, and suddenly thrust his left hand forward and placed it on her chest. The green glow pulsed from around Aerith's hand and spread across Hannah's body, engulfing her. Pain racked Hannah's body as every cell of her being became imbued with the power that Aerith was feeding into her. She could feel the change taking place, power flooding through her on a scale that she never imagined was even possible. After a few languid moments, the glow of energy shifted and took on a red hue, and Hannah felt a new pain began to contort her body. Her mind and body were both on fire, and she wondered if she would survive whatever transition she was going through. But the pain would begin to ease and abate as the enveloping glow turned blue, and a cool wave of refreshment and calm washed over her pained body. The fire in her stomach and mind had begun to lessen, but the pain was still with her, even though it was significantly diminished. The pulsating glow then shifted to white, and the pain began to ebb even more. It became nothing more than background noise. Hannah felt different, but she only felt half of what she should be. It was as though Hannah could now sense what it was that she was becoming and she knew that the power that had already flowed into her was barely a trickle, the warning for the flood that was to come. It was then that Aerith extended his other hand, and though Hannah tried to brace herself for the wave of pain that would accompany the infusion, there was no way that she could prepare herself for the torrent that would break across her like an unforgiving tidal wave.

Lightning, fire, ice, and smoke enveloped Hannah and though she tried her best to bite it back, she screamed in agony as the deluge permeated her body. The pain was so intense that Hannah thought she was dying, and perhaps in a way she was. The woman that she was before this moment had been devoted to nothing more than the service of the Creator, and now that Hannah would cease to exist. She would find a new purpose, a new voice, and a new life. Her heart beat hard in her chest, so hard that it threatened to burst right through her ribs. Breathing was a laborious task at best, and Hannah had to forcefully drag each and every breath in and out of her tired lungs. Then, just as suddenly as the pain began, it began to cease. When Hannah opened her eyes again, she saw the threads of lightning, fire and ice still fluttering around her, lazily entering and then exiting her body. Aerith no longer controlled the torrent of energy, but stood a step back, and watched the continuation of the process. Hannah felt a new strength begin to permeate her body, and a new window in her consciousness open. She could see the lines of power running through her, and she could also see where the different planes of energy intersected with the plane she called reality. It was like turning on the light in a dark room to see the walls adorned with the most beautiful paintings in the entire world. There was music in the motion of time, space, and reality. Life as she knew it began to take on a whole new meaning. It was as if in that span of a few moments, Hannah had become a god. But there was more, so much more than just the power. A whole stream of consciousness collided with her own, and her mind was on fire with the new infusion of knowledge. The history of a dozen lifetimes, battle strategies and tactics, skills that she could never learn if she lived a hundred lifetimes, and a wave of emotions so primal and powerful that Hannah didn't know if she could contain them all. She wasn't just the vessel of Aerith's power. In a way, she had become an echo of Aerith. She knew everything that he knew, felt everything that he had ever felt, but at the same time, she was more than Aerith. She had her own experiences in addition to his; her own thoughts and her own power. But that thought quickly vanished. The transition had not been one way. Though he had not gained nearly what she had, Aerith had gained insight into Hannah's mind and soul. He too had absorbed part of her during the process, and they were really and truly one person spilt in two halves. It was then that Hannah felt another stream of consciousness. There was another woman, a woman that shared Aerith's mind and soul. But it was not this woman Bryn that Aerith loved with more of his being than should have been decent to devote to one other person. Hannah had to suppress the rush of heat through her body the first time the thoughts of Bryn and the fire of her passion ignited within Hannah. But when Hannah's mind found Sabrina's echo in Aerith's soul, and now her own, for the first time in so long, she felt complete. Aerith in many ways was Hannah's father, brother, and husband all at the same time; and Sabrina was her mother, sister, and wife. Together, the three of them were complete, and when Aerith stepped to Hannah's side, and put his hand back on her shoulder, she saw her enemy with new eyes.

"How do you feel?" Aerith said, letting the blade of Blaze energy reform in his hand.

Hannah knew that there was no answer needed to the question. There were no words for how she felt. But then she heard Aerith's mind in hers. She could not resist.

"Like you."

Aerith laughed and took a single step forward and let his battle stance take over his posture. A heartbeat later, the second blade of energy appeared, and Aerith was ready to fight again. Hannah knew the propensity that Aerith had for fighting with two weapons, and she could feel all of his skills in the back of her mind. But Hannah was determined that no matter how much of Aerith had been imparted into her, she would still be the woman that she wanted to be, the woman that Aerith had chosen to trust with his abilities. So she brought Spirit to bear, and prepared herself for the assault that would come any moment.

The Will rushed forward first, his larger frame and power aimed right at Aerith, and the Voice flashed in behind, feinting first to Aerith's left and then darting back behind the screen that the Will was providing and streaked straight at Hannah. The Will's massive blade thrust forward, a giant sharp steel tip aimed right at the center of Aerith's chest. Aerith didn't move, and brought up both of his blades in an X. The tip of the Will's blade struck the very center of Aerith's crossed blades, and sparks flew in all directions, but neither man budged from their spots. Hannah had no time to react to the collision of power, and instead focused her attention on the blade of the Voice's crystalline sword that flashed down at her from above. The haft of Spirit was enough to block the blow, but Hannah was not content with blocking. Spirit was singing in her mind in a way that it never had before, a confident voice that told her she could do anything now that Aerith had blessed her. She pushed back hard with Spirit, and sent the Voice back a pace. In that space, Hannah swung hard with the head of Spirit. Her target however was not the Voice himself, but his sword. The mace head struck the flawless crystal and the sound of thousands of chimes being struck simultaneously at a hundred different octaves filled the chamber as the crystalline sword shattered. Neither Hannah nor the Voice had been prepared for the shockwave of power that would pulse from the broken blade, and both were tossed away from the center of the explosion. The Will too caught the full force of the explosion and was propelled into the wall of the corridor. Aerith however seemed to know what was going to happen, and instead of being caught by the explosion, leapt forward toward the floor, sliding along the stone on his belly before popping up on the far side of the wake of the explosion and letting the cascade of turbulent air carry him in pursuit of the Voice. The Voice's wings beat hard at the air, and he finally was able to right himself, but not before Aerith was upon him. A sword of pure energy flashed down, scarring the front of the Voice's gleaming breastplate, digging an ugly scar that dulled and tarnished the surrounding metal with its corrosive heat. The Voice howled and thrust both hands forward. A spray of white lights erupted from its outstretched fingers and caused Aerith to bring up his guard and fall away from the retreating form of the Voice. Both men landed on their feet, and when Aerith stood straight again, the Voice let another crystal blade appear in his hands, this time it glowed with a red hue, and there was a vicious sneer on the Voice's lips.

Hannah in the meantime was left with the Will, and he was just bringing his massive bulk back to bear. Whatever cleaver tricks Hannah was able to accomplish with the Voice's weapon, she knew she would not be able to repeat the performance with the Will. His blade was massive and solid, and as it whipped around in her direction, she could only dodge the blow as it collided with wall and ceiling bringing more explosions of rubble. Hannah could hear more creaking from the structure of the Heart of Stone, and it was trembling under the terrible torment the two Heralds of the Creator were putting it through. How many innocents would be killed if this confrontation were to lead to the total collapse of the palace? There would be no time to get anyone out, and dozens, perhaps hundreds would be buried alive. The Heart of Stone would become a tomb. Hannah felt rage bubble up within her, an anger of such magnitude that it bordered on hate.

The song of battle intensified in the back of her mind, and the powers that she had gained from Spirit flared. The Will brought its blade up for another hard strike, this one straight down on the spot where Hannah stood. Hannah leapt as the blade came crashing down, not away from the strike, but toward the Will itself. Spirit flashed in, crashing hard against the gleaming and pristine helm that covered the face of the Will, but the blow didn't leave a scratch, let alone a dent. But damaging the Will had not been Hannah's primary goal. Her other hand flashed forward, sliding in under the helm and above the Will's breastplate. Her hand found a chainmail shirt covering what should have been the throat of the massive beast, but no amount of armor could protect him from what was to come. She squeezed hard and felt something soft beneath the armor give. She channeled all of the new power that she had at her disposal into her touch, calling on the power that Spirit had given her access to, and pulled back hard. The massive form of the Will staggered back two large steps, standing like an empty shell. In Hannah's outstretched hand was an ethereal shape, the blazing white outline of the Will struggling to escape her clutches.

"In the name of Aerith Seth, and the true balance of this world, I consecrate the spirit of this creature and allow its soul to find peace in the bosom of the living Cosmos."

The spirit of the Will cried out so loudly that it shook the rafters of the whole of the Heart of Stone, but no matter how loudly it wailed or how much it struggled, it could not escape its fate. In a matter of moments, the spirit of the Will disappeared. After it was gone, the armor of the creature crumbled into a pile of scrap metal and dust. A body lay in the rubble, a little over half the size of the armor itself. The exertion caused Hannah to fall to her knees and use Spirit to keep her upright.

The Voice watched on in horror as the Will was destroyed. It saw the smile flash across Aerith Seth's features, and knew that if it stayed in this conflict, no matter its skill it could not combat both of the mortals at the same time. Without a word, it wrapped its wings around itself, and a pulse of light was all that preceded the Voice's retreat from the field. Aerith released both of the blades of energy from his hands, and turned to face

Hannah. He walked over slowly, shaking his head, the smile on his face beaming. He helped her to her feet and hugged her tightly.

"I knew I was right about you."

Hannah could not help but give into the hug. She felt as though she could sleep for a month and still not feel rested. When Aerith released her, he turned toward the body of the Will and knelt beside it, moving several of the pieces of rubble. He sighed hard, and motioned Hannah over. She made her way over to the other side of the Will as best she could, but she was not confident with her footfalls. When she saw the face of the man under the armor, she knew him. Hannah had personally never met the man before, but through Aerith, she knew his name.

"Taron."

Aerith nodded.

"This is the fate of anyone touched by the Creator. They become pawns, tools. They become expendable. Because Taron was the child of Halicon, the Creator could pull him back from the void and make use of him any way he saw fit. You've done him a favor Hannah. He's free now."

Hannah heard Aerith's words, but did not take solace in them. She detested killing at any level, even if it was to save another. That was one thing that she could never reconcile in Aerith's memories. Aerith thrived in battle, he thrived on killing his enemies, but only in the service of protecting the innocent and doing the right thing. But no killing was acceptable, no matter the reason.

"We need to go," Aerith said as he moved to collect Valor and Discipline from where they lay. "We have to make sure we get everyone out of the Heart of Stone, and we need to find out what happened to Tess and Camille."

Hannah nodded absently and followed Aerith as best she could back into the Heart of Stone.

Chapter LXV

Rising from a Fall

Year Forty of the Founding Wars, the Creator's Calendar Year 45

The lands of the Kingdom of Zevarit hemorrhaged blood from the field of the latest pitched battle between the forces of Terrik Lorien and those of the warlord Grawn. The rapidly approaching dusk had forced a cessation to the day's hostilities, but the morning would cause them to flare once again. Grawn's legions, flush with vicious and bloodthirsty soldiers and wicked conjurers who bent the arcane forces of the world to their whims had been making a concerted push toward the capitol of Zevarit. The whole of the southern reaches of the continent were in his control, every inch conquered, none taken through negotiation or alliance. Grawn did not value words, he valued only how much blood he could extract from the enemies that stood before him. On the field of battle, the banner of the Shark was feared and respected, and simply raising the banner before battle had caused many armies to break and run before him. However, Grawn was never satisfied with an ordered retreat. His cavalry would push forward and mow down as many of the enemy as possible. It would leave less to destroy in the days to come, and it would discourage more fools from raising arms against him. Neither did Grawn suffer the indignity of those who surrendered. Too many times the warlord had seen loyalty bought with coin or with an even more powerful currency, fear. While not considered a tactical match to Terrik Lorien, still the barbarian horde gained ground, pushing back the lines of the unified forces of the fragmented Kingdoms of the Cadarian continent. However, Terrik fought wars on multiple fronts, and the prolonged incursions by Grawn's forces were causing Terrik to lose traction with some of the more impatient kingdoms. Thorigald and Saldarine were already threatening to leave the alliance and go their own ways, which would put them at each other's throats within a month. Albitonin stood firm for now, but if Thorigald and Saldarine broke ranks, Albitonin would pull back its forces to protect its borders. Pellatori had already broken ranks and were pushing against Grawn's forces in Celidar and Rashaleb. There had been a rebellion in Iltorp, and the allied kingdoms were having to commit too many forces to bring those lands back under control, which had compromised the supply lines that Terrik Lorien desperately needed to continue his defense of Zevarit. Terrik's dream of a unified Cadaria was breathing its last breaths. The loss of Zevarit would fracture the alliance, perhaps for good, and there would be little to stand in Grawn's path to conquest.

Miles from where Terrik Lorien held his strategy session just before midnight in the capitol of Zevarit, a different sort of meeting was taking place. A short but broadly built man stood next to a great tree, irritation filling him as he dug his knife deeper into the tree's bark, carving a deep furrow. He wore simple leathers for armor, and they were stained with blood and ash from many battles. He greatly disliked waiting. A sound from the east caused him to stop all motion and listen. He started breathing again when he saw the man who approached. Dressed in common clothes, the man who now wore the name Dane was not certainly a threatening visage.

"You're late," Blade said roughly. "You should know better than to keep me waiting."

Dane rolled his head from one side to the other, stretching his neck, before sitting on an exposed root.

"It seems I'm not the only one. Looks as though you saw a little action today."

Blade frowned.

"Grawn doesn't like his generals to be above the fighting. I still don't think he trusts me. Probably wouldn't bother him if I were to fall in the next engagement."

"Can you blame him? You were only enemies for how many centuries?"

The two men fell silent. There were many things in that pregnant silence that went unsaid. Dane and Blade for many years were on opposite sides of conflicts, and had been the most intense of enemies. But like all beings that were wrapped up in this war, both recognized that a continent united under Grawn's banner would be one that would be soaked with blood from its beginning to its eventual end. His tyranny would only be suffered for so long before another with dreams of conquest would rise up. But would the person to throw down Grawn be a savior or just another tyrant. Regardless, war would be inevitable, and death would be the price of the change of leadership. The silence didn't last long before both men turned to the north side of the clearing. Moments later a swirling portal appeared and three men and a woman emerged. One of the men was chained by the wrists and ankles, while another wore a dark cloak that disguised his features. The young woman quickly covered the distance and wrapped her arms around Dane in a long and powerful hug. Dane found himself laughing when he separated himself from the young woman and kissed her on the forehead.

"Missed you too, Sabrina. It's been too long."

The young woman regarded Dane for a moment and then ran her hand over his cheek and chin.

"You need a shave, Uncle Logan."

Though he smiled, Dane bristled at the use of his old name. Since the fall of his world, he had not been comfortable with the name, and the only way to leave that life and those things that he lost behind was to craft a new identity for himself on this new world. He looked past Sabrina that next moment and found himself staring. One of his oldest enemies stood not twenty feet from him, and yet for the purpose of the moment, Jeroch Yetre would now have to be counted among his allies. Though he too wore a different name now, Dane would never see him as anything but the Shadow.

"Shadow," Dane said coolly, "I trust your errand to Iltorp went without incident."

Vallic frowned. He then put his hand in the back of the shackled man and pushed him hard. With his ankles bound, the man could not keep himself upright, and fell to his knees on the forest floor.

"I would appreciate it if you called me by my new name, Dane," Vallic said trying not to grit his teeth. "But in answer to your question, we discovered why Iltorp suddenly was embroiled in a civil war, and why one of the factions seemed intent on throwing its weight behind Grawn and his advance."

Blade took two long strides forward and took hold of the bound man by the hair. His features were non-descript, and certainly not threatening or familiar. Holding his head up, Blade slapped the man hard across the face with the back of his free hand. The bound man wrenched himself free of Blade's grasp and quickly spit a mouthful of blood onto the ground. When he looked back up at Blade, his features had changed, and were much more familiar to everyone in the small clearing.

"Was that really necessary?" the bound man said gruffly.

Dane took a step forward, Sabrina remaining at his side and let a low whistle escape his lips. He looked up first at Vallic and then to Blade.

"Well that explains everything, now doesn't it? How have you been, Erdric?"

The former member of the phasia, and now general in the service of Grawn, Erdric, looked up at Dane and let a broad smile curl his lips. He then took a deep breath and spat as much blood and saliva as he could onto the front of Dane's shirt.

"You can hide behind another man's name, Ranthall, but you'll never erase that stench. You heroes all smell alike."

Dane didn't react other than to shake his head.

"Charming as always, Erdric. But it makes sense you would throw your lot in with Grawn. You were never strong enough to stand on your own."

Blade took hold of Erdric's hair again and pulled back hard.

"Grawn had been hinting for months that he had someone high up within Terrik's inner circle, but within the last few weeks, Grawn had become increasing irritated with the reports of rebellion coming out of Iltorp. It didn't take much digging to figure out that Grawn's spy had gone rogue and tried to set up his own little empire. The options on the spineless coward list were pretty short."

Vallic folded his arms and tried his best to suppress a scowl.

"Once the information came from Blade, it didn't take long for us to ferret out the spy and we were less than surprised to find our old friend Erdric up to his old tricks. He didn't put up too much of a fight, especially when we made it clear that we were trying to take him alive. It always made Erdric more compliant when he thought there were options."

Sabrina looked up at Vallic and cocked her head slightly.

"What will happen now that Erdric has been removed from power?"

"Isa is picking up the pieces now," Vallic replied. "She'll be quite adept at restoring a stable power structure that will support Terrik and keep Saldarine and Thorigald from ripping each other's throats out until Grawn is dealt with."

Dane looked at Blade and then at Vallic.

"Isa?"

Vallic's frown deepened.

"Ellis."

Dane nodded.

"Have to start keeping notes," Sabrina mumbled.

Dane finally looked over to the cloaked man who stood silent and unmoving through the entire exchange.

"Do you have anything to add, or are you going to just stand there?"

Gwydeon gently pulled back the hood of his cloak and then took two steps toward Erdric. Blade retreated a step, his fingers pulling out some of Erdric's hair and he pulled away.

"I think our friend here will allow us to accelerate our plan."

Sabrina's posture changed slightly, a more aloof and light posture, one that the assembled former residents of Onea would have readily seen from Aerith Seth.

"You don't honestly think that Erdric can be trusted? Even if he is afraid of you, he would never consciously betray Grawn. And even if he would, you couldn't trust him not to just turn on you as soon as it became convenient. Better to just kill him now and get it out of the way and then focus on Grawn."

Gwydeon smiled and shook his head.

"Oh, Erdric will be quite happy to help us," Gwydeon then looked down at Erdric and his eyes began to glow brightly. "Won't you Erdric?"

The power in Gwydeon's voice was subdued, but still could be felt by everyone in the clearing. Soft white light radiated from Gwydeon's eyes and floated across Erdric's features like a soft mist. The bound man made no attempt to resist the light, and he seemed to be frozen in place; not even his chest rose and fell with breath. The exchange lasted for only a few moments before Gwydeon stepped away and pulled the hood of his cloak back up over his head.

"I think you'll find our friend much more compliant now."

Dane looked at Blade and then at Sabrina.

"Remind me not to disagree with him anymore."

Gwydeon growled lightly at the comment.

"This isn't a game," Gwydeon said, his eyes bright in the shadow of his cloaked face. "If Terrik falls, there will be no chance for us to do what needs to be done. We move against Grawn now, and ensure that the Cadarians have a chance. I've risked a lot putting this into motion, and I won't have any of you jeopardizing it because of old grudges."

Dane and Gwydeon's gazes remained locked for a moment before Gwydeon turned his back on the rest of the group and took one step toward the deeper forest.

"We have to go, Sabrina," he said without turning around.

Sabrina could not hide her scowl, but turned and hugged Dane before quickly walking to Gwydeon's side. The two began to walk together into the forest, where they faded from view. Multiple portals opened the next moment, and then closed. Dane felt his teeth grinding together. He dismissed the angry thoughts that filled him the next moment with a deep sigh.

"So the plan moves forward?"

Vallic's question was less a question and more a resigned statement. Toppling Grawn had been in the works for quite some time, and it had taken Blade many years to work his way into a semi-trusted position within Grawn's inner circle. It was clear that Terrik Lorien and his followers had the will, but did not have the power necessary to take on someone like Grawn who was at the height of his powers and cruelty. No, Grawn was from Onea, therefore the burden fell to Oneans to remove him as a threat.

"We move," Blade said finally, "but we must move tonight. If Grawn takes the field tomorrow commanding his troops, then Zevarit will fall, and if Terrik Lorien does not fall with it, then certainly his retreat will bring an end to the alliance. Any hope for him will end as soon as dawn breaks on the battlefield."

Dane rubbed his hands together absently. He suddenly felt cold.

"Can you do it?"

"I never had a problem killing," Blade said finally.

Vallic cleared his throat after a long silence.

"I'll head back to Iltorp and see how Isa is doing with the reconstruction. After that I'm heading for Bellnoc. There are reports of someone there using the Lion banner, trying to rally support for Terrik Lorien. I have to know if it's him."

Dane frowned.

"I don't know why you're so intent on killing him."

Vallic turned his back on Dane and let a portal form in front of him.

"He's my problem, just like Pike is yours. No matter what we might have been on Onea, all we are here is a plague. These people will never be free so long as any of us exist."

Vallic stepped through the portal, leaving Blade and Dane alone with Erdric. Dane looked over to Blade and frowned.

"A plague?"

Blade snorted.

"We've been called worse."

* * * * * * * * * * * *

In his command tent, Grawn Aplee sat in a high backed chair and stared out the tent flap in the direction of the keep that served as the capitol of Zevarit. He had sat like this on many occasions during his march to conquest, staring out at his enemy, envisioning their defeat at his hands. At times it felt as though he could channel his hate and decimate his enemies with only a thought. It had been too long since he had felt this kind of power at his disposal. For too long he had sat impotent in that castle in Frontier, trapped between the over-analysis and droning of Ellis and the incessant scheming and treachery of his supposed wife, Bryn. Neither of them was loyal to anything but their own plans and alliances were momentary at best. Mortal matters only interested Ellis insofar as they could be painted into the tapestry of greater meaning, and Bryn's only interest in mortality had to do with the anatomy of that bastard Aerith Seth.

Grawn had had many lifetimes to contemplate just how much he hated the man. But that was a different world, a different time, and a different situation. No longer was he restricted to dreaming of conquest. Now he could reach out and crush his enemies with his own hands, not act through useless intermediaries.

Grawn tensed slightly as he saw the tent flap pulled back, and the tension didn't ease when he saw the man who entered. The squat man wore the gray and black colors of Grawn's army, and proudly displayed the shark crest over his heart, but Grawn knew deep in his heart that it was allegiance of the moment. One day, the two men would be at each other's throats, and only one of them would survive the engagement. There was not a time that Warron Ysamaran was in Grawn's presence that he was not prepared to end the war that was started the day Warron was born. It didn't matter what name he wore now, and it didn't matter how much he tried to change his appearance with a long beard. Warron was still the Lord Boar, he was still a member of the phasia, and he was still a greater threat to Grawn's power than a hundred thousand Terrik Loriens would ever be.

"General Blade," Grawn said, spitting out the name as though it was a curse, "report?"

Blade snapped to a quick attention and then eased slightly.

"The perimeter is secured, and the troops are resting in shifts in case the enemy foolishly tries to attack this evening. It is not a tactic that they would normally employ, but I would put nothing past the mind of a desperate man."

Grawn scratched his chin.

"You feel Lorien is desperate now?"

Blade nodded.

"His back is to the wall, and if Zevarit falls while under his protection, many of the kingdoms that he has managed to keep under his banner will splinter. You are on the verge of victory."

Grawn fingered the hilt of his sword.

"So this is when you choose to move against me."

Blade stood firm.

"I'm not a fool, Warron," Grawn said, discarding courtesy. "On the eve of my greatest victory, you've put patrols out for an attack that only a fool would launch. The only reason you would do so is to keep the number of guards around to a minimum. You don't want anyone interfering while you take your chance. I'm sure a coward like you hoped that you would catch me sleeping. But it matters little what plans you may have made. This is my time, and none of you are strong enough to stand against me."

Grawn pulled his sword free the next moment and bounded the distance before Blade had a chance to react. The larger man feinted high and then struck low, opening a deep gash in Blade's left leg, just above the knee. A hard palm strike with his free hand gave Grawn an even larger advantage as Blade was taken off his feet and sent back first into a map table on the far side of the tent. The commotion drew the attention of the two guards that held the tent entrance, and then entered with weapons drawn. Grawn motioned for the two men to stand down, and they retained their positions and made no move to interfere. Blade managed to make his way back to his feet, but the wound in his leg made it difficult to move. In a normal fight he would have reached for the power of the Blaze, but a fight on that level would have brought the attention of the whole encampment and destroyed any chances for their plan to succeed. Grawn darted in again, his hard strike met with the haft of Blade's axe. The strain caused by the power of Grawn's strike was almost too much for Blade's weakened leg, and he fell to one knee. Grawn pulled back his blade and brought it thundering down again on the raised haft of Blade's axe. This time the blow could not be successfully blocked, and the haft shattered in Blade's hands, the tip of Grawn's blade carving a deep gaping wound down the center of Blade's chest. The tyrant stood over his defeated opponent, gloating for a moment before the final strike that would remove yet another obstacle from his path to victory. Blade looked up just in time to see the tip of a crossbow bolt erupt from Grawn's throat, blood spraying in all directions.

The shock of the strike caused Grawn's eyes to go wide, his hand flexed involuntarily, sending his sword crashing to the ground. But Grawn would not fall. He turned slowly, facing the direction the bolt had come from, only to see that one of the two guards who had entered just after the fight began was holding a crossbow. Grawn took a long step forward, his hands reaching out for the guard. As if not expecting Grawn to be on his feet, the guard hesitated for a moment, dropping the crossbow and reaching for the hilt of his sword. Grawn proved to be quicker than the soldier's draw, seizing the man by the throat and squeezing as hard as he could. The assault was short lived, as from behind Grawn, Blade recovered what was left of his axe and heaved it in Grawn's direction. The massive axe blade lodged deep in the tyrant's back, forcing him to release the soldier's neck and sending him to his knees. There he stayed, the last of his life fleeing from his kneeling form.

Dane removed the soldier's helmet and rubbed his throat, trying to alleviate the ache from the pressure Grawn had applied. He moved quickly to where Blade sat, running his hand over the wound in the smaller man's chest, channeling a little power to hasten the healing.

"For a second I didn't know if you were going to wait until he finished me off before you took your shot," Blade said, annoyance thick in his voice.

"For a second," Dane said, his voice sounding thicker and more gravelly, "I wasn't sure either."

After several moments, the wound in Blade's chest had healed enough that he could safely move without causing any more damage, and his own healing energies had been devoted to his leg while Dane worked on Blade's chest. By the time the two men were on their feet next to Grawn's fallen form, Erdric had removed the soldier's armor and stood looking at his fallen brother. Dane looked first at Grawn and then at Erdric.

"Are you ready?"

Erdric made no moves for several moments, and then slowly his features began to change. The smooth and boyish features that Erdric always favored began to shift and harden, and after a matter of moments, the hard face of the tyrant Grawn had replaced them. A few moments after that, Erdric's height and girth had adjusted accordingly, and the only missing feature was now the uniform. Dane nodded his approval.

"I'll make sure you aren't disturbed while you get into costume."

* * * * * * * * * * * *

By sundown the next day, the Kingdom of Zevarit would have earned its new moniker as the Kingdom of Blood. The forces waving the banner of the Shark fought with their typical ferocity, but also with a sense of wild abandon. Terrik Lorien's army, emboldened by tactical victories early in the day's battle pierced deep into the central lines of Grawn's army, and Terrik Lorien found himself finally face to face with the man who had proved to be the greatest threat to his dreams. Grawn had killed hundreds that day, the bodies of the dead littering the ground like broken dolls. But when the tyrant and the would-be savior crossed swords, it was as though the rest of the battlefield stopped and held its breath. In the end, it would be Terrik's sword that cut through the neck of the tyrant, sending his head flying and landing in a pool of the blood of his own victims. Despite the loss of their leader, Grawn's forces continued to fight for a while, but eventually their will and resolve were broken. Terrik Lorien had the victory he needed to keep his coalition fighting, and it garnered him the support that would eventually place him on the throne of a united Cadaria. When both armies had left the field, and night had fallen, Blade walked slowly through the carnage to meet Dane who stood looking up at the keep of Zevarit.

"It seems that Gwydeon's plan worked."

Blade snorted.

"Fat lot of good it will do. Just delays the inevitable, and I hate waiting."

The two men stood silent, so much unspoken.

"So, what will you do now?" Dane asked. "Enlist in another army? I'm sure one of them could use you."

Blade shook his head.

"No more war. Nothing to gain anymore. If I'm going to wait, I might as well find something that makes the waiting not as terrible. Think I'll go north and see what's there."

Dane nodded. Blade waited only a moment before letting his own question fill the empty air.

"What about you?"

Dane considered for a moment.

"I hear the Church of the Creator is getting pretty big in Albitonin. Thought I might cause some trouble."

Not All Who Wander

Year Three of the Just Emperor Kaitain "Dragonsbane" Lorien, Creator's Calendar Year 1870

Marlae Lorien awoke in her soft and luxuriant bed and felt the silk sheets lightly brushing against her pampered naked skin. She kept her eyes closed for several long moments, savoring the feel of the silk encasing her. The pillows that held her head were just soft enough, but not so soft that she felt as though her head had sunk into a cloud. Feeling the soft embrace of sleep beginning to flee from her muscles and joints, Marlae arched her back slowly, keeping her shoulders to the mattress and sinking her hips deeper into the featherbed. The covers pulled away from her body, sliding down from around her neck, across her chest, settling just below her breasts. The air in the room was cool, and she felt it tickle across her exposed flesh. Slowly she let her eyes begin to open and despite herself, she felt a smile come across her face. There was a soft light in the room, and it seemed to bounce off of the lightly colored walls, bringing the whole room the colors of early sunrise. Propping herself up onto her right elbow, she looked around her room and felt the smile deepen. A large wardrobe stood in the far corner of the room, the doors open, showing the collection of the finest gowns in the whole of the Empire. Hanging from one of the doors was a black and burgundy dress that once belonged to her step-mother, Dominique, but it was torn and stained with blood. A fitting monument to the end of the woman's life. From the other door hung the crown that her father once wore when he reigned as the Emperor of Cadaria. It was cracked and tarnished now, his name nearly forgotten in the shadow of the greatness that Marlae had brought to the title.

Marlae pulled herself from the bed gently and let her feet softly touch the cool floor. She stretched her toes apart, first on her left foot, and then her right before stretching once more and standing up. Her soft and curly hair cascaded down her back, long enough now to reach the small of her back. A nearly transparent robe hung from the gilded footboard, and she recovered it and slipped it gently over her shoulders, but didn't close it. Wiping the last bit of sleep from her eyes, while stretching one last time, she ambled slowly away from her bed toward the door of the warm bedchamber.

Two delicately featured female servants snapped to attention as soon as the door to the bedchamber opened. Marlae paused only a moment, inspecting their scandalous attire out of the corner of her eye before continuing on down the corridor. She suppressed a small smile when she heard to soft footsteps fall in behind her less than two paces behind. While the young women may not have looked like much, they were the deadliest of assassins that could be found in Marlae's empire, and they were not to be trifled with. At the end of the corridor, two more assassins waited, and then led Marlae out of the corridor into the large common room that waited beyond.

The room was filled with people, representatives from each of the great kingdoms, and all manner of people who wished boons from the Empress. As soon as the corridor door opened all in attendance fell to one knee. Marlae hesitated at the door, enjoying the adoration for several moments before slowly walking through the throng and ascending the dais and standing before the golden throne. She stood waiting, looking over the assemblage before perching herself on the very edge of the throne, feeling the cold hard metal against her barely covered skin. One of the attendants near the throne rose slowly and clapped her hands together sharply twice. However, the assembled mass did not respond and stayed kneeling. The attendant clapped sharply twice again, and again, there was no response from the masses. Marlae opened her mouth as though to issue a command, but her words were cut short as the massive double doors at the end of the common room opened to admit an unexpected visitor. Suddenly Marlae felt very naked, but made no move to cover herself.

Jaccob Aldora walked slowly down the thin purple carpet that led all the way to the foot of the dais. He was unarmed as was tradition when meeting the Empress in her receiving hall, but his brilliant platinum armor shimmered in the torchlight that illuminated the room. His eyes looked up at Marlae and looked her directly in the eyes, his gait confident and measured. When he reached the foot of the dais, he knelt smoothly, but never lowered his gaze to the ground as was befitting his station. He didn't wait to be bidden by the Empress or her servant before rising back to his feet. Marlae propped her elbows on the arms of the throne and steepled her fingers together in front of her face, waiting for the words of the Knight of the Flashing Blade.

"Hello, Marlae."

Marlae frowned at his voice. His tone was not formal, it was light and familiar as though they were sitting in a common inn and had been friends for many years. And yet, Marlae was the Empress of the land, and Jaccob was one of her servants. He owed his loyalty and his deference to her. The arrogance and disrespect he was showing her could not go unanswered.

"Guards," she trilled, "seize him!"

Just as when the attendant signaled for the assemblage to rise, neither the guards nor the kneeling mass made a move at the Empress's voice. Jaccob made no move to defend himself either, and simply smiled up at Marlae.

"You don't think this is real, do you?"

Marlae's eyes went wide for a moment, and then suddenly all of the kneeling people were gone. She looked quickly to the left and the right, and both her attendants and her assassins were gone. There was only Jaccob and her. Marlae's mouth went dry and she felt a cold sweat begin to break out all over her. For the first time, Jaccob took a moment to look around the common room as though he were seeing it for the first time.

"All of this is in your mind, Marlae," Jaccob said motioning to the finery of the room, "at present you're lying in a far more common than you would like bed deep in the bowels of the Heart of Stone. Luckily your lover and erstwhile protector decided that you would be better protected sleeping in your room than trying to get involved in fights that would almost certainly bring about your end. As it is, I can't see you lasting very much longer given the path you're on."

Marlae's self-consciousness suddenly began to overtake her thoughts, and she pulled the thin robe around herself hoping it would conceal far more than it was ever intended to.

"No need to worry about that, Marlae," Jaccob said, his armor suddenly gone, replace by a common shirt and pants. "First and foremost, as I said, you're dreaming. Secondly, and less impressively, I'm dead, so I doubt my first inclination would be to admire your nakedness."

Confusion painted Marlae's face, but before she could manage to form even the first of the thousand questions that had filled her mind, she found herself standing instead of sitting on her throne, and a common white nightshirt draped over her form. The throne room was gone, and instead the two stood in a rather non-descript bedroom. The only unusual thing in the room was the fact that a woman was tucked under the covers of the spacious bed. When Marlae looked closely she realized that it wasn't just any woman, it was herself.

"This is where you really are," Jaccob said after a moment, "somewhat safe and sound. Unfortunately, you won't be safe for much longer."

Marlae looked down at herself for another long moment, captivated. It wasn't like looking in a mirror, it was much more real, and she felt as though she was really seeing herself for the first time. She turned back to Jaccob, and his face had changed. He was no longer the young and vibrant man that she had briefly known. To her knowledge she had never directly spoken to Jaccob Aldora, and only knew him on sight because of his position. She hadn't even been at the ceremony that elevated him to the position of Knight of the Flashing Blade. His face was pocked and lined with age now, his features that of a fifty or sixty year old man, but his eyes had not changed. They were still filled with the youth and the vigor they had been moments earlier. His hair was now silver and hung long, to his shoulders and slicked back behind his ears. When Marlae's eyes found Jaccob's again, he smiled and moved to a small chair near the door and slowly sat down. A small grimace came to his face as he bent his knees to sit, but when he looked back up at her, his smile returned.

"We all have our destinies, Marlae," Jaccob said softly, "and there are some things that we pay for both on this side of life and on the Other Side. The more evil we do, and the more we fight out destiny, the less we are rewarded when we meet our end. I can no longer see myself as I was in life, and thank you for allowing me to be that idyllic young man again, even if only for a moment. And may I say, you should be quite proud of your own idyllic self. In our dreams we see ourselves as we would wish to be."

Finally Marlae found her voice again.

"What is this?"

Jaccob laughed.

"This is your chance, Marlae. Your chance to be more than the spoiled little girl you've always been. Even now the poison that Rhain gave you is having unintended consequences. You see, when Rhain's mother developed the poison, she didn't develop it to be used on mortals. No, it was intended to subdue those with power. Despite what you may think about yourself my little Empress-in-waiting, you do not have any real power. You wear a paper crown and sit on a make-believe throne. I'm afraid that this may be the most lucid you will be again for quite some time."

Marlae's eyes went wide.

"Am I going to die?"

Jaccob stood again, approaching her slowly and then putting his wrinkled and aged hand on the smooth skin of her cheek.

"My sweet little girl. There are far worse things than dying."

Tears began to roll down Marlae's cheeks, and her knees buckled under her. Before long, the shaking joints rebelled against her weight, and she collapsed onto the floor, unable to control her tears any longer. The sobs wrenched from her throat, and she felt in equal parts as though she were choking and hyperventilating. A feeling of euphoria flooded through her and her head swam. Suddenly Jaccob was kneeling there beside her, his features shifting from the older man back to his younger self and then varying amalgamations of the two.

"It's progressing faster than I thought it would," Jaccob said, his voice sounding very far away. "You have a chance, here and now to be more than the spoiled girl that you have always been."

He pointed at the wall. Marlae turned her head slowly, it feeling swollen and as though it were floating on a great tide. Beside where Jaccob was pointing stood a candle stand, and the light from the candle stand made a halo of light on the wall.

"Which is true, the light on the wall, or the light of the candle? Which is true, that which we show to the world, or that which we keep hidden deep inside ourselves? The brighter the light cast on the wall, the realer it may seem, so much so that people will confuse it for the truth."

Jaccob pointed again at the halo of light on the wall. There was such intensity in his motion that Marlae felt the haze clear from her mind slightly. His voice seemed closer now, but the words echoed in her ear.

"The light on the wall is the Creator. An image of a greater light that cannot be perceived. The closer we get to that reflection of light, the more we see our own reflection within it. That is why we all see the Creator as ourselves, and that is why we are seduced by the worship of Him. Deep inside, we long to worship ourselves. We long to elevate the very core of our being. I see you shudder, because it is an undesirable thought. Elevating yourself? Worshiping yourself? How can such a thing be lauded? How can such a thing be desired? All around us there are the false faces we show the world. But is that the truth? Is that any truer than the light on the wall? Do we only thirst for conflict, war, death, destruction? Do we need the pain that we live in every day? Is that all we are? Is there nothing more? To each other we talk of the want of love, and peace, and happiness, but we take up arms against one another with weapon, and word, and thought. That is the Creator's way."

Jaccob took Marlae's face in his hands, and his stare bore deep into her soul.

"Life, truth, wisdom; those things do not lie within the Creator's way. They lie somewhere in between; they lie in balance, and that is the true way of the universe. For all your flaws, Marlae, there is part of you that embodies everything that opposes the light you cast on the wall. But as long as all we see are the reflections in the darkness, as long as our eyes and our hearts cannot perceive that which is behind the reflection, this reality of war and pain that we have crafted will continue. The church tells us that the Creator made us, and that we are his children living in his image. No. The Creator was made in our image. Once his motives may have been the same as those of the universe. He may have sought only peace and balance and the furtherance of life. But our ambition, our arrogance, and our creative lusts have tainted the Creator, and so He is now a reflection of Us. There is no one true Creator any longer. We have become the Creator. We have become the foundation of our own demise. Until we understand that, until we understand that our divisions and our reflections have pulled us away from the truth of the universe, then we will never have the peace we wish for. And we will burn, when the Creator wills it."

Jaccob could feel Marlae beginning to slip away, a fog beginning to descend over her eyes. He put one finger to her forehead and enunciated slowly and clearly.

"You will have to make a choice, Marlae. Are you going to continue to be your father's daughter and a slave to everything around you, or are you going to stand up and make a difference. As of now, your fate is inextricably tied to your father. Make the most of these opportunities little girl."

As Jaccob said the final words, Marlae's form began to dematerialize before him. Within a matter of moments, she had disappeared completely, and Jaccob was left only with the slumbering form of the young woman in the bed several feet from where he knelt. Jaccob sighed and shook his head. There was so much more, so much more, and yet no more opportunities. It would have taken lifetimes to explain all of the things he learned at the point of his death. But now, the choice was Marlae Lorien's. Jaccob rose from where he knelt and moved slowly over to where Marlae slumbered and stood, looking down at her. Part of him wished that the rest of Cadaria could see the way that the spoiled girl looked when she slept, and perhaps they would not have so harsh of an opinion of her. But, no matter what true face the girl presented while she slept, the face that she showed to the world would not let anyone approach her true beauty. Suddenly Jaccob felt the presence that he had been expecting enter the room. He looked over his shoulder and saw the woman begin to materialize. With every step she took toward the bed, her form became more substantial. Her form was lithe but the muscle on her athletic form was lean and belied a strength that would match most men. Her face was without blemish, skin tan and toned, with full pink lips and charcoal colored eyes. Her straight brown hair was sun lightened and hung long to the middle of her back. She wore the clothing of a commoner, but her gait and posture were anything but common. She was however diminutive in stature, a full head and shoulders shorter than Jaccob. When she stood beside Jaccob, she placed a small delicate hand on his shoulder and he felt rather than saw her smile. The feeling of peace radiated through him, and whatever vigor had been lost by his changed condition was quickly restored. Without a word, the woman removed her hand from Jaccob's shoulder and looked down at Marlae. She leaned slightly over the bed, so that her face was mere inches from the younger woman's. Jaccob watched intently as the older woman regarded Marlae's sleeping form.

"She is not worthy," the woman said finally, her voice regal and wise. "Are you sure she is the one you wish me to bestow my gifts upon?"

Jaccob nodded slowly. His eyes suddenly filled with sadness. The woman looked up at him for only a moment and then turned her attention back to Marlae. She placed one hand on Marlae's forehead and closed her eyes. A slight glow emanated from the woman's hand, and Jaccob could feel heat radiating from the light. The light and the contact lasted for only a moment before the slight woman pulled her hand away and took a step back from the bed. When Jaccob looked at the woman, he could see that her features had aged slightly, her cheeks sunken, and her skin more pale; her form gaunt and diminished. She smiled ever so slightly and then turned to walk away the same direction from which she had appeared. Two steps from the bed, she turned back and extended her hand to Jaccob.

"There is still more to do, Jaccob. We must go."

Jaccob lingered for another moment at Marlae's bedside, noticing a small plume of white hair that had taken its place in Marlae's mane of brown. Her features too had become more pure, whatever minor imperfections that may have been there moments earlier, erased by the older woman's touch. When Jaccob finally turned away and took the older woman's hand, he noted that she had begun to regain some of her youthful appearance. She smiled and nodded to him as if she understood his thoughts.

"I am diminished, Jaccob, but not completely. My penance has yet to be served upon this world, but I am happy to have company again."

Jaccob nodded and patted her hand.

"After the gift you have given me, Temperance, how could I leave you?"

The woman smiled wider, and the two walked forward together, disappearing from the room.

* * * * * * * * * * * *

The whirling blue portal opened into the average-sized bedroom in the Heart of Stone in Albitonin, and a young man's form fell through. He was just on the edge of consciousness, and despite the best efforts of his friend at healing his rather extensive wounds; Ayden had still lost an incredible amount of blood. Emries had done his best to ensure that while the wound would not end up being instantly fatal, it would certainly kill Ayden after several hours. The crystalline sword had penetrated from Ayden's back to his front without striking any major internal organs or any other major structure. All it did was bleed, and bleed in copious amounts. Jaccob Aldora had done his best to slow the bleeding, and Ayden himself had drawn on what power that he could, but every application of power that Ayden tried only made the wound worse. Emries obviously had cooked up some new tricks over the millennia. He was a much more dangerous foe than the stories Ayden's mother and father had told him over the years.

Ayden lay on his back, running his fingers over the wound and feeling nothing but more hot blood oozing from the large gash near the center of his chest. The portal stone was supposed to take him to where his father was, but obviously in his weakened state, he was not able to control the portal properly. It shouldn't have been possible for the portal to end up off course, but Ayden's father had never said anything about going through a portal gravely wounded and barely on the edge of consciousness. Ayden would have thought that would have come up.

Ayden let his head fall back, and he felt the last grasp of death reaching for him. His breathing was already starting to become shallower and shallower, and the edge of his vision was tinged with white. Out of the corner of his eye, Ayden saw something moving. Despite his best efforts, all strength had fled from his body, and he could not even turn his head in the direction of the movement. A white haze had almost completely overridden his vision, and when the form entered his visual range fully, there was little he could make out for sure. It was a woman, that much he could make out from the long curly hair and the delicate features. She had this glow about her, almost angelic, and for a long uncertain moment, Ayden thought that he had already passed over the threshold into death. The look on her face was kind, but at the same time seemed devoid of the care and attentiveness that something deep within Ayden expected. However, that in itself was comforting as he had spent his entire life with his mother's cold yet caring eyes. He felt a warm hand on his left forearm, and felt the thin and delicate fingers lightly gripping. A moment later, the woman's other hand found its way to the wound in his chest. Suddenly, Ayden felt self-conscious, and wanted to lift his hand to pull her fingers away. Blood continued to ooze from the wound, but the pain had begun to ebb. The disorientation from the loss of blood began to fade and Ayden's vision started to clear. The woman's features started to become sharper, more in focus, and his eyes widened at the realization. Leaning over him was not an angel at all, but the infamous rebel empress, Marlae Lorien. However, there was something different about her. Something that made Ayden's original thoughts of an angel more fitting.

Over the next few moments, the pain began to ebb even more, and Ayden found more and more of his strength returning. Before long he was able to lift his right arm and he brought his hand to meet Marlae's above the wound that was quickly sealing. The flow of blood had ceased, and the skin began to slowly mend, leaving only the barest scar. Marlae turned her gaze away from the remains of the wound and turned her attention to Ayden's face. Their eyes met, and a simple and slight smile curled her lips. Though the smile did not curl her lips much, it did reach her eyes. Suddenly her eyes rolled back in her head and she collapsed forward across him. Her hair fell across his chest, neck, and face, and Ayden took a long deep breath, inhaling the scent of lavender. Despite himself, Ayden pulled his arm free of Marlae's grip and first brushed her hair out of his face, and then lay there for a long time, stroking her hair. It took only a few moments before Ayden's eyelids became too heavy to ignore. His eyes finally closed, and he joined the delicate empress in peaceful slumber.

Sons and Daughters

Year Three of the Just Emperor Kaitain "Dragonsbane" Lorien,
Creator's Calendar Year 1870

The Citadel of the Dark Gods was a structure that had stood proudly under the veil of darkness that perpetually covered the continent of Mythryn for almost two thousand years. Its proud blackened marble spires reached up to scrape the sky, and its trio of central domes was crafted with glass so that the sky could be seen clearly from most places in the palace. It was an architectural miracle that could only have been crafted by the application of power wielded by the Dark Gods. Gwydeon, Midarin, and Pike had spent months hewing stone and perfecting the framework while Diana and Aryx built the miraculous glass domes that would be lifted into place in the last days of the construction. Every member of the Dark Gods had something to offer in the palace's construction; all that was except for Wolf and Lissa. The fall from the heavens had done something to Wolf, and when they landed on Espre, he would not be awoken by any means. Lissa was early into her adjustment into parenthood when the Fall occurred, and so between tending to her ailing husband and ensuring that she could transition into raising her children alone, there was little that she had to offer the rest of the Dark Gods by way of support. In many ways, she felt like a burden to her family, but Diana and Midarin did their best to support her. But that was eighteen hundred years ago, and the explosions that were triggered deep in the core of the Citadel of the Dark Gods had caused the massive structure to being to crumble. The great glass domes had shattered under the force of the explosion, and at least one of the tall spires had fallen. Now though, Lissa was able to lend something to the construction of the palace, and more than that, her husband was as well. Naturally Lissa could not shake the thought that the timing of his revival from wherever he had been was beyond ominous, but there were many things about Wolf's nature that complicated matters.

When Lissa had met Wolf for the first time all those millennia ago on Onea, the war between the brothers Emries and Halicon was well into its first century of escalating conflict. Unbeknownst to Lissa, at least until several hours after their meeting, it was Wolf's uncle and father that had played crucial roles in the defeat of the Nightmare of Men, Shau-ling in the second generation of the Prophecies of the *Coromor*. According to the prophecies, Wolf was supposed to be the hero of the third generation, the one whose hand would be responsible for Shau-ling's defeat, as his uncle's had. But something in the second generation had caused Emries to change the rules. Perhaps Emries was afraid of the Ranthall family, and perhaps in the long run it was better for Wolf that he was able to make his own path. As it was, he became the fulcrum for a battle of a different kind. Because of the actions of the phase Basille, Wolf was granted powers that never should have been available to him, and that action caused the Creator to split Onea in two, a reality of light and a reality of darkness. In the light reality, Wolf existed and fought valiantly to beat back the darkness. However, in the dark mirror reality, Wolf's evil reflection, Draven, a phase in the service of Shau-ling, existed. The link between them was Basille, and Lissa's suspicions about Basille's involvement in Wolf's catatonia were confirmed when Wolf woke and Basille spoke through him. There were still so many questions that needed answers, but Wolf had either been unwilling or unable to provide any of them. For the past several days, he had spent most of his time working alone on the spire that had collapsed. The oldest of their twin daughters, Mirana had gone to work with him for brief periods. She was just returning from one of her attempts to assist the stranger that was her father as Lissa was just lifting a section of the ceiling back into place.

Of her parents, there was no doubt that Mirana had a stronger resemblance to her father than to her mother. Like her father, she had thick dark brown hair and clear blue eyes. She kept her bangs short in the front and slightly feathered, while the layers became longer as they moved back away from her face. At its longest, her hair hung to just below the level of her shoulders. Her strong chin and thinner lips were certainly characteristics that came from her father, but her nose was more like that of her mother with her nostril ridges a little higher and broader. Despite the work that they were doing, Mirana chose to wear what was her typical attire. The robe-like dress was white with a pattern like reptilian scales of silver shimmering through it. It was held tight at her waist with a broad gold belt, and flared open from the middle of her stomach and widened to her throat, leaving most of her upper chest exposed. Her breasts were completely concealed, and even when the breeze caused the golden central edges of the gown to move, the flesh-colored body-stocking that she wore beneath it allowed for no indecency. The dress stopped mid-thigh, and beneath it she wore a pair of her father's black pants. The sleeves of the dress were long and came to a wide cuff at the wrist that flared like a bell. On her right thumb she wore a wide darkened steel ring that had once belonged to her grandmother, Elwyne, a gift that Wolf had wanted his first born daughter to have. Lissa could always tell that her daughter was deep in thought when she would bring her hand to her chin and spin the ring around her thumb while staring off into the distance.

Lissa turned to face her daughter, and saw that there was a streak of dirt on her sleeve and a slight tear. The fabric around the area was tinged with red.

"Everything alright?"

There was no real concern in Lissa's voice. They were Dark Gods after all, and there was little that could do permanent harm to them. The girl blinked her cool blue eyes slowly and then spoke in a clear proud voice. The voice always reminded Lissa of her mother's voice, and Diana had taken great pride in teaching the girl how to read and write in the earliest years of her life.

"Father has finished rebuilding the spire," Mirana said, her voice smooth and proud, "but I think we both misjudged the strength of the structures around it. There was a collapse, and father had to shield me from a heavy piece of stone. He's working on repairing the surrounding structures now."

Lissa took hold of her daughter's arm and wiped some of the dirt away. Whatever cut had been below the tear in the fabric had already healed, and there was no trace of it left.

"And did you tell Wolf that we were ready to put the first dome back into place?"

Mirana pulled her arm away from her mother softly and brought her hand up, spinning the ring slowly around her thumb.

"He said he would come as soon as you wished."

Lissa nodded her head softly and turned to look over her shoulder.

"Liara? Where are we on those last pieces of glass?"

The youngest daughter emerged through the door to one of the inner chambers, two large panes of glass floating behind her. Like her sister, Liara was dressed in her typical fashion, an outfit more suited for the fineries of court rather than a construction project on a ruined palace. How the girl was forming glass in that dress was beyond Lissa. But then again, Lissa had never felt comfortable in a noblewoman's gown, and felt like a pretender in anything but her warrior-cut shirt and pants. If Mirana was the spitting image of her father, Liara was certainly a younger version of her mother. Flowing rivulets of red hair cascaded down her back almost to the level of her waist with two clusters that hung uncooperatively at the left side of her face and occasionally into her bright green eyes. No matter how many times she smoothed back the rebellious knot, it would make its way back to it precarious perch. While her skin was not overly pale, the brightness of her hair made her skin look more white than it would look ordinarily. The dress Liara wore was purple in color, but it was closer to red in hue. The bodice of the dress was tight, but covered her fully, leaving her throat and shoulders exposed. From the top of the bodice, a strand of antique slightly yellowed lace stretched across the gap to her arm and covered her upper arm in three intricate layers. The actual sleeve of the dress began at the elbow with a bunched sleeve that hugged her elbow and then flared wide, and by the time it reached her wrist, the sleeve was wide enough that it could have encircled her waist with room to spare. The lower half of the dress was almost completely comprised of a series of layered scalloped ruffles that continued to the ground. At her waist was a braided golden belt. If one didn't know that the two women were sisters, most would not have guessed that Liara and Mirana were even related except for some slight similarity in facial structure. The only identical feature the two women shared was their wide and intoxicating smile.

"These two are finished, mother. I have one more to form, and we should be ready."

Liara's head snapped in the direction of a chamber deeper in the palace, and the next moment a blade of lightning had formed in her hand.

"Portal."

The word came from her mouth softly, and the next moment Mirana had disappeared from view. Like Lissa, Mirana had learned to utilize her powers in a decidedly offensive capacity. One of the more unique ways that Mirana had learned to apply her abilities was to wrap ambient light around herself to make her functionally invisible. The ability was learned in Mirana's youngest days when the sisters would play hide and seek in the Citadel. However, what Mirana did not learn until many years later was that despite her invisibility, Liara always knew where her sister was. From her earliest days, Liara was possibly the most astutely aware of all of the Dark Gods. It was as though she could see and feel the use of power in a different way than any of the others. She could feel portals forming farther away and sooner than anyone else, and she had the uncanny ability to mimic any use of power than she had seen or felt. However, this perception did not lend itself to innovation. Liara may have been able to mimic any talent, but she was not possessed of enough control to create new techniques.

Carefully, Liara let the panes of glass gently hover to the ground, and subtly wrapped herself in a skin-tight shield of lightning that flickered softly. She was certainly not her sister's match in the martial, but she certainly knew enough to defend herself from any attack that would come. Lissa's hands were filled with fire the next moment, and the three women waited for the source of the portal to emerge from the darkness of the ruins. When the first of the forms emerged, Lissa relaxed for a moment, but that ease ended the moment that she saw that half of Alderin's arm was missing. Lissa ran to her brother's side, and Mirana reappeared and was also there. Lissa was so focused on Alderin, that she didn't see Darrien until Liara's gasp filled her ears. Hanging limp in Darrien's arms was the half-naked form of Tess Annis, covered in mud and gore. A moment later, Camille Renar limped into the room, her stark and beautiful white wings hanging limply from her back, and huge gashes on her stomach and sides mending themselves slowly.

"What the hell happened?"

Alderin looked up into Lissa's eyes.

"Hell would be the right word for it."

Darrien bristled a bit at Alderin's words, but then knelt down slowly and placed Tess's limp body on the floor. Liara recovered a cushion from one of the chairs that was still overturned from the explosion and brought it over to put under the girl's head.

"We went to Albitonin to recover Tess and Camille as father ordered," Pike's daughter said wiping a cold sweat from her brow. "As soon as we arrived we were ambushed by Talisia Masile and some man who called himself Lucian. We were able to fight them off. But Alderin was wounded by a dagger that Lucian had. Before either of us fully recovered from the fight, Tess just blasted out a section of the wall and walked out with Camille in her arms. Then things just went out of control, and I'm not really sure what actually happened. All I know is that Tess wasn't thinking straight because she attacked Alderin and I. Then a Knight of the Flashing Blade showed up."

Darrien's dark eyes flashed. Liara put her hand up and motioned in the direction of one of the opened doors, but no one noticed her.

"I'm pretty sure that Tess killed him."

"Good," a man's voice rang from the open doorway that Liara was facing, "we were going to take the fight to the Cadarians as it was. The fact that my daughter killed one of their champions couldn't make things any better."

Pike Rhuiden emerged from the shadows and covered the distance in several long strides. He knelt beside his youngest daughter, holding the back of his hand to her forehead for a long moment as if checking for a fever and listening to her breathe. When he looked up from Tess, he put his hand under Darrien's chin, turned her head from one side to the other and then back to the center looking into her clear eyes. He barely gave a glance to Alderin or Camille before shifting back around and setting his gaze on Lissa.

"What happened here? Where is Sadrina?"

Lissa fumbled for a moment with her words, not sure what to say, but it was Liara's voice that hit the air next.

"It was Ivan Quicksilver. He used some kind of arcane technique and ignited the bonding material that held the stones together in the throne room. Once that room ignited, he created a portal and took Sadrina. The explosions spread through the palace quickly and did an incredible amount of damage. We've been working trying to repair the damage and keep the place intact when everyone started to return."

Pike's eyes never left Lissa's and his face began to color with the fury that was building inside of him. A moment later, his axe was in his hands, and he was back on his feet and turning back the direction from which he came. The portal snapped into being the next moment.

"That bastard Kaitain has gone too far this time. This ends now."

"Pike, wait!"

Camille's cry fell on deaf ears. Pike was already through the portal and it was winking closed. A moment after Pike had gone, Wolf emerged from the darkness in the direction of the recently reconstructed spire. There was no way that he couldn't have heard everything that had transpired over the past few minutes, and Lissa was confident that he remained in the darkness so that he would not encounter Pike.

"Well, that was expected."

Wolf knelt down at Tess's side, and smiled up at Darrien.

"She'll be fine," he said, certainty filling his voice. "She just needs some rest. She's expelled more power than she ever has, and it's going to take her body some time before it adjusts."

Wolf was back to his feet the next moment, and he looked first at Alderin and then to Camille. There was a deep sigh that escaped his lips before he looked back down at Darrien.

"Tess's room was in the wing that wasn't impacted by the explosion. Maybe you should take her back there and make sure she's comfortable. You won't be able to stay here long though. The Citadel is no longer safe, and we need to relocate. Once Tess is awake or at the very least strong and steady enough to travel, you'll take her to Jerrard."

Darrien opened her mouth to protest, thinking that she was being excluded from something, but the words died in her mouth when she saw the look in Wolf's eyes. The concern that he had not only for Tess but for Darrien was clear. As if feeling the hesitation in the woman, Wolf smiled and placed a reassuring hand on Darrien's shoulder.

"I know you want to be charging into Aldere right there at your father's side, Darrien, but you know as well as I do, that if we're going to get out of this alive, we can't follow Pike into the heart of the fire. All we can hope for is that he doesn't get himself killed for no reason. Don't worry, you'll get your taste of this war soon enough."

Darrien's eyes fell, but she nodded. Wordlessly, she gathered up Tess's limp form and carried her in the direction of the bedrooms in the far wing. Alderin started to move in that direction, but Wolf caught him by what was left of his arm. Alderin watched Darrien go, and it was clear from the look in his eyes, that he didn't like being kept from her.

"Do you want to tell me what happened?"

Lissa asked the question before Wolf could take the initiative.

"I'm not sure," Alderin said finally. "Like Darrien said, everything was crazy. Tess was insane, and she sent this wave of power out of herself that just, I don't know how to say it, unraveled everything in its path. When it touched my fingers, there was pain, but the pain faded so quickly I wonder if the pain was in my mind and not actually happening. The best I can explain it, my arm simply was ripped out of existence."

Wolf nodded gravely.

"I need to be with Darrien."

Lissa hugged her brother for a brief moment before letting him pass between her and Wolf. While Lissa's eyes followed Alderin as he left the room, Wolf's full attention had turned to the wounded woman that supported herself on Mirana's shoulder.

"Seems you have an interesting tale to tell," Wolf said after a moment.

This seemed to draw Mirana's ire, as her face bunched up and her nose twitched slightly.

"She needs to rest, father. You sent Tess to bed, surely you can wait until Camille recovers before you start asking her questions."

Liara was there the next moment, placing her hand on Wolf's shoulder.

"Yes father, please let her rest."

Wolf opened his mouth to speak, when Camille pulled herself back to a standing position, no longer supported by Mirana. A moment later, the wings that had hung slack from her back pulled themselves into a more proper and controlled position, and though she was obviously in pain, Camille held herself at her full height.

"No," Camille said proudly. "Your father's right. There is danger coming, the likes of which we haven't seen since the civil war in the heavens. The Voice is back, and he had taken the body of Gregor Quicksilver. The Will is also on the move, and manifested in Albitonin. They both openly struck at Aerith. It's clear that the Creator intends to remove him from the game now that he had recovered his powers from Evan."

Wolf nodded.

"It was only a matter of time I suppose. Aerith can't be allowed to stay on the loose if the Creator is going to get his ideological war that he is craving so badly. Once he strikes at Aerith, he'll strike down everyone that has a connection to Aerith, including his children, Sabrina, and everyone else with a direct connection."

Lissa's face was blank.

"How do you know Aerith has children?"

Wolf turned to face his wife and his mouth widened into a smile.

"I seem to know a surprising amount about what has been going on in my absence. And I'll tell you something else; I'm not the only one."

Wolf's gaze fell back to Camille.

"Am I?"

Lissa could practically hear the winged woman grinding her teeth. Finally, as if she were trying to prevent herself from doing so, her head nodded ever so slightly.

"As much as I'm sure you would like to stay with Tess," Wolf said a somber tone coming into his voice, "I think you know why you need to be as far away from her as possible right now. Whatever this new power is that is taking hold of her, it seems to be tied to the way that she feels about you. Am I right?"

A slight color came to Camille's cheeks.

"You know she's been in love with you for years," Liara said breaking the uncomfortable silence.

"Lee!"

Mirana's shrill irritation was felt as much as it was heard.

"I'm not telling anything that everyone with eyes doesn't see, Mir. You'd have to be dead or ignorant not to see the way Tess's eyes follow Camille everywhere she goes. And you can't tell me that that is an innocently admiring look in her eyes either."

Camille put her hand up and ended the conversation.

"Where do you want me to go?" Camille asked.

Wolf's expression remained blank.

"I think you know who needs you right now. Aerith moved too soon. The whole wager is at risk. And to make matters worse, Sabrina has overstepped her place, and has made herself into a very inviting target for Seraphina and for Talisia."

Camille nodded.

"And what should I tell my mother?"

Wolf shook his head and spread his hands.

"As though I could tell your mother anything that she would listen to under the circumstances. Just tell her that if things are moving the way they should, we need to rally everyone in Rashaleb. We're going to find allies there we never expected. Lissa and the girls will meet you there, after we level this place. The Citadel will not stand as a target for the Cadarians any longer. They have to think that we can strike them from anywhere at any time if this war is going to turn back into the level playing field it has been for this long."

Camille nodded, squeezed Mirana's shoulder for a brief moment, and then turned toward the doorway, letting a portal form quickly. After she was through, Lissa put both of her hands on her hips and stared into Wolf's eyes.

"You have exactly three seconds to start explaining yourself."

Wolf's grim expression was not what Lissa expected. The threat in her tone was always a playful reminder between the married couple that secrets were not welcome in their relationship. This time though, Wolf's eyes flashed with a power that Lissa knew. He would not be bullied into revealing anything before he was ready. When that occurred, Lissa knew it was the gravest of circumstances.

"As soon as Darrien, Alderin, and Tess leave, take the girls and meet up with Jerrard. He's going to need help soon if what Pike is about to do has the impact I think it will. Kaitain's only next steps are to start directly seizing control of the kingdoms that are still loyal to him to ensure that no more slip into rebellion. That doesn't bode well for our friend, and we're going to need as many footholds in his domain as we can get when the time comes. This war is going to be finished within the borders of Cadaria."

Lissa nodded, waiting for the other shoe to drop. But it was Liara who's voice came next.

"Father, a portal is about to form outside the Citadel."

Wolf looked at Liara and nodded.

"I was beginning to wonder when he was going to show up."

Wolf returned his gaze to his wife.

"You know what to do. I'll meet you when I can."

He reached out, took Lissa's hand in his, kissed the back of her hand softly, and then simply wasn't there. Lissa and her two daughters were left looking at the empty air before setting upon the task of undoing all of the work they had been dedicated to. The Citadel would fall, but they would be the cause of it this time.

The Masks We Choose to Wear

Year Three of the Just Emperor Kaitain "Dragonsbane" Lorien, Creator's Calendar Year 1870

Kaitain Lorien slumped into the chair in his chambers in the Inn of Coventry and felt the cold steel of the mask itch against his deformed face. He would not allow the deformity to overpower him and give in to the phantom discomfort. So he sat, fire radiating through one side of his face, gaze transfixed on all that remained of the once Sacred Weapon of the Kingdom of Hedorah, Temperance. The shock had been palpable in the common room of the inn, most unsure how to react to the destruction of a weapon that had been the symbol of one of the great kingdoms for almost two thousand years. A riot nearly broke out, and Korin Melcab and the rest of the Imperial Guard had to work diligently to quell the crowd. However, threats of forceful conscription had been enough to cause most of the disgruntled crowd to make their way home. Jaccob's body was also quickly removed, and though he may have been a traitor, it certainly was not advisable to display his body as such. Kaitain left the matter for Korin to deal with, and he was assured that the Captain of the Imperial Guard would ensure that Jaccob would find his final rest to be a very brief and very hot encounter.

Sitting there in his chair, Kaitain was lost in many conflicting thoughts. What was strangest to him was that he was neither concerned nor worried about the reason for the shattering of the Sacred Weapon. All Kaitain really concerned himself with was to turn this incident to the best advantage possible. Leveraging the shattering of the Sacred Weapon had many ramifications, but with the splintering of the empire, Kaitain could think of only one possible course of action. He had just begun to pen a series of letters and orders when there was a knock at the door. Kaitain ignored the knock at first. When the knock came again, Kaitain put the quill down into the ink well and looked up at the door, and a thought came to him. He knew there had been a knock before, but had he ignored it, or had he simply not heard it, or did he only imagine the knock. Through the door, he knew that Geoffry Aramour was there, and perhaps that knowledge had caused Kaitain to perceive a knock that never occurred. Kaitain waited another moment, and as he expected, another knock came at the door.

"Enter, Geoffry."

The door opened slowly, and Geoffry Aramour poked his head tentatively through the opening. If he had been disturbed by the identification without announcing himself he did an admirable job of keeping it off his face.

"Alise Modrall awaits your leisure, my Emperor."

Kaitain looked down at the papers in front of him and then back up at Geoffry.

"Allow my daughter to enter," Kaitain said, his cold voice escaping the mask. "And once my audience with Alise has ended, I will see Dominique."

Geoffry bowed.

"And Geoffry," Kaitain said, allowing more steel to enter his voice, "I do not expect to wait long."

Geoffry bowed again, and lingered in the bow for longer than was normal, and Kaitain chalked it up to Geoffry's need to control the emotions of the moment. Finally the assassin straightened up and turned without letting his eyes find Kaitain's again. The door closed behind Geoffry, and Kaitain felt a smile curl his lips. Kaitain was enjoying the new level of respect and power that fear was bringing him. It was a different sensation than the simple application of power had brought him. His reverie was cut short, as the door opened smoothly admitting a new presence to the room. At first, Kaitain was surprised that he did not feel Alise coming, but then he was more than comforted in the fact that Alise was totally loyal to his will and would never have to be counted among the threats to his reign. The young woman moved with subtle grace, her footfalls making no sound, and not even her light white blood-stained dress made noise as it shifted with her movements. Her posture was tall and straight, her porcelain white shoulders totally exposed to the soft and subdued light of the room. Her light curly hair cascaded across her bare shoulders and her yellow eyes held a nearly permanent look of disdain. Even though she was entering an audience with the Emperor of Cadaria, she was still armed. The three pronged razor claws attached to leather gauntlets that started just below her knuckles ended just above her elbows. The weapons were graceful extensions of Alise's lithe yet powerful frame. After a moment, Alise bowed ever so slightly, not enough to show deference to someone of Kaitain's elevated position. When she straightened, Kaitain smiled behind his mask.

"I have come as commanded, father."

Kaitain regarded the young woman for another long moment. In every posture she was the antithesis of Kaitain's former daughter, Marlae. Where Marlae would whine and use her power and influence to make things the way she wished, and show impatience in the process, Alise was dutiful, reserved, and infinitely patient. Alise would never rise to become anything more than a servant and assassin, but then she would never thirst for more than the opportunity to be that servant. In time however, there would be no need for her services, and Alise knew as well as Kaitain did, when that time came she would lay down her life at his command.

"I understand you failed to take care of my familial issue."

Alise's eyes narrowed slightly, but she may no other outward show of annoyance.

"As Geoffry no doubt informed you, father, there was a complication. Geoffry was able to arrange for the personal guard of the Prince and Princess to be bribed into dereliction of his duty, but he was unable to account for a certain troublesome interloper. Geoffry's best assassin was effectively dismantled, and his sword taken. The man was quite adept at concealing not only his tracks, but the tracks of the untrained princess and the wounded prince."

Kaitain looked down at the papers in front of him, and then back up at Alise.

"So you would characterize this man…"

"Wynne," Alise interrupted.

Kaitain let some annoyance creep into his tone.

"You would characterize this Wynne as a threat to my throne?"

Alise frowned, the movement causing her full lips to thin slightly.

"Were this man motivated to do so, he would be a significant threat. But I have the taste of his blood. There is nowhere on this world that he can go that I will not find him. His skills are impressive, that much is certain, but he is no match for me."

Kaitain tilted his head slightly.

"Then why did you not defeat him when you had the chance."

Kaitain saw Alise ball her fists and heard the knuckles crack.

"The hunt, father, is not about killing the prey. If it were, there would be no animals left in this world, and the dragons would no longer be a threat. The hunt is understanding your prey, why it moves and when. How it fights and what its strengths and weaknesses are. Anyone can kill, not everyone can hunt. If a killer could have accomplished this task, then Geoffry's assassin would not be dead and your familial issue would be taken care of. I will hunt this man, and I will ferret out all of his secrets, and then, my dear father, he will be dealt with permanently."

It was then that Alise's hands finally relaxed and blood flowed quickly back into her stark white fingers. Kaitain absently nodded and then shuffled through the papers lying on the table before him. After a moment he recovered the piece of paper he was looking for and lifted it from the table. When he read the words that he himself had written, his voice again took on an ominous and cold tone.

"The Knights of the Flashing Blade have been an institution of this Empire since the days of its founding. However, it has become clear that the Knights of the Flashing Blade have become too powerful and derelict in their duties. As evidenced by the loss of the Sacred Weapon of the Flying Kingdom of Hedorah, the Knights of the Flashing Blade have lost their way. This has been proven not only by their failure to protect the life of the Emperor and the capitol of the Empire, but the traitorous and rebellious acts of members of their order. The one member of the Knights of the Flashing Blade that has shown true dedication to her sacred trust had been rewarded for her actions. In the judgment of the Just Emperor of Cadaria, the remaining members of the Knights of the Flashing Blade shall be stripped of their positions. The Sacred Weapons shall be recovered and returned to Imperial custody until such time as the rebellion is put down, and worthy successors can be found to revive the tradition and status that the Knights of the Flashing Blade should represent. Further, those currently holding the post of Knight of the Flashing Blade are to be considered traitors to the throne and are subject to immediate execution."

Kaitain regarded the paper for another moment and then placed it back onto the table before looking back up at Alise.

"You do understand what this means, don't you?"

Alise blinked slightly in response.

"It means that Geoffry's assassins will be quite busy for some time."

Kaitain brought his fist down hard on the table.

"I didn't have you made to be insolent!"

Alise didn't react to the Emperor's outburst. She knew what she was, and that would never be in doubt.

"What is your command, my Emperor?"

The simple phrase was enough to temporarily deaden the Emperor's fury. From the table he recovered five sealed parchments each affixed with the seal of the Imperial Family as well as Kaitain's personal seal.

"Deliver these into the dead hands of the five Knights of the Flashing Blade that still count their loyalties to the rightful Emperor. Start with the supposed Serpentine Knight Vallic Ultiv. I have been told that his ineffectual healing is to blame for the length in which I was trapped in that hellish dream. Let him be the first to feel the justice of the Empire reigning down upon him."

Alise bowed deeper this time, and then received the orders. She snapped her fingers, and a swirling red portal appeared to her right. Before stepping through, she hesitated and turned back to her father.

"And Vallic's companion? What of her?"

Kaitain seemed to ponder for a moment, and then looked back down at the table and recovered his quill.

"No witnesses. I want no one left alive that could claim vengeance in the future."

Alise nodded and then stepped through the portal. It closed only a moment later, leaving Kaitain alone. He knew that Geoffry was loitering nearby, his nature as a spy and assassin almost overriding his desire for self-preservation. It was arrogance to think that Alise would allow Geoffry to hear anything that was said in the room, and it was presumptive to think that the Emperor would allow him to exist knowing more information than the Emperor wished him to know. It was becoming clearer that Geoffry was rapidly becoming a liability that would have to be removed soon. Whatever usefulness the man had served before Kaitain's tortured slumber, it was clear he would only now be an impediment to the future. Perhaps that would become true of the whole of the Shadow Guild. But that was trouble for another time. As it was, the Shadow Guild held no power that the Emperor did not give it, and Geoffry could be easily exposed and discredited if the need arose. He would only be an irritant until the greater threats had been removed from Kaitain's path.

"Bring the Empress now, Geoffry."

There were only the barest moments of hesitation before the door to the Emperor's room opened. When Kaitain looked up, Dominique Lorien was attempting to stand tall, but her shoulders hunched slightly, and she seemed to have so much weight riding upon her. She was dressed in her maroon and black dress, but whatever sex appeal the dress normally evoked, her posture did not bespeak the confidence that she normally exuded. The way the fabric was draped upon her, it looked more like a burial gown. Guards flanked her, and though she was no threat to run or fight, the guards looked nervous. With a wave of the Emperor's hand, the guards bowed slightly and retreated from the room. The husband and wife looked at each other for a long moment, and finally Kaitain motioned in the direction of the chair that sat opposite the low table that he was working on. Dominique moved gracefully from the doorway and took the seat across from Kaitain. She sat on the edge of the seat and rested her hands delicately in her lap. For a long few minutes Kaitain said nothing, he continued to work on the piece of paper in front of him. He brought the quill up after signing his name and regarded the words printed there before setting the quill back in the ink well.

"Dominique," Kaitain said finally, his voice even and cool, "while I cannot agree with many of the actions you have taken while ruling Cadaria in my stead, I also cannot call any of those actions treasonous. You have ruled wisely, and perhaps with too much restraint. When the rebellion began in Albitonin, you should have acted more swiftly in dealing with them. Though your decision to send a spy with my daughter was well played. And perhaps by letting Marlae leave to go to Albitonin, you have spared me a threat later in my rule. Even more surprising was your decision to declare Seraph Kore a traitor to the Throne. I was disappointed though that you stopped short of ordering his execution. Your reputation is that of someone who chooses to display mercy at all costs. In the days to come, that will be a liability."

At this he looked up and met his wife's eyes.

"The Imperial lands are no place for you to be, my dear Dominique. And while I cannot have you killed, and I cannot dissolve our union because of your popularity, I will take every opportunity from this point forward to crush your reputation and everything that you think you have gained while I have been asleep. The people see you as some kind of savior, and those that do not lust after you would follow you because of your kindness and your generosity. I have already stripped away your protection by promoting Chelsea Zarova, and it will only be a matter of time before she is dealt with in the manner in which she most deserves. And once you take up your new post, it will only be a matter of time before someone finds their way to make you pay as well."

Dominique felt the fire burning her from the inside out, but she didn't allow her rage or her hate to manifest on her face or in her eyes. She simply bowed her head slightly as a show of respect and deference. It was time for a calculated gamble.

"And how," she said smoothly and softly, "could I find my way back into the good graces of the Emperor, and back into the trust of my husband?"

She nearly choked on the word husband, but was able to keep her voice even and calm. Kaitain had lowered his eyes back to his work and stopped just short of retrieving his quill from the ink well. For all Dominique knew, he could have been drafting the order that would end her life, or Chelsea's for that matter. It was not something that she wanted to think about, but death was staring her in the face as surely as if Kaitain was holding a dagger. He brought his hand back and then reached down to a bundle that sat just under his chair. He picked it up smoothly and put it onto his lap and then looked back up at Dominique.

"Is it truly your wish to act as my Empress? Is it truly your wish to remain my wife, knowing what is coming?"

There was a shudder than ran through Dominique that she could not suppress. She saw Kaitain's eyes glaring out from under the mask, hard as steel and boring into her like a knife intent on carving her heart out. If there had ever been gentleness within the man, it had been destroyed by whatever had waited for him in his slumber. There was no love possible in his heart any longer, no emotion of any kind that could be considered positive or tender. He cared for nothing save his own destiny, and there would be nothing that would stand in the way of that destiny, certainly not some peasant girl from a small farm town in the countryside. If Kaitain was willing to execute a member of the Knights of the Flashing Blade in full view of everyone on the slimmest of charges, what hope did Dominique have of escaping a similar fate? Dominique cleared her throat and put as much steel into her voice as she felt she could manage.

"When I agreed to become your wife and the Empress, I knew that there would be risks, and I knew that there would be responsibilities. When I was thrust into the position of having to make decisions I felt were in the best interests of the Empire and in keeping with the example that you set, I did what I felt was right, and I make no apologies for the manner in which I conducted myself. And now, my Emperor, that you have returned from your slumber, my intention is to continue to act in the best interests of the Empire, and I will do so at your direction. My wish is not to supplant you as leader of this Empire, and had I wished it, I could have followed Marlae into the Rebellion, or simply started my own. Or perhaps I could have found a loyal vassal like Chelsea to act against you directly and end your life while you slumbered. It is not out of the realm of possibility that I could have found one of the members of the Shadow Guild to end your life and make it look as though you had finally succumbed to the poison. But I did none of those things, as they are not in my nature. While I may not agree with your policies, and they would not be mine were I given the choice, I have given my word to be your wife and your fellow in the ruling of this Empire. And so, if you are asking me that given the choice would I follow your commands and do my duty as your wife and your Empress, then the answer is yes."

Kaitain nodded, and found himself quite impressed with how much Dominique had changed in the time that she had been forced to adapt to the pressures of responsibility. She had become stronger and more assured of her place in the world, but there was still naivety about her. She was still an innocent in a world of thugs and murderers. Either she would shed the innocent doe-eyed nature of hers, or she would be devoured by the wolves like all the others that underestimated the demands of power. Either way, Kaitain would not shed a tear.

"Very well, Dominique," Kaitain said finally, "I will accept that you do mean what it is that you are saying, and that your intentions are only to follow my orders and do what is best for the Empire. To that end, I have an assignment for you. As you no doubt have become aware, I have outlawed the worship of the Creator within the bounds of the continent of Cadaria, and I have also set steps in motion to permanently, and forcefully if necessary, disband the Church of the Creator within this empire. Additionally, you are no doubt aware of the death of the Topaz Knight, Jaccob Aldora and the destruction of the Sacred Weapon Temperance."

Dominique nodded.

"Good. There have been many wild speculations that have cropped up over the last few hours about the reasons and motivations behind the destruction of the Sacred Weapon, and while I would have taken the opportunity to squelch them at one point in my rule, I have decided that the uncertainly actually benefits us. And so, I am going to issue a declaration that the breaking of the Sacred Weapon, Temperance is a sign that the Flying Kingdom of Hedorah has been hopelessly tainted by the Church of the Creator, and can be no longer trusted to govern itself as a great kingdom of the Cadarian Empire. To that end, the ruling council and royalty of Hedorah will be removed from their positions, and Hedorah will become an Imperial Province in the same way as Aldere is. You, my good wife, will be dispatched to oversee the transition of Hedorah to an Imperial protectorate, as well as the dismantling of the current power structure. There has been a great deal of graft and vice in the Flying Kingdom, and it will be your task to stamp it out."

Dominique frowned, and for a moment, Kaitain interpreted the gesture as dissatisfaction with the task, until such point as she began to speak.

"I understand why you would take these steps," she said slowly but calmly, "but you must understand that my gentle touch will not be enough to quell many of the problems within Hedorah. As you say, the practice of bribery and usury is well known within the power structure there from the royalty all the way through the Flying Guard. Stamping out all of the issues there will take political cunning as well as force of will to bring the Flying Guard in line. I'm afraid I am going to need someone with a military background to assist me with this."

Dominique could feel Kaitain's scowl even if she couldn't see it.

"I'm afraid many of the military assets that I have at my disposal are not available to assist you. You're just going to have to make the best of the situation and find allies there that you feel you can trust."

Dominique smiled her best smile.

"I know that you have promoted Chelsea to the position of Lady of Saldarine, but in doing so you did not remove the current power structure, you simply decreed that they would not report directly to her. Could Chelsea not fulfill that role in absentia, the reports of the royals sent to her in Hedorah? Surely they are competent enough for that during the securing of Hedorah?"

Kaitain crushed a piece of paper in his hand, and let it fall to the table. His eyes burned, and Dominique could practically feel the heat radiating from them. But after a moment, the glare softened, as though he had thought of something.

"Very well, my Empress," Kaitain said, his voice filled with contempt. "But if there is any delay from Saldarine in the commission of my orders, or I feel for one moment that they could become disloyal, I will march the Imperial Guard into the capital, have all of them executed, and absorb Saldarine as an Imperial protectorate as well. And be assured that your precious Chelsea will be the first to feel the knife at her throat."

Dominique nodded.

"But for the time being," she said calmly, "you will give me your word that you will suspend any action that would result in the death of either myself or Chelsea. You have been honest with me thus far about your intentions, and so I trust now that if you tell me you will take no action, or by inaction support any attempt on my life, or the life of Chelsea Zarova."

Kaitain nodded.

"I will accept your condition, Dominique. But now you must accept a condition of mine."

Kaitain took the package out of his lap and placed in on the low table in front of him. Dominique regarded the parcel for a moment before retrieving it and placing it in her own lap. The package was bound in simple tan colored cloth and held with a simple brown ribbon. Dominique's nimble and delicate fingers shook the slightest bit as she untied the ribbon and began to unwrap the package. Her breath caught in her throat when she saw what lay in her lap, but she did not gasp. Her heartbeat pounded in her ears, and her head swam. For a moment Dominique felt as though she was going to pass out, but she would not give Kaitain that satisfaction. What lay in the bundle in her lap was a light, simple and elegant mask. Unlike Kaitain's it would not cover Dominique's entire face, and would leave most of it in open view. The mask itself was in the shape of a butterfly. The central body was designed to fit over the bridge of her nose, leaving most of the tip of her nose exposed. The wings swept out, the upper part of the wing arching over her eyebrow and sweeping up to the crown of her head. The bottom swept over the middle of her cheek, down to her jaw-line just below her earlobe. The sides ran straight from her crown to her jaw. The outline of the mask itself was the color of the sharpened edge of a sword, and glistened slightly in the light. The rest of the mask looked like it was covered with spider webs made of onyx. She tentatively reached out and picked up the cool mask, and was surprised by how light it was. It also flexed gently in her hands, and did not appear that it would be uncomfortable to wear.

"As you are my Empress, you will wear this in all public forums, and only take it off when you are in private. You are an extension of my will, and of my power, and thus you will present yourself as such. Do we understand one another?"

Dominique nodded and brought the mask to her face, then gently tightened the straps that would be easily hidden under the cascade of her hair. When she removed her hands, she looked up to see Kaitain nodding. Sensing that their conversation was at an end, Dominique rose and waited to be dismissed.

"I am sure you will be successful in Hedorah, my Empress," Kaitain said in a quietly mocking tone, "I look forward to glowing reports of your progress."

Dominique bowed and then turned to the door. When she was gone, Kaitain rose from his chair and turned to a door on the far side of the room that led to an adjoining room. He opened the door slowly and stepped through to find the former Ruby Knight Ivan Quicksilver standing behind a chair where a bound and gagged Sadrina Annis sat, tears streaming down her face.

"That is one Empress dealt with," Kaitain said, cruelty filling his voice, "and now to deal with another."

Chapter LXVI

Uneasy Lies the Head
that Wears the Crown

Year Three of the Just Emperor Kaitain "Dragonsbane" Lorien, Creator's Calendar Year 1870

Gabrielle Peregrim brought a presence to the room that Quyhn Ravenheart had never been exposed to before, at least not for any length of time. After the death of her mother, Quyhn had a shortage of strong female role-models in her life. The most senior advisor to her as a woman was Aris Ebonsight, but Aris was more an academic whose presence extended more to the intellectual and not to the regal. Even when Quyhn was around Chelsea and Dominique, the way they carried themselves was unique. Chelsea was a soldier, every bit a soldier from the way she breathed, to the way she sat, to the way she ate. She exuded military precision from every pore. Dominique, while she was training to be royal, was certainly not raised in the regal manner. There was so much casual nature in Dominique's mannerisms, and even in the finest silks, the now Empress presented herself as though she were wearing common clothes. Gabrielle Peregrim on the other hand exuded nothing but the most refined and dignified air, a life-long member of the royal class who would not display one moment that was not perfectly rehearsed and controlled. She sat on the edge of Quyhn's bed, her shoulders back, her hands in her lap, and her ankles crossed. The look on her face, controlled, calm, and inviting was designed to set everyone around her at ease. She wore a two-tone green dress, which was cut long to the level of her ankles, where upon her left ankle she wore a small band of gold with inlay filigree of emeralds. The flowing skirt was a light green and was gently pleated. The bodice of the dress was a darker forest green with a panel of the lighter green that ran from her stomach to just over her bust in a triangular pattern. Crisscrossing embroidery of gold transected the light panel like the laces of a corset, and made it appear as though the darker green material was like an open vest simple draped over the lighter green dress. This illusion was furthered by the golden tie at the bottom of the light green panel, in the shape of a knot with trailing loops. The dark green of the dress covered her shoulders and arms to the elbow, but left her upper chest and throat completely exposed, while showing only the slightest bit of cleavage. She wore a broad choker of green and gold that accented the rest of the dress perfectly. On one forearm Gabrielle wore a thick bracelet of silver, gold and emeralds, while on the other a weave of gold that snaked around her wrist and ran up the back of her hand where it met a broad gold ring with a multiple karat diamond set upon it. Her long brunette hair flowed and cascaded down her back like a waterfall of curls. One small lock of hair fell across her face to the left of her eye, and gave almost a disarming quality to her appearance. It was calculated of course, but no less effective.

Quyhn sat opposite Gabrielle, still trying to wrap her mind around her sudden change in situation. To her left stood Rhionna, her face impassive, but there was color in her cheeks that had not been there before the more than intimate conversation with her charge. Gabrielle didn't press, nor did she say another word before sitting on the edge of the bed. She knew that Quyhn would come to her own conclusions, and when she was ready the conversation would continue. Finally, Quyhn shut her eyes for a long second, nodded her head silently, and then opened them again. When she refocused her gaze on Gabrielle, a new determination was etched on her face.

"Alright, explain this to me. Slowly."

Gabrielle kept her hands folded on her lap like a proper lady. She nodded her head twice slowly, and then began to speak. Her tone was even and measured, each word chosen for precision and with clear purpose. She knew the impossible position that the young woman, not really much more than a girl, had been placed in, and regardless of what Gabrielle said in that moment, it was the young woman herself that would have to determine whether she would rise to meet the challenges now placed in front of her, or if she would crumble under the incredible pressure.

"The simplest way to explain that, my dear Quyhn, is for you to understand Kaitain. As Rhionna no doubt has told you, or as you had probably learned before your travels here, I am a first cousin of the Emperor. While that gives me no standing in the framework of the Imperial Family, it does however give me insight into the inner workings of not only the Imperial Family, but also how it impacts those around it. My mother was the sister of the great Emperor Ender Lorien, perhaps one of the finest members of the Lorien family to wear the crown. Great things were expected of Ender's children, and perhaps that was the problem."

Gabrielle shifted slightly, uncrossing and re-crossing her ankles. She gently smoothed the rogue lock of hair back behind her ear and then let her hands come back to rest in her lap.

"Perhaps if it had only started with Ender," Gabrielle said, continuing her voice remaining calm and even, "then the expectations might not have been as high as they were when Kaitain was born. But as with all things, circumstances conspire to make us what we are, not the other way around. The real root of Kaitain's problems can be traced back to his grandfather. Kaldawyn Lorien was one of the most beloved emperors in the history of the Cadarian Empire, and was so beloved in fact that his death started a war. There aren't many who can say that. In fact, Kaitain's name is a derivative of Kaldawyn, one of the many unfair circumstances to befall our beloved Emperor."

There was the slightest bit of venom attached to the word 'beloved', but none of it ever showed in the older woman's eyes. Quyhn knew that Gabrielle was much older than she looked, and only the barest evidence of wrinkles had begun at the corners of her mouth and the corners of her eyes. They could be easily hidden if the woman wished to, but perhaps she felt on this day that the more honest she was with her appearance, the more force her words would have.

"When Ender took over from his father, he had equal opportunities to fail as he did to succeed. But where Kaldawyn was a practical man who used logic and expediency to solve disputes, Ender was a wise man who tried to see situations from all angles and ensure than any decision he made would have the best long-reaching results. Ender was willing to sacrifice the moment for the justice and peace of the future. It took little time for Ender to be loved by his people, and it took little longer for Ender to be known as 'the Just Hand'. It was not a name he gave himself, unlike Kaitain, but a name that grew when everyone saw that regardless of status, people were treated as they deserved. This was the man that Kaitain learned at the feet of, this is the man that everyone idolized, that everyone loved. That was the template that generations of people who lived and died in Cadaria expected their Emperors to follow. But whatever opportunity was ahead of the young Kaitain, he saw only obligation."

Gabrielle paused here, allowing her audience to drink in her words. Before she could continue, it was Rhionna that added her voice.

"We all live with expectation. I was born the daughter of a pair of warriors, and so I was destined to be part of the military. Quyhn was born the daughter of two great masters of the arcane arts, and so her path would one day lead her to take her place on the Masters Council."

Gabrielle frowned.

"And the current Empress was born the daughter of a farmer and a former whore. What does that say for her path? Tolon Morr, now a member of the Knights of the Flashing Blade was a common gladiator who killed for his food. Devlin Rannoch is a hated half-breed who many thought should have been killed at birth to prevent the threat that he would pose in his later years. Now he too has worn the title of Knight of the Flashing Blade. As I have said, we are the culmination of not only that which we are born to, but the circumstances that we put ourselves in, as well as those circumstances that the Creator places before us. Some people call it fate, others call it destiny. Those that follow the teachings of the Creator like to think of it as a grand plan. Whatever your personal beliefs lead you to call it, there is no denying that our paths through this life are not set. What lay behind us is certainly not what must lie before us."

There was a slight chiding tone in Gabrielle's voice, but it was not harsh. Rhionna's jaw remained set, and she took the slight reprimand in stride. Gabrielle exhaled slightly and slowly, as if calming herself.

"I was raised with Kaitain in the Imperial Court. I saw what he was and what he became first hand, and believe me, there was no power on this world that would have prevented what would come later. I fear that it was simply sped along by the emergence of the Crawling Plague. Perhaps some would have been spared the suffering that they endure now, but believe me, there would have been suffering no matter when Kaitain took the throne. That much I believe now was certain."

Quyhn felt the color drain from her face, and her mouth go dry. Her mind swam, and her insides clenched with anxiety. Gabrielle spoke as though the man who sat on the throne, her patron and now her adoptive father was born to be a monster.

"How is this even possible? Kaitain had everything!"

Quyhn's voice was incredulous, despite how she tried to make sense of it all, she couldn't. Gabrielle waited until Quyhn calmed before continuing. She wanted to ensure that her words would be taken for what they were, and that her meaning would not be misconstrued.

"I want you both to understand," she said slowly and calmly, "that I am in no way excusing Kaitain's behavior. In fact, I find it as deplorable as you do, and I know far more about his wretched deeds than anyone. You must learn how and why Kaitain makes his decisions, and the tactics he will employ on his favored battlefield. You have to know what lengths he is willing to go to. And you have to know just what lines you have to be willing to cross to defeat him. There is an old axiom in the Lorien family, one that Kaitain has taken to heart. Blood cannot stain hands that do not hold the blade."

After another long pause, Gabrielle looked first to Rhionna and then Quyhn, and seeing no cause for delay in their eyes, she continued.

"Kaitain may have been born with every advantage, but he was also born into a competition. Not only with the legacy of his ancestor and his father, but also with his younger brother. Twins were not uncommon in

262 – ASHES AND ECHOES

the Lorien family, but it was the first time that succession to the throne would be determined by a matter of minutes. From the moment of his birth, Kaitain felt the comparisons drawn by those around him between he and his brother. More often than not, the comparisons were phantoms in Kaitain's mind, and more than once, those phantoms lead to the dismissal of tutors. Kaitain was quick to point the finger of favoritism when Feyd excelled at anything above and beyond Kaitain's abilities. If anything, Kaitain was by far the more talented of the brothers, and the constant need by everyone to placate his ego stunted Feyd in many aspects. Feyd was a calm and mild boy who wanted so much to please everyone, but never grasped many of the concepts that his brother did. The only place that that Feyd ever excelled was training with weapons. He was not a prodigy, but he was far more capable than Kaitain, but that was only because Kaitain viewed martial training as beneath him. And I can assure you that Kaitain held his accomplishments over the head of his brother at every opportunity, mocking and belittling him. Among the circles that Kaitain frequented, Feyd was known as the little barbarian."

Quyhn immediately felt sorry for Feyd and for what the years of taunting and tormenting must have done to him. However, in the short meetings that she had had with not only Feyd but Felicia, the younger of the Lorien brothers seemed to have learned his limits and was comfortable within his own skin where his older brother was still searching for something that he quite possibly would never achieve. His thirst for power was like his thirst for attention and acceptance; seemingly endless. Gabrielle paused only slightly this time before advancing her tale.

"However, there were areas of life that Feyd found coming to him in abundance, and that drove the first true wedge between Feyd and Kaitain. Feyd was a strong and beautiful boy, and his training with the Imperial Legion filled out his muscles and his form. Kaitain was thinner, perhaps weaker, and while in his face he was no less attractive than his brother, his demeanor hung on him like a shroud of blackness. Young women do not want to have melancholy draped over them in the arms of their lover, and so Kaitain did not receive the attention that I am sure that he wanted from the young women of the court."

Quyhn unconsciously raised an eyebrow.

"Don't mistake my words," Gabrielle clarified. "Kaitain had plenty of attention, and never needed suffer from an empty bed. But as one would expect, these women wanted him not for the man but for the title and the influence that being the concubine or the betrothed of the heir to the throne could bring. Feyd on the other hand needed worry about nothing but who he wanted to receive attention from, never their motivations. But both men shared a common want. Her name was Teairra."

Quyhn nodded a small knowing nod, her mind immediately recognizing the name from Feyd's story during the less-than-cordial meal prior to Dominique's wedding.

"Teairra was as much royalty as I was, and in those days she and I were close. The kind of close that only women can be growing up together. We were sisters in every way except those that would have bound us by blood. There was nothing that we did not share with one another, and from the moment that we as young women began to look upon boys as young men, Teairra's eye would not leave Feyd. Just as I must say that Kaitain's eye never left Teairra. Teairra's father was the economic advisor to the Emperor, and as such, Teairra received a lot of attention from those suitors who wanted a closer alliance to the Lorien family. She received much in the way of attention from common men as well, but not for her beauty, which was considerable. Teairra's mother was from Galateria, and as such, Teairra's skin was darkened slightly, more the color of milk-lightened chocolate. It was an exotic beauty that brought her a mixture of fascination and scorn. It was this exotic nature that Kaitain saw, and the same nature that Feyd never saw. Moreover, what Kaitain saw, and what Kaitain hated, was the spark of love that was undeniable between his brother and the young woman."

"And so he sought to destroy that love," Rhionna added.

Gabrielle's eyes shifted to Rhionna for a second and let a small smile creep to her lips.

"Eventually," she allowed. "His first goal was to make Teairra see the error of her ways. To see that she had fallen in love with the wrong brother."

Gabrielle opened her mouth as to continue her story, and then stopped, bringing a finger to her lips for a moment before smiling.

"Do you ever wonder why Kaitain has dark hair and Feyd has red?"

Quyhn nodded slightly.

"Before it became clear to Kaitain that it would be impossible to tear apart the love between Feyd and Teairra, Kaitain tried all manner of schemes in an attempt to dampen Feyd's attractiveness. The most long-lasting of these schemes involved a barrel of ink. Kaitain lured Feyd to a storehouse and sat in wait. When his younger brother finally appeared, Kaitain ambushed him and attempted to shove his head into a barrel of ink. Of course, Feyd was much stronger than his brother and was easily able to turn the conflict to his own advantage. So it was Kaitain whose head wound up submerged in ink, and from that day forward, it was Kaitain and not Feyd who had blackened hair. But, in true Kaitain fashion, he never told the truth about the radical change in his appearance, instead beginning the lie that he wanted to create a new identity for himself that would set him apart in the minds of the people he would one day rule. Feyd, being the man that he is, told no one. I know the truth, only because I was there that night and saw the whole thing. Of course, out of respect, I too told no one, and would never openly have challenged the word of the heir to the throne."

Though she tried, Quyhn could not suppress a giggle, and brought a hand to her mouth to help her regain a small measure of control. But then the words from Feyd came flooding back to her mind, and any comedy was purged. She knew what would come next.

"Kaitain had Feyd sent to the front lines with the Imperial Legions to quell the conflict between Saldarine and Thorigald, didn't he?" Quyhn asked.

Gabrielle's eyes showed some surprise, but then finally she nodded gravely.

"It was the only avenue left open to Kaitain. He could not act directly against his brother, no matter how much he might want to, but sending him into dangerous situations would serve the purpose well enough. I knew from the moment that Feyd was dispatched that he would not be coming home, and Teairra knew it too. She spent the first week crying, most of it in my arms. Of course Kaitain was by her side every day, consoling her, sowing the seeds of his scheme in her misery."

Gabrielle faltered here. Obviously mulling over her next words.

"I was there the morning after. I saw the cut on her lip, the swelling around her eye, the bruises on her arms and legs. We disguised it the best we could, even arranging for a carriage accident that morning. But with every look, Kaitain tried to tear down her resolve, her pride, and her passion for life. But when word came of Feyd's return, and the proposal of marriage that would be on his lips, any leverage that Kaitain felt he had over the soul of the woman was erased. Teairra told Feyd as soon as he returned that she had a moment of weakness in the arms of another man, and though Feyd wanted to take revenge upon his brother for this, Teairra would not allow him. Had she told Feyd the truth, nothing would have prevented Feyd from killing Kaitain. Had that happened, the whole of Cadaria would have been thrown into chaos."

Rhionna snorted.

"Perhaps that would have been better."

Gabrielle regarded the blond woman for a moment and then smiled.

"Perhaps it would have at that."

Quyhn however did not share the ironic comedy of the moment. She was focused on the next part of the story. The part more terrible than a man taking liberties with the beloved of his brother.

"So when Kaitain knew he couldn't have her, and had no leverage upon her, he had her killed."

Again Gabrielle found herself surprised by the young woman.

"There is no proof of that, but the actions of the man since that point make it a near certainty. Kaitain has become the kind of ruler that removes obstacles from his path by the most expedient methods at hand, as well as disposing of those things that no longer serve a purpose. And so, dear Quyhn, this brings us back to your situation. Marlae was an irritant to Kaitain, and she made her choice. To that end, now that she has betrayed his love and thrown herself body and soul into the lust for power that he himself bred in her, Kaitain must ensure that she cannot take action to bring a premature end to his reign. She is a threat to him, and must be destroyed."

Rhionna snorted again.

"She is a spoiled girl. She rages, she curses, and she knows nothing but venom pouring from her tongue."

Quyhn looked up at Rhionna and smiled.

"And that's why Kaitain has to remove her from the equation. She is every bit her father's daughter, and if she were to be able to bring to bear her considerable skills of manipulation and cunning, she could turn that rebellion in the west into a force that could take the throne. She knows all of her father's tricks, and whatever restraint Kaitain may have within him is certainly not within Marlae. She is perhaps more vicious and vindictive than her father, and less shy about acting on those impulses. It makes perfect sense that Kaitain could not allow the viper to remain in her nest with the ability to gain from striking at his heart."

Gabrielle nodded.

"And that is why you, dear Quyhn, have been placed in this awkward position. You are the heir to the throne of a murderer, and as long as you are useful to him, Kaitain cannot have you eliminated. There is no clear succession after you, were Kaitain to die. No matter what others may think, unless Kaitain reverses his decree, Marlae cannot be reinstated to her previous position. Not even Dominique can undo the decree, even if she wanted to. Even if Dominique were to have an heir now, legitimately by Kaitain, you would still become Empress upon Kaitain's death. So long as Kaitain believes you will do nothing to hasten that day, I believe you are safe."

There was something unspoken hanging in the air, and Rhionna obviously picked up on it.

"But Kaitain cannot allow his heir to be in the hands of people whose loyalty is in question."

A grave pall came to Gabrielle's face, and finally, she nodded.

"The rumors of a possible uprising in Lordhill have been persistent for some time, I'm afraid," Gabrielle said in a nearly conspiratorial tone, "and though there is no evidence for such claims, that does not make it untrue. Connor and I have been gathering forces ever since we were sent here. We both knew that one day Kaitain would become a threat, and we wanted to be ready to defend ourselves were it to become necessary. Quyhn, I give you the choice now, probably one of the most important you will ever make. We received word from our spies in the Imperial Court that a detachment of the Imperial Legion has been dispatched to Lordhill to collect you and return you to Coventry. It seems that the Emperor wants to continue your tutelage personally. These soldiers will not be turned away. They will either leave here with you, or with your body."

"Or they will not leave at all," Rhionna added.

"And so it is to you, Quyhn," Gabrielle said rising, "we will defend you. We will stand by you, and we will help you to return this Empire to the greatness that it once held. Or we will allow you to return to Kaitain."

"You would let me go?" Quyhn asked, disbelief thick in her voice, "knowing what I know now? Knowing that you have been gathering forces to oppose Kaitain?"

"We would be gone long before Kaitain could act on such information," Gabrielle responded. "We have allies that you do not know about that would gladly give us shelter while we continue to marshal our forces."

Quyhn fell silent and nodded her head.

"I give you until the morning," Gabrielle said softly, moving toward the door. "Past that I am afraid you leave us little in the way of options. We are prepared to draw blood in your name, Quyhn, and we are prepared to go to war to defend you. That is the depths of our devotion to the Lorien family and the Throne of Cadaria."

With that Gabrielle opened the door to the small bedroom and left closing it gently behind her. Quyhn watched the door for a long time after Gabrielle had left, her thoughts leaving her mute. Finally she rose from the small wooden chair and turned to face Rhionna.

"Will you fight and die for me?"

The blond woman's jaw tightened, and her answer came with only a curt nod of her head. Quyhn nodded in return.

"I will not serve at the foot of the man who arranged for the murder of my father. Nor will I stand for the humiliations of the woman I now call my mother."

Rhionna looked down into the very serious eyes of the shorter woman for a long moment, and saw the hot tears beginning to collect in the corners of her eyes. The proud Saldarian woman bowed her head and eased slowly to one knee.

"I pledge my life to defend you, and so long as I live, no harm will come to you."

Rhionna kept her head bowed, and when Quyhn looked down, she could keep her tears from falling no longer. Cheeks flushed, tears streaming down her face, Quyhn fell to her knees and threw her arms around Rhionna's neck, the emotions of the moment overwhelming her. Her sobs came rapid and uncontrollable, her face buried in the blond woman's hair. For a long moment Rhionna was paralyzed, then finally one hand wrapped around the smaller woman's waist, while the other hand gently stroked her hair. Finally, Rhionna put her hand under Quyhn's chin and lifted her face so their eyes met. Quyhn's cheeks burned and her eyes were already beginning to get puffy. A long second later, Rhionna leaned in and pressed her lips to Quyhn's, and in that instant all of Quyhn's pain went away.

Restrain of the Ephemeral

Year Three of the Just Emperor Kaitain "Dragonsbane" Lorien,
Creator's Calendar Year 1870

The third year of the rule of Emperor Kaitain Lorien was growing late, and finally the Emperor had been roused from his slumber and he had returned to his rightful place ruling his empire. However, the cataclysmic events that helped to hasten his awakening had shaken the core of the already fractured empire. The Imperial Palace of Aldere had stood for over two thousand years, before the Lorien family had united the kingdoms of Cadaria in to a cohesive unit. Originally it had been the capital of the Kingdom of Iltorp, and had been one of the most well-defensible strongholds in the whole of Cadaria. When Terrik Lorien and his allies finally defeated the last of the warlords trying to wrest control of Cadaria for themselves, the key members of the Lorien Alliance: Zevarit, Iltorp, Pellatori, and Thorigald; each sacrificed a portion of their own kingdoms to form the Imperial Province of Aldere. As Terrik Lorien was a member of the royal families of Iltorp, the palace of Aldere became the new capital of Cadaria. In the beginning, the fact that the Palace of Aldere was the new capital had caused some disquiet among the Great Kingdoms, but when the royal families saw that Terrik ruled with an even hand, that disquiet quickly faded. There were few that even remembered that Terrik Lorien was born in Iltorp, and it was only noted as a foot note in a few history books. Now, the great and historic Imperial Palace of Aldere had been reduced to several smoldering piles of rubble and shattered ruins of wood, metal, and stone.

Two detachments of the Imperial Guard had been dispatched to start the process of excavating the site, and while any discoveries and recoveries were welcome, they had standing orders to recover the Imperial Throne, the Imperial Sword, crown, and the body of the Ethereal Sorceress Irene Drage. Those orders had brought a round of uncomfortable looks, but none of the soldiers were foolish enough to give voice to their concerns. If the Court Sorceress had indeed died in the destruction of the Imperial Palace, then it was a massive loss to the already fragmented Imperial Court. However, that was not what concerned the soldiers that were digging through the rubble. There were rumors that one of the Dark Gods was in the Imperial Palace. Worse, there were rumors that the creature calling itself Death was also seen in the palace. If Irene Drage had been killed by either the Dark God or Death, it would have sparked another conflict somewhere else, and the Cadarian Empire was already fighting a war on two fronts. Could they really afford to fight a war on three, or even four? Most of the soldiers searching did not want to find the body of the Ethereal Sorceress, and they hoped that even if they did, her body would have been so badly damaged that it could not be identified. No one held out any hope that she would be found alive.

Sundown was rapidly approaching, and while the soldiers knew that there was urgency in their task, working after dark had not been ordered yet. However, after word of the death of the Topaz Knight Jaccob Aldora for dereliction of duty, many were sure that those orders would be coming soon. Others wondered whether they should start working after dark even without an order to ensure that there would be no judging eye cast in their direction. However, because there were so few soldiers assigned to search the massive area that was the ruined Imperial Palace, working at night was too dangerous. The three man search teams were often out of the sight line of other search teams. The ranking officer of the search detachment had requested reinforcements for the effort, however the request had been denied. Every soldier was needed to protect the tactically weak position of the Inn in Coventry, those that weren't assigned to the protection of the Emperor were sent to bolster the ranks against the rebel army. Already there was word that the forces of Thorigald were marching on Saldarine, and the rebellion was moving from a war of words to a war of arms. It was only a matter of time before the battle lines extended to include Galateria and Albitonin.

One search party had struck deeply into the rubble, finding a pocket of space under several large slabs of marble that were precariously balanced over several fallen pillars. One of the soldiers shifted a piece of the marble and uncovered a body. The soldier turned to wave over the other members of the search party and then to call for help, but standing in front of him when he turned was a woman. She wore a padded smoke-colored bodysuit that had the physical characteristics of light leather armor. Her black boots stretched up the length of her calves to the center of her thighs where they ended in a thin cuff. She also wore long black gloves that stretched up her forearms, past her elbows to the center of her bicep where they ended in a similar thin cuff. The bodysuit continued across her entire form, all the way to her throat. What struck the solider was that the woman's eyes were the same color as the bodysuit, with the color identical in both her pupil and iris. She had long black hair that was pulled back and wound into a bun at the back of her head. Her face was tan as though she was no stranger to the sun, and her lips were bright red. The soldier faltered for a moment, and then suddenly realized there was a pain in his chest, and when he looked down, there was a dagger sticking out of his chest just under his breastbone. He looked back up into the eyes of the woman only to find that she had disappeared. The blade across this throat the next moment was the only clue that she was still close to him. His cries gurgled and died in his throat as his blood spilled in every direction.

The two other members of the search party arrived several moments later, only to find a puddle of fresh blood near the void under the collapsed pillars. There was a blur of motion from the soldiers' left. The first soldier was dead before he had a chance to act, his neck snapped in a single deft and brutal motion. The second soldier was not afforded the same mercy, as two quick knife slashes across his throat severed both his esophagus and the primary arteries in his neck. Several moments later the trio of guards was wedged into the void under the collapsed pillars, and the woman's body was gone. It took very little effort to cause the void to collapse in upon itself, crushing the three guards and disguising the true cause of their deaths, at least for a little while. At the rate that the ruins of Aldere were being uncovered, it would take several days at the minimum before their bodies were discovered, and several more days before they were identified, if ever. By then, the trail would be so cold that Liandra Nightshade's tracks would never be able to be uncovered.

* * * * * * * * * * * *

Irene Drage's head hurt. She could feel her heartbeat in her ears, and the pounding behind her eyes. There was nothing but blackness in her field of vision, and though she tried, she couldn't force her eyelids to open. It hurt to think, it hurt to breath, and it hurt to move. It was then that she realized that she couldn't move. She could feel the chair underneath her, and the wood felt cool against her exposed arms. There was something rough and biting at both her wrists and her ankles. After several attempts to rotate her left wrist, and to pull away from the restraint, it became clear that some kind of rope was holding her down, and one that burned against her skin. After several moments of purposeless struggling, Irene concentrated on trying to open her eyes again. No matter how hard she tried the pounding in her brain kept preventing her from restoring her vision. Panic began to set in. She couldn't move, and the more she tried to breath, the more helpless she felt. It felt like walls were crashing down upon her; like the walls of the whole of the Imperial Palace were falling in upon her. Then the memory hit her. She had been in the throne room of the Imperial Palace, fighting against a Dark God, and then something happened. Something dreadful. Something terrible. She felt as though she were burning from the inside out. Like her head was going to explode, and then just as suddenly as the physical torment began, it was over, and she was sitting, bound in that chair. It was then that she heard breathing in the room that was not hers. Someone was close to her, watching her, but making no movements, a man by the deep tone of his breaths. Her captor was close enough that if her hands were free she could reach out and touch him. There was shuffling behind her as well, and then there was a set of warm hands on each side of her head. The pain in her head began to ebb, and suddenly the pounding in her ears had vanished. It was then much easier to open her eyes. There were two bright torches near her, behind the form of a man who stood in front of her. Irene could tell it was a man because of his stature and his build. He wore a flowing robe of some kind, and though there was something familiar about the man, Irene couldn't place it. Then he took a step forward, and recollection filled her.

The robe was heavy and thick, a dark purple in color bordering on black. It was bound with a black belt and complimented with black gloves. But it was the mask over the lower half of the man's face that ignited Irene's memory the most. Torda Safrick was the master of secrets for the Hand of Chaos, working to keep the secrets and uncover the secrets of the world for Talisia and Seraphina Masile. He had been the one that had delivered the dagger capable of killing a god to Irene. She had gleefully given in to Kaitain Lorien, adding fuel to the fire that was raging between Cadaria and Mythryn. His long dark hair framed his lean face. One of the torches behind Torda was extinguished, and that was when Irene noticed something distinct that she had never seen before. Torda's eyes were a brilliant violet. Torda looked up past Irene, presumably at the person who stood behind her, and then nodded. The warm hands left Irene's face and then a soft rush of air moved down her forearms. The bonds on her wrists loosened slightly, enough that Irene could rotate her hands and wrists without furthering the burning of her skin. Torda reached up and pulled away the mask over the bottom part of his face, and Irene could finally see the full face of the man. He smiled down at her, and slowly pulled the gloves off his hands and untied the belt at his waist. He slipped the robe off his shoulders and let it drop to the floor, revealing black pants and a simple gray shirt. The man also wore a sword belt that had the symbol of a striking viper on the scabbard. Another form entered the room, features obscured by the light of the torch flickering in Irene's still unadjusted eyes. However, Irene could tell that the form was of a woman, and that the clothes she wore clung very tightly to her body. The new arrival handed a chair to Torda, and he quickly accepted it and sat down in front of Irene.

"I'm sorry for all of this, Irene, I really am. But you have to understand that I had to be sure you had been cleared of all of Talisia's influence before I let you regain consciousness. Otherwise you would have been too much of a threat to me, and to the operation I built here."

Irene's eyes widened, but she tried hard to keep the panic out of them. Now that her hands were free, she would be able to prepare simple enough spells to free herself. Perhaps even some powerful enough to render all three people in the room unconscious. That was when she felt something small and sharp at the back of her neck. It pushed in just above the level of her shoulders and would only need to push in a little farther before it would pierce her spine.

"Please, Irene," Torda said after a long look behind Irene at the form behind her, "my associate is quite capable of killing you before you are able to finish drawing on any of your abilities. Your hands and your lips are being watched every moment, and if we so much as think you are trying to escape, I am afraid we will have to take punitive measures to prevent it."

Irene frowned, and nodded slowly, ensuring that she didn't shift enough to give the blade at her neck any excuse to advance.

"Good."

The man leaned forward, and his violet eyes shimmered. He arched his hands together under his chin and rested his elbows on his knees. He sat there like that looking at her for a long time before speaking again.

"You have to understand something, Irene. I don't want you at all. In fact, it was because you were victimized by Talisia that you have been spared this long. I have been close enough to you over these past few years that I could have slit your throat. But, you are as much a victim in this as all the others that Talisia has inhabited since her exile here. It was difficult to watch you adjust to the possession, and I wish that I would have been able to prevent you murdering Estelle Ravenheart. She was a valued friend, and her loss is still felt by those who knew her."

Irene opened her mouth to speak, but her mouth went dry. She remembered. For so long she wanted to believe that it was just some terrible nightmare, or some unrequited guilt. But it was true. In her jealousy she had murdered Estelle Ravenheart.

"It wasn't your doing," Torda continued, "no more than it was your doing when you arranged for Alistair Ravenheart to be murdered, or when you seduced Kaitain Lorien, or any of the other things you have done since your meteoric ascension to the rank of Court Sorceress. Anyone who knows you as long as I have, knows that you were an average student at best, and you were never destined to be anything other than ordinary. It was Talisia that made your ascension possible, and you will have the rest of your life to come to terms with both your horrible deeds, and your inability to prevent them. I am not here to clear your conscience, or to absolve you of blame."

Irene swallowed hard. She wanted to scream. She wanted to let the tears fall from her eyes, and she wanted to let her heart explode. But there was a defiant streak within her still, despite her innocence and relative naiveté. She would not give this repugnant man the satisfaction of seeing her break down. The woman behind Torda handed him several sheets of paper, and he accepted them without looking at them. She smiled a vicious viper's smile.

"You want to know how I know all of these things. Fair enough. I'll answer that in a show of my good faith. I invented a technique called face dancing. Well, in truth I stole it from my brother; and while he was born with the ability and could do it at will, it seems that my version required a little more of a cost. Any person I kill, I can assume the identity of. I can speak with their voice, mimic all of their facial expressions, and inherit enough of their memories to fool even their closest acquaintances. I can recall all of the identities I have ever copied. Unfortunately, those I have taught the technique to have never been able to recall previous identities, and so their use is limited and very expensive. And so, I have identities that allow me to get into most places without being noticed. Though I must say it cost me far more than I care to admit to find and subdue your friend Torda. He was quite the troublesome little nuisance. But it got me closer to you, and it allowed me to identify those members of the Hand of Chaos that had been eluding us for quite some time. And it is always beneficial to know everything you can about your enemies."

The smile faded, and a stern look came to the man's eyes. They burrowed into her soul as though they could get the answers that he wanted whether she wanted to surrender them or not.

"Now, you're going to tell me everything Kaitain knows about the Dragon's Tear."

Irene gritted her teeth and narrowed her eyes. The man in front of her exhaled slowly, lowered and then shook his head. When he looked back up and locked his violet stare on Irene, she could almost see a level of pity in his gaze.

"I could take the information from you, Irene. The woman behind me here, if you were as knowledgeable about the agents at Kaitain's command as I think you are, then you would know who she is and what she is capable of. Her name is Liandra Nightshade. While she is just as talented as most other assassins at ending lives, she is most adept at creating poisons and other concoctions from her collection of rare plants. Her ointments and tinctures can cause you more pain than you ever thought possible. They can render you blind, mute, paralyzed, or unable to feel pain. Once I watched her carve up one of her victims, and he was laughing as she displayed each of his severed body parts to him. It is not a fate I would want for you, Irene, but if you leave me no choice, then I will have to travel down that road with you. But, if you cooperate, I will make sure that you are released, unharmed, somewhere that Kaitain can never touch you."

Finally, Irene clenched her fists and ground her teeth tighter together. She would not be used again, no matter what happened to her. The man before her frowned, and she felt a small victory stir within her. The next thing she knew, searing pain rocketed through her body from her head down her to feet. Even her long hair hurt down to the tip, and she could feel every part of her body on fire and freezing at the same time. No matter how she fought, she could not keep her eyes from closing, and the next thing she knew, the blackness took her, and she slumped in the chair.

* * * * * * * * * * * *

Saurn Macco slumped in his chair as he heard the screams coming from the next room. It had been three hours since Liandra had started her interrogation of Irene Drage, and Saurn knew that Liandra hadn't even asked a question yet. Torture never gave reliable information, but Saurn had to follow through on his threat, otherwise the next time he sat in front of Irene, his bargaining posture would be impotent at best. He had to admit that the woman was strong. She hadn't passed out once since she had been revived when Saurn left the room. Suddenly the screaming stopped, and Saurn looked up to see Natalia Pressen exiting the room. Thick red blood covered her hands, and she was wiping it onto a torn fragment of Irene's dress. Natalia was shaking her head, but Saurn knew that the Sunstone Knight's constitution for scenes of torture would not have allowed her to feel anything for a monster like Irene Drage. It didn't matter that Talisia Masile was guiding her actions. Irene still was a conscious being and could have fought back. But she didn't. On some level Irene enjoyed the power that her merging with Talisia had brought her, and it was on that level that she deserved to be punished, even if on other levels she was a victim too.

"We're letting her rest a bit," Natalia said in answer to the unspoken question of the Grand Master of the Shadow Guild, "Liandra is sure that we can break her any time we please. But if we don't give her the illusion that she has some will and some resistance, then when we do finally break her, we can't rely that the information we glean is genuine."

"Make them think they have a chance before you rip them to shreds. A time honored tactic."

Natalia frowned.

"You don't sound like you approve, grandfather. Aren't you the one who taught all of us these techniques?"

Saurn nodded.

"Knowing the depths of human weakness leads to overconfidence. If all humans were as fragile as we believe them to be, it would completely destroy the possibility of heroism. But I know more than most that heroes come from the very places that they should not be possible. That is why someone like Irene is so maddening. She was controlled. And yet, the human will still gave her the choice to break from that control and show a streak of that heroism that is bred into all of the human race."

Natalia frowned.

"But Talisia would have simply destroyed her as a matter of course and moved on to another victim. It would have done Irene no good to resist."

Saurn snorted once.

"Heroism rarely is a self-preserving stance. The heroes I have known have always been too eager to destroy themselves for their cause. It is at the heart of why heroes can exist. People who believe that an idea or an ideal is greater than the cost of a single life are the most dangerous weapons, and the most destructive force in the universe."

Natalia tried her best to stifle a groan.

"He who is willing to bring change must also be willing to bring destruction. Yes, grandfather, we all know your first precept."

Saurn straightened and then stood, taking two long steps toward Natalia. He took her hands into his and raised them so that she could see the blood still dripping from them.

"If you're not careful, little girl, this can change from a tool to a badge of honor. Irene Drage is not an innocent, and she has done shameful things in her life to this point, but it only takes a push to send her over the edge to becoming one of the most deadly forces in your life, one that will be willing to walk into the Great Dark One's pit and back just so she can have the opportunity to bathe her own hands in your blood. I've seen it before, and you have met the result. You need only think back to the Dark Goddess that effortlessly and gleefully threw you around the room like you were an insignificant worm. Believe it or not, she was a disgraced princess, relegated to a life of ignominy waiting tables in an insignificant bar in the middle of nowhere. But she too was pushed, and she decided to push back. She was given the chance to be more than her situation allowed, and she became that very bringer of change that you scoff at."

Natalia tried to pull her hands away, but Saurn held her firm.

"Never underestimate what those with power can do when they have the opportunity. Overconfidence and carelessness will end your life long before the sword will. I don't want to have to train another successor because you lost sight of what we are trying to accomplish."

Finally Saurn released Natalia's hands and returned to his chair on the other side of the room. If Natalia was frustrated or irritated with her grandfather's actions or words, she didn't let it show in her face or in her body language. She simply returned to cleaning the blood off her hands. A knock came at the door, and Saurn motioned in that direction causing the door to slowly slide open. This deep in the inner sanctum of the Shadow Guild, there was little need to worry about people who knew enough to knock. One of the junior assassins entered, a young boy whose name did not immediately come to Natalia's mind. He had a letter in his hand that he quickly and dutifully delivered to Saurn before bowing first to the Grand Master, and then to Natalia before just as quickly and wordlessly departing. Even though Natalia and Saurn treated each other with an informal ease, Saurn was still the Grand Master of the Shadow Guild, and Natalia still had the rank of Master. The minimum respect afforded to them was a bow of acknowledgement.

Saurn opened the letter and read it quickly, and then placed a finger to his lips regarding its contents with a look of almost amusement. He dropped the letter and it floated across the room to where Natalia stood. She snatched it out of the air without a word and read the contents. It was a letter from Chelsea Zarova addressed to Natalia in care of the Shadow Guild. There were few who had the arrogance to send a letter this way, and even fewer that were afforded the respect to ensure that the letter would be delivered as intended. Natalia's eyes widened at the contents of the letter.

"It seems that our dear Garnet Knight has found herself pushed to that line of heroism too," Saurn said idly. He turned and looked directly at Natalia. "And the unexpected can often be the result. You'll see to this personally."

Natalia bowed smoothly, feeling the color rush to her cheeks. Whether she was embarrassed or furious would be a matter for another time.

The Only Truth of War

Year Three of the Just Emperor Kaitain "Dragonsbane" Lorien, Creator's Calendar Year 1870

A dense and foreboding fog had descended on the battlefield that now filled the Plains of Steam. The Army of Fire of Saldarine and the Army of Water of Thorigald were well into their charges into each other's ranks and they seemed to care little about the titans that were seconds from attempting to tear each other apart. The creature War stood like a massive sentinel of death at the edge of the battlefield, and where moments before he stood only twelve feet in height, over the moments after the huge dragon's appearance, he had grown in both stature and girth so that the top of his massive head rose above the long broad head of Thalasia Steelbiter. Steelbiter pulled itself up to its full height, its two-tone bronze scales catching some of the light that filtered through the dense fog of steam that filled the plains. The dragon roared, the green crest of feather-like scales at the back of his head shaking with the fury of the roar. Steelbiter beat its huge wings, a blur of green and bronze. Dark talons dug at the ground, and trails of steam clung to the long green and bronze whiskers that hung from its lower jaw. The broad blade in War's hand stabbed out like a lance through the fog, aiming straight for the dragon's head. Steelbiter dodged to one side, but was not fast enough to completely avoid the blow. The tip of the sword collided with one of Steelbiter's long horns. The horn broke off almost at the level of the dragon's head, and the roar that broke from the dragon's jaws changed in tone to reflect the sharp pain. However, Steelbiter was not content with being wounded by War's blade. With its right foreleg, Steelbiter raked its claws across War's breastplate, a hissing sound accompanying the sound of bone scraping against steel. Huge furrows were dug in War's breastplate, but the creature didn't react at all. All Steelbiter had done was draw itself closer to War, and the reflexive attack could have proven to be the end of Steelbiter's offense against Dorovar's chosen. War reached out with its free hand and seized the dragon by the throat. However, Steelbiter beat hard with its wings to pull away, but War proved to be strong enough to hold the dragon in place. Moments later however, it became clear that Steelbiter's intention had not been to pull away, but rather to reposition itself so that its gaping jaws were pointed at the already damaged breastplate of the hulking colossus.

A spray of viscous green liquid belched forth from Steelbiter's open mouth, coating War from its shoulders to its waist. On contact, the metal armor coating War began to smoke and steam, burning away where the liquid struck. Again Steelbiter beat its wings and pulled hard against the grip of the colossus, this time however the strength of the great dragon won out. War's arm pulled free at its smoking shoulder, and Steelbiter came to rest on the ground several yards away from the smoking form of War, with its disembodied hand still clutched tightly around the dragon's neck, and tree trunk of an arm trailing behind. With a shake of its massive head, the arm fell away, crashing to the ground like a great felled tree. Seconds later, the whole of the arm disintegrated. War's breastplate melted away as well, falling like large steel rain on the ground before it. Beneath the massive plate was a core of roiling blackness punctuated by flashes of lightning. However, the great tumult was only visible for a few seconds. War's breastplate began to reconstitute itself, and in a matter of moments, had been completely reformed. The monster's arm too instantly regrew from the shoulder, this time sporting large deadly looking spikes on the outer plates. Its hand too was different upon reforming. The hand, instead of an oversized gauntlet was now tipped with razor-sharp blades that ran the length of each finger, inside and out. Protruding from the palm was a cruel looking spike that would easily rip through anything it was thrust into. Whatever damage Steelbiter had done was quickly undone and nullified.

* * * * * * * * * * * *

Jillian watched in horror as the two beasts tore at each other. For a moment there was a feeling of triumph when the large dragon seemed to have taken the upper hand through its cleverness, but that advantage was short-lived at best. Now that War was back at full fighting strength, it would only be a matter of time before it would adapt its tactics and fell the large winged beast. So far, the armies of Thorigald and Saldarine had paid no mind to the small fragmented band, but Jillian's fellow dragon hunters were well prepared if the situation were to quickly shift in a bad direction. Dane was still sprawled out on the ground, and from where she stood, Jillian could not tell if the man were dead or alive. She could not see him breathing, but knowing the nature of the man may well have rendered that fact irrelevant. He was a Dark God after all, or at least that was what he seemed to be considering he had been consorting with one of them. Blade on the other hand was lying face down, and he too had not moved an inch since War had overcome whatever tactic he and Dane had cooked up. Jillian could only hope that whichever of the mammoths emerged from the conflict of titans would be so weakened by the exertion that the handful of mortals would be able to prevail. However, Jillian did not hold out great hope for their chances. But then, out of the corner of her eye, there was a hint of movement from Dane's prone body. It was more than the muscles twitching in a dead body. It was more deliberate. Jillian wanted to sprint over to the fallen man to help him up, but she never had the chance.

The small band of dragon hunters were in the bubble that was being afforded to the clash of monsters as the two enemy armies threw themselves at each other with reckless abandon. A great shadow moved over the swelled ranks of the fighting and dying, and then suddenly crashed down in the very center of them, sending a shock wave of wind and dirt flying in all directions. Again Jillian and her band were knocked off their feet. It seemed that Nessus the Hovering Rain was not about to allow her mate to do the fighting alone. The nearly translucent white dragon with its great long neck and doubly long tail waded into the ranks of the hopelessly overmatched soldiers and began to mow them down by the dozens. Her powerful tail cut through bodies like a scythe though wheat, and her mighty jaws broke ten men in half in a single bite. And still the ranks of soldiers threw themselves at one another, paying no mind to the massive interloper.

The death toll was staggering, and in less than an hour, there would be no armies left to hoist the banner for either of the Great Kingdoms.

There was a quick unspoken communication between the four women, and they knew what needed to be done. The closest siege assets to them were being wheeled through the mud by a group of soldiers from Thorigald. Either they had forgotten that they had such a weapon at their disposal, or the fog that War had placed upon their minds made it impossible for them to think of anything other than getting close to their opponent and trying to draw blood in the quickest way possible. Angelina and Jacqueline darted out in the direction of the massive ballista that seemed to be easily finding every hole and furrow in the land, delaying the five soldiers that tried to push it without watching where they were going. Jillian held the hilt of Scaleripper tightly in her hand and darted off toward where Nessus was eviscerating another group of soldiers who died without screams or probably even realizing that it wasn't their enemies who were ending their lives. Kiara, sensing that she was needed in another capacity carefully picked her way across the battlefield of the titans and tried her best to give aid to the fallen Blade.

Angelina and Jacqueline got to their goal first. Angelina took one side of the war machine while Jacqueline took the other. The soldiers fell without even realizing they were dead. In a matter of moments, Angelina had set the support legs of the massive bow in the ground, while Jacqueline with her more developed muscles cranked back the great tensioned arms that set the iron tipped spear in place. The spear itself was greater in diameter than some of the larger trees Jacqueline had ever seen, and it would be perfect for bringing down a beast the size of Nessus. All Jillian had to do was keep the foul beast's attention for long enough for Jacqueline to line up the shot. Angelina gave the signal that the supports were in place. Even though it mattered little if the great machine tore itself apart after one shot, what did matter was that Angelina and Jacqueline would easily be killed by such an event. All they had to do was wait.

Jillian knew her job, and as she darted in and out of the mindless ranks of soldiers to where Nessus was laying waste to both armies she started to feel the bursts of nervous energy fluttering through her muscles. It was always this way when she was about to engage a dragon. The anxiety seemed to make her faster and stronger; ready to face the dangers that awaited her. Nessus had just lifted her massive head with another batch of unfortunate souls trapped between her teeth when Jillian got close enough to strike. Scaleripper longed to taste the blood of the great dragon, and Jillian was quite ready to appease the weapon's thirst. She flashed in, her goal the great gleaming white fore-claw of the beast. The slash would cut a massive gash across the top of the clawed foot, forcing bright blue blood to seep in all directions. Nessus howled in pain, sending broken bodies falling from her jaws and crashing to the ground. Jillian dodged the falling debris as well as the blind slash from the damaged appendage. She rolled quickly out of the way, coming back to her feet covered in blood, gore, and mud. The great dragon was intelligent though, and quickly found the woman's form standing beneath her. The dragon roared again and struck straight down at the ground with its huge mouth. Jillian rolled away again, narrowly avoiding an intimate engagement with a shimmering white fang. Scaleripper found the beast's flesh again, this time creating a jagged scar on the underside of the dragon's jaw. When Nessus straightened again, another roar billowed from its open maw.

This was the moment that Angelina and Jacqueline were waiting for. The dragon was totally distracted by Jillian's tactics, and she had the beast on the defensive. Angelina held fast to the firing arm, while Jacqueline expertly lined up the shot. She only needed a few more seconds before she would be able to end Nessus's reign of terror in the Plains of Steam. She raised her hand slightly, waiting for just the right moment. Her eyes widened when she saw it, and hurriedly dropped her hand. Angelina didn't hesitate, and pushed forward hard on the firing arm, setting the siege machine into its deadly action. The taught and tortured wood released, sending the deadly bolt streaking across the distance, toward the back of Nessus the Hovering Rain. The bolt was nearly upon her when both of the beast's massive wings beat hard against the air, propelling her backwards. It changed the angle at which the bolt struck true. Instead of piercing the dragon in the back and going straight through to her heart, the bolt instead struck the thick fleshy bundle of muscles that held her left wing to her body. A plume of blue blood sprayed in all directions, and the wing collapsed like a ruined sail. The roar that came from the dragon's throat was a mixture of rage, pain, and hatred. But instead of turning to see where the vicious attack had come from, the dragon was more in control of its actions than the dragon hunters had expected or had ever seen in all their hunts. Nessus's long tail rose quickly into the air and slammed down on where the ballista had launched the crippling bolt. Jacqueline and Angelina had no chance to get out of the way of the attack, and even if they had, once the incredible girth of the tail had struck down hard once on the site of the ballista, it then rose into the air, waved to one side, and then swept the whole area clean of both war machine and soldiers alike. The crushed bodies of the dragon hunters were thrown clear, landing hundreds of yards away, battered into nearly unrecognizable mounds of flesh.

Jillian could only watch in horror as two of her closest friends and allies were swatted like flies into nothingness. She screamed some guttural rage-filled cry and threw herself forward at the great foot of the dragon. Scaleripper plunged downward, piercing through the hardened scales into the flesh below. But Jillian didn't stop there, she kept driving the sword deeper and deeper, pushing all the way through, the point of Scaleripper bursting through the palm of the great clawed hand, and then into the ground below. The tip of the sword struck some boulder and thrust into it. Nessus roared again, and pulled up on its pinned foot, and Jillian could hear and feel the flesh and scales ripping. She backed away slightly from the thrashing appendage, feeling the ground beneath her shaking. She barely saw the flash of light from the head of the axe as it struck true, sending blood spattering in all directions.

* * * * * * * * * * * *

Tolon Morr carefully picked his way down the side of the cliff-face, keeping the nearly limp form of Jerrica Maldovrin bundled tightly in his arms. It seemed the closer they got to the battlefield, the weaker she became, and the less able she was to fight against whatever was draining her. When they reached the bottom, Tolon placed Jerrica carefully on the ground and turned in time to see the Lady of Cadaria, Jillian Corven, charge in to engage the second dragon that had intruded on the mindless warzone. She was either incredibly brave, or incredibly stupid, but no matter what she was, Tolon could not allow her to be it alone. Gripping hard onto the hilt of the Sacred Weapon Strength, Tolon charged in, trying to cover the distance between himself and the dragon in as few steps as possible. He saw the strike from the ballista, and had to move as quickly as he could to avoid being swept away by the dragon's mighty tail. The sound of armor sailing through the air was nearly as sickening as the echoing crunch of breaking bones and stifled screams. Leaping over several broken bodies of soldiers, Tolon closed the distance just as Jillian's sword plunged through the great foot of Nessus. Seizing that opening, Tolon swung with all of the might that he could manage, unleashing the fury of the Sacred Weapon strength on the pinned limb. The hardened steel of the battle axe Strength bit deep into the leg of the creature, burrowing all the way to the bone. The roar from the dragon became a scream, and the massive beast's one good wing batted hard, and it pulled again at the pinned limb, trying to dislodge it. Finally the sword was pulled free from the stone that held it, and Nessus leapt away. When she landed back on the ground, the three good feet crushed dozens of soldiers, and the sweeping tail sent dozens more flying in all directions. The slaughter may have been unintentional, but it was no less effective.

Tolon looked over in Jillian's direction, but she was already dashing toward the wounded dragon. He stifled a curse, but found himself running after the mad woman. He could understand what she was feeling. Many times in his previous life as one of the most feared gladiators to ever set foot in an Imperial fighting pit, he had felt the red rage come over him. In his early days before he learned the truth about fighting for the sport and amusement of others, Tolon was so assured of his abilities that he often underestimated the skill of his opponent. Because of it, he was wounded far more often than he should have been. Those wounds often pushed Tolon into a kind of red rage. He knew nothing but the thirst for blood and the revenge of the moment. That rage, once harnessed was an incredible weapon, and more than once, Tolon had used to crush his opponents with his bare hands. It could be a powerful weapon when harnessed, but it could also blind a person to the needs of the moment.

Nessus planted her back feet and her one good front foot and roared in the direction of Jillian and Tolon. Dozens of yards separated them, but the force of the roar could be felt as though she were right on top of them. The next moment, her long horn covered head rose into the air for a moment before it darted back toward the ground and then leveled out. Her jaws opened the next moment, and a swirling funnel of steam burst forth. Tolon was only a step or two behind Jillian when the cone of death erupted from the dragon, and he was able to gather his legs underneath him enough to leap forward and tackle Jillian, dragging her to the ground. The hot steam just barely missed enveloping them both, and from where Tolon lay in the mud, he could see hundreds of soldiers caught in the exhalation, their flesh melting from their bodies, and even the strong steel of their weapons and armor nearly liquefying from the intense heat. The ranks of soldiers melted like candles, leaving pools of unspeakable horror as the only proof of their existence. Once the heat had abated, Jillian pulled herself from Tolon's grasp and continued sprinting towards the wounded dragon. This time Tolon made no attempt to stifle the curse that came to his lips, and he sprinted after her.

* * * * * * * * * * * *

Kiara deftly dodged her way to Blade's side, and after quite a bit of effort was able to turn the stocky man over on his back. Despite the brave appearance she was trying to put forth, her hands shook with the fear that was radiating from her core. Even as she worked to revive Blade and mend the severe wounds on both his chest and his forehead, she repeated the blessings of the Creator to herself in an effort to calm her nerves. Moreover, she tried to concentrate on her work, and tried hard not to look at the battle that raged all around her, or at the battle of colossi that raged behind her. She nearly jumped out of her skin when she felt a hand on her shoulder. She was relieved when she heard Dane's soothing voice in her ear.

"Just like you to lie down until a pretty girl comes to wake you up."

Blade's eyes opened, and he pushed himself to a seated position. Though Kiara was a little shocked, she brought her hand to her chest and said a short soft prayer of thanks. It was then that Kiara heard the roar of pain come from Nessus, and she looked up to see the massive ballista bolt jutting out of the dragon's back. She could only watch in horror the next moments as her friends were crushed in retaliation. As much as she wanted to scream, to run to their broken bodies, Kiara stayed kneeling at Blade's side, the prayers for the dying feeling empty in her mind and heart. As an acolyte of the Church of the Creator, she knew what she was supposed to do at that moment. She knew that she was supposed to help ease the transition of the lost souls into the embrace of the Creator. But with death all around her, and more death coming with every second that passed, it seemed like she was helpless and worthless in the moment. Dane's hands on her shoulder gave her little comfort, but it did help, more than she should have admitted.

She didn't know when Blade got back to his feet, and she didn't know when Dane pulled her to hers, but all of a sudden Dane turned her around and locked his eyes on hers.

"You have to put it out of your mind, Kiara. You have to let them go now. They're dead, and there's nothing you can do. But that," he said pointed back at where Steelbiter and War were trading blows that could have caused mountains to crumble, "that we have to deal with right now. The longer War is residing on this battlefield, the longer those two armies will keep dying. The only chance we have to stop this is to stop him."

Kiara blinked hard, but she couldn't stop the tears from streaming from her eyes. What Dane was saying made sense, but it didn't matter. How could they, the three of them, hope to fight something like War when a monster like Steelbiter hadn't been able to make so much as a lasting dent? The odds were hopeless, the task was hopeless, and more than that it defied even Kiara's staunch and supposedly bottomless faith.

"Direct won't work," Blade said gruffly, an axe seemly made of pure green fire in his hands, "he'll just swat us away again."

Dane nodded. His fists started to glow bright green, the fires dancing across his knuckles and the back of his fists. He looked over his shoulder at where War had absorbed another of Steelbiter's massive blows, rocking back on his heels. When Dane turned back, there was a slight smile on his face.

"Then we won't worry about direct. Steelbiter's been softening War up, and he'll be ready to try that corrosive breath again. When he does, we have to be ready. We won't get another shot. The last time, War came back stronger, and I don't think that Steelbiter will survive another exchange."

Blade nodded and moved toward Steelbiter's left flank, leaving Dane with Kiara.

"I know you want to do something Kiara, but believe me when I say that the best way you can help is to be ready to pull us out if we fail."

He squeezed her shoulder hard once and turned to move toward Steelbiter's right flank. He stopped for only a moment and looked back over his shoulder.

"I'd ask you to pray for us, but believe me, it won't help."

* * * * * * * * * * * *

Thalasia Steelbiter could feel the drain on his body. This creature calling itself War was unlike anything it had ever fought before, and had taken everything the dragon was able to muster and still kept coming. Its blows seemed to get stronger and stronger, while Steelbiter's only got weaker. But the dragon had wounded the monstrous creature, if only for a moment. So he had been gathering his strength for one more assault. He only needed the proper opening. War swung hard with the gigantic sword, only missing by a hair's breadth. It was a small opening, but Steelbiter was sure he wouldn't get another. He swung hard with his damaged left forearm, causing War to move to block. This move to parry left War's breastplate exposed, and created the target Steelbiter wanted. A moment later, Steelbiter's jaws opened wide and the massive stream of corrosive acid burst forth, coating War from its neck all the way to its waist. As before, the breastplate dissolved, and Steelbiter made a move to strike at the storm of black energy in the creature's chest. War was quicker than the dragon had anticipated, its free hand rocketing forward, razor-covered fingers slicing the throat of the dragon and bursting the sacks that contained the corrosive acid. Steelbiter's most effective weapon would slowly eat the dragon from the inside out, but it mattered little. The great dragon was dead before its head hit the ground, his spine ripped to shreds by War's strike.

* * * * * * * * * * * *

Dane and Blade saw the opening at the same time. Even as Thalasia Steelbiter's corpse collapsed to the ground, the two former members of the phasia struck, unleashing massive torrents of pure Blaze flame into the storm of black energy and flashing lightning within War's chest. They both drew as deeply as they could manage, drawing more and more power from the supposedly limitless source. Dane felt as though his skin was on fire, and he continued to draw deeper, just to the edge of fatality. An earthshattering combination of screams and shattering metal roared from inside of War, and the massive form of the creature exploded. A backlash of energy burst in all direction, sending Blade and Dane, as well as thousands of troops sailing through the air in all directions. For several long moments, Dane didn't know if he was dead or alive, and the only thing he could see in front of his face was white light. Finally, his vision cleared, and he was looking at a steam-filled fog obscuring the mid-day sky. He sat up slowly, feeling like one gigantic bruise, and saw that the creature that called itself War was gone. Looking around, it appeared that Nessus was gone as well, and the battle that had been sparked minutes ago had suddenly come to a confusing and bloody truce. Dane took a long deep breath, closed his eyes, and laid his head back on the ground. It wasn't until he felt cold steel pressing against his neck that he was forced to open them again.

The Good Fight

Year Three of the Just Emperor Kaitain "Dragonsbane" Lorien, Creator's Calendar Year 1870

Midarin pushed hard, sending the form with her husband's eyes skidding across the floor. She was back on her feet the next second, one sword of pure dark energy forming in each hand. She pointed the tip of one blade at the still-unmoving form of Felicia Lorien, and the other at the prone body of the man who couldn't have been Gwydeon Sandar. To the man's credit, he stayed on his back looking up at Midarin for a long moment before sitting up slowly and then putting his hands at his sides. Whoever this man was, he obviously didn't want to further incite Midarin's anger. Without a word, Midarin motioned with her sword for the man to get to his feet. Slowly and deliberately, the man got back to his feet, but kept his hands at his sides. Out of the corner of her eye, Midarin saw Jerrard and Erika enter the now ruined audience chamber along with another man that Midarin didn't recognize. The unfamiliar man pushed forward, presumably in the direction of the fallen princess, but Jerrard smartly held him back. Confident that the unconscious form of the princess would not be returning to the fight any time soon, Midarin allowed the blade to disappear from her left hand, and with it pawed at her eyes to clear the last bit of haze from them. The man standing opposite her was standing stark still, his mouth closed, waiting for Midarin to make the next move.

"I am about thirty seconds from burning this entire palace to the ground, and there is not a thing that any of you can do to stop me. So I'm going to ask several questions, and either I get the answers that I want, or I'll make sure that the price paid is higher than any of you can stomach. I've already destroyed one palace today; don't think for a moment that I won't do it again."

Midarin first looked up at Jerrard and Erika and then back to the man who wore Gwydeon's face. When there were no objections or motions of any kind, Midarin nodded slowly.

"Alright, the first question is very simple. And this is the one that I promise you will get you all killed if I don't like the answer. Jerrard, you have been a friend to me and a friend to the Dark Gods for a very long time. Is this man standing in front of me Gwydeon?"

Midarin's eyes didn't leave the man standing in front of her, and the tip of her sword didn't waver from where it pointed.

"I didn't believe it myself at first," Jerrard said clearly. "When he came into the palace earlier today with the prince and princess, I thought my eyes were playing tricks on me. But once I looked in his eyes, once I heard him speak, there was no doubt in my mind that he is in fact Gwydeon. He as much told me so without telling me."

The answer seemed to shake Midarin for a moment, and the tip of her blade dipped ever so slightly. There was a long slow exhalation of breath, and then the sword steadied again. Midarin blinked slowly and then refocused her eyes on the man before her. His face was blank of expression, and there was no emotion in his eyes. If he wasn't Gwydeon, he was smart enough to play the situation as coolly and calmly as possible.

"If I believe Jerrard, you're Gwydeon," Midarin said, her voice low and cold, "but you can't be because Gwydeon has been dead for eighteen hundred years. So, if you aren't Gwydeon, give me one good reason why I shouldn't gut you right now."

The man kept his hands out at his sides, making no move to lower them or to advance or retreat. When he began to speak, his voice was calm, and as soon as she heard it, she felt the cold shock running through her. It was her husband's voice, burned in her memory over many years together.

"I would say I'm sorry, Midarin, but I know you well enough that you would only see it as an insult."

Midarin realized that she was nodding.

"The truth of the matter is, Midarin," Gwydeon said, finding some strength to put into his voice. "I did die that day at the hands of Terrik Lorien in an effort to assure the truce between Cadaria and Mythryn. Well, at least I thought I was going to die, and maybe what happened was much worse. When Terrik struck me with his Imperial Sword, while it may not have been able to kill me because of my nature as a Dark God, it certainly had an impact. Most, if not all of my abilities were removed, other than my immortality, and even that I have questions about. From what I assume, I don't age, but significant injury could end my life. I haven't really tested the theory."

Midarin wanted to smile. She wanted to give in to Gwydeon's terrible sense of humor, his dry and sometimes totally misplaced attempts to make tense situations lighter. But the anger that was rising within her was not going to let her see anything other than the lies and the betrayals that she had been subjected to for a longer period of time than could be easily swallowed. Midarin redoubled the glare at Gwydeon. There was no doubt in Midarin's mind that was the identity of the man who stood before her. It was Gwydeon, and the bile rose in the back of her throat at the realization.

"Tell me what happened, tell me why you stayed away, and tell me where you've been all this time."

Gwydeon nodded slowly, as though he knew the question was coming. He started to lower his hands, but stopped halfway through the motion and the unspoken question entered his eyes. Midarin gritted her teeth but finally nodded and lowered her sword. Gwydeon lowered his hands to his sides, and took a long deep breath before starting his tale.

"It started before there was even a Cadarian Empire to negotiate with. It started before the Fall. I think in some ways it started in the final days of Onea. When we all found out about the fact that we were just a playground for Emries and Halicon to fight out their personal grudges. But we didn't even know how deep things went. We didn't know about the other members of the Creator's chosen, and we certainly didn't know about the heralds or the dragons. My elevation to the so-called Brother of Angels was just a step below the power available to the Voice and the other heralds. Evan took the role of Voice, and Sabrina allowed herself to be chosen as the Spirit. The original plan was that they would gather as much information as they could about what was going on. But hell broke loose, and Dorovar started destroying worlds."

Midarin remembered it well. All of the Dark Gods at one time had been dispatched either to work damage control to pick up the pieces, or in an attempt to stop Dorovar's path of destruction. Of course no one had succeeded, at least until Evan and Meredith were dispatched. Of course, the price for that mission was high.

"What no one expected was for Talisia and her dragon allies to take the ideological battle further than it had ever been taken before. Emries taking a shot at destroying Halicon was the most direct attack against one of their own, and while it had resulted in Emries' defeat, it had also damaged Halicon to the point where he had gone into seclusion. He had been redeemed from the path that Shau-ling had led him down, but he was never the same after that. Emries was gone, Halicon was in seclusion, and Raenera had been missing since the death of Dorovar's world. Talisia saw it as the prime opportunity to strike at Pyrrus."

Finally Jerrard added his voice.

"We did everything we could, Gwydeon. There were too many dragons fighting on Talisia's side, and too few on Pyrrus' side. Even when we got involved, we had no chance to turn the tide. Pyrrus never had a chance, and we could only stand by and watch as Talisia cut him down."

Midarin remembered the scene clearly. Dragons and angels alike lay dead at each other's hands, and even more lay dead at the hands of the Dark Gods. But Talisia had set the situation up too perfectly, and Pyrrus ended up isolated against her. Pyrrus may have been a child of the Creator, but he was not as skilled as Talisia in personal combat, and he had no chance to defend himself against her assaults. Gwydeon was the only one close enough to try to make a difference, but he could only watch, a handful of paces away. After Pyrrus fell, Gwydeon was going to take Talisia's head, but the remaining heralds swooped in to prevent it.

"But before Pyrrus' death, the gears were already in motion for the creation of Espre. Sabrina had been planting the seeds in the Creator's ear for quite some time that his children would never be able to come to some decision about whose view of the cosmos was correct. The Creator would never have His answers. Talisia's actions pushed it over the line, and that was why Espre was created as a free world and Talisia was banished here. That was also why Dorovar was imprisoned here, and the reason that the dragons were lured here as well. All that was left to set the stage was the Dark Gods being cast out of the Heavens. Sabrina made sure that my expulsion trapped the dragons here so that they had no choice but to play out the game."

Midarin's eyes widened, and her frown deepened.

"You and Sabrina engineered this. I knew that we were pushing for a resolution, but I didn't know you were being this arrogant!"

Gwydeon took the angry tone in stride, and nodded.

"It had to be put to an end before more suffered. How many died on Dorovar's world? How many died on Onea? How many died on the dozens of other worlds that the children of the Creator failed to protect from one another? How many millions were killed by Dorovar on his rampage to get justice? It couldn't go on any longer. That is why we rebelled. That is why Sabrina made the bargain with the Creator to step down from her position as the Spirit. That is why the Creator lied to Evan about our fall. It had to be engineered to keep all the players in check."

For the first time, Midarin felt puzzlement fill her. Almost everything Gwydeon said made sense to that point.

"What does Evan have to do with all of this? And what do you mean all of the players?"

Gwydeon looked over to Jerrard and for the first time realized that Feyd was there. He grimaced and then looked to Jerrard again. There was suddenly a flash of light and Feyd collapsed to the ground. Jerrard seemed surprised but then Erika was at Feyd's side ensuring that he was comfortable on the stone floor.

"I'll make sure he doesn't remember any of this later," Jerrard said finally.

Gwydeon nodded and then turned his attention back to Midarin.

"You know that Evan was not just the Voice. He also had Aerith's powers. Ensuring that Evan would not feel some misplaced loyalty to Aerith or to our cause was the only way to ensure that the Voice would remain loyal to the Creator and ensure that control of the experiment would be maintained. Especially once the Creator ensured that all of the players were in place. Raenera was lured here, so was Halicon, and so was Emries. The remaining children of Halicon were brought here too, so the phasia had to be brought here to ensure that everyone and everything related to the children of the Creator would be in the battleground. That is why Talisia's servants are here. That is why Dorovar is here."

Midarin opened her mouth to speak, but Gwydeon waved her off. It annoyed her, but even after all this time, she knew he would not do it without good reason. Gwydeon was a man of few words in the best of times, and his explanations never included more information than necessary. However, now was a time that he needed to be specific and explicit.

"But we weren't alone. It couldn't just be those of us with power left to slug it out and kill each other for the sake of an ideal. That doesn't make someone right. It just makes you stronger. So there had to be more. There had to be a stake."

Midarin's eyes widened in realization. Her mouth was suddenly dry and revulsion filled her. Gwydeon recognized the look on his wife's face and nodded somberly. That was the great truth that Gwydeon had been wrestling with for so long, one that he had to wrestle with in isolation. The truth that kept him away from the rest of the Dark Gods; that kept him away from his wife and his daughter. The truth that made him plot the deaths of people he had once counted among his friends and allies.

"That's right. The Cadarians. The humans of this world are the stake. If they are wiped out by any side, no one wins. But they are the only way someone can be right. They have to be swayed to one side or another. Why do you think we fell in the middle of a civil war? It was the perfect opportunity for someone to take control and mold the people in their image."

"But you fought so hard to keep us out of it. You made sure we didn't fight," Midarin countered. "Couldn't we have made sure that none of the other groups took control?"

Gwydeon smiled.

"If only I could have trusted the other Dark Gods the way I trusted you, Midarin," Gwydeon's words were clipped, and she could tell by his tone that he genuinely regretted the words that were going to come from his lips next. "But there was no trusting Pike, or Aryx, or Diana, or any of the others. Midarin, I trusted you with my life, but if I included you on any of this, one of the others would have found out. As it was I had to find allies outside of the Citadel. The only person I dared trust was Sabrina, and that was because she could come and go from the Citadel without anyone knowing, and she had figured out that damn doubling skill that Basille always used."

Jerrard took two steps toward where Gwydeon and Midarin stood, but a stern look from Midarin told him not to come any closer.

"What about us? Why couldn't you trust us? We made it clear we wanted nothing to do with the Dark Gods or anything else on this world."

Gwydeon sighed hard.

"I couldn't trust the Forgotten. I didn't know where your loyalties lay, and I didn't know how close the Creator was keeping track of your movements. After all, Aerith and Bryn technically counted themselves as members of the Forgotten. You needed to be left to do what you needed to do when the time came. I proved to be right when I saw what the

Creator did after the civil war was over and the Loriens were in control of Cadaria. But I'm getting ahead of myself, aren't I?"

Midarin nodded, but found herself smiling a little, even though she didn't want to. She was close to the man she loved once again, and no matter the time since his death, what she felt for him had not diminished one iota.

"As I said, all of the phasia were brought back, but knowing that this was a game, and knowing the track record of the phasia, we had to take them out of the equation as quickly as possible. So, with the help of Sabrina, I pulled in the one person I knew I could trust."

Midarin wanted to scream.

"Logan."

It was Jerrard's voice that matched Midarin's thoughts. In the last days on Onea, in the dark mirror reality, the hero Logan Ranthall, a broken and wounded man, had used the powers of the Blaze to refashion himself into a member of the phasia, calling himself Lord Phoenix.

"When Logan embraced the Blaze, he opened himself to being called back from the void. When Sabrina and I explained the situation, Logan agreed to join us in hunting down the phasia and eliminating them one by one. I couldn't act too directly, so I left most of the business in Logan's hands. We were both a little surprised when we found out we weren't the only ones who had come to the same conclusion."

Gwydeon saw Jerrard nodding out of the corner of his eye.

"Jeroch."

Midarin looked first at Gwydeon and then to Jerrard. Before Gwydeon could provide more detail, Jerrard continued.

"As the lord of a kingdom, I have had the pleasure of entertaining members of the Knights of the Flashing Blade. Jeroch may be quite adept at making himself look ordinary to the people of Cadaria, but when you put him within view of someone who knows what the power of the phasia looks like, he has no chance. He was never as adept at hiding who he was as Erdric or Aldridge, and his pride in his powers and his position were often his downfall."

Midarin was stunned.

"Jeroch is a member of the Knights of the Flashing Blade?"

Gwydeon nodded.

"And has been for quite some time. He changes his face and his name every generation and insures that the title of Serpentine Knight will find its way back to him. Now he's Vallic Ultiv. And you probably won't be utterly surprised that his companion Isa is one of the phasia too. Ellis was quick to sign on to help Jeroch and Logan track down and eliminate all of the phasia. But Jeroch was obsessed with making sure that Saurn and Cedric were dealt with. As far as I know, we've gotten most of the phasia, and those we haven't gotten are dug in pretty deep, or got themselves killed without us."

"Meaning Logan is still out there," Midarin added.

Gwydeon nodded.

"He's got concerns of his own when it comes to the role of the Dark Gods, and he wants to make sure that when things come to a head, that people do exactly what they are supposed to."

The pieces were starting to come together in Midarin's mind. Gwydeon's logic was smooth, flawless; but there were still too many pieces missing for the whole picture to come to clarity. But her head was starting to hurt.

"It still doesn't answer why you stayed away. It doesn't tell me why I've had to mourn for you all this time, and why you couldn't have taken me with you into hiding."

Gwydeon swallowed hard and hung his head. His chest hurt, and he could feel the anxiety and regret and remorse building inside of him. He had been practicing this part for generations, and no matter how many times he went over it in his head, the words still sounded hollow. It was an excuse, nothing more; and an excuse that was based on eventualities that may never have come true. But it was all he had, and at the end of the day, she was either going to forgive him, or she was going to hate him for the rest of their lives, even if that meant for the rest of eternity.

"Once Terrik became Emperor, I thought we would have time to gather our forces and make things right. I thought that perhaps one of us could approach Terrik and create an understanding. But I never planned on Liette showing up. Liette was a creation of the Creator, a direct measure of control. Grawn had done the Creator a favor by killing Terrik's wife and child during the war, and left the newly minted emperor open to being paired to a suitably pliable spouse. Except it would end up being Terrik who would be the pliable one. Liette would manipulate Terrik, just like the rest of the Seers that would come after her, to ensure that Cadaria would remain in the middle of the war. The Creator stacked the deck, and then went farther when he allowed that thief to get a hold of Arturious Demascious' journal."

"The man who forged the Sacred Weapons and the Imperial Sword?" Erika asked.

Gwydeon nodded.

"For a long time, I thought the Sacred Weapons were just what they seemed to be on the surface. But then Jeroch and Ellis started doing the research that they are so famous for. Turns out that the weapons are more than just for the protection of the Empire. They get their powers from souls that are imprisoned inside. But not just any souls."

Gwydeon's next words were like an explosion in Midarin's mind.

"The reason Dorovar's world was destroyed was because Emries and Talisia interfered and gave power to Raenera's chosen followers. Power enough to defeat the dragons. Dorovar was the only one who didn't take the offer. It turned out to be enough power to destroy their world. They were touched by Raenera in word only. They were touched by Emries in action. Like the *Erieal* from our world, but to a much different and deeper degree. Like an Emries version of the phasia. So, when this world was created, they were brought here too, all thirteen of them. But somehow, they were trapped between this world and the Other Side, and I'm guessing that had something to do either with Raenera, or Dorovar or maybe both. That crazy weapon smith, when Dorovar touched his mind, learned about the souls of Dorovar's fellow acolytes and used them to ensure that either Dorovar would never get out of his prison, or would get out of his prison, depending on your point of view. The weapons are the keys. When they are broken or destroyed, the souls are released, and Dorovar's prison weakens. Not just the prison inside the Vault of Terrors, but this entire world. If they all are broken, nothing will prevent Dorovar from making good on his threat to use the souls of this world to fuel him into the Heavens where he can take on the Creator himself."

Midarin was dizzy, more than that she felt sick. But Gwydeon kept going.

"I had to stay away, because I had to make sure that balance was maintained until Emries and Raenera revealed themselves. I also had to make sure that Pike stayed right where he was. And as far as why I didn't take you with me, well, other than it would have been pretty damn peculiar that both you and I disappeared, without you there in the Dark Citadel, who would have been able to stop Pike from making war when the Cadarians broke the truce?"

She didn't want to understand. She didn't want to agree. But as usual, Gwydeon's logic was sound. More than that, he was right. Without Midarin's council, Pike would have launched his assault on Cadaria generations ago, and wiped the whole empire off the face of the world. That would have been the end of the game, and probably would have meant the death of everyone, including the Dark Gods. That was why Gwydeon fought so hard for the truce to begin with. There had to be peace, and there had to be more than just a physical battleground to fight on.

"But now Aerith has gone and turned everything sideways," Gwydeon growled. "Evan is dead, and Kaitain had gone off the deep end trying to search for this Dragon's Tear. I'm pretty sure that either Emries or Talisia has gotten to him. It's the only thing that explains all of the erratic behavior he's been displaying. So, I thought that I would try to get close to

Feyd and Felicia here in order to ensure that a more level-headed member of the Lorien family sat on the throne once Kaitain and his daughter were through destroying each other and trying to take the better part of the continent with them. I don't know how much of Cadaria would be left once the civil war has burned itself out, but I figured if one of them was around to pick up the pieces, we would have a better chance of getting things to fall our way."

Midarin looked at the fallen from of Princess Felicia Lorien and felt the frown return to her face. The sword suddenly disappeared from her hand, and she took a long step forward toward Gwydeon. They were standing nearly face to face, and Gwydeon could practically feel Midarin's annoyance like needles pressing into his skin. She leaned in conspiratorially, her mouth close to his left ear.

"If I so much as imagine that you touched that girl," she said, the venom practically dripping from her lips, "we're going to test to see just how immortal you are."

When she pulled back, there was no levity in her eyes, nothing that gave any indication to Gwydeon that she was anything but deadly serious. Resignation filled his eyes, but a moment later, he felt the soft and smooth skin of her hand on his cheek. When his eyes met hers again, the subtle softness of his wife's eyes had returned. He opened his mouth to say something, but her finger was at his lips almost immediately. She just stood there looking into his eyes. So much passing between them, so much time and so much distance, and yet it was as though all the years and all the lifetimes didn't exist. They were standing there together, and her heart raged. His arms reached out for her, and suddenly she was in his arms again, and he was holding her tightly against him. She could feel the way his muscles flexed, the way he smelled filling her nostrils. Then she could resist no longer. Her lips pressed against his. The sweetness of his lips, the taste of him stoking long-dead embers within her.

She was whole again….

Chapter LXVII

Who's More Foolish

Year Three of the Just Emperor Kaitain "Dragonsbane" Lorien, Creator's Calendar Year 1870

The Heart of Stone was crumbling, that much was certain. Hannah Ironheart didn't have to be an expert in stonemasonry to know that the damage done during the fight deep in the western wing of the keep had weakened the foundation, nor did she have to understand the source of the explosions that had ripped through the Heart on its eastern perimeter. Her home, and the home of the Church of the Creator within the borders of the Cadarian Empire, was shaking itself to pieces around her. It would not be a slow death, but it certainly was an inevitable one. The only thing to do now, as her new patron had said, was to save as many people as possible. However, even that task had proved more difficult than Hannah had anticipated. After all, Aerith Seth was still carrying the label of a traitor, and the newly named Empress Marlae Lorien had not reversed the order of death against him, nor had she had any reason to do so. Where Hannah tried her best to talk their way through the guards and the clerics who were doing their best to maintain some level of normalcy and sanity as the Heart of Stone disintegrated around them, Aerith's inclination was to break through first and talk second. The guards were already nervous enough without seeing Aerith with two weapons drawn ready for a fight. In some cases, Hannah was able to talk their way out of conflict, but only in those situations where Hannah knew the guards and the clerics personally. She seemingly held no sway over Gregor's men, and they barely allowed a word or two to come from either Hannah or Aerith before they charged into a battle they were hopelessly outmatched in. Both were now hopelessly stained with what could be construed as innocent blood.

Aerith leaned up against a cracked pillar, wiped sweat off his brow, and then shook his hair out sending pieces of plaster and dust in all directions. Hannah could tell that he was tired, and more to the point, she could tell that there was something more to his fatigue than just the near constancy of battle over the last hour. As though he felt her eyes on him, Aerith cocked his head to one side and let his eyes float over to Hannah. When Aerith's eyes met Hannah's his lips immediately curled into a cocky smirk. She didn't need to ask him if he was alright, Hannah knew now that she would never get an honest answer. The important thing now was that they had saved hundreds of innocent lives, and Hannah only hoped that in some small way it made up for the dozens of lives they had taken in the attempt. After a long moment, Aerith pulled the huge blade of Valor free from its sheath that hung on his back. He felt the weight in his hands and brought it to a guard position, having to shift the weight between his feet several times before finally finding the appropriate balance. Finally Aerith stood straight again, letting the tip of the blade rest against the stone floor.

"How did Gregor ever wield this thing?"

Hannah could feel Aerith's mind working. Since her inheritance of Aerith's mantle, Hannah had had little chance to think about what had happened to her. Of course there was the quick adjustment brought on by the necessity of battle. The powers were strange and exhilarating, but frightening at the same time. But her consistent exposure to Spirit had given her a taste of extraordinary power. What was most jarring was the access to memories and thoughts that were not her own. Memories on their own would have been easier to integrate into her own mind, but memories were not facts as though they were read out of dusty tomes. But Aerith's memories, and those that were part of her through the other bearers of his mantle, were all colored with the emotion of the moment, as well as the contextual memory of one looking back fondly or with horror on the past. Again, the complication was with the volume and not the information. Given enough time and familiarity, Hannah would be able to interpret Aerith's moods and thoughts, and be able to see through the color that his emotion lent to the accounts in his memories. However, there were four other tracks of thought in her mind, two which were incredibly similar, as if from sisters. The emotional swing was obviously feminine. As for the third and fourth, they were unquestionably male. Only one of the tracks of thought, one of the feminine ones, continued to add fresh content to her mind, but even those thoughts seemed to have trailed off. It wasn't as of the woman's life had been snuffed out, but more as though her thoughts were being hidden somehow from Aerith's view. Or maybe it was just hidden from Hannah's view. There was no telling how much that Aerith's mantle actually allowed those whom Aerith had chosen to see into his mind, or into the minds of the others that Aerith had touched, and already Hannah had begun to feel as though things were being hidden from her. Yes, there were the uncomfortable recollections about Aerith's intimate moments with Bryn and the emotions connected with those thoughts, but Hannah saw those as more of a shroud that Aerith's true thoughts could hide behind.

One thing had become clear to Hannah in the few hours that she had been able to spend with Aerith, there was more to him than even he wanted to admit. There in his mind were all of the marks of brilliance. He could speak dozens of languages, and the amount of information he had available to him concerning military theory and tactics, as well as individual combat abilities with a myriad of weapons were staggering and perhaps unparalleled. In addition, Aerith had access information about classical literature, poetry, and music. Moreover, Aerith had knowledge within him to play at least a dozen instruments. But all that was clouded behind the smug arrogance and nonchalance in which he looked at life. Perhaps it had been all the years that he had lived, or perhaps it was the fact that Aerith no longer saw life as a valuable commodity. In some ways the two were linked. Aerith had been alive for over two thousand years. He had seen wars, death on a scale that would make even the most battle-hardened soldier pale, and had known centuries of love and bliss with the only woman that truly mattered in his heart. He had children that he loved more than even he would admit, and yet, there was something about the relationship with his children that concerned him.

Ayden and Rhain were their parent's children in many ways. Ayden was a mirror image of his father, from his irreverent nature, to this aloof manner in which he viewed life. But there was a streak of his mother in him as well, because Ayden was not shy about the application of his powers in his everyday life. The casual nature in which he approached power concerned Aerith, and there was something in Aerith that believed that such a view would bring Ayden to a bad end. Like his wife and their children, Aerith had been born with his abilities, but they did not truly manifest until he was in his teens. Bryn, who never had a childhood, raised their children as though they were just smaller adults, and though she tired of them quickly, her patience proved to be more than Aerith had expected. But Bryn was not shy about using her powers, and she would use them for anything from levitating a glass of water from one side of the room to another, to leveling a city. To Bryn, both applications were reasonable and similar. Ayden shared that view. His powers were tools, and he would apply them in every means available to him. That is why Aerith had pushed for Ayden to attend the Academy of Arcane Arts. Perhaps there he would learn respect for his abilities, and not allow them to override his good sense in situations where the application of power was unwarranted or ineffectual. Aerith knew from personal experience that power in and of itself was never the answer to difficult situations, and more often than not made those situations worse.

Rhain was a completely different matter, and her situation troubled Aerith far more than Ayden's did. Like Ayden, Rhain saw her abilities as completely natural, but where Ayden used his extraordinary powers with impunity, Rhain was more judicious with her applications of those powers. It was the use of her very natural feminine physical prowess that Aerith found disconcerting. Bryn had never been one to be shy about her sexual nature, and many times would walk around the simple cottage that was their home in the nude. Naturally this powerful female role model had set an interesting precedent for the impressionable girl as she matured, and Bryn was never one to shy when tales of her role in the rise and fall of kingdoms were told. And like her mother, Rhain took these lessons to heart, and began to use her body as her tool of choice to infiltrate into the places of power and exact change. First this led her into the employ of the Shadow Guild where she assassinated high profile members of the Cadarian royalty, sometimes under the direction of the guild, and sometimes to further her own agendas. Now though, her casualness had led her into the bed of the woman who could well be the Empress of Cadaria. The knowledge made Hannah uncomfortable as well, but at much different levels than it did with Aerith. Hannah was a proud woman who had kept herself chaste under the direction of the Creator until she was bound for life with Gregor Quicksilver. But faced with the knowledge imparted by Aerith, she now had to live with the memories of a life that once would have qualified as wicked, devilish, and at the least hedonistic. Hannah was lost in her own thoughts when Aerith laid a hand on her shoulder.

"Are you alright? You've had to deal with a lot today."

Hannah looked up into Aerith's eyes, and felt the smile come to her face.

"I'm better than I thought I would be considering the circumstances," she said finally. "I'm not sure what you think of me, Aerith, but I do not like killing, no matter what the reasons. And no matter what I may have thought about the Creator before today, or after today, that feeling will not change. I know enough that you revel in battle, that you revel in killing, and regardless of how long I wear your mantle, I will never feel that way."

There wasn't a change in Aerith's expression, but Hannah knew that there was more venom in her voice than she had wanted. Perhaps it was frustration at the path her life had taken and the necessity to be both a priest and a warrior at the same time. A holy warrior was one that fought the battles of faith, not the battles of the flesh. And yet her role as a member of the Knights of the Flashing Blade made the battles of the flesh more important than the battles of faith. Moreover, serving at the leisure of immoral men made consistency of purpose in the eyes of those that required spiritual guidance impossible. Now Hannah found herself serving another immoral man, and yet immoral in a way that befuddled her. Was he truly immoral? Could he be immoral if he patently rejected the whims of a being that created the morality? Could those morals be true if they were imposed as a measure of control by an abusive Creator? These were all questions that ignited fierce frustration and conflict within the core of what Hannah Ironheart had always been. But was Aerith truly the one she wanted to vent these frustrations upon, or was he simply a convenient target.

"Good."

Hannah felt her eyes widen. She was too shocked for her expression to change more than that, and it wasn't until her chest started to hurt that she realized she was holding her breath. Aerith gave her shoulder a reassuring squeeze and returned to where he leaned against the column. He looked older now, gentle lines at his temple more apparent in the close torchlight. He smoothed his hair back twice before sighing deeply. He didn't look at her when he began to speak, but instead looked down the hallway that led to Marlae's bedroom. That was their last stop before heading in the direction that Tess and Camille had fled. Aerith was adamant that Marlae would still be in her room, and it seemed as if he knew he would not like what he found there.

"This isn't my life, Hannah," Aerith said, his voice thick with pain and sorrow, "I wasn't even supposed to be alive by my tenth birthday. And like so many children then, I had no idea why I deserved to die. But I was special."

The word rolled off his tongue as though it tasted vile. He nearly spat the word.

"Like the phasia before me, the *Coromor* after me, the *Erieal*, the Knights of the Flashing Blade, the Dark Gods, the touched of the Creator, Dorovar, his heralds, and all the rest. Special. Elevated above the rest by the Creator, for no other reason than because it served his whim. And what do the special bring in the Creator's universe? Do we do good works? Or do we just bring pain and destruction in our wake of change?"

Hannah felt there was overstatement in his words, but Aerith seemed to sense her trepidation and turned to face her with his palms turned toward her.

"These hands have felt the blood of so many on them, and the stains of the blood that were not drawn directly by me are the ones that will never be cleansed. My father and mother, a mother I never knew, and a father whom I would never know as a father, were taken from me when I was barely two years old. They were taken because my father was a powerful warrior, and his enemies wanted to make him pay by killing his family. I was sent to an orphanage, and it was burned to the ground by those same enemies who somehow learned I lived. How many innocent children died that day just because I existed? When I was sent to the mines, and I continued to survive, mine workers wanted to work my shift because they thought I was lucky. But time after time, the things came from the darkness, and the tunnels collapsed, and I continued to walk away, and those people who thought I was lucky didn't."

Hannah found herself wanting to argue, wanted to try to refocus his thoughts, but he continued, his thoughts taking a new direction that Hannah didn't expect.

"But it wasn't just those actions that caused death and suffering. My release from the mines found me in the arms of a woman I didn't know was a princess and bound to be the wife of the king of the lands. She had two children. My children, one of which would become another doomed hero in the war between the children of the Creator. My first born son, Cedric, led troops against Shau-ling and killed and lost thousands. That blood is as much on my hands as his because I know now that it wasn't chance that I met that woman in that town on that day. It was all engineered. I was a puppet on the string acting out his role. It could have ended there. If Emries hadn't manipulated the phasia, I could have just died. Cedric would have been spared his fate, as would everyone that came after. Espre probably never would have been created, and this ideological warzone wouldn't have existed. Maybe Halicon would have finished Emries off and the whole thing could have stopped there. Pyrrus wouldn't have died and things wouldn't have spun so far out of control. But no, it couldn't be that way. I had to die. Not for the wrongs I had done. Not for the death I had been responsible for. Not even for anything that I might have done in the future. No, it was because a pawn had to be sacrificed so that the game could continue."

Hate rolled off of Aerith like a fog. It clung to Hannah like grease and turned her stomach with every word. She was feeling the pain from his voice, feeling his emotion twist her stomach from recalling all of his stories in her own mind. She shared his revulsion and was horrified by it.

"But then once the pawn was sacrificed, something happened. Maybe it was the Creator's doing, or maybe it was something else," Aerith continued.

"But I was still alive, and still able to make changes. And how did I choose to do that? How did I choose to continue my legacy? I did nothing. I sat and watched as the world tore itself apart. And then the second generation came along, and I sat again, watching. But this time I chose to act. But of course I was too afraid, too ignorant to understand what was expected of me. So I gave away my powers, tied my anchor around another life. A life I eventually had to end because the Creator perverted my intentions."

His eyes lit up now, a flash that burned through the irritation and the pain.

"Then I was ready, perfectly ready to give it all up and just die. But I stumbled into the middle of something I shouldn't have, and I ended up saving the life of one of the Creator's children. I saved Halicon from the blade of one of his own children, and I realized that I had the power to work outside the wishes of the Creator. There was no plan guiding my fate, so I created one of my own."

He drew a small dagger from his belt and quickly ran it across his palm. Blood flowed from the wound for a long moment before it started to seal itself. But it wasn't that the skin pulled itself together. Hannah was unsure if mortal eyes could have seen or understood what actually happened. Tiny peaks of green flame simply created new skin in place of that which was torn, reversing the damage done.

"I'm not sure who had the plan first, or if there was even one plan. But Sabrina has taken another step. There are five of us now, and we have the power to change the world. More than that, we have the power to change everything."

The pause was pregnant.

"You surpassed your children."

Aerith frowned.

"Why do I always pick the smart ones?"

The frown reached Aerith's eyes, and some of the color drained from his face.

"Rhain and Ayden were born after I had given most of my powers to Evan, and Bryn had only the powers that her birth as a member of the phasia had granted her. She had no access to the Blaze, and as we learned later was unable to pass on the ability to touch it. Ayden and Rhain have powers, but they will never be able to be more than they are now. They are not like the children of the Dark Gods, and cannot compete with them on any level. But now, Bryn and I have returned to what we once were, and our children will forever be in that shadow, and there is nothing we can do. We are destined to outlive them, a fact that Bryn will never acknowledge, and one I can never forget or forgive myself for."

Finally Aerith fell silent. But there was something more there, Hannah was sure of it. There was something he would not, or could not say. Did he not trust her fully yet with his plan? Did he even know that there was a plan yet, or was she beginning to see the flaw and the brilliance of a life without a true fate? He stayed that way for a long moment until another rumble came from deep within the Heart, and more plaster and stone fell from the ceiling.

"We should get moving."

Hannah nodded and tightened her grip on Spirit, uneasiness filling her. The weapon had never been silent this long. It was more than just silence, Spirit was resisting her, ignoring her, and trepidation began to grow in Hannah that given the chance, the Sacred Weapon would work to betray her.

* * * * * * * * * * * *

Marlae's eyes snapped open as she felt the ground beneath her rumbling. It took a few moments for her to realize that she was laying on the cold stone floor, and only a few seconds longer to realize that she was doing so naked and atop the body of a strange man. She sat up and reached out toward the bed to pull a sheet down over her, when she saw that her hand was covered in dried blood. The shock of it was enough to stay her hand and keep her staring for a long time, until she felt the form beside her begin to stir. A small groan escaped the man's lips, and Marlae finally shook herself enough to pull the cover down around herself. Finally his eyes opened, and the angry recriminations that were perched on the tip of her tongue died in her mouth. Their eyes met, and though she didn't know his name, she felt suddenly as though she knew everything about him. His pain, his torment, and the greatness that was locked away inside of him. He smiled and started to sit up.

"Good morning, Empress," Ayden said in a weakened voice. "I owe you my life."

She was suddenly aware of the scar on his chest, and then the horror of the blood on her hand leapt back into her mind. She reached out with the bloody hand, pressing it against his chest. It was his blood, and he had been hurt. It all seemed like a dream. He fell from the sky like an angel, and she had been there to save him.

"The Creator brought you to me," Marlae said, finding her regal voice once more. "All my protectors have gone, and the Creator sent you to take their place. It could only mean that here, in this place, in the Heart of Stone, the most holy of the sites dedicated to the Creator, that He has ordained that I should be the Empress of these lands."

Ayden finally got to a fully seated position and felt his heartbeat surge with Marlae's hand upon his chest. So many of his memories were jumbled and didn't make sense. He knew that he was at the Imperial Palace, learning about the Emperor's dark academy, where he was teaching those with the talent for touching the arcane to use their powers for destructive purposes, to loose against the Dark Gods and the dragons. Before that he had been in the Academy of Arcane Arts where his parents had sent him to learn to control his abilities. His powers that were gifts from his parents who themselves were akin to the Dark Gods. And then he had been face to face with Emries. He had been face to face with the evil that his father had warned him about, the child of the Creator that wanted nothing but to annihilate not only his father, but his whole family and everyone that he had ever loved or would love. Emries had cut him down, and cut him down easily. Had it not been for Jaccob, the good man Jaccob Aldora that he left to die an ignominious and humiliating death at the hands of a monster, Ayden would have died there on the floor of the Imperial Palace. Ayden had known Jaccob's fate long before he ever met the man. It was foretold to him by the Dark Seer, Jehna Feris. She told him the role that he would play in Jaccob's demise, but that only through Jaccob's death would

Ayden's true path be revealed. Perhaps this was it, perhaps Marlae was right. The Creator had saved him, saved him from Emries, and put him here to protect Marlae. That was why the portal did not go where it was supposed to. The Creator wanted him here, and He made it so. Ayden scrambled to his feet, and pulled Marlae to hers quickly.

"I'm sorry Empress, but I have to get you out of here while I can. It's not safe."

Marlae nodded, and pulled an elegant gray dressing gown from the bench at the foot of the bed while Ayden recovered a stone from his pocket. She watched in amazement as the young man pulled the stone open to a swirling blue portal. He smiled at her, took her hand and led her to the event horizon of the portal.

"Just stay with me, and you will be fine. I'll take you somewhere safe until we can rally your troops to take your empire from your father."

Marlae reached out and clung to Ayden's arm and the two stepped through the portal together.

* * * * * * * * * * * *

Debris had fallen in front of the door that led to the bedroom that had been given to Marlae Lorien for her stay in Albitonin. It took only a moment for Aerith to clear it with his abilities, and Hannah opened it quickly. They both rushed into the room to find the bed mangled, and a large blood stain on the floor. Hannah knelt by the dry pool of blood fearing the worst, but when she looked back at Aerith, she saw that he had his eyes closed and was concentrating. As if feeling her uncertainty, he opened his eyes and turned to face her.

"There's been two portal opened in this room. And not just any portals either, they were made by the stones. Rhain must have come back for Marlae."

Hannah didn't feel any better.

"What about the blood?"

Aerith frowned.

"It's your choice, Hannah," Aerith said finally. "Marlae or Tess. Your call."

Were she another woman in another place in another time, Hannah probably would have allowed herself to curse under her breath. But she was not. She was Hannah Ironheart, and she would remain that until the end of her days. Which left her only one choice.

"Tess."

Aerith nodded, reached into his pocket and pulled out a black stone. He tossed it to Hannah in one quick motion.

"Time for you to start learning my good tricks."

Drifting Souls Collide

Year Three of the Just Emperor Kaitain "Dragonsbane" Lorien, Creator's Calendar Year 1870

Sabrina Binosear sat on a small wooden chair in the corner of the captain's suite on the *SeaFox* and rubbed her temples. She had never been at sea before, and between the rocking of the waves and the new powers that were blossoming inside her, it felt like her stomach wanted to come out her nose. It had taken her time even to get enough of her balance underneath her to walk to the captain's quarters, and Taya had been more than generous about extending the courtesy. As it was, Taya had been busy marshaling her forces and pushing through the forward naval lines of the Cadarian Empire. By this time, Taya had had generations to ply her trade as a pirate on the high seas, and she had become an expert on naval tactics. The flotilla under her command was not nearly as large as the one that could be brought to bear by the Cadarians but her knowledge of tactics and the manner in which the Cadarians operated gave her enough of an advantage that sheer numbers were not an issue. However, even Taya knew that taking her entire flotilla into Cadarian waters and into the docks of one of the Great Kingdoms was not without significant risk. However, once they had made berth in Celidar, they would be a lot harder to deal with without the bulk of the Cadarian fleet to oppose them. Already Sabrina had heard the powerful cannons of the *SeaFox* ring out and the shouts of the crew members under Taya's command. Battle had been joined at least twice so far, and there was no indication that the rest of the journey would be without bloodshed. Now though, at least for a few minutes, the guns had fallen silent. There came a quick knock at the door of the quarters, and Sabrina had enough time to look up before the door opened. She had expected Taya to walk through the door, but instead, it was Rhain. Sabrina was able to manage a weak smile to the much younger woman. Rhain closed the door behind her and walked half-way across the room before perching herself on the edge of the map table that stood in the center of the room. That table was also where the Snag had chosen to make its own bed, and Sabrina heard the pitch of its normally deep constant purr elevate slightly in recognition. Rhain reached out and gently stroked the Snag, an act that to Sabrina seemed both absurd and comforting. The Snag was a creature bred to kill, and there was nothing gentle in the creature's physical nature, from its razor-sharp teeth, to its deadly tail, to its blood that could burn through the bodies of its enemies even in death. But for Rhain, the big black ball of fur had always been like a member of her family. Not a pet, because the word implied responsibility for the creature's wellbeing, but more like a strange sibling.

"You look terrible."

Sabrina looked up into Rhain's eyes and did her best to smile weakly. Rhain had obviously spent enough time at sea that the transition did not bother her, and her eyes were as bright as ever. One thing had changed about her though. The bright red hair that she had been displaying when she and Sabrina first met had been toned down since their arrival on the *SeaFox*. The predominant color was now a slightly more brown shade of auburn with deeper red streaks shot through it. She looked much more like her mother now, in both her attire and her posture. The white dress she wore looked like it could have come right out of Bryn's wardrobe. As if sensing Sabrina's puzzlement at her change of attire, Rhain smiled and smoothed the dress at her stomach.

"Taya keeps clothes for Aerith and Bryn on board in case one of them happens to drop in. Mother and I are close enough to the same size that I can fit into all but her most scandalous dresses. Well, what little modesty I have really prevents me from trying to fit into those."

Sabrina laughed slightly, and her stomach lurched. Her skin felt like it was on fire and even her hair hurt. Hanging her head again, Sabrina closed her eyes and rubbed her temples again. It wasn't helping, but at least the discomfort of the pressure on her temples was distracting her from her stomach, at least for a few seconds. Her long brown hair hung down over her face, and when she looked up again, she brushed some of the strands out of her face. Rhain remained where she was, a bit of concern creeping onto her face.

"I assume this isn't just sea-sickness."

Sabrina shook her head.

"The human body was never intended to house the kind of power that was given to a child of the Creator," Sabrina began, looking as much down at the floor as she was at Rhain. "When I was possessed with the power of the Spirit, I held only a fraction of the Creator's power and even that felt like it was going to tear me apart. With Halicon's power, I'm not sure I'm ever going to adjust to it. But at least I can try. Aerith's powers are helping a little. I've lost his mantle, but the memory of how he uses his powers to hold himself together is helpful."

Rhain nodded. Though her parents were diminished when Rhain and Ayden were born, they were able to impart at least some ability to touch forces similar to those granted to the Dark Gods. One of the first lessons that Aerith taught to both his son and his daughter was the ability to channel the powers within them to knit wounds and to overcome illness. Small wounds were easy to deal with, and the powers could be leveraged to heal even wounds that would be considered mortal. Aerith once told the story of how he once reconnected an arm that had been severed during a battle.

"Whatever Halicon's power is doing to me," Sabrina continued after a moment, "it feels like it's completely destroying every part of my body and then remaking it piece by piece. I'm using all the power at my disposal just to hold the rest of me together as it continues its work. I hope by the time we get to Celidar, that the process will be complete."

Rhain shifted uncomfortably.

"What is it?" Sabrina asked meekly, trying her best to raise her eyes to meet Rhain's.

"I'm concerned about you, and I'm concerned about the others who came through with us. Gabriel and Devlin for everything they've done are still members of the Knights of the Flashing Blade. Taya had to put them below decks under guard to make sure that none of the crew tried to take out a vendetta on them. Taya trusts her crew, but there are some things that can cause even the most rational man to lose hold of his senses. And we are talking about pirates after all."

The unspoken thought hung in the air between them.

"And Aerith too," Rhain finally added.

This caused Sabrina's color to return to her cheeks a little.

"Aerith's fine. He lives to be in the middle of impossible situations. Why do you think he stayed married to Bryn?"

The joke didn't elicit a response from Rhain, and the younger woman kept her eyes trained on Sabrina's face. She could see the weakness in her eyes, and the way that her features had been ravaged by her new powers. She was so pale, and it looked as though many great weights had been placed upon her shoulders, and it was a monumental effort just to lift her head. It looked like the life was being squeezed out of her moment by moment. Sabrina didn't need to be able to read Rhain's thoughts; the sentiment was painted clearly on her face and was practically being screamed by her eyes. There was concern there of course, but underneath the concern for a woman who had every right to be called a member of her family, there was fear. Fear at what Sabrina was becoming, and fear at what that becoming was doing to her.

"I'm not sure how Halicon lived with this," Sabrina said finally, rubbing her temples again. "It's like I can feel everyone who can touch the Blaze in my head. But it's not like the connection that I had with Aerith. When I wore Aerith's mantle, I could reach for his thoughts and feel them run through my mind, but at the same time I had access to all of his memories and his emotions whether I wanted them or not. I know he got glimpses into my head too, and in a lot of ways we shared so much that we were like two halves of the same person. I could feel everyone else that wore his mantle before me too. Not in the same way that I felt Aerith of course, but I could access their thoughts and their memories from the time that they wore the mantle. It was overwhelming dealing with the emotions of all the different people. It could be confusing too, especially because everyone that held Aerith's mantle before me was a man. I have to tell you that that can cause some real interesting thoughts to cross your mind. But I don't need to tell you about that."

For a moment Rhain didn't know how to take the comment. Was it a subtle insult, or was it just an expression of shared experience? There would be time enough to figure that out later. For that moment thought, Rhain kept her own council and continued to listen to Sabrina.

"I talked to Bryn once a long time ago about the Blaze, and what it felt like to her. She always told me that it was this raging fire in the back of her mind that never went out. It was comforting and soothing, and filled her with the sense that as long as she held on to it, she could do anything. But there was a deeper part of the Blaze too, a control that Halicon put into place to prevent his phasia from becoming too drunk on their own power. The power of the Blaze is not like a siren-song. It isn't seductive. It's a living thing that reacts to being used. The more you want its power, the more it pulls away from you. You have to surrender to it for it to be at its most potent. And once you've taken hold, you can continue to draw upon it. I have memories of the first of Halicon's scions. The ones that first fought against Emries on a world far from Onea."

Rhain perked up a little. There were scarcely few stories about the times before Onea existed and the lives of the Dark Gods. Though they had been thrust into the war between the children of the Creator, the mystery of its origins continued. As Sabrina began to speak, Rhain saw the door to the captain's quarters open slowly, and Taya entered. Sabrina looked up at Taya, but did not stop her tale.

"For most of the first hundred millennia, the conflicts between the children of the Creator were largely of words. But as time wore on, the battles of ideology and philosophy began to spill out into each of the sibling's worlds. It wasn't until Onea of course that two of the siblings would actually directly clash, but there was an incident before Onea, a direct attack by Emries against Halicon's ideology that was very nearly the last. When Halicon created his scions on each of his worlds, he linked them to the Blaze, which was essentially his own life force. The phasia were a much more militant version of these scions, bred for the specific purpose of battling Emries, and were the extension of the nightmare that was Shauling. Halicon's scions on other worlds were artists, scholars, diplomats, and philosophers. They could draw on the Blaze freely and used that power to explore the depths of their own existence and to create wonders of art and architecture. But Emries warned Halicon that granting his followers access to his own life would be dangerous and that given the opportunity, even his own creations would turn on him. They debated furiously over this linking technique. Emries saw betrayal and greed in every creature, and so in his followers he bestowed only a finite power, and sought to control and protect himself from those most base impulses."

Sabrina paused here, as though the memories were difficult and painful. But after a long, slow, deep breath, she pressed on.

"Halicon's trust in his scions in those days was limitless and he felt that the level of control that Emries sought was not possible with intelligent beings. Free will would only allow them to be lead to a point, but never truly controlled. Control was an illusion of a weakened mind, and the arrogant desire of those who have no mastery over themselves. Of course Emries resented this characterization and sought to prove his point in the most direct way possible. Under the guise of a prophet of the Creator, Emries visited the scions of Halicon and began to convince them that their own ambitions were being thwarted; that the powers they were granted did not give them freedom, but were actually a leash. These scions had the power to change the face of the world, to fix what was broken, and to make everything right for all time. Halicon knew immediately of these attempted manipulations, and the faith in the motivations and loyalty of his scions was absolute. Emries' attempted manipulations were rebuffed at every turn until Emries himself was convinced that his initial plan was a failure. However, this only strengthened his resolve. Emries became obsessed with tearing down Halicon's shadow of control and prove that faith and trust in lower beings could only lead to betrayal."

Tears began to well in Sabrina's eyes, and as her story came to its conclusion, they began to fall freely down her face.

"Emries took his message as the prophet to the other beings of the world. His role as a prophet and his message preaching the evil of the scions struck a jealous chord in the hearts of most beings. Emries convinced hundreds of thousands that they were slaves suffering under the yoke of the false and evil powers of the scions. A revolution was born, a full-scale world-wide rebellion against the scions in the name of the 'One Who Brings Change.' The rebellion raged on for years. The conflict was assisted by the fact that Halcion's scions refused to use lethal force against the innocent beings who were hopelessly manipulated. Halicon had hoped that eventually the scions would find a way to break through Emries' lies. However, Halicon would not recognize his mistake until it was almost too late. Greed, resentment, and lust for power had taken hold, and reality had warped to the point where the lie had become the truth. Halicon's trust and belief had been his undoing by the hand of Emries' indoctrinations and when the rebellion reached its climax, Halicon's scions found themselves overwhelmed by sheer numbers. Finally, left with no choice, and driven by the unrelenting need for self-preservation, the scions struck back. But at this late hour, there were just too many to stand against them. The scions fell under waves of rebels. Tens of thousands died."

Rhain was starting to feel the oppressive sadness that was radiating from Sabrina, and one look over at Taya, and she knew that her much older niece was feeling the same way.

"In a last gasp attempt to salvage their own lives, as well as the innocent beings on the world, the five remaining scions drew deeply on the Blaze, deeper than they ever had before. Despairing, lost, and filled with fear, the words Emries left to fester in their minds suddenly had fuel to stoke the flames. Their intentions were to remake the face of the world, to turn back the hands of time and bring peace back. But no matter their exertion, they saw only more death mounting around them. So the scions drew deeper still, so deep their hearts stopped beating and their lives were buoyed on the raging flames of the Blaze. And still only death swirled around them, so they drew deeper still. One of the scions simply ceased to exist due to the exertion. Time slowed, seconds passed as though they were minutes, and the whole of the world shivered. Continued exertion vaporized another of the scions, the roaring flames of the Blaze consuming her from within. The three remaining scions drew on the new reserves of anguish and pain, finding the will to draw even deeper."

Sabrina's face was flushed now, her voice quavering and the tears streaming down her face. For a long moment her voice caught in her throat and she had to pause, waiting for the wave of emotion to subside enough for her to continue.

"Worlds away, Halicon was paralyzed in pain and weakness, his life force being drained as the seconds passed. The scions that he had trusted were now robbing him of his life. But as he reached across the void to touch their minds, to implore them to stop, he felt no malice, only deep pain and regret. They understood their mistake. Their fear and arrogance had been their undoing. Halicon had no choice but to sever his connection to his scions, killing them instantly, and nearly extinguishing the Blaze in the process. Halicon was so overwhelmed with sadness that he withdrew into the formless Cosmos for millennia before reemerging at the call of the Creator to become Shau-ling."

Sabrina's eyes closed, and she hung her head at the conclusion of her story, not even having the strength to paw at the tears that were staining her cheeks. The three sat silent for a long time before Taya finally cleared her throat to gain the attention of the other two women. When Sabrina finally looked up Taya did her best to force a smile.

"I was just coming to tell you. We broke through the last of the sentry lines, and by nightfall we'll be in the harbor at Celidar."

For the first time since their arrival on the *SeaFox*, the rumbling in Sabrina's stomach began to quiet.

* * * * * * * * * * * *

It was late into the night when Felicia Lorien woke. Her mind had been filled with such miraculous and terrifying dreams; a woman knight with incredible powers that she wanted to pass on, a demon made of metal, and a Dark God. Part of her fully expected to see the familiar walls of her quarters in Lordhill, normalcy returned to her life from the nightmare of a year that had consumed her. But when her eyes did finally open, the single flickering light of a candle illuminated the sparse walls of the little room in the royal palace of Celidar. When she sat up, she realized firstly that she was fully dressed, and secondly that she was not alone in her room. Sitting at the foot of her bed was the woman whom she had fought, the one who identified herself as a Dark God, and behind her stood the man who had been her protector on the journey here, Wynne. She remembered suddenly that the fight, and Diana, and Nightwing were not dreams, but in fact very real. She wanted to jump out of the bed and grab for her sword, but it was then that the pain returned to her. It had never really stopped, but the dreaming had kept it at bay, at least for a little while. Perhaps it was the jittery nature of her movements, or perhaps it was the mixture of panic and confusion in her eyes, but Wynne gently raised one hand, and that simple gesture seemed to ease Felicia. The princess thought she saw the woman bristle at his ease with the girl, but perhaps that was her nature.

"You've been asleep for perhaps an hour," Wynne said gently, and in a quiet tone, "and we wanted to make sure that we were here when you woke up."

He put his hand on the woman's shoulder for a long moment, and then as if finally acquiescing to the queue, she began to speak.

"I don't know how much you remember," Midarin said calmly, with more gentleness creeping into her words as she continued. "You took a pretty nasty blow to the head when you went crashing through the wall. I knew that Nightwing was a tough creature, but you obviously haven't had it at your disposal for very long, and so we did not know how well it would have protected you."

"The important thing," Wynne said in a tone that bespoke steering a conversation back in a less confrontational direction, "is that you are alright."

Felicia finally was able to get to a full seated position. Her head did hurt, but that was the least of the pains that wracked her body. She felt like one large throbbing bruise, but she knew that by morning all of the pain and external bruising would be gone. The healing abilities that Diana had given her had already mended the largest part of the damage.

"You've taken a step into a much larger world than you can imagine, little princess," Midarin said, careful to keep any mocking out of her tone. "Diana was one of the oldest members of our group, and she had fought in wars that my husband and I could never have dreamed of. Not only do you have her powers, but you have those of Nightwing, who was created to kill people like us all those millennia ago. In mortal terms, Felicia, you may have been a formidable woman before. But now there are few that could stand against you in combat, and as you have seen, you can even hold you own against a member of the Dark Gods. With some practice, you will do much better than you did against me."

If there was a compliment there, Felicia had a hard time finding it. Then the word husband resonated through her mind. Jerrard had said that Wynne was married, but Felicia never dreamed that he was married to a member of the Dark Gods. If perhaps she had had more time to delve through Diana's memories, or the memories of the Blaze she wouldn't have been as shocked. But as it stood, her mind was racing and unable to grasp any of the information that flowed through it. There were a thousand questions that she wanted to ask that she didn't honestly want the answer to. Then, as if in answer to some unspoken prayer, the salvation to her racing mind came in the form of a quiet knock at the door. Wynne and Midarin both turned their head just as the door opened. Jerrard Mistic didn't enter the room, he only ducked his head in far enough that he could be clearly seen.

"We've just received word that Taya's flotilla has docked at the harbor. They'll be coming to the palace soon. But Taya sent word ahead that she has two members of the Knights of the Flashing Blade with her, as well as Sabrina and another woman that she refuses to name through the page. What she did say was that Sabrina has some very interesting information concerning the whereabouts of an old friend of yours."

Wynne's jaw visibly tightened, and he let his head bow slightly before looking back at Jerrard and nodding. He put his hand back on Midarin's shoulder, and the woman rose from where she sat.

"We may have to go away for a while," Wynne said softly. "You get some rest, and make sure your father remains protected. I have a feeling that in the days and weeks to come, he's going to be very important."

CHAPTER 67

Midarin was the almost through the door when Felicia's feet hit the floor and she forced her way to a standing position. She was just reaching for her sword when she spoke.

"Wherever it is you're going, you're not leaving me behind."

What the Mind Forgets
the Heart Remembers

Year Three of the Just Emperor Kaitain "Dragonsbane" Lorien, Creator's Calendar Year 1870

Bryn realized that she was crying moments after Vallic had finished recounting his final moments with Cedric Binosear. Of course, she did not weep openly, and for her the massive display of the raging emotions inside of her consisted of a single tear that ran slowly from the corner of each eye. Even to the trained eye the tears would not have been visible under normal circumstances, but with the soot and dirt on her face, Bryn was sure that the streaks were more than noticeable. While Bryn had never been close to Cedric, she did respect the fact that Cedric was Aerith's son, and Aerith would always have a soft spot in his heart for his first born son. There were times that Bryn wished he had shown the same kind of affection for their first son, Gideon, but she had given up that argument a long time ago. Isa had her hand on Vallic's shoulder through his whole tale, and there were many times that she winced right along with Bryn at the description. It was as though she was hearing parts of the story for the first time too. Perhaps Vallic and Isa were truly in love with one another, and they were trying to push through the parts of their nature that made them both impossible. Isa had an insatiable thirst for knowledge, and she would ferret out any piece of information that she thought was relevant. The unfortunate part was that

Isa thought everything was relevant. That was how she found out about Aerith Seth, how she found out about the game between Halicon and Emries, and obviously how she found out about the nature of this world. Vallic was just the opposite. When he was the leader of the phasia, Vallic excelled at keeping secrets, and was never thought of as one of the more intelligent or insightful members of the order. Most members of the phasia simply looked at him as Halicon's pet that was called upon when something needed to get done. The infuriating part of that equation for the more volatile and ambitious members of the phasia was that Vallic usually got the job done. Together they would be a formidable pair, and obviously they had learned to coexist while still keeping their cores intact.

"So where do we go from here?"

Isa's question was not idle. Bryn had been dispatched to start the slaughter of the members of the Knights of the Flashing Blade, and no matter his past, Vallic Ultiv was still a member of that order. Now there were additional complications. If Vallic was right, Cedric had taught a mortal how to touch the Blaze, and she too was a member of the Knights of the Flashing Blade. This job was getting better and better all the time.

"So no one else knows you're here? None of the Dark Gods?"

Vallic sighed.

"Sabrina knows we're here obviously and Pike found out a great many years ago. He was good enough to keep things quiet, but he does have a tendency to call in favors now and then. If I didn't like him before when he was just a troublesome farm boy, I like him much less now that he has the powers of a god."

Bryn could see the fury burning in Vallic's eyes. But it was Isa that spoke.

"You've been away too long, Bryn. Pike Rhuiden, or whatever name the Creator has forced him to wear on this world, is not the headstrong boy that followed Logan and the others into hell. He isn't the same young man who carved his way through so many of us when he shouldn't have had a chance to keep standing. The power and the position within the hierarchy of the Dark Gods has turned him into the worst thing that he could be. It has unlocked his true nature and that in and of itself is disgusting. What is more revolting is that he had used this position to take advantage of those who have no way to protect themselves, including his current wife."

Vallic reached up and put his hand on Isa's forearm. Isa was not prone to such emotional outbursts, and Bryn knew there was more of a story there. One that she was sure would never be told.

"We have some measure of our powers left," Vallic said, some strength seeming to return to his voice, "but even together, as you've seen, we're no match for you, let alone a full member of the Dark Gods. You have power Bryn, probably more than you had when you were a member of the phasia, but you know that pales in comparison to what Pike and the others have available to them. They could each crush us like bugs if they wanted. Pike knows it, and while he doesn't fully know why, Pike understands that we desire to remain on this rock until the game is at an end. He uses that against us."

Bryn's stomach lurched.

"Are you telling me that Pike is extorting from you in exchange for your lives?"

Vallic put both hands flat on the table, and pushed back slightly. The chair made a horrible scraping sound in the silence that held the room, and then Vallic pushed his way back to his feet. Obviously, Vallic had been able to use the limited powers at his disposal to speed the healing of the wounds that Bryn had inflicted in their brief encounter, but Bryn could tell by the way he was bracing himself, he still had a fair amount of healing to go before he would be back in full fighting shape.

"It started out simply. He just wanted information, and we were happy to oblige. The threats came later. We helped him amass troops for his armies on the Dark Continent, and kept our eyes out for those who were discontented with the rule of the Lorien family. But then the demands became more twisted. He would invite himself to royal functions and use us as either alibies or scape goats when a princess or a lady left without her virtue. If only Pike dedicated as much of his focus to solving the real problems as he did to indulging his libido."

Vallic reached over and put a reassuring hand on Isa's shoulder. For a moment it seemed as though she was going to shrug it off, but then she remained firm in her stance. Her frown deepened.

"Part of it is my fault," she said finally. "He knew that I had continued to gather information after the Fall, and he knew that if there was any place that he would be able to learn how to hurt the Creator and his children, it would be here. So he raided my library and then me in order to get the information he wanted. Finally he came across the ramblings in a few journals about something called the Dragon's Tear. It was a legend from the beginning of this world, and probably from a few others, but Pike became obsessed."

Bryn stood finally and smoothed her dress. It was all she could do to contain the fury in her, and no matter how she tried to construct her next words, they would not come out the way she wanted. She was never one, even in those long years with Isa and Grawn in Frontier, to sit around and listen as Isa droned on endlessly, and she could not abide another history lesson. There had been too much talking already. Those days the talk and the planning was about the way to overthrow Shau-ling and to put the phasia in their rightful places. If they had only known then half of what they knew now, the phasia would have united under the banner of their maker and wiped Emries and his followers off the face of Onea. But they were stupid and short sighted. They only wanted power and control. And now, one of the heroes that had a hand in their defeat was acting just as they would have all those millennia ago. What's more, he had the power to make good on his threats to upset the whole world, and perhaps the whole of creation. It was time to act. It was past time.

Bryn set her jaw firmly.

"Pike didn't tell me to avoid coming here, and he didn't place any restrictions on my targets, so I'm sure he knew that I would come here, and I'm sure he hoped that I would destroy you before I realized who you were. For that, and for that alone, I want him dead."

Isa's eyes widened, and Vallic opened his mouth to speak, but Bryn held up a hand. She was so angry that her body was shaking. After a moment, she lowered her hand, took a deep breath, and continued on.

"I've had enough of conspiracies, and I've had enough of being part of a game that I didn't know was going on around me. I was managed by my husband because he knew that I would act rashly when patience was needed. I was managed by my children so they could get themselves in the right positions to continue this absurd plan. And now I've been managed into nearly eliminating two people that I love dearly, regardless of our past."

Bryn looked over at Isa, and clicked her tongue.

"Don't look at me like that, Ellis."

The name felt good coming off her tongue. It felt more natural, and it felt right. She would have no more of this Isa and Vallic nonsense.

"I've never been sentimental, and I've burned down more sentimental fools than I can remember. But we are phasia. I'll say it again. We are phasia. We're not humans, we don't think like the humans, and our hearts don't rage like theirs do. We were bred to make them our slaves, and we were bred to crush their belief in the false god Emries. But we aren't on Onea anymore. We made our mistakes and lost our world. And now we have another chance. The Dark Gods are our enemies, Emries is our enemy, the Cadarians are our enemies. Aerith may not have wanted me as part of his plan before, but now that I know there is a plan, I'm going to make sure that I am there when it comes to fruition."

Her eyes passed from Ellis to Jeroch.

"Come with me. Leave all this behind. Leave the lies and the false names and the pain behind. Stop hiding and come with me."

For a long moment silence held the room. Jeroch first looked from Bryn to Ellis and the two long time companions held each other's gaze for a long time. Finally Ellis closed her eyes, bowed her head and nodded. Jeroch nodded sharply once and then returned his gaze to Bryn.

"Vallic Ultiv is dead."

"It's not nice to deprive a woman of her enjoyments," a strange woman's voice came from the darkness at the edge of the room. "And preventing me from saying those words to my Emperor is certainly high on that list. Second of course to the actual act of cutting you to pieces."

Bryn immediately turned to the doorway and fire launched from her hands and crossed the distance in a heartbeat. The entirety of the doorways was engulfed in flames, but the woman's voice rang out against the next moment.

"Come come now," the feminine voice called out from seemingly everywhere in the room at once, "you don't think I would let myself be taken by such an obvious attack. I am the Emperor's top assassin, and I have killed very talented wielders of the arcane arts. None of them have even scratched me yet, and I don't think the lackeys of a masquerading member of the Knights of the Flashing Blade will put up much more of a challenge. But I would be disappointed if you didn't try."

Jeroch's eyes widened and he put both hands under the table in the center of the study and sent it flying toward Bryn. She fell to the floor at the last moment, the table passing over her head and slamming into the wall. Half a heartbeat later, a portal opened where Bryn's head would have been. Another portal opened behind Jeroch the next moment, and a three-pronged set of claws emerged first, just missing his spine, but ripping through his already damaged side. Ellis was the next to move, pushing Jeroch clear of the follow-up attack mere moments before it would have ended his life. As it was the claws ripped across his shoulder as he was falling away, and then the hand and cruel weapon disappeared back through the portal and it winked out quickly. When the portal opened again, it was on the far side of the room, away from where the three members of the phasia stood.

Like the portals that the phasia used the portal was filled with a swirling blue color, but to Ellis' trained eyes, there was something different. The rotation of the color in the center of the portal was slower, and the color was also not uniform. It was like a film of grease had dried upon the surface of the portal and had begun to crack. A woman's shapely leg emerged from the portal, and as more of the leg became visible, Ellis wondered if there was going to be any clothes on the rest of the woman as she emerged. Finally a gauze-like gown appeared clinging to the woman's hip. It took only a few seconds for the rest of the woman's svelte form to appear, the simple sheer white gown sticking to her like it was an extension of her skin, from the middle of her chest to the middle of her thighs. Her dirty blond hair cascaded from her head around her like a waterfall. The hair itself may have been clean, but it didn't shine and looked as though it could have been shot through with sweat and grime. In many ways the woman could have been described as beautiful, her features flawless with pouting lips and high cheekbones. She had all the visual characteristics of the aristocracy, but there was nothing but hate in her eyes. The weapons strapped to each of her hands were unlike any that Ellis had ever laid eyes on. Three broad bands of leather circled her hand and forearm. The highest band was just below her elbow, the second at the middle of her forearm, and the third and widest wrapped completely around her hand below the wrist. Her fingers were completely exposed, and her thumb snaked through a hole cut into the band. A broad leather strap ran across the top and bottom of her forearm, bonding the three straps together. Attached to the top of the hand strap were three shimmering claws that seemed to be at least ten inches, and perhaps a foot long. They gleamed brightly, the blade and tip looked sharp enough to cut through anything. Her posture was like that of a feral beast, muscles taut and ready to strike at any moment. When she spoke, her dispassionate expression didn't change, but her hate-filled eyes flared.

"Vallic Ultiv, Serpentine Knight of the Flashing Blade, Protector of the Kingdom of Iltorp," she paused for a moment and regarded Jeroch where he lay on the floor bleeding, "or whatever name you choose to go by, you have earned the respect of your Emperor and he feels that after so many fine years of service both to himself and to his father that you have earned a long retirement. But of course, the Emperor knows that a man like you would not take such a reward in the spirit in which it was offered, so he sent me to insure that you understood the true veracity of his magnanimous gift."

Jeroch rolled over onto his unwounded side, his right hand clutching his wounded flank. With some effort he got to a half-seated position, but not without causing more blood to spew from the three gaping wounds.

"In other words," the assassin concluded. "He sent me to kill you."

She leapt the next moment, traveling faster across the intervening distance than should have been possible, both sets of cruel claws racing toward Jeroch's throat. Midway to her target, her foot lightly touched a chair that had been thrown across the room when the table was upended, and used it as a bracing point. The trajectory of her attack changed that instant, and a set of claws slashed for Ellis' heart. Though combat had never been her prowess, Ellis let both of her hands fly forward, and a blast of frigid air caught the wind, sending shards of ice blasting out toward the attacker. Alise Modrall had no counter for the assault, but wrapped her arms around herself and let her body weight carry her through the wind. Shards of ice ripped at the white dress and the skin beneath, causing blooms of red to stain the surface. While Ellis' attack had prevented Alise from striking with her deadly claws, it did nothing to change to direction of her strike or the force that was behind it. The assassin barreled into Ellis, sending them both sprawling. The smaller and lighter Alise however was able to control her fall, as though the forces of gravity bent themselves to her bidding. Somehow the assassin ended up on top of Ellis, claws poised for a strike. One clawed hand jabbed toward Ellis' throat, and the much older woman brought the palm of her hand up to loose another wintery blast. In counter, Alise changed the direction of her strike and let the claws rip their way through the center of Ellis' palm. Blood spattered in all directions, but from Ellis' palm and also from the back of her hand. Ellis could not help but to cry out, but the cry lasted only a moment, as she immediately had to defend against the other clawed hand. It would have shredded her throat the next moment had she not shifted her body weight at the last possible second. The strike instead connected with Ellis' right shoulder, the claws sinking in all the way to the bone, ruining muscles and nearly rending the whole of her arm from her body. Finally the lips on the assassin's face curled into something other than an impassive glare. The predatory smile spoke of what she thought was an impending victory. But Ellis was not one to lay down her life so quickly. For the first time in centuries Ellis reached down deep inside herself and found the softly flickering green flame of the Blaze. She felt its potency fill her, and felt whole again. Unlike most of the applications of the powers of the Blaze, what Ellis released upon her attacker that next moment was certainly neither elegant, nor focused. The unfocused flash of Blaze energy seemed to leak from her pores and then burst and burned in all directions. Alise had no option but to pull back or be consumed by the fires. The woman practically floated back across the room, landing lightly preparing herself for another assault.

By this time, Bryn had found her way to her feet, and was preparing an assault of her own. Ellis however would not allow herself to remain on the ground for longer than a moment, and when she stood again, her right arm hung limply, but already the flesh was beginning to bind itself. Flames raged around her wounded hand, and Bryn could see the fires of the Blaze alight in her piercing blue eyes.

"Bryn," Ellis said her cold voice strong, "take Jeroch out of here. There is much he must still do if you are to succeed in eliminating our enemies and ensuring your husband is successful in his endeavors. I'll deal with this woman."

Bryn wanted to object, wanted to argue, but one look at Jeroch and she knew what had happened. The man was pale, paler than even the loss of blood should have been responsible for. There was no doubt that the blades of the woman's weapons had been envenomed, and without swift treatment, Jeroch would die. Though Ellis fought to heal her own wounds, it was obvious that the poison was powerful enough to resist even the potent force of the Blaze. If Bryn added herself into the fray, with this woman's skill there was a good chance that those claws would find her flesh as well. Ellis was volunteering to hold the assassin at bay while the others escaped, a tactic that practically sealed Ellis' fate. And yet as Bryn looked at her sister, she saw even more. Not only had Ellis drawn deeply on the Blaze, but she had drawn so deeply that the powers were beginning to eat her from the inside out. It was as if the Blaze and the poison were starting to compete as to which could kill the woman the fastest. It seemed that only Ellis' considerable will was keeping her on her feet. There was a sidelong glance between the two women.

"We said our goodbyes long ago, sister," Ellis said finally, the flows of the Blaze filling her. "Don't insult me by not doing what is right."

A moment later, twin portals opened in the room, one beneath Jeroch and one beneath Bryn. Jeroch was in no position to risk his falling through, and while Bryn could have made some attempt to stay there, she resigned herself in that briefest moment that she had set her eyes on her sister for the last time. The two portals closed, leaving Ellis facing off with the assassin. Alise Modrall looked first to where the former Serpentine Knight lay, and then to where the woman in red had stood, a frown coming to her face.

"I was sent here to kill a Knight of the Flashing Blade," the assassin said mockingly, "not his companion. You are so far beneath notice that you will die here, alone and forgotten. No one will know your name, and no one will care that you are gone."

Alise leapt the next moment, but this time Ellis was ready. The shield of Blaze energy flared around her, and when the gleaming silver claws struck, there was a bright flash of light, and Alise was cast across the room. But the woman was crafty and perhaps Ellis had underestimated just how powerful the woman truly was. Though flying through the air, she somehow summoned a portal to appear behind her, she disappeared through it, and reappeared behind Ellis, the force of her impact sending both women sprawling to the ground. In her weakened state, Ellis was not able to react quickly enough to block the blow that ripped across her stomach. Alise mounted her prey again, and this time her kill would not be denied.

"These are your last breaths," the assassin cooed, "give me the name of the woman I am ridding my father's world of."

From somewhere behind Alise the hard haft of the scythe Harmony came cracking down hard on the back of the woman, and then again to the back of her head. She fell limply to the ground.

Her name is Ellis Chandara," a deep and resonate man's voice said.

Ellis exhaled sharply, but her vision clouded and her eyes rolled back in her head as a form leaned in and swept her up off the ground.

* * * * * * * * * * * *

Alise Modrall woke, fires raging around her. All of her prey was gone, and she had failed in her task to eliminate Vallic Ultiv. But if what she had heard was true, Vallic had not been the Serpentine Knight, but had been masquerading for quite some time. His true name was Jeroch, and unless she missed her guess, the true nature of the man was more akin to Dark God than human. Her father would need to know this information, need to know that the Dark Gods had infiltrated the ranks of the Knights of the Flashing Blade. But to return now, with this information, would mean admitting her failure. She sat up and ran her tongue over the dried blood on her claws. The woman that she had struck, the woman who was a self-espoused sister to a Dark God, was dead. That much was certain. Her blood was cold and the trail along with it. The man however, this Jeroch, was very much alive. And she knew just where he was. A smile came to her lips, one that would not leave no matter what feelings ran through her. And where this Jeroch was, so too was the man she wanted to kill more than anything. Where Jeroch was, so too was Wynne.

* * * * * * * * * * * *

When Ellis' eyes opened, she saw only the cool blue sky above her. She was only half laying on soft grass, her upper body supported by the strong arms of a man, and her head was rested on his chest. His heart beat steadily, but there were ragged beats with half-caught breaths. The strong man was crying. When she moved, he looked down on her, and for the first time Ellis met her savior's eyes, and she could not suppress her smile. Though she had little strength left, and her smile was weak if it curled her lips at all, it filled her from her eyes to her heart. Wordlessly he smoothed back her white hair, gently kissed her on the forehead. His strong proud eyes were filled with tears, and she reached up the best she could to wipe some of the tears from his cheek.

"I never thought to see you again," she said in a weak voice, "but I'm glad you're the one. I'm glad it's you who is here. After all the terrible things I did to you."

He kissed her again on the forehead and then let his lips brush across hers.

"You never did anything but love me," the man said finally, his voice barely above a whisper. "No matter your motives."

Ellis blinked and found that she could barely force her eyes open again. Time was growing short, and she still had so many things she wanted to say. So many things she needed to tell him, so many things she needed to tell Bryn and the others. She had been alone for so long, empty for so long, even after her heart had found Jeroch. But she had only truly loved once. Only truly felt alive once. In the arms of a man that she should have hated. A man that she should have been trying to kill. But night after night she lay beside him in their bed, and he never even knew her true name. Not until long after. Not until just before his death. And yet there, on his deathbed he forgave her.

"And I never stopped," she said weakly, "loving you."

Light sparked in her eyes for the briefest moment, and then finally they closed. There was one last exhalation of breath, and then the proud Ellis Chandara, daughter of Halicon, Lady Leopard of the Brotherhood of Phasia, was gone. The man held her close for a long time, stroking her hair and letting the waves of emotion fall through him. Finally, he lay her back onto the ground, and pulled himself back to his feet. Tears stained his face, and he looked over into the distance where there was a softly falling waterfall and knew that this would be the perfect place for Ellis to be laid to rest. When he turned back to Ellis' body, several small balls of fur had accumulated around her. One of the larger ones was almost black in color, with a bright streak of silver forming a perfect circle around its center. The eyes, teeth, and tail emerged from the Snag's body the next moment and the man smiled down at his old friend.

"I knew you would want to see your creator off," he said wiping his eyes again. "Make sure the grave won't be disturbed. By anyone."

The Snags went to work quickly, and Arin Ranthall turned to face the direction of Cadaria, lifting the haft of the Sacred Weapon Harmony and feeling comfortable with its weight in his hands as he watched the sky light up with falling stars.

Brothers in Arms

Year Three of the Just Emperor Kaitain "Dragonsbane" Lorien, Creator's Calendar Year 1870

Dane Rhuiden sat on the hot muddy ground wanting to be anywhere other than where he was. They had just fought two dragons as well as a herald of the abomination known as Dorovar, while two armies were clashing all around them trying to kill each other. In the process, two of their own number, young women who had dedicated their lives to fighting the scourge that the dragons had become, had met their end. Dane knew that Jillian and Kiara would both be hurting from their loss, but the time for those emotions was not now. If they lived through the next few moments, then perhaps time could be made for grief. They had been gathered together at the heart of the temporary camp set up by the surviving members of the Army of Fire from Saldarine. The Army of Water from Thorigald had withdrawn from the field, leaving the Plains of Steam under their ancient enemy's banner. A quartet of soldiers surrounded them, but a dozen more were in close proximity. In top fighting condition, that many soldiers would not be a challenge for Blade and Dane combined, but the two were nowhere near peak fighting condition. Kiara and Jillian were also being held, but they were bound, as they were still technically fugitives from the Throne, and Saldarine was still one of the Great Kingdoms that was loyal to the Emperor. The man who had identified himself as the Amethyst

Knight of the Flashing Blade from the Kingdom of Celidar was shown to a private tent with an unidentified woman whom from the short glimpses that Dane had gotten, looked worse for wear. However, Dane could not remember seeing the woman engaged in the battle at any level. But then again, Dane had not been conscious for a portion of the battle and had not even known that Tolon Morr had joined the battle until it was over.

The two men sat back to back, their hands and feet bound, and then the bonds at their wrists were tied together. From one of the tents, an officer in glistening armor emerged, flanked on each side by rank and file soldiers. The officer pointed to Dane, and one of the soldiers leaned in and quickly separated Dane and Blade's bonds. The other soldier then joined the first, and took hold of Dane by the elbows and lifted him to his feet. His back ached and his knees wanted to buckle underneath him, not that it mattered much as the soldiers chose to drag Dane behind the officer toward what had to have been the command tent. Once inside the surprisingly well-lit tent, the two soldiers forced Dane to his knees. There was another officer in the room who had his back to the tent flap leaning over a table studying what were probably maps of the surrounding area. The first officer in his armor that obviously had not seen action in the most recent conflict, saluted, turned on his heel, signaled to the two soldiers, and then walked briskly past Dane and out of the tent with the two soldiers in tow. For a long time, Dane knelt looking at the back of the officer as he mulled over his maps. Finally the officer turned and regarded his prisoner. Even in the tent, the officer wore a small helm. The metal swept down from his head in a smooth arch to over his ears and came to an end just above his shoulders. It also covered his eyes leaving a small slit for visibility, and also swept downward to create a guard over his nose. He took two long steps toward Dane and then stood looking down at the captive. Finally, the officer shook his head.

"You're always finding new and interesting ways to get yourself into trouble."

The voice flooded into Dane's ears, familiarity filling him. Dane looked up, and when he did the officer smiled and removed his helmet.

"Korrd…"

Dane's voice was filled with a mixture of shock and genuine happiness, and he could not keep the smile off his face.

"Hello, little brother," Korrd said finally, "but its General Arin Chandara, now; leader of the military of the Kingdom of Saldarine."

Korrd waved one hand, and the bonds holding Dane's hands and feet untied themselves and fell limp to the floor. A chair slid over from the corner of the tent, and Korrd helped Dane into it before leaning against the map table.

"Using your mother's name now?" Dane asked.

"And father's," Korrd answered. "Seemed appropriate somehow. But I've been using the Chandara name for some time. Of course I have to lay low every generation or two just to make sure that I keep people from getting suspicious. I usually go back and forth between a few kingdoms, but Saldarine is home. There are some people I like to remain close to. In fact, I'm my own nephew this time around, if you can believe it. But what is it with you using Pike's name?"

Dane shifted uncomfortably in his seat.

"A long story. I thought maybe I could remind Pike what he used to be. But I see now that's impossible. I never imagined after all this time that Pike would become exactly what he hated most."

Korrd bowed his head thoughtfully.

"Just like one of the phasia?"

Dane frowned.

"I'll try not to take that personally."

Korrd looked up and met his younger brother's eyes. Both men smiled and Dane did his best to suppress a laugh.

"Well," Korrd said smoothing back his helmet matted hair, "you can't blame me for forgetting. After all, I was dead through your whole transformative phase. No pun intended of course."

Dane lowered and shook his head, a small chuckle escaping his lips.

"And none delivered."

There was a very long moment of silence. When the awkward pressure built up too much, Dane cleared his throat, and rubbed at the remaining irritation in his wrists.

"The Creator exercised his sick sense of humor on us after Shau-ling fell at the end of our generation. That was our first real taste of the games and the power struggle between the Creator and his children. The Creator split our reality right down the middle, one where the followers of Emries had prevailed, and one where Shau-ling's forces ended up with the upper hand. Who would have figured that it would have been the Pike from the light side of things that would have ended up being the bastard? He was a power-mad drunk, letch, and so involved in his own agendas that he couldn't see more than the twelve inches in front of his face. Pike, our Pike, had to stare down that part of himself and I thought when we left Onea that he would have ended up on the right path after seeing what power could do to him."

"No such luck," Korrd replied.

Dane nodded.

"He isn't the Pike you knew," Dane continued, "and now I guess he isn't even the Pike I knew, even though we're from the same reality. We both had to scratch and claw just to survive through the years, dodging the phasia and the Shadowwalker patrols. It was terrible in a way that I never thought I would see again. Then there was Dorovar."

Dane could practically hear Korrd's teeth grind together. He turned away and looked at the map again, his fists balling on the table. Dane dragged himself back to his feet and half walked, half stumbled over to his older brother's side. What stretched on the table before them was something Dane knew that he was not supposed to be seeing, but it didn't really matter. The tactical map of the whole of Cadaria showed troop movements in all of the Kaitain-controlled kingdoms as well as a best guess of the movements of rebel forces. What was also on the map were small notations of sightings related to the heralds of Dorovar, including the most recent and very deadly confrontation with War.

"From what I can gather, Dorovar's people are just trying to stir up unrest and prevent anyone from consolidating power. The kingdoms hardest hit weren't the power base of Kaitain's empire, but it caused enough uproar that more splintering could happen at any time. But I have a sinking suspicion that there is more to it. Pestilence hits the fertile farmland, but not the major food producing centers. Just some of the outlying areas. See here?"

Korrd indicated a section of the map near the borders of Aldere.

"He hit the small independent farms, but didn't actually cross into Imperial controlled farmlands. More people would have been effected if he had gone after the real supply lines, like we would do in a military action. Then you have Famine."

Korrd moved his pointing finger to the Kingdom of Ice, Rashaleb.

"She turns Rashaleb into a ghost town, but other than creating fear and unrest, it doesn't damage Cadaria as a whole. By even our standards, Rashaleb is backwater. Makes Aradon look positively regal. Then you have Death. Yeah, he hit the center of the Church of the Creator, but that does nothing to Kaitain's establishment. Knowing the little I know about Dorovar, that smacks of a personal statement. And now War strikes here. Just to keep us all fighting each other and looking over here when he's going to be doing whatever he wants to do while our back is turned."

Dane drank it all in.

"Seems like sound tactics. He knows what he's doing, and we have no idea what he's doing. In the mean time we continue to do the best we can killing each other."

Korrd pounded his fist on the table again, retreated back two steps and then slumped into the chair that Dane had been sitting in only moments before.

"For all this time I've been skulking around on this ball of dust, I feel completely left behind. On Onea I was the Dragon, the only one who could defeat Shau-ling. Everyone wanted me. Saurn, Shau-ling, Emries, Basille, Bryn... Everyone either wanted to use me or kill me. I've been here a little over a thousand years now, and the best I've been able to manage is some military post in the greater cog of the Cadarian machine."

Dane turned around and regarded Korrd for a long moment. He looked much the same as he did the last time Dane had set eyes on him, and not much different than the last time they were together on Onea. But this Korrd was different in all the ways one would expect a grizzled war veteran to be. The eyes that had seen a thousand years of war and strife could never be filled with anything but strength and fear. It was a strength needed to face every situation upright, and a fear of that strength. Without that fear, everyone with that kind of strength would become a tyrant or a dictator.

"You could have gone and joined the Dark Gods. You didn't have to be alone."

Korrd snorted and shook his head.

"Could you see me taking orders from Pike? Besides, I'm not like them. Whatever little bit of power I have left isn't like what I had on Onea. I can change my appearance slightly, mostly just let myself look older or younger, I heal rapidly, and as far as I can tell, the only way I can die is if someone cuts out my heart or cuts off my head. Other than that, I'm just a regular person. But, to your point, I wasn't alone. I see Vallic and Isa when I can, and it's actually nice to have a relationship with my mother. And then I do have an occasion to see Jerrard and Erika. It's not that bad being one of the outsiders in this sometimes. And I don't have to worry about accidentally using my powers like the rest of them. I can have a wife, a family, when it works out. But now things are changing. Now that it's obvious that Dorovar is stepping up his assaults... Well, and the two of us running into each other is anything but a coincidence."

"Two Ranthalls in the same room is never a good thing,"

Korrd crossed his arms and leaned back in the chair. There was a slight grimace on his face, and Dane could tell that there was so much that Korrd wanted to say, so much that had been waiting for the right moment and the right audience. If there was any opportunity better than the one he had in front of him, he would never see it.

"You've been doing your outlaw agitation thing for a long time, Logan," Korrd said finally, placing heavy accent on his brother's name, "and I know on some level that you're just trying to agitate the Creator and the Chosen. But I know you. Even after all these years, I know you. There is more method to your madness than you care to admit, and now that I know you've thrown in with Warron, there is definitely more. So, you tell me what's going on."

Dane looked past Korrd for a moment at the tent's entrance and then back at Korrd.

"Now isn't the time, and this isn't the place, but your suspicions are right. It's about Dorovar, and it's about what his real motivations are. But if I tell you, you have to understand that you can't just stay on the edge of the fight. And I'm going to have to know what you've been up to all this time, and why you've stayed away. More than that, if you've seen Vallic and Jerrard, you had to have sworn them to secrecy about your being alive. Either that, or you didn't let them know who you were. I didn't feel your power at this battlefield, so either you've gotten very adept at hiding it, or it's so low that it escapes notice. So it seems like both of us have secrets to protect."

Korrd nodded.

"Where are you bound for next?" Logan asked, letting the difficult conversation evaporate like smoke.

Korrd pointed back at the map and found his way back to his feet.

"We have orders from Chelsea," Korrd's brow furrowed a little, "Lady Zarova, to push forward into Thorigald and take part in a series of take and hold engagements. We're supposed to be getting support from Iltorp, but the last word I received from Vallic was that he was unwilling to commit very many of his forces to the joint venture. And with the losses that we've taken from this engagement, I doubt we'll be able to strike very far into the Kingdom of Water's territory."

"Chelsea?" Dane had easily caught his brother's slight slip of the tongue. "A little familiar when discussing a superior officer, isn't it?"

Just then the flap of the tent was pulled back and two men entered. Korrd quickly turned, his hand going to the hilt of the sword that lay on the map table, while Dane remained where he was. The first man who entered Korrd recognized immediately. While he had never formally met the new Amethyst Knight of the Flashing Blade, he knew Tolon Morr by reputation. He had been a renowned and feared gladiator in the Kingdom of Steel and throughout all of the recognized fighting circles. His records were impressive, and while it was no surprise that he was able to win his freedom, his ability to ascend past his station to become one of the most powerful knights in the whole of Cadaria was nothing short of miraculous. When the thickly-muscled man was named to his new position, many thought that he would become the new Emperor's enforcer and executioner. That opinion had been strengthened when the newest member of the Knights of the Flashing Blade had been immediately dispatched on some secret mission for the Throne. The man that followed the frowning form of Tolon Morr was Korrd's second in command.

"I'm sorry general, but he insisted. There was nothing I could do to stop him."

From the look in the eyes of the Amethyst Knight, Korrd was sure that his subordinate was quite correct in his assessment of the situation. Korrd nodded and waved a dismissive hand. The officer saluted and then left the tent.

"General Chandara," Tolon started, "I demand to know why I've been detained, and further I demand to know what you intend to do with these wanted criminals."

Korrd motioned to the chair, and when Tolon did not move from his spot, Korrd instead took the chair and eased Dane into it. Korrd himself took position at the map table.

"First of all, Sir Tolon, I apologize if you feel you were treated in any way that was beneath your station, but you did wander into a warzone and we had to confirm your identity. As for these criminals as you call them, you are in my camp, and this is my jurisdiction, therefore I will deal with them as I see fit. My orders are to deal with the incursion by the rebel forces into the Plains of Steam. I also have standing orders to engage any dragons that attempt to impede our progress. These are orders from the Emperor and Empress. And while I am sure these fugitives are an issue that should be dealt with, you must agree that they are a minor consideration in the grander scheme of things."

Tolon balled his fists and generally seemed barely on the edge of control.

"Besides," Korrd said after a moment, "I would think after what happened to Jaccob Aldora you would be more worried about your own neck than these people."

Tolon's eyes widened.

"What are you talking about?"

Korrd reached behind him and collected a series of dispatches, and handed them to Tolon. While Tolon scanned through them, Korrd began to quickly summarize.

"We received these dispatches before this morning's engagement. It appears that Emperor Kaitain has awakened from his slumber, and his mood certainly was not improved by the extended rest. Of course, I'm sure that the loss of the Imperial Palace did not improve his mood to any great degree. Jaccob Aldora was named a traitor and executed for his role in the loss of the Imperial Palace. Irene Drage, the Ethereal Sorceress is still missing and presumed dead. Marlae Lorien was declared a traitor to the throne and her membership in the Imperial Family was revoked. In the Emperor's words, she has been rendered a non-entity and sentenced to execution."

The words hit Tolon in the chest like a great hammer. Even as his own eyes were struggling to believe what they were seeing, his ears and his mind rebelled against the words that the general was pouring into them. It was the perpetuation of some great cosmic joke. The Emperor had executed one of his principle protectors. One of the Knights of the Flashing Blade.

"But it doesn't stop there. The one there in your right hand. The decree that makes worship of the Creator illegal and demands the conscription or forced servitude of those who are connected to the church, if not their executions. Those orders sanction the mass murder of men, women, and children. I haven't shared these orders with my men yet, but before long, once we press further into rebel held territory, I will have no choice."

Blood drained from Tolon's face, and though he did not look up, he questioned Korrd all the same.

"What right do you have not to pass on the orders from the Emperor to your men? Withholding these orders or preventing the execution of them is treason."

Korrd leveled his eyes on Tolon.

"No more than abandoning your post in time of war."

Tolon looked up, and the papers dropped from his hands. Anger flashed through his eyes, and his fists balled again. Korrd put up and hand and retrieved another piece of paper from the map table and extended it toward Tolon. For a long moment Tolon stared incredulously at the paper before finally snatching it from the general.

"That is a missive from Lady Chelsea Zarova, now the autonomous ruler of the Kingdom of Fire Saldarine. It accompanied the dispatch from the Emperor detailing her change in position. That letter gives me control of the Army of Fire. I'm directed to act in any way that I feel best benefits my men so long that it does not directly countermand her orders. In effect, she has named me her successor until a new Garnet Knight is named by the Emperor, or until that position is returned to her."

Tolon regarded the paper for a long moment, and then let it fall from his hand.

"Very well, I suppose you have the rights you claim."

Korrd nodded slightly, an acceptance of an apology not offered.

"So, now that we have those things out of the way, Sir Tolon," Korrd said finally, "I suppose that you will want to get underway. I appreciate your assistance in the conflict with the dragon, and if you would like I can either include or preclude your name from the report that I will send to Lady Zarova, as well as the Emperor."

Tolon stiffened.

"Of course," he said, a frown coming to his face. "I suppose there is no need to mention that I was here, nor anything about my companion."

Korrd nodded.

"And of course," Tolon continued, "if I was never here, then I would not have seen the fugitives."

"My thoughts exactly," Korrd added.

The tent flap pulled back once more, and a woman stumbled into the tent. She looked frail at best, and her color was pale except for a slight pink in her cheeks and her lips. Her long straight dark hair was bound in a bun at the back of her head and still flowed down her back like a waterfall. Whatever luster her features had lost due to her recent travels, her hair had lost none of its own. She was wrapped in a simple lavender robe that looked slightly large on her, and had long sleeves that stretched down over the heels of her hands. She held herself upright the best she could, but it seemed that the weight of her own body was more than her frame could handle. Tolon was at her side the next moment, supporting her, and she leaned into him, as though she drew strength from his closeness. For the first time, her almond shaped eyes looked up and met Korrd's. They widened slightly, and then widened even more when they crossed to Dane's. She stumbled backwards slightly, losing her balance and causing Tolon to catch her.

"The brothers!"

Dane and Korrd looked at one another, and Dane found his way to his feet. Tolon seemed to be more distracted with Jerrica's condition than to concentrate on her words, but it took only a moment for his glance to follow the direction of her wide-eyes stare. She clung to the Amethyst Knight now, the slight pink draining completely from her lips.

"They can't be here, Tolon. They can't be here, not now. It's not time yet for them to be together. What have I done?"

Her eyes rolled back in her head the next moment, and she fell limp in Tolon's arms. Korrd fetched the small basin and pitcher of water as well as a cloth and moved to the limp woman's side. He dabbed at her sweat-covered brow, and then place the back of his head at her forehead.

"She's burning up."

Tolon's look was grave.

"She's been getting weaker the longer we traveled. I had initially thought it was just a weakness in her constitution. She's not used to long journeys, and we have been traveling at a substantial pace. But now I fear that she has been ill for quite some time."

Korrd looked back at Dane. The younger of the brothers also made his way to the fallen woman's side.

"Who is she?" Korrd asked.

"Jerrica Maldovrin."

Dane stole a look at Korrd, one he hoped Tolon would not have seen because of his concentration on Jerrica.

"A seer," Korrd said finally. "The fever must be causing her abilities to manifest in delusions. I can only imagine how real they must feel to her."

Tolon took hold of one of the cloths that Korrd had brought, bunched it under Jerrica's head and laid her gently onto the ground. It took him only a moment to find his way back to his feet, where the Sacred Weapon Strength was in his hands the next moment.

"I don't know what's going on here," he said finally, the blade leveled firmly at the back of Korrd's neck. "But whatever it is, I'm sure that I don't like it. So, one of you better start talking, and soon, otherwise I'm going to have to start using this."

Chapter LXVIII

No Strength Without Unity

Dominique Lorien sat in her tiny room in the Inn of Coventry, the butterfly-shaped mask sitting on its wrappings on the small table that stood against the far wall of the room. Looking at the mask filled her with a sense of revulsion, and yet she couldn't pull her eyes away from it. She would be acting from that point forward as an extension of Kaitain's will, and that in and of itself sickened her more than she ever could have imagined. Now even the memory of his hands upon her turned her stomach. But at least she was being sent into exile rather than to her death. Hearing the guards talking about Jaccob Aldora's execution and the destruction of the Sacred Weapon had been terrifying enough, and knowing that her fate was completely in his hands sent shivers through her. But Chelsea had been spared, and even though Kaitain had tried to humiliate her, Chelsea was not the kind to give in to that kind of manipulation. There was nothing that Kaitain could do to her, not even sentence her to death that would break her considerable will. Perhaps the worst thing Kaitain could do to her was to take away the very thing that she defined herself by. Chelsea was a soldier, and had been a soldier for most of her life. To take that away from her and turn her into a politician was perhaps the cruelest joke. She would be fierce no matter where she was placed, but without her weapon in hand staring across from the clear enemy, she would never be at peace.

When Chelsea and Dominique first had come to the Imperial Court, it was Chelsea that was most out of her depth. In politics there were no clear enemies, and no clear rules of engagement. The only truth was that winning was a series of holding actions, truces, and compromises. The Wolf of Saldarine was not one to compromise, nor was she one to stop advancing on an opponent that seemed to be in a weakened position. She was always out for blood and the quickest victory possible. In the political arena, Dominique had learned rather quickly that the quick were most often the first ones to feel the sting of carelessness; and that the more patient one was, the more often they got what they wanted. Many times that was how Dominique found herself frustrated. For all of the annoyance that Irene Drage and Marlae Lorien brought into her life, Dominique often found herself astounded by how astute the two women were in navigating the political waters in Aldere. Hopefully Chelsea had learned as much from the insufferable women as Dominique had and would be able to transition those skills to her new role as sovereign of Saldarine. At least they would still be together for a little while longer.

Rashaleb was the destination often inflicted on those who were either too incompetent or intolerable to serve real functions in the machine that was the Cadarian Empire. Malcontents and troublemakers found themselves shipped off to work the mines in Lordhill, and those that were better off dead in the eyes of their superiors got extended tours of duty in Galateria, keeping the southern borders safe from monsters, dragons, and pirates. The life expectancy in the southern reaches of Cadaria was about six months. Galateria was the kingdom that had had the most representatives wearing the title of Onyx Knight, and for good reason. Rashaleb on the other hand was stable, but undesirable. It had little in the way of natural resources or any profitable attribute except for the wild horses that called the frozen tundra home. It was said that horses raised in Rashaleb were the heartiest and the most durable in all of Cadaria. The best were taken for the Imperial Cavalry, and others sold for ten to twelve times what other horses fetched at market. Illegal trading of those horses was considered treasonous and was one of the few theft related crimes that still held a penalty of execution. Dominique herself had ridden a Rashaleb stallion once. Seraph had been given one as a gift for his service to the Kingdom of Thorigald, and he wanted Dominique to go on a late ride with him. She had been impressed with how powerful the beast was and at the same time how elegant and regal. That was shortly before they had all been summoned to the Imperial Court and Dominique's new life began. From time to time she wondered what had happened to that horse, and to all of the beautiful things that Seraph had added to his estate for Dominique. Once Dominique had asked Seraph why he insisted on buying tapestries, paintings, and sculptures when he did not even like them. He had simply said that in order for true beauty to be appreciated, it had to be surrounded by beauty. Seraph had never been practiced at sentiment.

Dominique stood and went to the small wardrobe in the corner of the room and opened the doors wide. The only garment hanging there was a simple white cotton dress with simple stitching. It had been taken in slightly at the waist, and had most likely been a favorite of the person that was the occupant of this room before Kaitain annexed it. The dress reminded Dominique of her days before coming to the Imperial Court, and the days before she was the lover of a member of the Knights of the Flashing Blade. That life seemed so distant to her now, so many lifetimes away, and a hazy memory at best. Had she ever worn such a simple garment? Had she really been a common woman at all? Unconsciously she felt the color come to her cheeks and a tear streak from the corner of her eye. Why was she crying? For the man she loved? For the life she once had? For the woman that she had been so long ago?

A knock came at the door several moments later, and as Dominique blinked away the tears, she realized that she had been standing there for quite some time looking at the dress. She had been so lost in her thoughts and in that brief moment of weakness that time had slipped away from her. Using the back of her hand to dab at her eyes, she cleared her throat and spoke.

"Enter."

Dominique heard the door open and then promptly shut, and as soon as she was sure that the emotion was no longer showing on her face, she turned to greet her visitor. While at some level she may have been prepared for Chelsea to visit her, she certainly was not ready for how the former Knight of the Flashing Blade looked.

The first time Dominique had encountered Chelsea Zarova, she had been intimidated and worried that the fierce woman would leap across the table and slit her throat. It was a formal dinner on the anniversary of the peace between Thorigald and Saldarine that was solidified by the marriage between Chelsea and Seraph. Dominique came as a guest of the Emerald Knight, and she remembered fondly that it was one of the first times in her life that she had ever worn a fine gown. In fact, it had been fitted just for her, and Seraph made sure that he spared no expense in the tailoring. Despite her own finery, Dominique felt positively common as she watched each of the lords and ladies of the royal families stride proudly into the dining hall and be announced one by one. They all sparkled like the stars in the sky. Then the Garnet Knight, Lady Chelsea Zarova, the famous Wolf of Saldarine was announced. It wasn't until the assembled royals began to cheer that Dominique realized that she was holding her breath. When Dominique was preparing for dinner, she watched as Seraph got dressed. She had laid out his finest dress uniform, but Seraph instead opted for something far less military. The outfit was still formal, but he looked more like royalty than a military officer. For that reason, Dominique had had expected Chelsea to be wearing some kind of dress, one that would put the rest of the royalty and pretenders to shame. Dominique could not have been more wrong.

Chelsea strode into the room proudly in what Dominique learned later was ceremonial armor. She was covered from her shoulders to her feet, and the leggings and body suit were gray in color with a darker charcoal sewn throughout to add texture. The texture was subtle and barely noticeable, but it made an unconscious, almost instinctive impact. She wore crimson boots that came up to just below her knees and buckled once at the top of the boot, and then once over the ankle. Around her waist was a thick belt that had three separate buckling strands over a wide leather base. The base extended down the sides of Chelsea's legs almost like fabric, and continued into a teardrop-shaped panel that trailed behind her. The base was crimson as well, with a slightly lighter red at the edges. A crimson breastplate with gold accents stretched from her throat, across her chest, and swept down to a point under her ribs to the center of her stomach. Her shoulders were exposed to the top of her bicep where a set of bracers circled each bicep to the elbow. They too were crimson with gold accents. Her hands were clad in gauntlets that stretched all the way up her forearm.

A light purplish-red twisted silk band crisscrossed her hips meeting in a knot. From this silk band hung the Sacred Weapon Tenacity; one blade on each hip. Her features were stern and sharp, clear and sober eyes staring out into the room, hair barely shoulder length, and swept back away from her face. When Chelsea's eyes met Dominique's the first time, an unconscious shudder ran through her to the very core.

Now as Dominique looked at the former Garnet Knight, the intimidating edge that the woman had in armor was replaced with a more feminine edge, one that even in her most unguarded moments Dominique had never seen in her friend and protector. She wore a long flowing satin gown, crimson in color with a very high neckline that came to nearly the bottom of her jaw. It flowed down, leaving her shoulders and arms completely exposed, hugging her form as though it had been sewn to the contours of her body. It cinched in tighter at her waist, so that when the fabric flowed across her hips, it seemed to hug her that much tighter. Two slits were cut in each side of the dress that went from where the fabric stopped just above her ankle to the middle of her thigh. The edges of the dress were black, and a broad black silk belt wrapped around her waist. The crest of the Kingdom of Saldarine was carefully stitched in black on the front of the dress. With her hair brushed out straight, she looked vulnerable and feminine, and even to a degree naked. When their eyes met, Chelsea unconsciously bit her bottom lip and folded her hands at her waist, smoothing down the dress that could not have bunched even if she had wanted it to.

"This is your husband's idea of how I should dress to fulfill the responsibilities of my new position. The seamstress has been torturing me. This is certainly not my idea of dignified."

Dominique crossed the distance between them in two long steps and threw her arms around the taller and more muscular woman. For a long moment, Chelsea didn't move, and Dominique could feel her holding her breath. A few moments into the hug, Dominique felt Chelsea's hands snake around her waist, and Chelsea joined the embrace. It was all too much for Dominique, and she felt the strength drain from her and the tears begin to flow in earnest. Even in her new attire, Chelsea was a rock of normality in a world gone mad. No matter what happened from that point forward, as long as they were together, Dominique knew that she had a chance to get through. They stayed that way for several long moments until Chelsea became too uncomfortable to continue. She let her hands run up Dominique's arms and pulled her back. There was resistance to the movement at first, and then Dominique relented and allowed herself to be pushed back. Dominique started to speak, but Chelsea put her finger to her lips. A puzzled look came onto Dominique's face for just a moment until Chelsea pointed first at the door, and then to the wall behind the wardrobe. The implication was clear enough, and it was something that honestly Dominique herself should have considered. They were after all in a small inn in the middle of the countryside, with two detachments of the Imperial Guard, as well as the Captain of the Imperial Guard, and the Emperor's master assassin and spy in residence. They would have to be quite insane to think that they weren't being watched every single moment. Once the realization had crept in, Dominique pulled herself back to her full height and stepped two steps away from Chelsea. She did not however make any attempt to clear the tears from her eyes of from her flushed face.

"Well I think it looks splendid on you," Dominique managed in her best voice. "Be thankful that you don't have a mask to complete your new look. I assume that since you are still going to act as my protector that I will not have to wear it when we are alone together. There are some concessions I must be allowed for my sanity."

Chelsea nodded but the color that leaked into her cheeks told a different story than that of acceptance. She narrowed her eyes and mouthed a question.

"Does Kaitain have my weapon?"

"I understand we are leaving in the morning for Rashaleb," Chelsea said a moment later.

"I didn't see it"

"Yes," Dominique answered. "From what I understand it will be a long trip, especially since we will both be required to travel in a litter. After speaking to the leader of the detachment of the Imperial Guard that will be accompanying us, I understand that they were given strict instructions not to allow you to ride."

Chelsea's brow furrowed a bit, and Dominique could not tell if the irritation on her face was from the answer to the silent question, or to the revelation that Kaitain was doing everything in his power to destroy the former image of Chelsea as the great and feared Wolf of Saldarine.

"Korin doesn't have it either."

Chelsea's statement was met by another frown.

"Perhaps they should call me the Puppy of Saldarine now, or maybe the Bitch of Saldarine."

Dominique's eyes went wide and she felt her cheeks color in embarrassment, due largely to the fact that she had just been thinking the same thing. Then the idea came to her head.

"The basement armory."

"I think a woman can be just as fierce riding from place to place on a litter as they can be on the back of a steed. Perhaps even more so, given the right conditions."

Chelsea nodded her ascent, and from the look on her face, Dominique was quite sure she had ignored Dominique's last words. It was just as well, they came out a little sharper than she had intended anyway. Perhaps there was still a little resentment left that had not been purged by their long close friendship.

"I have some arrangements to make, Empress," Chelsea said in her best formal voice, "I will see you early in the morning when we depart."

Dominique felt crestfallen for a moment, and then Chelsea flashed a quick smile and gave her a wink before turning toward the door. Dominique went to the table and claimed the mask off the table and brought it to her face for the first time. Despite the velvet lining on the inside, it felt cold and hard when it touched her skin, more an emotional disturbance than a physical one. The thin straps slid across her face under her hair, and tightened easily. She saw Chelsea's eyes widen briefly, but a curt nod showed at least some level of approval. Perhaps she did not look like the monster she felt like.

Chelsea opened the door, but did not close it behind her as she stepped through. As expected the guard ducked his head in the door and quickly his eyes found the Empress. His jaw went slack and he stared for a long moment before remembering who he was and what he was supposed to be doing.

"Was there anything you needed, Empress?" the guard asked, his voice thick with nervousness.

"As a matter of fact, there is. Bring me all of the seamstresses in the area. I will not arrive in Rashaleb without proper attire. Tell them they better be prepared to work all night, and alert the guards to expect a lot of comings and goings all night long."

The guard nodded and hurriedly shut the door before scrambling off to do his duty. Dominique found herself smiling. Whatever Chelsea had planned tonight, there would be a little more distraction to keep the guards occupied.

* * * * * * * * * * *

Chelsea left Dominique's room, her spirit lifted slightly at seeing the woman who had quickly become her closest friend. There was no reason that the two of them should have tolerated each other, let alone come to rely on each other so much. But despite herself, Chelsea understood what Dominique was going through. She was trapped in her duty no differently than Chelsea was trapped in hers, and the grace in which she did it was a testament to just how strong of a woman that Dominique was. But it wasn't Dominique that Chelsea would be demanding unrelenting strength out of.

Upon returning to the common room, Chelsea found who she was looking for. A small and frail looking serving maid was doing her best to clean up the scuff marks and mud that the soldiers had tracked into the room as they changed shifts. There were fresh bruises on the woman's arms and wrists, and it was obvious that she had been handled very roughly.

It did not take much inquiry to discover that this little serving maid had been a favorite of the Captain of the Imperial Guard, Korin Melcab, since his arrival at the Inn of Coventry. It seemed that his manner in private was not much different than his manner in public. When Chelsea approached, the serving girl rose from where she knelt on the floor, but kept her head down respectfully.

"What is your name, girl?"

"Shilenda, my lady," the girl said in a meek and quivering voice, "how may I be of service?"

Chelsea steeled herself. She knew what needed to be done, she knew what the stakes were now, especially after she saw what had happened to the Sacred Weapon Temperance once it had been used to murder Jaccob Aldora. She kept telling herself that it was a war, and in war, there were losses. It was unfortunate that the battlefield had spilled out to affect the innocent. But perhaps Kaitain was right and there were no innocents any more. Everyone had to pick a side, and those who didn't would be trampled every time the sides met on any battlefield.

"Shilenda," Chelsea said, chewing the name over in her mouth, "that is a beautiful name."

The girl colored slightly, but Chelsea tried not to feel anything for the girl, even though her face would be etched in Chelsea's mind for the rest of her life.

"I need your assistance in ensuring that the Empress's litter is properly prepared for tomorrow. You are roughly her size, and so you should make a good substitute. Meet me in the stables after you have finished here."

The girl curtsied and vowed that she would do as ordered. Chelsea nodded and walked past the girl, careful not to step on a part of the floor that she had already cleaned. There was no point in making the girl's work more miserable than it already was. Once outside the inn, Chelsea was comforted to see a few familiar faces from her personally trained guards. They had been integrated into the Imperial Guard, but no matter what Korin Melcab or Emperor Kaitain may have wanted to think, the former members of the Army of Fire were loyal to Chelsea first and foremost. She had spent most of the morning, when not at the mercy of the harpies calling themselves seamstresses, ensuring that as many of her soldiers from Saldarine were assigned to protect the twin litters on their way to Rashaleb. Luckily, Chelsea had managed to ensure two-thirds of the detachment would be personally loyal to Chelsea. It would make things easier when the time came.

Two trusted members of the Imperial Guard escorted Chelsea to the stables where the litters sat waiting for their use early the next morning. Chelsea waited out of sight until the perimeter was secured and there was no chance that anything that was about to happen would be overheard or interrupted. Leaning back against the back wall of the stable, Chelsea closed her eyes and breathed deeply. This was the longest that she had been separated from Tenacity, but what was striking to her was the fact that her senses had not diminished. Her hearing was still sharp, as was her sense of smell, and eyesight. It was as though that the abilities had been permanently imprinted on her, and no matter where she was, Tenacity was still with her, at least in spirit. It was only because of her enhanced senses that she knew she was not alone in the stable. Two people had entered quietly, their footfalls barely rustling the dry hay that covered the ground. When Chelsea opened her eyes, she smiled, recognizing one of the two people. Natalia Pressen, though she was not totally trustworthy because of her position within the Shadow Guild, was at least still a member of the Knights of the Flashing Blade, and Chelsea felt that her loyalty to that order was much stronger than any loyalty she still may have felt for Emperor Kaitain. The woman standing beside Natalia was dressed in a seemingly one piece black bodysuit that covered every part of her, including her throat. Her face and head were shrouded under a mask and hood.

"Nice to see you are punctual when you choose to help."

Natalia frowned at Chelsea's jibe.

"There was nothing for me to do there, Chelsea, you know that as well as I do. I had to make sure that the Guild knew what was happening. If I hadn't, you wouldn't be getting the assistance you requested. Though I have to say, that the Grand Master was surprised to receive your request. He always has looked at you as some kind of incorruptible straight arrow. The Grand Master doesn't like to be wrong."

Chelsea shook her head.

"There are times in war when the unpalatable must be done."

There were three hard raps on the wall of the stable, which was the signal that the serving girl was entering. Chelsea had turned her head to look in the direction that the girl would be coming from, and when she turned her head to speak with Natalia again, she found that the two women had disappeared from view. Her disquieted stomach would not allow her to smile, but instead she walked somberly and soberly to where the litters stood. As expected Shilenda was waiting there, and as soon as she saw Chelsea, the girl reverently lowered her eyes.

"Please," Chelsea said, the bile rising in the back of her throat, "lift your head."

Shilenda raised her eyes, and though she smiled, it was her eyes that Chelsea focused on. Those bright and big blue eyes were so full of innocence and caring, and Chelsea knew that her life, though a simple one, was probably filled with more happiness than Chelsea would have been able to see in a dozen lifetimes. With her enhanced vision, Chelsea tried hard to memorize every line and blemish on the woman's face. Calling her a woman was being kind, she was really just a girl. It was then that Chelsea saw the black clad form rise up from behind Shilenda.

"I'm sorry," Chelsea heard herself saying, "if there was any other way, you have to know that I would find it."

The girl's eyes went wide the next moment, and her mouth opened and closed, but no sound came out. Her mouth worked once more, and then she collapsed to the ground like a marionette that had its strings cut. The next moment, the black-clad figure removed her hood, revealing the stolen face of the now departed serving girl. The copy was perfect, Chelsea knew, but all Chelsea could see was an imperfect reflection of the stolen innocent life. Natalia was there the next moment, and she obviously saw the trepidation in Chelsea's eyes.

"The face-dancing technique can only be done at the expense of the life of the person copied. I'm sorry Chelsea, but you knew this was the price."

Chelsea nodded.

"Don't worry, Deidre will get the job done. She is one of the most skilled assassins in the guild and was personally trained in the face-dancing technique by the Grand Master. She won't fail."

There was nothing more Chelsea could do for the fallen barmaid, and nothing more that could be done to lessen the guilt and shame that she felt. Perhaps she had crossed a line. Perhaps there were still more lines waiting to be crossed. Tomorrow was New Year's Day, a day that was supposed to mark a start of new chapter in every life. It was by Chelsea's actions that she had ended one woman's story, and the chapter that she would have to write in the coming year was going to be darker than any in her past. If Natalia was right, the assassin's dark work would be completed without fail, and Natalia would be able to easily recover Tenacity from where it sat in the basement armory. Her skin prickled with the coldness of their deeds. She knew that Natalia would ensure that no one ever found the barmaid's body, or any trace of the blood that slowly leaked from the wound in her back. And that thought brought Chelsea no comfort.

"The Nights of Star Fire begin tonight," Chelsea said looking out the front of the stables to the darkening sky, "and Korin Melcab will not see another sunrise."

One Crow Sorrow

*Year Three of the Just Emperor Kaitain "Dragonsbane" Lorien,
Creator's Calendar Year 1870*

A cold winter wind whipped through the empty buildings of Rashaleb, and despite the chill in the air, Orren Eldrath didn't know that he would ever be able to feel cold again. The power of the Blaze filled him now, and it was a warmth and a power that he wanted and at the same time wondered if he truly deserved. Perhaps that had always been the way things have been in Orren's life. He was born under strange and powerful signs, and all of the so-called fortune tellers and prophets had labeled Orren as the fulcrum that would bring about true change. That he would be a man who great things would be seen from. And though there were some that saw Orren's ascension to the rank of Sapphire Knight of the Flashing Blade as the fulfillment of this prophecy, Orren knew better. Deep in his heart, he knew that appointment to the Knights of the Flashing Blade was merely a conduit to a greater purpose. What Orren had always wanted was an audience with a true prophet, a true seer, to try to confirm this prophecy. But no matter what he tried, he would never be able to arrange such an audience. The Maldovrin Triplets were elusive at best, and had turned away his three attempts to get information, and the Dark Seer Jehna Feris had not been seen since her disappearance from the Imperial Court before the death of Ender Lorien. Now, though, Orren knew the truth. Orren as a member of the Knights of the Flashing Blade, was spared the destruction in Rashaleb, and his guilt over the devastation put him in the right place at the right time. The right place to be approached by the man who called himself Aryx Terian. The right place to be the recipient of the new power that now filled him. A power that Aryx himself said would give him the ability to fulfill his prophesied greatness. The power to change the world.

Despite himself, Orren found himself smiling at the characterization, and then when he realized where he was and what he was doing, the smile was just as quickly suppressed. He was knee-deep into digging a grave for his benefactor, and the frozen earth was rebelling against the steel head of the shovel that Orren had found in a nearby barn. In the back of his mind, he knew that he could simply reach for the new power that he had been granted and just lift the rock and soil out of the ground with a minimal amount of exertion. But somehow that wouldn't be right. From all of the memories that Orren had inherited from Aryx Terian, he knew that such use of power was undignified. Using power simply because it is available can lead to recklessness. Power can corrupt, and furthermore, the more incredible the power at a person's disposal, the more radical and intense the possibilities for corruption. Orren didn't need to think very hard about the possibilities of how his new powers could be used for evil. All he needed to do was comb back through Aryx's own memories to see destruction, devastation, murder, and suffering caused by men and women who wielded the power of the Blaze.

"So this is how he ended up," a strange voice said from somewhere behind Orren, "how pathetic."

The shovel slipped out of Orren's hands, and he reached for a small bit of the power that was now under his control, and propelled himself into a long, if slightly clumsy leap and somersault with a twist. Orren had never prided himself on his physical conditioning, and what little skill with a sword he had for wielding Courage was granted from the Sacred Weapon itself. Now though, things were different. Orren had the abilities and skills of a sword master at his disposal. A man who was so in tune with what his body could do, that he could push himself to the brink of physical exhaustion without any fear of his body betraying him. Orren however worried that his own slightly frail physical form would not be up to the task that he would be demanding of it. When Orren's feet hit the ground, he faltered slightly before getting himself into a passable fighting stance and drawing Courage from the scabbard at his side. The weapon felt different in his hands now. It did not seem to want to be within his hands, nor did it seem to want to lend its strength to his cause. The hilt seemed to slip from his grasp for a moment, but Orren redoubled his grip.

The man who stood on the far side of the half dug grave wore no expression other than an aloof amusement at Orren's display. His dark hair hung long to the level of his shoulders, and was straight with slight curls at the end. His skin was not tan, but not pale. Almost all of his physical features were ordinary; the kind that the eye would pass over if they were scanning over a crowd. He could be described as the last person that would ever be picked out. All except for his eyes. His eyes were such a telling feature, so distinct and so stark, especially against the white of the background and the falling snow. The bright clear blue eyes were disarming and comforting, while at the same time being completely and totally frightening. The man wore a simple white shirt that tied closed at the front, but the laces were undone, and the shirt fit loosely. He should have been freezing, but the man showed no evidence of being discomforted at all by the temperature. Orren did not have to search far for the man's name, he knew him immediately.

"So, you are Emries."

The child of the Creator smiled slightly.

"I see that you have command of Aryx's memories. Good. That will make this much easier. My patience with ignorance I'm afraid has not been hampered by my time away from the mortal world. Tell me where I can find Logan and Saurn, and I may even let you live through this. And then again, I might not."

A blade of pure crystal and energy appeared in Emries right hand. With his left, he reached out toward the ground near his feet and finished excavating the grave that was to house Aryx Terian's body.

"You see how easy this can be, Orren," Emries continued. "I can just as easily dig another one for you."

Suddenly Orren felt there was another presence close by. He looked over his right shoulder to find a form clad in a non-descript white robe, the hood drawn tight around his head so that no features of his face could be seen. Orren assumed it was a he because of the person's posture, but he could have just as easily have been wrong as right. What was clear was that the person was possessed of great power, and was not making any attempt to suppress it. When Orren turned his attention back to Emries, there was a slight smile on the man's face.

"You don't need to worry about my newest protégé there," he said smoothly, with just a hint of malice in his voice, "he is only there to ensure that you don't attempt something as stupid as trying to run."

Orren tightened the grip on Courage, but did not find the familiar flows of power there waiting for him. If he was going to face down Emries and his protégé, he was going to do it on his own. Even with his new powers, Orren knew that he was no match for Emries in a one on one confrontation, and if the protégé decided to make his presence felt, it could end up being a one-sided slaughter. While Aryx had been possessed with great powers at one point in his life, he had been diminished, first by his defection from the service of his maker Shau-ling, and then from his turning against his benefactor Emries. All Aryx had left were the very powers that were granted to him as a child of one of the Creator's chosen, and in the scope of things, those powers were less than those available to the Dark Gods. In the end, in a bit of a cosmic joke, Aryx was closer to the mortals that he revered than the god-like creation he was intended to be. But it would not be those powers that would allow Orren to survive this situation. Orren would have to rely on those things that got him to this point, not the new gifts at his disposal. Slowly Orren returned Courage to its scabbard and let his hands fall to his sides.

"I'm afraid you may have underestimated how much information my benefactor was willing to trust me with. He no doubt must have known you would come looking for him at some point, and he obviously had this succession plan in place for some time. So, I'm pretty sure you're going to leave here disappointed."

The condescending smile on Emries' face disappeared that moment and was replaced by a frowning snarl. He would not be made a fool of in this manner, and he would not allow some mortal who had accidentally fallen into power make a fool of a child of the Creator. It was bad enough that blasphemies like Aerith Seth and his brood existed, or that the idiotic former heroes that could not just die still walked free. There was no room for pretenders like Orren Eldrath in Emries' conception of the universe. He was a bug that needed to be squashed. Emries opened his mouth to speak again, but Orren held up his hand and smiled.

"But then again," he said, his eyes staying trained on the man who could easily snuff him out of existence, "I may know something about Logan after all. I mean, Aryx and Logan were allies, one might even say friends, and if anyone alive knew something about Logan's whereabouts, it would certainly be Aryx Terian."

There was a sniff from behind Orren.

"He's lying," a grim voice said quietly, "kill him."

Orren smiled and held his hands out wider from his body.

"You could do that, but then you'll never be able to be sure about just what I did and didn't know. And from what I know about you, Emries, you don't like to tread in uncertainties. Control is your currency, Emries, and as long as you allow the control to be taken out of your hands by your little puppet here, you'll never know just how close or how far you were from the truth."

Orren could swear he heard the grinding of Emries' hand against the crystal hilt of the sword.

"This is a dangerous game you're playing, Sapphire Knight. And no matter how far ahead you think you may be, never forget that when the game ends, you will lose, and I will be waiting there at the end to collect."

Orren felt the figure behind him move closer, and then saw Emries' hand extend in the man's direction. Whatever the mysterious protégé's identity, what was clear was that he was constantly on the edge of restrained violence. Malice was his default posture, and Orren knew in his heart that there was nothing this man would like more than to rip Orren apart with his bare hands. What's more, was that Orren was completely and totally sure that he could do it with minimal effort.

"I'll make a deal with you Emries," Orren said finally, his mouth suddenly dry, "you tell me how it is that you escaped your judgment after the fall of Onea, and I'll tell you what I know about Logan and Saurn."

Emries tilted his head slightly and regarded the insolent human. The frowning snarl disappeared, and Emries' more neutral expression returned. The crystal sword blinked out of existence from Emries hand.

"Very well, human. I will accept the terms of your deal. But understand this. If you try to run; no matter where you go, no matter where you try to hide, I will find you. There is nowhere in this universe that you can hide from me. No one with any kind of power on this rock will be able to protect you from me."

Orren nodded in reply. He didn't feel that there was anything his words would add at this point, and he knew without any doubt that Emries meant every word.

"You humans," Emries said, disgust thick in his voice, "no matter what, everything comes down to loyalty. Loyalty to your flags, your royalty, your gods. But in the end, none of that means anything. You can all be separated into two groups because of loyalty. One group can be loyal to an ideal or a principle, and that loyalty will extend until death and beyond. The other group, well there is nothing they prize more highly then themselves. That is their only treasure, their only loyalty, their only god is themselves. You call it arrogance; I call it the truest beauty of the human condition."

Orren felt his blood boil at the words.

"But I should have expected nothing less from you. After all, humans wouldn't exist without me. You are all my children, and you behave exactly as I expect you to."

At that, Orren could not help but smirk.

"For behaving how you expect us to, we seem to want to kill you an awful lot."

If the comment had any impact on Emries, it didn't show. He continued on with his explanation undaunted.

"You are a disease. An infestation. A destructive sickness that I've introduced to the worlds of my lesser siblings to upset their perfect balances. You see, this is all just a game. All of this. All of this stupidity and war. If my brothers and sisters would have seen the light and accepted that I and I alone understand the true nature of the universe, then there would be no more need for you pathetic humans and your selfish devotion to everything self. But no, it couldn't be that simple. My idiot siblings would rather make war on each other, make war on the Creator, and get involved in your petty little conflicts than deal with the true issues. I am the visionary. I am the one who understands the truth. I was sorry to learn that my brother Pyrrus had to pay for the mistakes of Raenera and Halicon, but someone had to pay. Talisia could have been the one to pay the price, but she was too smart for Pyrrus and the insufferable heroes of Onea were too late to prevent the horrors that followed. And all it cost Talisia was her banishment to this nightmare. In the end, she will be able to go home, and all of the other Fallen will burn with the rest of you."

Orren's frown deepened.

"You're not telling me what I want to know, Emries."

Emries shook his head.

"And impatient too. But then again, when you have a lifespan as short as you humans do, I suppose that is to be expected. Even your counterparts who fell to this world who have tasted immortality are still as impatient as they were in their mortal lives. But, that matters little. Very well. At the end on Onea, I was reckless. I was perhaps contaminated by your human failings. And so, that bastard Aerith Seth and his equally frustrating protégé Evan Sinn caught me at my weakest and most vulnerable point. A point mind you that should have been the scene of my greatest victory, and the ultimate end of my brother Halicon. But it wasn't to be. I was defeated, not by cunning, or will, or skill, but by my own confidence in my abilities. For a long time, I floated, in nothingness. I was vaguely aware of time passing around me. It was like it was in the beginning. When the universe was young, when we children of the Creator were first learning about ourselves and our nature and powers. It was when I discovered the fundamental truth. A truth that you humans could never understand if you lived a thousand lifetimes. But it didn't help me in the wars before the creation of these worlds, and it certainly didn't help me on Onea, or on Loinn. In the end, it only helped me to get back to where I was. Back to the nothingness. Back to the void. This time though, I was not alone in the void. There were others in the void. Others that had been cast out, cast away, hoping that they wouldn't be forgotten when the ending times came. That is where I found my protégé. He too wanted to get revenge for his lot in life. For the failure that he was destined to be. Isn't that right?"

Orren felt the irritation long before the person behind him moved. Before Orren knew it, Emries' protégé was standing right beside him. The hood of his white cloak still pulled up over his head, but the movement had dislodged some of the stark black hair from under concealment.

"Emries rescued me," the gruff and hate-filled voice said, "rescued me from being forgotten. From being left out of the end. Prevented me from not being able to make up for the slaughter at the hands of my oppressors. That was stolen from me on my world. Now the only way I can find peace is to burn all of those who had a hand in my fall. And I will kill them all."

Orren felt hate-filled eyes staring at him.

"And now you hold the soul and the stink of one of them. I will enjoy flaying the skin from your body and making you beg me for death. I will slowly cut off every piece of you, healing you just enough to keep you from dying. Over and over again, the torment will go on until there is barely enough of you left to support life. It will take you days, weeks, maybe even months to die. But you will die. And I will be the one to kill you."

Emries growled something unintelligible, and the robed man took a step back.

"Enough of this. You have heard what you wanted to know. Now tell me what I want to know. Tell me where Logan and Saurn are. Tell me now!"

"No!"

Emries kept his eyes trained on Orren, but made no moves against the man. Similarly, the robed figure made no aggressive action, though Orren was sure that his restraint was much more difficult to come by.

"We had a deal, human."

Orren frowned, reaching for the hilt of his sword.

"The deal was that you tell me how you escaped your judgment. You tell me how you survived Evan Sinn's blade in the final battle on Onea. Why are you still alive and so many others are not? Tell me the truth, or let's find out if you really are willing to kill me, or if it's just more of your talk."

Orren never saw the blow coming, and he barely felt it connect. The next thing Orren knew, he was tumbling through the air, and his shoulder hit hard against the outside wall of the barn that he had gotten the shovel from. The barn wasn't protected against the ravages of the storm, and so its supports were weakened by the cold and the wind. When Orren impacted the side of the barn, the whole wall gave way and the ceiling collapsed down upon him. Orren barely had time to pull his hand to his chest and reach for the powers that had been given to him by Aryx Terian. The shield of lightning flared up around him a moment before the beams of the ceiling crashed down upon him. But Orren didn't have to wait long buried in the pile of debris. A massive explosion of wind and fire followed shortly after Orren's impact, blasting all of the boards and beams in all directions. The man in the white robe crossed the distance between where he was standing and where Orren lay in the blink of an eye. His white gloved hand piercing through the shield of lightning and seizing the Sapphire Knight by the throat. For the first time, Orren saw the flash of yellow eyes from beneath the hood of the cloak. Orren could see smoke rolling from the glove and the cloak of the protégé, and while the man may have been biting back the pain, he was unable to prevent the physical repercussions from showing. His grip was powerful, close to collapsing Orren's windpipe, but as the heartbeats flashed by, Orren could feel the man's grasp weakening. Seizing on that moment of advantage, Orren called forth more of his new powers, doubling the intensity of the lightning field. Finally the man grunted in pain and released his hold on Orren's throat.

The robed man leapt backwards and stopped just a few feet from where Orren lay.

"Enough!"

Emries' shout echoed through the empty city, shaking walls and windows alike. The robed man seemed to debate for a moment whether or not he was going to obey the command, but finally lowered his hands and took three steps back from his position and stood still as a statue. Emries too remained where he was positioned and waited as Orren forced his way back to his feet. It wasn't easy, but Orren managed to get back to a standing position. He felt as though his whole body was bruised. As much as he wanted to keep the lightning shield up and around him, the pain his body was in made concentrating on something that required that much exertion all but impossible.

"You are stubborn, human. But stupidly so. Very well. In answer to your irrelevant question, there was no judgment to escape. The Creator was not going to let one of his children die at the hand of an insignificant being like a human. If it would have been a dragon that tried to kill one of us, then perhaps I would have passed on into nothingness. Pyrrus was only allowed to die because it was Talisia that ripped his heart out. When I destroyed one of Halicon's worlds long ego, he went into seclusion and came back stronger than I had ever seen him. So I took the opportunity after my defeat to take my own seclusion. What is a few thousand years in the span of my life? Now human, I have lived up to my end of the bargain. Now it's your turn. Tell me what I want to know."

Orren pulled himself up and drew his sword. He knew what would happen as soon as he told Emries what he wanted to know. As subtly as he could, he reached into the back of his mind and took hold of the energies that would be required to open a portal. If he was quick enough, he would be able to open it beneath his feet and get far enough away that he would be safe to open a properly targeted portal.

"As far as Saurn, I have no clue. But Logan. Well, let's just say that Logan is looking for you, probably as hard as you are looking for him. He has a score he'd like to settle for you. If you were half as smart as you think you are, you would have already found him. The crest of the phoenix shouldn't be that difficult to track down."

As soon as he said the last words, Orren reached for the flows of power in the back of his mind and started to open the portal beneath his feet. The swirling blue portal appeared, but just as soon as it had opened, it slammed shut. Orren looked up and saw Emries clenched fist and knowing wide smile.

"Not as clever as you thought you were, now are you, you pathetic waste of flesh? No matter. My real issue is with Logan and the rest of the refugees from Onea. Once I have dealt with them all, then I will be sure to tend to my siblings. For now though, I will leave you in the capable hands of my protégé."

Emries started to turn his back, thought better of it, and then turned back to face Orren.

"And, I wouldn't bother trying that portal trick again, or next time you'll find it slamming shut on your neck or some other vital part of your body. You see, I've learned how to counter the portals, and I can feel them forming before they become viable. My protégé here also has that ability. And believe me when I say that he will not use it just to keep you in his sight. He will most certainly utilize the ability to its most lethal outcome."

Emries turned away and the next second was gone. Orren turned his attention to the white robed man, who had not moved. For a long moment the two simply stared at one another, until the robed man reached up with his gloved hands and pulled back the hood of his cloak. Orren's jaws went slack, and his eyes widened. It wasn't possible. But those sharp features, the long stringy black hair, and the piercing yellow eyes. There was only one person whose cruelty was so plainly written on their face.

"Prepare yourself, Orren Eldrath of the Knights of the Flashing Blade," Draven Batoe said, his smile showing bright white teeth, "to cross swords with the king of the devils."

In the Lap of the Gods

Year Three of the Just Emperor Kaitain "Dragonsbane" Lorien, Creator's Calendar Year 1870

The darkening sky over the mountain city of Jelan held all manner of terrors suspended within it, while below on the fields outside the Academy of Arcane Arts, the three armies had taken a respite from the conflict that had held them the better part of the day. The Days of Star Fire were upon the world of Espre, holy days and days that evoked a combination of fear and awe at the power and majesty of the Creator. To that end, the darkening sky could just see the streaks of fire beginning to set the dark firmament alight. Rael and Trece Starlin, still recovering from their conflict with the Jade Knight Leonora Wastri and her command of the Blaze, could only look up in horror at the hovering form of the Goddess Talisia Masile and her dragon retinue. While Rael and Trece were thought of as gods by the mortals on Espre, they knew that Talisia was a god to them in the same way. The little amount of power that the two retained after their expulsion to Espre paled in comparison to those granted to a child of the Creator. It had been another child of the Creator, the god Halicon who had been the source of the powers granted to Rael and Trece, and now to Leonora, but they were only shadows of the source. Talisia bristled with unrestrained power, her dark hair graced with gentle streaks of gray fluttered around her as though she were submerged in water. She floated on the air as though she weighed nothing, and her dress of black and silver fluttered and flowed like the spectral gown of a wraith. Her large piercing green eyes could be seen even where she hung in the air, and her black lips were curled into an impassive frown. She would have been intimidating enough floating there in the void alone, but she had not come alone. Her three massive dragon companions beat wings in lazy patterns, holding themselves aloft with her.

The first of the three dragons floated above Talisia, a sinister backdrop to her malevolent appearance. Its skin was smooth by standards of dragons, no scales apparent, but rather smooth red skin that stretched tight over bulging musculature. Its limbs were thinner than the other two dragons, and it appeared to have none of the bulk, but rather was lean and limber. Four long taloned fingers emerged from both hands and feet, and cruel bone spikes jutted from both knee and elbow joints. Black veined wings in the same dark crimson color swept from the beast's back, and its long neck sported a lean head with long mouth and nose. Long horns curled back from the crest of the dragon's head, as well as a single horn that emerged from its chin. The dragon looked every bit like a massive bird of prey. Rael knew this dragon by sight, an ancient beast that had fought by Talisia's side during her failed coup that ended the life of the god Pyrrus. Its name was Karasut the Devourer. That day it had been the end of a great many angels, and was feared and respected among the ranks of its own race.

The second dragon was also known to the twin Dark Gods, and had also been on the field of battle at Talisia's side in the rebellion in the heavens. Like Karasut, Phantasma Graverobber was an imposing sight. It floated nearest to the mortal armies, its white, nearly translucent form hanging like a shimmering image reflected in a pool of water. The only definite feature was the creature's huge head which jutted out from its body on a short neck, but its large jaws held razor-sharp teeth that it could bring to bear quickly. Blue light seemed to envelop the whole of the dragon, and as the light pulsed and faded, different pieces of the spectral body became apparent. Sometimes the sky behind the dragon could be clearly seen through its membranous skin, while other times, the body was as substantial as stone. While the creature did have wings, they did not seem to beat as the other two dragons' did, Phantasma floated in mid-air through sheer force of will, much as Talisia did.

Hovering nearest to the Academy of Arcane Arts, the great bulk of the largest of the three dragons was held aloft by massive purplish wings whose attachments stretched the length of the dragon's back from its front shoulders all the way to its long tail. Pandesmos the Light Render was easily the size of its two fellows put together with room to spare. Most of the dragon's great bulk was contained in its barrel chest that could have doubled for a mountain face. The great long stalk of the dragon's neck emerged from between its upper shoulders, and unlike Karasut, Pandesmos' neck was not lean and serpentine. The neck was nearly the thickness of its massive chest, stretching long and tall with a ridge of multicolored fins running from the middle of its shoulders to the top of its head. The giant head was a sight to behold as well. Looking more like the head of a fish than that of a dragon, it sported dorsal fins on both side of its head, as well as long flowing fins like a fish's tail hanging from its chin. Its deep-set eyes glowed violet in the advancing darkness, and the iridescent scales shifted through spectrums of color like an oil slick on water. Without needing any further indication, Pandesmos was the first to act, letting its wings hesitate in their beating for a moment, the great bulk dropping out of the air like an anvil. It spread its wings at the last moment, catching enough air to slow its decent to prevent injuring itself. A large group of Jeresei and Kalbraks were not as lucky, and were crushed under its great weight. A long hard swipe of one of its fore claws shattered a Stone, and sent the pieces flying in all directions.

The cue for the battle to begin was as abrupt as it was brutal. Phantasma swooped down the next second, but it was more like a strobe effect. It jumped across the sky like a lightning bug, shining brightly in one place and then suddenly in the next a blink of the eye later. The tangled mass of soldiers from the Iron Legion and the Jade Army scattered when it finally flashed into a striking position on the ground, unnerved by the spectral dragon's appearance. Some ranks held, but their strikes seemed as ineffectual as one would expect when fighting what was for all intents and purposes a ghost. The twins broke from their position the next moment, Rael and Trece both sprinting in the direction of the massive form of Pandesmos. The Jeresei and Kalbraks were flashing in; cutting at the creature's bulk, but not able to penetrate the armored hide. Stone were converging on the dragon's position, but they were slow and lumbering while the dragon was surprisingly agile for its size. As they ran, Rael looked over his shoulder at Trece who nodded in ascent. The plan was hatched. Rael put his head down and continued to sprint toward Pandesmos. Trece changed her trajectory, heading for a large rock outcropping. At a full sprint she reached the peak of the outcropping and leapt high into the sky.

* * * * * * * * * * * *

Much like her transformation into her tiger form, Trece's transformation into a massive hawk was smooth and striking. At the peak of her long leap, her arms stretched wide, elongated, and her long fingers became long white feathers. The transformation of her arms into wings was completed first, while her long red hair grew in length and wrapped around the rest of her body. She brought her knees up, almost to her chest and her boots fell away, revealing yellow three-toed feet with bright green talons on the end. The broad fan tail erupted the next moment as her head shrank and narrowed, her chin collapsing and her mouth elongating and joining with her nose to form a silver beak that hooked slightly at the end. The hawk was red and brown in color and was nearly as large as a Shadowwalker, as it joined the conglomeration of flying creatures that began to mass like a great cloud of death. She led the leather-winged creatures in an assault on Karasut, who seemed eager to try its hand at engaging a hundred Shadowwalkers.

The dragon swooped in first, its lean form twisting and leaping through the air as though it weighed no more than a feather on the breeze. It pulled its wings in around itself as it hurtled toward the mass of Shadowwalkers, presenting a minimal target to strike. At the last moment, it opened its long lean jaws and sent a stream of black-peaked fire rushing deep into the heart of the formation. Trece dove to avoid the blast, and most of the Shadowwalkers were able to scatter in all directions to avoid the assault. However, the few that weren't fast enough to escape the flames were reduced to ash in a matter of seconds. Karasut let its wings hit the air again, acting like massive sails that pulled the dragon to a stop in mid-air. Dozens of Shadowwalkers dove in the next moment, raking with razor-sharp nails on hands and feet, few able to score direct hits. Still others flashed in, letting streams of pure fire erupt from their jaws. The lithe form of the dragon was able to dodge all but the point blank gouts of fire, leaving some of the compact blasts to strike other Shadowwalkers. While the

Shadowwalkers themselves were immune to their own attacks, they were not immune to the kinetic force that sent them sprawling away from the conflict. Trece let herself be buffeted by the changing breeze, staying well out of the fight, but waiting for her opportunity. One of the Shadowwalkers flashed in close to the dragon and was unable to pull away in time as the great jaws of the beast snatched it out of the air. However the extended wings of the Shadowwalker had created a small sliver of blindness in the dragon's field of vision. Trece soared low under the dragon and flashed up at the last possible second behind the twitching wing and over the nose of the dragon. Her glowing talons were poised to strike, and the dragon's eye caught the glint off of her claws the second before they dug deep into the tender eye. The dragon roared and brought its wings in tight, rolling into an instinctive dive. Trece was forced to pull her claws away before she could completely blind the eye, but it would be enough to give the mass of Shadowwalkers a slight advantage.

Karasut righted itself just before impacting the ground, and twisted so that its back was parallel with the ground, its wings inverting in mid-flight to hold the dragon in the amazing position. Its jaws widened again, sending a cloud of the blackened flame into the sky. Several hundred feet into the sky, as the strike approached the scattering Shadowwalkers, the gout of flame sparked and exploded, spreading in all directions like a blanket of super-heated plasma. The curtain of death rushed upwards, and Trece cried out in her mind to all of the Shadowwalkers to climb. Many were too committed to dives toward the wounded dragon to pull out in time. They were vaporized on contact with the advancing barrier. More however were able to pull up at the last second and tried hard to stay ahead of the deadly sparking plasma. Trece did her best to climb as high as she could, but her eagle form was not as nimble or powerful as that of the Shadowwalkers. Many of the larger creatures passed her, streaking towards the tops of the clouds. At last she could feel the heat of the barrier approaching, and her tail feathers twitched against the heat. Her wings buckled against the pressure of the air, and the wind was conspiring to throw her back into the field that held only annihilation. At the last possible second, a set of claws enclosed around the roots of her wings, and whipped her upwards. The Shadowwalker who saved her from the barrier himself was consumed, but the few feet of altitude she gained was enough to escape the field, as it dissipated moments later. Already dozens of Shadowwalkers were diving, their wings pulled back, and they hurtled to the ground at dizzying speed. They quickly reached terminal velocity, and Trece didn't have to think hard to understand what was about to happen. She too folded her wings back and dove, though her dive was much more controlled than that of the Shadowwalkers. Karasut was just righting itself from its assault, but had no defense for the suicide attack that the Shadowwalkers would loose the next moment.

Two dozen Shadowwalkers pulled out of their dive several hundred feet from Karasut, and let fly long streams of fire that created a nimbus around the lithe dragon, one that would keep it in the strike zone long enough for the other Shadowwalkers to do their worst. Karasut understood too late to do anything, and the first of the Shadowwalkers impacted Karasut directly in the flank. The dragon roared in pain as another and then another of the speeding Shadowwalkers barreled into it. The sixth such impact caused Karasut's wings to falter, and the dragon fell to the ground. This didn't stop the onslaught of the Shadowwalkers, as they were now committed to their course. More of the large black beasts impacted the body of the dragon, the sounds of bones shattering filling the air. When the last of the Shadowwalkers struck, Karasut's head lulled, its neck barely able to lift it from the ground. That was when Trece struck. Her massive claws ripped through the damaged neck, sending blood and gore spraying in all directions. The eagle screeched in victory a moment before a beam of pure dark energy struck the massive bird in the back. The explosion of power sent the eagle hurtling through the air, along with pieces of the dragon, and when Trece landed on the ground, she had returned to her human form. Her naked body bled from a hundred small cuts, and breath barely escaped her lips.

"Foolish girl," Talisia said coldly as she turned her attention to the battle that raged on with her remaining escort.

* * * * * * * * * * * *

Hundreds had died in the moments since the battle was joined, and as Rael let another burst of pure Blaze fire erupt from his outstretched hands, he began to wonder if anything could damage the massive form of Pandesmos. One of the huge hulking forms of a Stone had come into striking distance and brought both of its fists slamming down on the shoulder of the dragon near its neck. The dragon didn't even flinch before ripping its long claws across the chest of the Stone, shattering it utterly. The great wide mouth of the dragon opened the next moment, a stream of bright violet light spilling in all directions. Whatever the light struck flashed brightly and then disappeared. Dozens of Kalbraks and Jeresei met their ends that way. Dozens more Kalbraks were trying to scale the towering form of the dragon, their two foot long claws digging into the flanks of the dragon as though they were scaling a mountain. In answer, the dragon brought one of its massive wings slamming to its side, crushing not only the beasts foolish enough to try and climb, but also those that were on the ground who were close enough to be claimed by the strike. Gore coated the dragon from its feet to its neck, a testament to the many who died in the assault. But no matter how many the dragon killed, more kept coming. Out of the corner of his eye, Rael saw a half-dozen forms flash by. Three panthers and three white tigers bounded through the air, and began to scale the massive form of the dragon. Rael found himself nearly holding his breath as his children leapt from one cluster of muscle to another, dodging beats of wings and strikes of talons. The Jeresei and Kalbraks continued to pour on the assault as the great cats dodged their way to the neck of the dragon. Two of the panthers made for the throat, ripping and tearing, trying to expose some of the soft flesh beneath the scales. One of the tigers scaled the long ridge of fins at the back of the dragon's neck. The remaining panther had its jaws firmly closed around one of the broad muscles at the base of the dragon's wing. However, he was not able to hold his grasp for long. One long bat of the wing sent the great cat flying high into the air, and before the panther could right itself, it was impaled on one of the long bony protrusions jutting from the tip of the massive wing. But finally the dragon roared in pain. The ripping and clawing at its throat finally drew the dragon's blood. Pandesmos clawed at his own throat, trying to rid itself of the parasites, but the cats were too clever and too quick for the strikes. One of the tigers got careless however and was crushed between the dragon's teeth after a quick downward strike. The distraction was enough for two Stone to surge forward, each taking hold of the dragon about the neck. They pushed and pulled with all of their might, twisting at the neck of the great beast. Kalbraks and Jeresei struck at the feet of the dragon while panthers and tigers clawed at the thick trunk of a neck. The tiger that had scaled the ridge of fins finally made it to the top of the dragon's head and began to claw at its eyes. With another great roar, finally the great dragon toppled and fell. When it struck the ground, the force of the impact shook the ground in all directions and nearly took Rael off his feet. One of the Stone that held the dragon by the neck was crushed by the impact, and a great many more Jeresei and Kalbraks found themselves unable to escape the falling girth. With the dragon's underbelly exposed, the forces of the Dark Gods rushed in to take advantage of the situation. But Pandesmos would not allow itself to be vulnerable for long. It gathered its legs underneath it, and beat its wings hard twice, quickly righting itself. Another hard beat of wings, and the dragon was in the air and gaining altitude. Rael knew that another strike from the beam of purple light from the dragon's jaws was coming, and at that height, there was nothing anyone was going to be able to do to prevent the majority of their forces from being wiped out.

* * * * * * * * * * * *

Phantasma ripped through dozens more of the human troops from the mixed armies from the Kingdom of Iron Pellatori and from the Kingdom of Soul Oradrim. Her ghostly claws left after trails hanging in the air for several long seconds after her strikes, blood and gore splattering from vivisected mortals. The ranks of the two armies had already been thinned by their own conflict, and now that the dragon had set her claws to them, barely a hundred remained. Leonora watched in a mixture of awe and horror as the troops refused to run, but instead redoubled their efforts and launched a second and third assault at the shadowy beast. While not nearly the size of the other two dragons, Phantasma was still of impressive size, and a single sweep of her clawed hand could strike down eight to ten men. If she did nothing, Leonora would watch as the rest of the brave troops were wiped out. Though she was still significantly weakened from the assault by the twins Rael and Trece, Leonora had no choice but to try. She had one chance, and it was a technique that Cedric had taught her long ago, one that was to be used only as a last resort.

Reaching deep into herself, Leonora drew on the powers of the Blaze. She felt the intoxicating power run through her, and she continued to draw deeper and deeper, and in a matter of moments she was filled to the brim with power. And still she drew deeper. For the technique to work, it would require every bit of power that she could muster, and if she miscalculated by a hair's breadth she would either burn herself to a cinder before she was able to launch her attack, or the backlash of power would consume her. Deeper and deeper she drew, the sweet call of power starting to sour in the pit of her stomach. Leonora knew that the power of the Blaze was seductive, and as the blood pounded in her ears, the implication was clear. She had reached the edge, she had reached that moment where if she drew one iota more, that it would rip her apart from the inside. Cedric had taken great pains to teach her this point, and the learning had very nearly killed her in the beginning. The lesson had left her in a coma for nearly a month, but it was a lesson she would never forget.

Leonora's eyes fluttered closed, and in her mind's eye, she could see the ghostly form of Phantasma ripping apart more of her troops. Barely two dozen remained now, but they had passed the point of flight. They would fight to the last man in the futile attempt to salvage a victory out of the rout. Locking the dragon's form in the back of her mind, Leonora began to channel her power. Suddenly dozens of portals snapped open within the body of the dragon, several bisected her neck with more emerging from deep within her body. Phantasma barely had time to roar before the portals began to close, collapsing upon themselves with no destination. Blood billowed in all directions as the dragon was ripped apart from the inside out. Its wings slumped, uneven holes ripped through the translucent membrane. All light had gone out of the creature's eyes, and it fell to the ground, life stolen from it. Despite themselves, the remaining troops from the two mortal armies sent up a meager cheer. Unseen by any of the troops was the form of the Jade Knight slumping to the ground.

* * * * * * * * * * * *

Rael watched in horror as Pandesmos' mouth opened wide, and he could see the violet light collecting and expanding like a ball on the massive dragon's tongue. There was a bright flash of light, and Rael instinctively closed his eyes. For a long moment he thought he was dead, but there was no pain. Against everything his mind was telling him should have been, he was inexplicably alive, and Rael forced his eyes open again. Pandesmos still hung in mid-air, but his wings no longer beat, and his jaws while open no longer glowed with the eerie violet light. His scales were darkened, almost tarnished, the myriad of colors reduced to a lifeless gray. It took Rael blinking his eyes several times before he could get them to focus on something small that hovered just above the dragon's massive head. Channeling a little bit of power, Rael sharpened his eyesight, and locked his gaze on the form hanging small against the fire-streaked night sky.

The woman's white-gray dress hung limp, rebelling against the wind that whipped around her. Her stark white skin and stark white hair stood out in the night, and her bright eyes rivaled those of the goddess Talisia. It looked as though the woman had all of the color drained from her, with the exception of the blood that coated her fingertips. The dispassionate look on the woman's face was clear, and her gaze was locked on the woman that floated in mid-air a hundred feet from where she levitated. Talisia had noticed the intruder to the battlefield and maneuvered herself over toward the stranger.

"You dare interfere in my victory?"

The new arrival made no motion. Talisia looked down at the frozen form of Pandesmos and frowned.

"So you have the power to freeze a dragon. Impressive. But how long can you hold something as powerful as Pandesmos at bay? And how much could I shorten that time if I chose to attack you now?"

Talisia's eyes flashed and a beam of emerald light flashed from each of her eyes and cut through the space where the mystery woman hovered. However, the pale woman disappeared a moment before the beams hit, and then reappeared in the same place after the strike had passed. Still the dragon hung motionless. Finally the mystery woman cocked her head to one side and motioned with one hand toward the frozen form of Pandesmos. She slowly closed her fist and the sound of shattering filled the air. It was loud and stomach churning, and beneath the pale woman, the massive form of the dragon began to crumple in on itself, compressed by some great force that even the dragon's ancient bulk was not proof against. After Pandesmos had been quartered in size, the pale woman opened her hand again, and Pandesmos began to shred like burned paper in the wind. Ashes rained down from the sky, a black snow falling on the bloody plain.

Rael's eyes immediately went to the incredulous look on Talisia's face. Her body crackled with power, and her eyes glowed with hatred.

"Tell me who you are before I kill you!"

Talisia's voice shook the sky like a hundred peels of thunder. Lightning flashed all around them, causing the sky to glow and shake with fury. The flashes were so bright that they obscured the impossibly bright trails of burning meteors passing into the atmosphere, and nearly blinded Rael's enhanced sight. When the pale woman's mouth opened and worked her lips to form a single word, it was as quiet as a whisper, but filled Rael's ears as though it had been shouted right next to him.

"Jerah."

All Bargains Have Their Price

Sadrina Annis sat, her hands in her lap, feeling that moment as though her hands were bound behind her back. Her bonds had only been released a moment earlier, but the gag was still firmly in place. As soon as Kaitain entered the room, she tried her best to find the defiance and the strength to arrest the fall of tears from her eyes. For all the freedom she had in that small inn room, she may as well have still been tied to the chair. Ivan Quicksilver's massive hand on her bare shoulder was as stern as an iron claw would have been, and no less relenting. Her long dark hair had been pulled over her left shoulder, and cascaded across half her chest. She wore a simple, for her, gold colored dress with a fur frill at the top of each sleeve. The dress left her shoulders and throat completely exposed, and clung to her tighter these days than it once did. The hem of the dress was much lower than her husband would have liked, but when Pike was away from the palace, she was more comfortable in formal type dresses rather than the more revealing ones he always wished her to wear. She was thankful that her modesty won out this day. As she was growing up, her younger sister Hannah had always been the more adventurous and free spirited of the two. Naturally, all of that changed when she joined the Church of the Creator, and that too perhaps was a shock to the rest of the family. Sadrina wanted nothing more than to be the one that elevated the family to a more prominent status through marriage. She saw herself in a role in which she would marry into the aristocracy of one of the Great Kingdoms, perhaps even into the royal family. She never saw herself as Empress per say, but perhaps to one of the cousins. In her teenage years she fell madly in love with Feyd Lorien. They met just briefly on Ender Lorien's visit to the Kingdom of Albitonin to dedicate the completely refurbished Heart of Stone, and the great cathedral that stood in its center. Kaitain Lorien had also made that trip, and the young man then seemed as though he wanted to be anywhere but there. Now Kaitain Lorien stood before her again, this time he was Emperor of the whole of Cadaria, and she was the Lady of Mythryn, and they were mortal enemies. The cruel mask that covered Kaitain's face should have sent a shiver through her, but Sadrina had witnessed far more horrible things in her years with the Dark Gods, powers the likes of which even she could not admit truly existed on this world. What did however cause Sadrina's blood to freeze in her veins was the very real possibility that Kaitain would kill her. She was not a Dark God, she was very mortal, and if either of the two men wanted her dead, it would have been as simple for them as swatting a fly.

For a long moment Kaitain stood in the doorway, just looking at her. Finally he took several steps into the room until he was standing right in front of her. His hands were clad in black leather gloves, and he reached out with his right hand and placed it under her chin. Gently he lifted her chin so that she was looking right up into his eyes. Behind the mask, at this distance, she could see his eyes clearly. The iris was nearly the shade of ivory with an umbra of light blue at the edge to create separation between the iris and the rest of the eye. His eyes were clearly bloodshot, and the red tint almost glowed. He held her chin firmly, and let his thumb brush across her full lips. He looked up at Ivan and nodded his head. A moment later the gag was released, but it did not fall free of her. Kaitain released her chin for a moment and allowed the leather gag to fall down to her neck, where Ivan pulled back hard, half-restraining and half choking her. The Emperor's left hand was at her throat the next moment, and then his face was inches from hers. She could feel cold rolling from the metal mask, and when his voice hit her ears, the malice was clear.

CHAPTER 68

"I could kill you now," Kaitain said coldly, "and there would be nothing that your husband could do to save you. I could do all manner of horrible things to you, and there would be nothing that your sister would do to save you. Your existence is an affront to everything this empire stands for, and every breath you take is treason."

Sadrina kept her breath as steady as should could, despite the pressure on her throat and the fear that was causing her heart to race. Though the threat was there, there was something more to Kaitain's posture. He wanted her to be afraid, he wanted her to think that any moment he could end her life. But from everything Sadrina knew of Kaitain, he was not a stupid man. He may have been impulsive, but when he had something as valuable in his grasp as the wife of the leader of the Dark Gods, he was not going to simply destroy that leverage. Not only that, if the rumors were true and Hannah was one of the leaders of the rebellion against Kaitain's reign, it would give him leverage against her too. Sadrina was the perfect bargaining chip, and her supposed ally, Ivan Quicksilver had delivered her right into Kaitain's hands. He straightened finally, and withdrew a dagger from his belt and held it to her throat.

"Because you are a traitor to not only the Throne of Cadaria, but also to your family, I hereby strip you of all title and position afforded to you by your familial ties. Like those heretics that will continue to worship the Creator, you are nothing. You are less than a person, and as such have no rights. You belong to the Throne of Cadaria, and more to the point, you belong to me."

Kaitain looked up at Ivan, and he removed his strong hand from her shoulder. Ivan bowed and turned to leave the room through the other door, but no doubt would not go far. Once the door was closed behind him, Kaitain moved the blade up her throat, across her chin and up her left cheek. He dug the point in right above her cheekbone, and Sadrina could feel the tip rip through her flesh, and a second later a hot drop of blood slowly streaked down her cheek. Over the next agonizing few seconds, Kaitain dragged the tip of the dagger across her cheekbone toward her ear, opening the cut wider. Just past the level of the corner of her eye, he pulled the dagger away from her face and looked at the blood covered tip for a long moment before returning the blade to her throat. He held it there for a long time, staring into her eyes. Sadrina tried her best not to move a muscle, but she could feel herself trembling. The blade of the dagger dropped lower, and was turned so that the tip slipped just under the upper hem of the dress. She heard rather than felt the fabric being torn by the cruel blade, and tried to keep her eyes from widening with shock and fear.

"If you struggle, I'll give you more than a cut on your cheek," Kaitain chided. "And there are many worse things I can do to you than kill you."

The tearing of the fabric continued until Sadrina felt the dress begin to fall away from her body. Kaitain did not look down, but continued to stare into her eyes. She could almost feel the smile that was behind the mask.

"But feel free to scream as much as you like."

* * * * * * * * * * * *

Korin Melcab returned to his tent, a box under one arm, feeling satisfaction at the service he had provided to his masters on that day. His place as the captain of the Imperial Guard had been assured by the work he had done, and he had taken pleasure in wielding the blade that had ended the life of the traitorous knight Jaccob Aldora. Whether or not he was really a traitor was immaterial. The important part of the situation was that the Emperor saw him as a traitor, and now the man was dead. That was all the Korin cared about, and all that truly mattered at the end of the day. As Korin expected, the little serving girl whom had caught his notice was waiting for him when he returned to his tent. When she saw him enter, she knelt and began to unlace the bodice at the front of her serving girl's uniform. It had not taken her long to learn her lessons, and Korin had only had to apply a few open hand slaps for her to take the lessons to heart. But tonight he did not want only her obedience. He wanted more.

A low table stood near the entrance of the tent where he placed the hinged wooden box as well as his scabbard and sword. He walked to where the girl knelt and she kept her eyes down waiting for the captain's instructions. A cruel smile coming to his lips, he grabbed the girl by her hair and lifted her to her feet. One of her hands instinctively went to her head, while the other braced herself on his shoulder. He pulled harder, lifting her completely off the ground, prompting her other hand to leave his shoulder and go to her head, trying desperately to keep him from ripping her hair completely out. The cruel smile on his face widened, and he carried her over to the table where the wooden box lay. With minimal effort, he lowered her back to the ground and then pushed on the back of her head until she was on her knees again. With his free hand, he pulled the wooden box over to her.

"Open it."

Hands trembling, the serving girl reached up and took hold of both sides of the box. It was hinged in such a way that the upper half of the box flipped open, and when she lifted it, and got a glimpse of what was inside, her stomach roiled. She wanted to let go of the top of the box. She wanted to let the thing fall closed and shut her eyes. But she knew he would beat her harder if she failed him in this. She knew that his violent streak was barely restrained as it was, and to give him cause to do more than he already intended was to invite certain death. As it was she would only remain alive so long as she amused him. And it certainly amused him to paralyze her with fear.

Laying on red satin cloth was the head of the former Topaz Knight of the Flashing Blade, Jaccob Aldora. His eyelids were sown open so that his dead eyes could stare out. The man's skin was already pale from the lack of blood, and the haunted look on his face spoke more than just the horror of his death, but perhaps the truth that he saw with his last breaths. The girl could feel the pride rushing through Korin, his trophy proudly displayed. Finally he pulled her back to her feet and again lifted her off the ground. This time he pulled her close to him, and she could smell the sickening scent of death all over him. His eyes blazed, and the taunting smile hung on his lips like a cruel mask.

"If you please me," he said in a low growling voice, "perhaps when I am done with you, you will deserve having your head in a box right alongside his."

The assassin's mind took over at that moment. This close it would be a simple matter to end the life of the Captain of the Imperial Guard. He had fallen into the trap, but perhaps not the way that the assassin would have liked. The dagger materialized in her hand the next moment, and she plunged it into Korin Melcab's chest, right into his heart. But instead of a shriek of pain and blood spraying in all directions, Melcab smiled wider and slammed the girl's head against the table before tossing her to the other side of the tent. Deidre tried to roll with the impact to the ground as her masters had taught her, but the blow to her head had thrown off her equilibrium, and as she came back to her feet, she found her legs were rubbery and the vision in her left eye was foggy. No doubt her skull had been cracked by contact with the table, and she could feel where splinters from the wood had lodged themselves deep in the side of her face. She could see the hilt of the dagger emerging from where the man's heart should have been, and yet he seemed to pay it no mind. Wordlessly he reached over to the table to recover his sword, but found only his empty scabbard. He returned his gaze to the wounded assassin, and balled his fists. The assassin formed two more daggers in her hand and charged. She feinted high and then went low, sliding through Korin's legs, slashing at each of his hamstrings as she passed behind him, before gathering her feet under her and pushing off hard, springing high into a backflip. She pulled her knees in so that her feet barely scraped the top of the tent before coming down in front of the Captain of the Imperial Guard, dragging one dagger across the side of his face, and burying the other in his gut. The controlled fall continued, and she kicked out with her legs, her feet catching the larger man in the shins, sending her backwards, while he fell forwards. As she recovered into a crouch, Korin lay flat on his face, the dagger in his chest and the one in his belly piercing deeply. To Deidre's amazement, no blood flowed from either of the wounds on the back of the man's legs, and no blood was pooling on the ground under him. A moment later, Korin's hands pressed against the ground and he pushed his way back to a kneeling position, the cruel smile still painted on his face.

"What are you?" Deidre cursed, forming two more blades in her hands.

He was on her quicker than she could blink, and she never felt his hands around her throat. A sickening snapping sound filled the tent, and blood trickled from the dead girl's mouth as he let her corpse fall to the ground. Finally the smile faded from Korin's lips, and he quickly removed the dagger from his chest and from his stomach, letting them fall to the ground beside the body of the assassin. He would call for one of his lieutenants to arrest Geoffry Aramour, and before the light of dawn he would have another trophy to sit upon his table. First though, he had to find out what happened to his sword.

* * * * * * * * * * * *

It was just before midnight when Dominique dismissed the last of the seamstresses for the night. They would all be working until dawn she knew, but she had had enough for one day and needed the rest. Tomorrow at least she would be on her way away from the Inn of Coventry, and at least ostensibly out from under the thumb and constant gaze of her husband the Emperor. Whatever the long slumber had done to the man, only the first ramifications of it were being felt. Before long the Imperial Legions would be enforcing his will on those kingdoms that were loyal to his name, and the gathered armies of the Great Kingdoms that were still under Kaitain's banner would mobilize and crush the rebel kingdoms one by one. Perhaps in the cold reaches of the Kingdom of Rashaleb she would have opportunities with Chelsea by her side to make enough changes to prevent the whole of Cadaria from falling into Kaitain's madness.

She had already changed into a sheer nightshirt and was just settling into her bed when there was a noise from the far side of the room. There was a chill in the room that had not been there several moments before, like that of a draft from an open window. However, Dominique had been sure to ensure the window was closed while she was changing. The small candle that stood on the table by the bed didn't cast enough light to see the area around the window, and the curtains had been drawn to prevent moonlight from seeping in, or the spectacular lights from the Nights of Falling Stars. Dominique had never been able to sleep when there was too much light in the room, and at the first streams of light peeking through the window in the morning, she would awaken. It had led to a maddening first few nights in the Royal Palace of Aldere, as the Imperial Bedroom had large picture windows that let in an incredible view of the moonlit night sky on all but the cloudiest of evenings. Finally she had been able to convince Kaitain to have curtains installed in the room. Of course, the servants constantly were opening the curtains to let in the bright morning light long before Dominique would have preferred.

Picking up the candle from the table, Dominique started toward the direction the sound had come from before a voice stopped her.

"Please stay there, Dominique," the familiar woman's voice said quietly. "Don't make this harder than it has to be."

The shadows in the far corner of the room seemed to melt away to reveal a woman's form. Moonlight flooded in from the window, a window that had obviously been opened briefly under the cloak of the assassin's abilities taught to a master such as Natalia Pressen, illuminating the woman's form. Her features were haunting in the moonlight, he long brown hair pulled back tightly against her head and her eyes filled with a mixture of pity and resignation. In her hand was not the Sacred Weapon of her station as the Sunstone Knight of the Kingdom of Gold, but rather a simple sword that bore the Imperial Crest. It was a weapon that was given to officers only, and would be unmistakable to anyone who saw it.

"What's the meaning of this?" Dominique said, raising her voice.

"Don't bother trying to alert the guards," Natalia said, a frown coming to her face. "No sound will leave this room until I permit it. Unfortunately, the situations that have transpired tonight have required me to enact our backup plan. That, I'm afraid, will require your life to end."

Dominique was shaken by the steel in the woman's voice, and the manner in which she spoke of ending a life. Until that moment, Dominique had no reason to suspect that Natalia was anything other than an ardent supporter of the work that Dominique had done while in the position of Empress, and the woman had even been present during the negotiations with the Dark God Midarin. She had had plenty of chances to betray not only Dominique, but Chelsea as well.

"I don't understand."

Natalia sighed slightly.

"Your friend and protector asked the Grand Master of the Shadow Guild for help in eliminating the Captain of the Imperial Guard. It was a bold plan, but certainly not without risk. The best we could hope for was that the plan would go through as intended, and Korin Melcab would have been eliminated. It would have been simple enough to frame a jealous subordinate, or perhaps a religious zealot who was rebelling against Kaitain's recent declarations. Either would have served the purpose of sewing dissension into the ranks of the Imperial Guard, and robbing Kaitain of one of his weapons. Worst case, the assassin would fail, and we would still be able to plant the story about the disgruntled members of the Church of the Creator. But Korin has proven to be cagier than we would have expected a thug like him to be. I suppose one does not rise to the ranks of the Captain of the Imperial Guard simply by being a blunt instrument. Moments after the death of the assassin, Korin ordered the arrest of Geoffry Aramour, the resident Master of the Shadow Guild who reports to the Emperor."

Dominique's eyes widened. She had always had her suspicions about the man who was the court musician and advisor to the Emperor, but she never would have pegged him as a member of the Shadow Guild, let alone one of their Masters. Natalia took two steps closer, brandishing the weapon in her hand so that Dominique could see clearly.

"This has left the Grand Master exposed to possible charges of treason, and threatens the whole of the Shadow Guild. And that is something we can't allow to happen. Shortly after the fight started, I took Korin's sword to give our assassin a better chance, but also to use just in case the worst happened. The Grand Master always taught me to be prepared. It will be a simple matter to eliminate everyone who has seen you over the last two hours, and make their bodies disappear so that no one will even miss them until it's too late. As for you, I'm afraid you will be found dead in your bed with the Captain's sword through your heart."

Dominique's mouth dropped open, and she could not bring herself to form any words to communicate her shock.

"I promise you, it will be painless. Or as painless as I can manage," Natalia continued. "When it is discovered that he is responsible for your death, it will be a simple enough matter to show that he arranged for the attempt on his life, that he escaped without a scratch, and was going to blame the Shadow Guild for both crimes. I just happened to discover the truth before an innocent man could be punished. Korin will no doubt be executed and the court will be thrown into disarray. More kingdoms will rebel against Kaitain after your death, and it will give us more opportunities to move directly against him. Once we have properly conditioned his heir of course."

Natalia stopped in her tracks and gave Dominique her best pitying glance.

"I'm truly sorry it has come to this Dominique. I was really starting to like you. But the Shadow Guild must be protected at all costs."

The door to the room opened just as Natalia started to move in. Dominique instinctively darted toward the door, and Natalia was quickly on her heels. Chelsea Zarova burst through the door the next moment, tackling Dominique to the ground just before the sword would have cut her down. Before Natalia could react, Chelsea was back on her feet and had a dagger in hand. Though the Sunstone Knight prided herself on her abilities, she was not fast enough to prevent the blow that would end her life. The dagger thrust upward into her chest, piercing her heart. The sword fell from the woman's hands the next moment, clattering to the ground noisily. Chelsea and Natalia fell to the ground, Chelsea still hanging on to the dagger. Dominique for her part scrambled over to the door, closing it quickly and bolting it shut.

"What's going on?"

Chelsea's mind was racing. She had just killed another member of the Knights of the Flashing Blade, and that had never been her intention. She had only wanted to disarm the woman and figure out what was going on, but her body would not obey her thoughts. Instinct had taken over when Dominique's life was threatened, and she could only answer deadly force with deadly force. Dominique was still on her hands and knees, scurrying over to where Chelsea and Natalia lay.

"Were there guards at the door?" Dominique said in hushed tones.

Chelsea stared at her blankly for a long moment, before Dominique's insistent gaze caused her to answer.

"No, I sent them to assist with the search of the camp. Someone tried to assassinate Korin Melcab."

Dominique nodded.

"I know."

Dominique was back to her feet a moment later, recovering the sword that Natalia had dropped. The blade was heavy in her hands, but she managed to bring it over to where Natalia's body lay. Wordlessly, Dominique fell back to her knees, and placed the tip of the blade of the sword where the hilt of the dagger was plunged into the assassin's chest. Chelsea understood the next moment what Dominique intended, and took the sword from the smaller woman's shaking hands. Keeping the angle the same as the dagger's, Chelsea plunged the sword into the dead woman's chest, and then recovered her dagger. When Chelsea looked back over to Dominique, she was just staring down at Natalia's fallen form, her features stark white. After a moment, Chelsea put both hands on Dominique's shoulders. That seemed to shake the woman from her daze.

"We're leaving," Chelsea said quietly, "tonight. Get only what you need, and I'll take you down to the stable. When all hell breaks loose in the morning, we don't want to be anywhere near here. I've made some arrangements for some trustworthy protection to meet us on the road."

Chelsea helped Dominique to her feet, and the look that passed between the two women communicated something that mere words could never have embodied. A conspiracy of silence, complicity in murder, and a pact that understood the high price they would both face if the path before them ended in failure.

Epilogue

The Days of Star Fire

Year Three of the Just Emperor Kaitain "Dragonsbane" Lorien, Creator's Calendar Year 1870

The sacred grove of the dragons stood eerily silent. One of the most holy times in the estimation of the small minded beings that roamed the world known as Espre was about to begin, and while the dragons paid it little mind, it was because they understood its true significance. When the dragons came to Espre, they chose it for a number of reasons, and despite what many of the younger members of the council thought, it was not solely out of desperation. There were other options as far as homes, but Espre was unique in several regards. The first and probably most important was the fact that it was an independent world. Most worlds in the Creator's universe were tended to by his children, very few of them were independent worlds that were controlled by the Creator alone. Many times over the millennia since the formation of the Creator's universe and the birth of the first dragons, the breeds had come into conflict with the children of the Creator. Most often these were common ideological conflicts, but they always ended the same way, in a war the reduced the world to a cinder. Here, on a world without the single-minded ideological posturing, the dragons would have a chance to make a real home for themselves. The other factor that made the world inviting and desirable was its unique physical and astrological characteristics.

Espre was a large world comprised mostly of water, and because of the small amount of land mass, all of the waters were connected into a single ocean. All of the land mass on the face of the world was concentrated into two continents and a smaller chain of islands that stretched between the large continents. Large polar ice caps covered the northern and southern poles of the world, but rather than forming contiguous tundra, they instead were formed by a series of interconnected icebergs, which themselves were comprised predominately of water. Due to the sheer amount of water on the face of the planet, rain was the dominant weather condition, with the exception of a large arid desert in the southern reaches of Mythryn. A thin equatorial zone was marked by very violent storm fronts that often became hurricanes, which though several parts of the year rendered several of the islands in the Pritan Island chain almost completely uninhabitable by any but the sturdiest of creatures. The equatorial zone itself in the heat of the long summer could be as much as twenty degrees hotter than the rest of the world on the longest days. The opposite was true for the northern and southern polar zones. Both areas were constantly in states of severe and extreme winter, where blizzard conditions were the norm. These variant conditions as well as consistent access to extreme weather made the world of Espre perfect as a home for the race of dragons.

The conditions on the world were created by the somewhat unique astronomical conditions that held Espre. Espre was the largest of the three planets that orbited a set of twin stars. The twin stars orbited about each other, drawn together so closely that from the surface of the world, the naked eye could not distinguish more than a single point of light. Because of the small size and the relative youth of the stars themselves, they did not generate much heat. The heat they did generate however was focused into a tight area, which was the reason for Espre's small yet volatile temperate zone, and the larger polar stretches. At the closest approach of Espre's orbit to the binary stars, the naked eye could distinguish between the two stars, but the close approach had a more spectacular result for those creatures on the world's face. Espre's one small moon normally orbited slowly, and on every fifth close approach to the twin stars, the orbit of the moon caused it to pass through the haze of stellar matter expelled by the twin stars. The moon would pass through the dense hot cloud leaving a fiery trail across Espre's sky. This process slowly degraded the dense and normally invulnerable surface rocks, stripping away pieces of the moon, creating a fireworks type of display in the sky as tiny meteors burned up when they passed through the atmosphere. During this show of fire, there was a near total solar eclipse, marked by incredibly powerful storms, winds, heat, and lightning. This pass of the moon through the nimbus of the stars became known by the humans of Espre as the Nights of Star Fire.

Through the high tree canopy, the start of the streaks of fire and smoke could be seen high in the sky. The small moon was clearly visible even in the daylight, surrounded by the nimbus of flame that marked its entry into close orbit of the twin suns. From the edge of the sacred grove, a pair of ancient eyes watched. It had been a long time since Dorovar had tasted fresh air, and even longer since he had felt anything other than the cold foreboding of his prison pressing in around him. It felt strange to have the scents of nature in his nostrils again, as well as the feel of grass and moisture on his bare feet. The plain black robe with grey borders that adorned him was simple and light, allowing the soft breeze that barely disturbed the leaves to encircle him and hold him. Most would not have seen the lines of the protection and detection spells that hung in the air around the sacred grove, but Dorovar knew they were there long before their phantasmal forms became apparent to his eyes. One step further forward would alert the dragons and their guardians to his approach, and would begin a chain of events, that once started, could not be stopped before its inevitable conclusion. It was fitting that the sky was burning. It would mark the coming of a new time on the face of Cadaria as well as in the universe itself. It was the time of Dorovar, and it was the time of reconciliation. A cessation of everything that had come before, a transition from the old to the new. The desiccated corpse of the Creator's universe would be washed away, to be replaced by the pristine and gleaming architecture that Dorovar would forge from the bones of the old. Unconsciously holding his breath, Dorovar stepped over the invisible line into the Dragons' Sacred Grove.

* * * * * * * * * * *

Orren Eldrath stood dumbfounded. In a matter of minutes he had been engaged in combat with a child of the Creator, and now was about to battle a child of another of the Creator's chosen. While Orren had never set eyes upon the creature known as Draven before, thanks to the memories granted to him by Aryx Terian's powers, he was well acquainted with the man. Draven was an evil unlike any that Orren had dealt with before. He was the personification of all of the worst fears the people of Cadaria had about the Dark Gods. He was brutal, precise, malicious, and conniving. Nothing that the man did was without purpose, and he would stop at nothing to ensure that his schemes came to fruition. Stunningly Orren thought that Draven and Kaitain had a lot in common. But those thoughts were for a time when Orren did not have the evil man's yellow eyes focused on him.

Courage felt numb in Orren's hand. It had ceased actively trying to pull itself away from the moment, but was simply a dead piece of metal. It would be of no use to him in what was to come. Keeping his eyes locked on Draven, Orren returned Courage to the scabbard on his belt, and then with a single deft motion, unclasped the belt at his waist and let the Sacred Weapon fall to the ground. Draven was on him the next second, flashing through the intervening space as if it wasn't there. A single fist flashed forward, striking Orren hard in the chest and sending him sprawling backwards several feet. Orren braced himself finally, but Draven was upon him again, another hard open-hand strike aimed at his throat. This blow the Sapphire Knight was able to quickly intercept with a punch of his own that targeted the palm of the demon's hand. The two men's hands collided, but Orren was not ready for the other man's strength. His hand hurt, and several bones could have been broken. If Draven was affected by the impact, he gave no sign. The determined snarl was on his lips, and he lunged in again, a hard right to Orren's chin. This time the Knight of the Flashing Blade did not underestimate his opponent's prowess. He called upon the new powers at his disposal and hardened his hand while at the same time anchoring his body. Orren successfully caught the strike, but Draven was one step quicker. Using the point where their two hands met as a fulcrum, Draven channeled energy into his limbs, and leapt straight up. The man once called the Lord Crow felt the tearing in his shoulder, but he paid it little mind. Draven's shoulder pulled free of the socket, dislocating totally while the man flipped backwards, but his attack proved to be as damaging to his opponent as it was to himself. Both feet caught Orren under his chin, shattering it, and sending the Sapphire Knight sprawling backwards. He landed flat on his back, spitting blood and teeth in all directions, his bottom lip and jaw hanging slack. Draven continued through a long arching back-flip, landing some fifty feet away from the fallen knight, his right arm hanging obscenely limp and lifeless at his side. A moment later however, the arm simply slid back into it proper location, healed by the barest application of power.

Orren tried to pull himself back to his feet, but it was no use. Pain radiated through his body, and the damage caused by Draven, as well as that caused by Emries and his unfamiliarity with his new powers put the still very-much mortal Sapphire Knight at a huge disadvantage. He tried to concentrate some of his powers to heal his extensive wounds, but he wasn't able to concentrate enough to form the pictures he needed to in his mind. Already his right hand was beginning to swell, his tongue lulled in his ruined mouth, and his back ached because of whatever he had landed on. The best Orren could manage was to pull himself into a half-sitting position, and that was tenuous. Draven was already approaching, and a haze of dark energy encased each of his hands. The strike that would end Orren's life was rapidly approaching. Suddenly Orren saw Draven's eyes go wide, he looked in all directions, and the haze around his hands quickly coalesced into two long crystalline blades that had a smoky quality to their coloration. From somewhere behind Draven, an arrow sped past, just clipping the top of the demon's ear.

* * * * * * * * * * * *

Dorovar felt the arrow coming a moment before it materialized. It was of no difficulty to snatch the piece of wood out of the air, and snap it in two. The first of the four guardians of the Sacred Grove had come much faster than Dorovar had expected, but their competence was still somewhat lacking. The shot had been intended as a warning, not to kill. That was the first mistake. The second of course was thinking that something as simple as an arrow would delay Dorovar for more than a second. Even now, Dorovar could see the four guardians emerging from the trees, ready to do their best to defend the sacred ground from the intruder. It would have been a simple enough matter for Dorovar to dispatch the four of them, but that would give his quarry more time to flee, if flight was his true intention. Dorovar had an appointment and a promise to keep, and nothing was going to delay him from it. A moment later, Dorovar was not alone at the edge of the clearing. His four heralds had been drawn to this place, the same as

Dorovar had been, and they were already moving to end whatever resistance the guardians would be. Their deaths were assured, and would certainly not be swift in the grander scheme of things. But that was not Dorovar's concern. Not now, not this close to his first taste of vengeance after so long.

Dorovar walked slowly and deliberately through the clearing, his footsteps leaving brown and dead imprints behind him. Underbrush fell away from his advancing form in all directions as though his very presence was poison to life. In a matter of minutes Dorovar was standing before the most beautiful sight he had seen in a hundred lifetimes. The Great Tree stood before him, beautiful and glowing in the haunting late light of the day framed high above by the glowing red and yellow embers of burning stone falling through the sky. Dozens of ancient trees curled together to form the trunk of one greater tree, a collection of life so grand that it altered all of the life around it. The great root system stretched in all directions, creating a massive clearing where no other life could be sustained. Huge spires of living branches scraped the sky, bursting forth with broad leaves that drank in light and moisture that fed the rest of the greater structure. In some places, the bark of the spires were a birch white, glistening like ivory in the light of the sun, and gleaming like marble in the moonlight of advancing night. Only beauty held sway in this ancient clearing, and even Dorovar's footsteps could not push back the abundant and powerful life. His hands extended to his sides, palms out, a mockery of a sign of peace, Dorovar advanced into to the Great Tree, the way to the council chambers of the Dragon's Council seared into his brain.

As Dorovar emerged through a great arch, he stood on the floor of the council chamber, the great walls of the chamber stretching high in all directions, with openings large enough for the members of the council to perch. On the other side of the chamber stretched the equally ancient form of the Lord Dragon Tarot, the leader of the dragons on Espre and elsewhere throughout the Creator's universe. His long white beard was brighter than his ivory white scales, and his huge blue eyes gleamed in the dim light of the chamber. The high-arching semi-transparent membrane that served as the roof of the chamber was starting to dim, but the flashes of light and fire from the meteor storm were clearly evident. The flashing light added a strobe effect to the movements of the combatants, Tarot's long almost lazy breaths dragging into incredible slow motion. The dragon raised its massive head and stared in Dorovar's direction.

"So, you've finally come."

Dorovar kept his hands at his sides, the robe billowing softly in the gentle breeze that swirled around the chamber. His dark eyes boring daggers into the hard flesh of the dragon.

"One day, I knew that I would be standing against a dragon again, my only hope that the first of your kind I would have come across was the deceiver Shadowweaver. But perhaps it is better that it is you, Tarot. I will rid your kind of their leader, and then one by one I will rip each of you apart until all that is left is the one that condemned my world to death. And once I am standing over his rotting carcass, I will have vengeance for the people of my world."

The dragon's wings drooped slightly.

"There is no one more responsible for the fate of your world than yourself, Dorovar," Tarot said in a somber tone. "You and all of your people could have left us in peace. You could have abided by the terms of the agreement. But your own leaders turned their weapons upon us. They created the war that brought ruin to your cities. They created the battles that left millions of broken bodies lying at our feet. Ultimately it was the thirst for power and mindless revenge that gave your own religious cult exactly what they wanted. They wanted the power to destroy us, and they didn't care what it cost. The cost was your world, Dorovar, and as much as you may want to lay the blame totally at our feet, it was you, and your race that is truly to blame. Why do you perpetuate this misguided hate? Why do you make world after world suffer?"

Dorovar's hands lowered slightly, and he bowed his head.

"Is that how you rationalize your crimes? Is that how you sleep at night after all the worlds you've destroyed? That it wasn't your fault? That if the humans had simply left you alone that things would not have happened the way they did? Should we ignore that you encroached on every part of the world from the seas to the air? That you fed on the livestock that meager families depended on to survive? Where were your attempts to coexist with us? Where were your attempts to leave the people of those worlds in peace? No, dragons do not want to coexist with anything. You are superior. You are the first race. You are the blessed of the Creator and touched by the will of his children. So loved are the dragons that they can even assist in rebellions against a Child of the Creator and escape punishment. And yet my world burns. Now I will burn you all down. I will seek you out to the last hatchling. No dragon will draw breath in this universe once my work is done."

Tarot roared and drew itself up to his full height. Razor-sharp ivory teeth gleamed and golden talons glowed with deadly power.

"The rest of my kind have scattered to the corners of this world to prepare for you and your servants. We were told of your coming, and we were told how to defeat you. I do not fear you. I have faced Emries in single combat. I have stood tall against Halicon's monstrous horde and survived with not even a scar. One such as you holds no fear for me. Your world was insignificant. Your existence is an abomination, and I will gladly end it. You were a fool to come here alone."

Dorovar lifted his head once again, locking his eyes on Tarot. His look was impassive, but there was a slight curl at the corner of his mouth, something vaguely resembling a smile.

"Oh, you are mistaken, ancient one. I am not alone."

Almost as though commanded, four shadowy translucent figures appeared flanking Dorovar.

"My friends have suffered mightily for their role in the destruction of our world. Their names stolen from them, the powers granted by that traitor Emries turned to the will of corrupt men and fools who served a crown. Every moment in those Sacred Weapons, holding my prison, they were tormented and tortured. All they knew was the moment of their own deaths, and the pain that every soul on our world felt in those last moments. Were it in my abilities, I would sentence every last one of your race to the same torment. But sadly it is not. My goddess is harsh on those who shun her love. So my fellows have suffered."

The four figures fanned around the room, their footsteps trailing flame. The flames blackened the ground and began to stretch across the face of the chamber. In a matter of seconds, the whole of the council chamber was set ablaze, and Dorovar and Tarot stood facing each other in the center of a raging inferno. Tarot roared again and stretched across the length of the chamber, its massive jaws ready to close around Dorovar's head. The man was fast enough to catch the tooth-lines jaws before they could close around his head, holding the gaping maw open. Dorovar's strength was not infinite, and was perhaps less than those who called themselves Dark Gods, but calling on his inner reserves, he was powerful enough to hold an ancient dragon at bay for a few moments at least. However, Tarot would not be denied his strike. A moment before the deluge struck, Dorovar heard the rumbling from deep within Tarot's gullet. That next moment, a torrent of wind so cold that it burned burst forth. Within the hurricane force winds were shards of ice no bigger than a needle that cut through Dorovar's flesh as though it were paper. Yet Dorovar endured. Even as the ice and burning wind cut at his flesh and threatened to flay the skin from his bones, the powers of immortality and perpetual healing granted by his deal with the dragons were mending the damage almost as fast as it was being inflicted. Not willing to undergo the assault without retaliation, Dorovar set his feet and braced himself. He drew on as much of his power as he could and with a single great motion twisted his body as fast and as hard as he could. The motion wrenched the head and neck of the great dragon, snapping resounding through the entire length of the neck, and the torrent of wind and ice being instantly interrupted. Sensing the advantage and the end of the battle, Dorovar pulled as hard as he could, ripping the massive head of the dragon clear from the shattered neck. The rest of the body of the Lord Tarot shuddered and twitched, finally collapsing to the floor, dark blue blood pouring in all directions from the headless neck. The great tongue curled out from inside the disembodied jaws, and wrapped itself firmly around Dorovar's throat, and squeezed as the last bit of light fled from the dragon's massive eyes. After several long moments, the muscles in the forked tongue went slack, and it fell limp over Dorovar's left shoulder. The head was left to fall to the ground moments, later, and lay there as a silent witness as the beautiful spires of the Great Tree burned.

As Dorovar watched, the first feelings of vengeance being quenched in his heart, the four phantoms looked on wordlessly, tears slowly falling from the eyes of the woman who until now could only answer to the name Temperance.

* * * * * * * * * * * *

Draven felt the tip of the arrow rip through his ear and the soft trickle of blood that followed. When he turned, he saw the portals closing, and the two people who stood in their wake. The owner of the bow did not take much imagination to identify. Midarin Rice stood proudly, bow in hand, long brown hair whipping behind her in the breeze. But the man beside her, a delicate curved blade in one hand made Draven's blood go cold. Part of Draven knew that this would come to pass. Part of Draven knew that he would not be able to move on in this new existence until his nemesis was dealt with. Gwydeon Sandar stood between him and the future that he was destined for. And if the two men crossed blades again, one of them would fall, and this time it would be forever.

"I should have known you would come running to defend this filth."

Draven's taunt went without answer, at least from the two people standing in front of him. Suddenly a burst of power shot from somewhere behind Draven, catching him firmly in the back and sending him sprawling face first to the ground. His back burned, and when the demon was able to scramble back to his feet, he saw the feminine form of Nightwing standing, her jaws slowly coming to a close. Draven looked over the three opponents, and one corner of his lips drew up in a smirk.

"Well, Gwydeon," Draven said, staring down his old enemy, "I see you are still not man enough to face me yourself. You've always hidden behind your woman, or your principles, or whatever else it was that kept you from dying. Now, old man, come and face me. Let me send you to your final rest."

Gwydeon raised his blade and advanced a pace, but jumped back at the last moment as a broad gout of fire erupted from the ground where he would have been the next heartbeat. Draven tilted his head to one side and then cocked a single eyebrow. With one hand, he pointed upwards, and when Midarin and Gwydeon both raised their eyes to the heavens, Midarin had to fight hard to retain control of her bow. A boy, no older than perhaps fifteen floated in the air above where Draven stood. His sandy colored hair short and wavy, his brown eyes filled with nothing but malice.

"Hello mother. Hello father."

Gwydeon's blood went cold, and he could not form the words. It was Midarin who spoke.

"Nathanial?"

"Nathan, mother, try to remember. Emries promised that I would have a chance to punish you for everything that happened on Onea. I just never thought I would get a chance to do it this soon."

The young boy once known as the Ram floated to the ground and stood just a few steps from Draven. The white cloaked demon regarded his counterpart for a moment, and then smiled wider.

"As much as I would like to stay, I think I will leave you to your family reunion. Enjoy yourselves, and Gwydeon, I hope you survive so that you and I can finish our own business."

The portal opened under Draven that next moment and he was gone. Nathan let a pure crystalline blade form in each hand and the sneer peeled back his lips.

* * * * * * * * * * *

Draven emerged from a swirling portal thousands of miles away at the southern tip of the so-called Dark Continent of Mythryn. He knew from Emries that the Dark Gods were on the defensive, and it was time to put the dagger in the hearts of the few stragglers that still clung to the husk of what had once been their domain. He was standing on a large cliffside overlooking the ruined towers, and he felt a smile creep to his lips. He would be on them before they knew what was happening, and he would be able to strike several of them down thanks to the dagger that Emries had given him. The thing had tried to exert some kind of control over him when it first was put in his hand, but the malice and hate in the dagger was nothing compared to the malice that already resided in what passed for Draven's heart. When he turned, he saw a man sitting several paces away, his head down, and his hands resting on the rock upon which he perched. After a moment, the man reacted as though he were being looked at. He raised his head slightly, and Draven's eyes widened and he felt the sick feeling twisting his stomach.

"Well, Draven," Wolf said after clearing his throat, "I think you and I have some things to discuss."

Appendicies

Dramatis Personae

The Knights of the Flashing Blade

Bernhardt Yeoman
The Moonstone Knight
Kingdom of Iron, Pellatori
Wielder of the Hammer Gravity

Chelsea Zarova
The Garnet Knight
Kingdom of Fire, Saldarine
"The Wolf of Saldarine"
Wife of Seraph Kore
Wielder of the Katars Tenacity

Devlin Rannoch
The Onyx Knight
Kingdom of Night, Galateria
Half-Dragon
Wielder of the Kopesh Discipline

Gregor Quicksilver
The Ruby Knight
Kingdom of Blood, Zevarit
Husband of Hannah Ironheart
Paladin of the Church of the Creator
Son of Ivan Quicksilver
Wielder of the Greatsword Valor

Hannah Ironheart
The Celestine Knight
Kingdom of Stone, Albitonin
High Priestess of the Church of the
Creator
Wife of Gregor Quicksilver
Wielder of the Mace Spirit

Jaccob Aldora
The Topaz Knight
The Flying Kingdom, Hedorah
Former Member of the Academy of
Arcane Arts
Wielder of the Double Sword
Temperance

Leonora Wastri
The Jade Knight
Kingdom of Soul, Oradrim
Wielder of the Naginata Wisdom

Natalia Pressen
The Sunstone Knight
Kingdom of Gold, Bellnoc
Master of the Shadow Guild
Wielder of the Rapier Perseverance

Orren Eldrath
The Sapphire Knight
Kingdom of Ice, Rashaleb
Former Member of the Academy of
Arcane Arts
Wielder of the Long Sword Courage

Seraph Kore
The Emerald Knight
Kingdom of Water, Thorigald
Husband of Chelsea Zarova
Wielder of Twin Sword Patience

Tolon Morr
The Amethyst Knight
Kingdom of Steel, Celidar
Former Gladiator
Wielder of Battle Axe Strength

Vallic Ultiv
The Serpentine Knight
Kingdom of Steam, Iltorp
Wielder of Scythe Harmony

Xaran Firesoul
The Tiger's Eye Knight
Kingdom of Knowledge, Menoris
Blind Since Birth
Wielder of Staff Faith

Ivan Quicksilver
Former Ruby Knight
Father of Gregor Quicksilver
Advisor to the Dark Court

Tutio Illik
Former Onyx Knight

Heremon Tal
Former Amethyst Knight

The Seers
Jehna Feris
The Dark Seer

Jania Maldovrin
Oldest of the Maldovrin Triplets

Jerrica Maldovrin
Youngest of the Maldovrin Triplets

Jordyne Maldovrin
Middle of the Maldovrin Triplets

The Academy of Arcane Arts
Alistair Ravenheart
Grandmaster of the Academy of
Arcane Arts
Master of Water
Imperial Sorcerer
Husband of Estelle Ravenheart
Father of Quyhn Ravenheart

Estelle Ravenheart
Sorceress
Wife of Alistair Ravenheart
Mother of Quyhn Ravenheart

Fiona Ebonsight
Master of Fire
Mother of Aris Ebonsight

Aris Ebonsight
Master of Air
Daughter of Fiona Ebonsight

Jastra Mythryn
Master of Energy

Ashinica Maupin
Master of Stone
Member of the Imperial Family

Ayden Seth
Son of Aerith Seth and Bryn Aplee

DRAMATIS PERSONAE

The Dragon Hunters

Jillian Corven
Self-Titled Lady of Cadaria
Wielder of Scaleripper
Leader of the Dragon Hunters

Kiara Aren
Dragon Hunter
Former Priestess of the Creator

Angelina Lynn Sydor
Dragon Hunter

Jacqueline Escandi
Dragon Hunter
Former Member of the Iron Legion

The Chorus

Dorovar
The Destroyer of Worlds

Pestilence
The Grey Man
Carrier of the Crawling Plague

Famine
Formerly Isabel Relin
Carrier of the Wasting Disease

Death
Formerly Ardis Franel
The Collector of Souls

Jerah
The Woman in White

The Hand of Chaos

Dimitri Sulano
The Voice of the Lost

Syren Belloch
The Priestess of Blood

Torda Safrick
The Master of Secrets

Xavier Cormea
The Corruptor of Souls

Erik Relcan
Pursuer of Lost Love
Former Personal Assistant of Hannah
Ironheart

Seraphina Masile
Second in Command of the Hand of
Chaos

The Children of the Creator

Emries
The First *Coromor*
Creator of the *Erieal*

Halicon
Formerly known as Shau-ling
Master of the Shadows
Father of the Phasia

Talisia Masile
The Dark Goddess

The Court of the Dark Gods
Sadrina Annis
Queen of Mythryn
Wife of Pike Rhuiden

Darrien Annis
Half-Dark Goddess
Daughter of Pike Rhuiden

Tess Annis
Half-Dark Goddess
Daughter of Pike Rhuiden

Alderin Parran
Dark God
Son of Aryx and Diana Terian
Protector of Darrien Annis

Camille Renar
Dark Goddess
Daughter of Gwydeon and Midarin
Sandar
Protector of Tess Annis

Serrina Mistic
Dark Goddess
Voice of the Dark Council
Daughter of Jerrard and Erika Mystic

The Dark Gods
Aryx Terian
White Lightning
Fire *Erieal* of the First Generation of
the Prophecies
Husband of Diana Geoffry Terian
Father of Lissa Terian
Father of Alderin Parran
Former Host of Nightwing

Diana Terian Geoffry
Wind *Erieal* of the First Generation of
the Prophecies
Sister of Arathorn Geoffry
Wife of Aryx Terian
Mother of Lissa Terian
Mother of Alderin Parran

Pike Rhuiden
Water *Erieal* of the Second
Generation of the Prophecies
Refugee from the Dark Mirror
First Cousin of Logan Ranthall
Eldar Merin's Former Husband
Husband of Sadrina Annis
Father of Darrien and Tess Annis

Gwydeon Sandar
Brother of Angels
Husband of Midarin Rice Sandar
Father of Nathaniel Sandar
Father of Camille Renar

Midarin Rice
Wife of Gwydeon Sandar
Mother of Nathaniel Sandar
Mother of Camille Renar

Lissa Terian
Fire *Erieal* of the Third Generation of
the Prophecies
Daughter of Aryx and Diana Terian
Wife of Wolf Ranthall

Sabrina Binosear
Third *Chosen One* of the Prophecies
Refugee from the Dark Mirror
Daughter of Cairyn Binosear

Wolf Ranthall
Son of Logan Ranthall and Elwyne
Tamerlane Ranthall

The Forgotten
Aerith Seth
The First *Chosen One*
Husband of Bryn Aplee
Father of Ayden Seth, Cedric
Binosear, Anabel Binosear, Gideon
Viruci

Bryn Aplee
The Lady Fox
Member of the Brotherhood of Phasia
Wife of Aerith Seth
Mother of Gideon Viruci
Mother of Ayden Seth

Taya Viruci
Daughter of Gideon Viruci and Erika
Belnosian
Refugee from the Dark Mirror

Logan Ranthall
AKA Dane Rhuiden
Second *Chosen One* of the Prophecies
Brother of Korrd Ranthall
First Cousin of Pike Rhuiden
Father of Wolf Ranthall
Leader of the Order of the Flickering
Flame
Refugee from the Dark Mirror

Jerrard Mystic
Son of Basille Mystic
Husband of Erika Belnosian
Father of Serrina Mistic

Erika Belnosian Mystic
Wife of Jerrard Mystic
Mother of Serrina Mystic

Other Cast
Cole Breon
Freelance Assassin
The Living Shadow

Liandra Nightshade
Freelance Assassin
Death Blossom

Alise Modrall
Assassin

Wynne
Farmer

Dane Rhuiden
Monk
Leader of the Order of the Flickering
Flame

Blade
Merchant
Purveyor of Oddities

Isa Shar
Companion of Vallic Ultiv

Evan Sinn
Inheritor of Aerith Seth's power
The Voice of the Creator
Husband of Meredith Heron

Meredith Heron
Emissary of the Creator
Wife of Evan Sinn
Murdered by Dorovar

Tera Dawnrunner
Guardian of the Council of the Winds
Guardian of the East
Last of the Tigrelle

Jander Eveningstar
Guardian of the Council of the Winds

Eldar Merin
Best Friend of Elwyne Tamerlane
Wife of Pike Rhuiden
Killed by Taron Steen at the Battle of
Taren

Heralds of the Creator
The Voice
Formerly embodied by Evan Sinn

The Will

The Wrath

The Spirit
Formerly embodied by Sabrina
Binosear

The Council of Winds
The Elder Dragon Tarot
Leader of the Council

Mariti Brightblade
Second in Command of the Council
Companion of Tarot

Khalas Skydancer
Friend of Xaran Firesoul

The Demon Dragon Shadowweaver
Chief Opposition to Tarot

Krangoth Granitewill

The Arcane Dragon Serentis

Brux Mightytide

Charnada Ivorytooth
Ally of Shadowweaver

Stormbane the Traitor
Ally of Shadowweaver

Sheyruushk Bottomdweller
Ally of Khalas Skydancer

About the Author

Brian Kershner is a life-long dreamer, writer, and problem-solver. He grew up absorbing anything and everything he could get his hands on, and as a child of the Star Wars era he constantly wanted to see the worlds beyond the little Indiana town he grew up in. There was no adventure too far, and no problem too big.

Emboldened by parents who always supported his curiosity and his thoughtfulness, Brian found himself bounding from Space Camp to Laser Summer Camp to Athletic Training Camp to Piano Lessons to Football Practice to Basketball Practice to Choir Practice and back again. Despite all of the roaming and traveling, his family remained close-knit and supportive.

Though he flirted with the idea of becoming a doctor, Brian's attentions always fell back to the computer world. He got his first computer when he was six, and not long after found his way into a word processing program and began crafting his own fantastic worlds and even more fantastic characters.

As he has grown and changed and experienced life, so too have his characters. He continues to write, craft, and create; whether it is websites for his customers, or characters and worlds for his audience.

www.ingramcontent.com/pod-product-compliance
Lightning Source LLC
Chambersburg PA
CBHW021123260626
47169CB00005B/1423